Facing the Music

FACING THE MUSIC

Mary Sheepshanks

St. Martin's Press ✹ New York

A THOMAS DUNNE BOOK.
An imprint of St. Martin's Press.

Lines from *The Highwayman* by Alfred Noyes are reprinted by kind permission of John Murray (Publishers) Ltd.

Lines from *Johann Joachim Quantz's Five Lessons* are taken from *Selected Poems* by W. S. Graham (Faber 1996) and are reprinted by kind permission of Nessie Graham and Faber & Faber Ltd.

Library of Congress Cataloging-in-Publication Data

Sheepshanks, Mary.
    Facing the music / Mary Sheepshanks.
      p. cm.
    ISBN 0-312-16832-2
    I. Title.
    PR6069.A399F33   1997
    823'.914—dc21   97-16647
                                            CIP

First published in Great Britain by Century Ltd, a division of Random House UK

First U.S. Edition: September 1997

10 9 8 7 6 5 4 3 2 1

To
George and Patricia
with love

ACKNOWLEDGEMENTS

Though I have of course drawn on my own knowledge of boys' schools for writing this novel, needless to say both of the schools and all the characters in this book are entirely fictitious. I should like to thank Nick, Tim and Prue Dawson and the staff of Sunningdale School, and also Richard Foster, Tim and Patricia Piper, and the staff of S. Anselm's School, Derbyshire for their help in bringing me up to date.

Many friends patiently discussed music with me, but I should like to thank Rosemary Pickering of The Young Concert Artists Trust for her help and advice, and a special debt of gratitude must go to my neighbour Stina Bisengaliev, principal flute with the English Northern Philharmonia (the Orchestra of Opera North), for all her help and interest. Any mistakes will be entirely my own.

Ardvrechan is an imaginary island, but I am grateful to Colin and Caroline Stroyan for kindly allowing me to visit Pait, and to Dougie Lipp for taking me there by boat.

As ever, I am indebted to all my family for their love, laughter, and encouragement and to my grandchildren for updating my vocabulary.

My special thanks to Sarah Molloy my agent, and Kate Parkin my editor.

THE REHEARSAL IN the morning had gone brilliantly. As the last notes died away and the tension broke, all the members of the orchestra were smiling at Flavia.

'If you play like that tonight, we shall have a sensation on our hands,' said Antoine, kissing her hand, not with the polished social flourish that was habitual with him, but placing the kiss in her palm and curling her fingers over it as though to keep a precious coin safe.

Everyone in the orchestra knew she was having an affair with their conductor – Antoine's affairs were usually public knowledge anyway. Flavia didn't mind; she felt like shouting it from the rooftops herself. It was amazing, the most wonderful thing that had happened in her twenty-one years. She would have been appalled to know that Jim Barnard, the respected leader of the orchestra, had said, 'I give it six months – a year at the most, and I tremble for her.' The orchestra hated Antoine, though even Jim, who had played under many conductors, had to admit that he made exciting music, and his appointment had given the orchestra a much needed injection of new energy.

There was bustle as they all packed away instruments and gathered up their music. Antoine watched Flavia put her flute in its case. There had been a coolness between them earlier in the morning caused by Flavia's refusal to tell Antoine which dress she intended to wear at the Festival Hall that night. He had very definite views on what kind of image he thought she should project, and in any case he now liked to control everything connected with her. She was not at all sure that he would approve of the slinky little black number that she had fallen for in Paris and secretly bought, at great expense, to be a surprise for him. It represented a small gesture of independence on her part that was important to her. She was besotted about Antoine but she did not want to become anyone's dummy.

'So, is it to be the red or the pale blue this evening?' he had asked as she lay in bed watching him brush his sleek black wings of hair back behind his ears.

'I shan't tell you – it's a secret.'

'But of course you must tell me. It's most important that you consult me.'

'You must wait and see,' she had teased, but Antoine did not like teasing, unless he was the one to do it. He had not been pleased by her obstinacy, and had tried to bully her into telling him, but she had held out, and Antoine, who was rehearsing the rest of the programme first that morning so that Flavia did not need to get up too early, had gone out with a face like a thundercloud. It was the first little spurt of defiance she had shown since their relationship started and – though it made her more interesting – had he not been in a hurry he was convinced that he would soon have got her to cave in.

Now he was too delighted with her playing to bring the matter up again. She would do him credit and justify his confident predictions about her to the press. Antoine du Fosset was proud of his ability to pick talent early – and not just musical promise, his detractors might have said.

Before they left he sent her up to stand at the back of the auditorium.

'I want to show you something. You are really going to hear a pin drop,' he said. Flavia jumped down the steps and ran up one of the aisles. She was alight with happiness at his approval and looking forward to the evening's performance with new confidence.

'Ready?' he called.

She looked down at him laughing. 'Ready.'

Antoine took the pin out from the carnation he always wore in his buttonhole – in homage to Malcolm Sargent, he said, though some people thought it was just to give himself airs. He held it up and dropped it. Flavia could clearly hear the tiny sound as it hit the floor of the stage.

'Wow! What a responsibility!'

'*Tu ferais bien de t'en souvenir.*'

She came back and joined him but before they went backstage she took a final look at the tiers of empty seats rising up before them and the boxes at each side, which stuck out like open chests of drawers, and thought with awe that this evening they would all be filled with people who had come to hear her play.

'Let's go.' Antoine took her hand and led her after him into the conductor's room and took her in his arms. He was only a little taller than she was. Because he had such an aura of vitality, it often came as a surprise to people who had only seen him conduct that he was not a larger man when they actually met him in person. Flavia closed her eyes and gave herself up to his kiss.

'Now you must get your coat.' Antoine held her away from him. 'We can't have you getting a chill. Come – we will have a delightful lunch together before I go to my meeting, and then you must rest, my darling.'

'I am very pleased with you,' he told her as he swept her out to the waiting taxi he had ordered.

After lunch she went back to the flat which she shared with Tricia, though Flavia had been a rare visitor there lately. Tricia was washing her hair.

'Hi, Trish – how lovely! What on earth are you doing home at this time of day?'

'Oh well, I knew you'd be back this afternoon, and I got fed up with the gallery.' Tricia pulled a face and wound a towel round her hair. 'Work is boring, boring, boring. So how is the Great French Lover, then? God, you look like a Christmas Tree – all that sickening sparkle makes me green. Wish Roddy did that for me. I'm thinking of giving him the push.' Tricia was always giving Roddy the push. 'Bet you've learnt more than just music from your conductor.'

'Umm.' Flavia stretched out on her bed. 'Oh Trish, you don't know how happy I am. I'd no idea life could be so brilliant – and it isn't just sex, though I have to say that's terrific – but Antoine and I breathe the same music all the time. He's the most marvellous man I've ever met and he's made me a different person. I'd die if anything happened to him.'

Tricia thought that given his track record, something, almost certainly another woman, would inevitably happen to Antoine soon, but she could see that it would be quite pointless to tell Flavia in her present state. She had an electric fence of private happiness round her that kept everyone else out.

'So what's the latest Roddy saga then?' Flavia was guiltily aware that she had become out of touch with all her old friends lately, not because she had ceased to care but because her life was just too full of music and Antoine to allow room for anything else. A few months ago she would have known exactly what the state of Tricia's eventful love-life was; they would have talked endlessly about whether it was fair of Trish to keep the faithful Roddy hanging about like a useful spare wheel in case she had a puncture screaming round corners on more exciting tyres. Once they had talked about Flavia's boyfriend, Guy, too, a shy, serious fellow student to whom Flavia had given her virginity while she was at college – not that he had seemed all that keen to receive it. He felt more confident playing the harpsichord than trying to make love. Tricia had christened him Gloomy Guy of the Guildhall, and teased her for being unadventurous. Now Flavia found she did not really want to discuss Antoine with Tricia. He was too precious, too private: it would seem like tempting fate.

All the same she enjoyed Tricia's breezy company, and was touched to hear that she was coming to the concert that evening, though classical music was not really her scene.

'Your ma offered to buy me a ticket so I'll be sitting with your parents and Matt and Di. I gather they're bringing quite a party. Haven't seen Matt for ages.'

Matt was Flavia's older brother and he and his girlfriend, Di, were both junior doctors at St Thomas's.

Tricia thoroughly approved of the slinky black dress, and chatting to her helped to take Flavia's mind off her nerves and stopped her looking at the clock too often. She was secretly relieved that her parents would not have time to come to see her before the concert began. Her ambitious mother had very ambivalent feelings towards Antoine. On the one hand she saw him as a wonderful stepping stone in Flavia's career, but on the other, was extremely jealous of his influence, and having what her children thought were Victorian standards on sexual morality would have disapproved violently of the liaison had she allowed herself to admit that it existed. But also like the Victorians, she had some double standards, and on the whole thought Antoine's usefulness made it expedient to turn a blind eye to his reputation. Antoine for his part made no pretence of even trying to like Hester Cameron and to be in their joint company was torture for Flavia. She dreaded the thought of dinner after the performance when they were all going out to celebrate together.

Just before she left the flat, Flavia had a choking fit. Tricia plied her with water, and hit her on the back.

'You all right now?' Tricia looked at her anxiously.

'I think so, but I feel as if something were stuck.' Flavia patted her chest, and coughed cautiously. Her eyes looked wide with anxiety. The coughing fit hadn't lasted long, but it left her with a curious feeling of pressure in her chest.

'We had fish for lunch. Do you think I could have swallowed a bone?'

'Of course not. You'd have felt it at the time.' Tricia sounded more certain than she felt. 'It's nerves.'

Antoine was already there when Flavia arrived at the Festival Hall.

'I've got this funny feeling in my chest,' said Flavia.

Antoine was bracing and not at all sympathetic. 'What were you doing this afternoon then?'

'Nothing – I was just at the flat, chatting to Trish, practising. It was all right then.'

'I told you to rest, not gossip to that silly girl. Pull yourself together.' Antoine was sharp. 'Don't fail me,' he added warningly. A little shiver of apprehension ran through Flavia.

When he came in to see her in the soloists' dressing room after she had changed he kissed her and told her she looked stunning in the new dress, but did not ask how she was. He was always preoccupied before a performance and she did not dare say anything more. The strange constricted feeling in her chest seemed a little better, though she did not feel very happy with her sound when she practised. She went to the performers' bar to get some Coke, feeling a fizzy drink might help, and also to breathe some fresh air. It seemed terribly oppressive in the dressing room, though it was not in fact a particularly hot day, but when she went back in she could feel herself breaking out in a sweat. I must stop this, thought Flavia, trying not to panic. She took some deep breaths to calm herself, but as she breathed in, a sharp pain shot through her.

When the Orchestra Manager came to tell her that the concert had begun and to give her the exact timing, she felt very lonely. She suddenly longed to have her mother with her.

After a Rossini overture, Antoine came to collect her, sweeping her along with him.

'*Tu es ravissante, chérie,*' he whispered as they went on stage to a burst of applause.

Though it was the first time some of the audience had heard her play in person, many of them had been enslaved by her charm and her playing on television a few years earlier when she had won The Young Musician of the Year competition. The panel of judges, who had been bowled over by her too, had not only commented on the sensuous, imaginative tone of her playing, but on her sparkling personality as well.

As she took her A from the oboist she could see her family contingent sitting in the centre of the orchestra stalls only about thirty metres away. Apart from Matt and Di, her eldest brother, Peter, and his wife, and Tricia, her parents had brought several members of staff from Orton Abbey, the school of which her father was Headmaster, and she noticed Gervaise Henderson, Headmaster of the feeder prep school for Orton, who was a great family friend. Gervaise was so tall that it was easy to pick him out, and the fact that he had brought several little boys with him made him look even taller. Flavia guessed they would be potential music scholars, and was touched that so many friends were supporting her. Her father gave her a little wink.

Flavia nodded to Antoine that she was ready, and he held her gaze for a long moment, that moment of tension and silence that is so important before the start of any performance, and then brought the orchestra in for the quicksilver opening.

At the morning rehearsal she had been thrilled to feel that though the concerto was so technically demanding, she still seemed to have plenty of spare fire to concentrate on performance and interpretation, and she knew she was playing even better than she had done in France with Antoine's other orchestra, L'Orchestre de l'Opéra de Nîmes, a few weeks earlier. She adored playing such a virtuoso piece as the Ibert and the result had been a triumph.

Now it was a relief to find she started well – the constriction in her chest must have been imagination, she thought. But soon things became very different and she was struggling with her breathing. If it's like this already, she thought, playing the lyric passage in the first movement, whatever shall I do in the next? Antoine gave her a puzzled look. His sleek wings of hair had broken loose and flapped wildly on either side of his head like those of a demented blackbird. By the time she was halfway through the second movement his expression had turned to one of incredulous anger. During the last movement Flavia could only concentrate on surviving. Play through the pain, she told herself, her one thought that she must somehow get to the end of the performance. Antoine looked like a jockey desperately trying to whip a flagging favourite to the winning post.

Afterwards Flavia had no recollection of taking her only bow before somehow walking off the stage again and falling into Antoine's arms as he stood ready to join her for their joint call.

He pushed her off furiously. 'Stand up!' he hissed at her, but she was quite unable to, and the orchestra manager had to take her from him and half carry her to the dressing room while Antoine went on stage alone. Her family arrived almost immediately, knowing from her performance that something was badly wrong. It took them less than a minute before they were with her, so they were all there when Antoine returned and stood in the doorway. His voice was icy.

'Whatever happened to you? That was a terrible perform-ance. Terrible.'

'Oh Antoine, I'm sorry. So dreadfully sorry – I feel so ill, so awful – but at least I managed to get through it,' she whispered.

'It would have been better – far, far better – if you had not,' he said brutally, white with disappointment and fury. 'If you had collapsed on stage at least perhaps people might have excused you, and we would all have been saved from that dreadful display of mediocrity. Don't ever expect me to conduct you again.'

Flavia gazed at him in horror, too stricken to speak.

It was her father, Andrew Cameron, who said, 'That's quite uncalled for. Perhaps you would leave us, Antoine. Can't you see my daughter is ill?'

And Antoine in a voice that chilled Flavia's bones answered: 'Certainly I am going. I have a symphony to conduct. You have made a complete fool of me, Flavia!'

He turned on his heel without a backward look, closing the door with a deliberate carefulness that was far more menacing than if he had stormed out and slammed it.

II

BEFORE THE GOVERNORS' Meeting, Gervaise Henderson rang Orton Abbey. He was devoted to all the Cameron family and had been greatly distressed for them by the disasters and dramas of the night before. He dialled the number of the Headmaster's House and got through to Andrew's secretary.

'I'm afraid the Headmaster's teaching this morning. Can I help?'

'I just wanted to know if there was any news of Flavia. How is she?'

'Well, Mrs Cameron has stayed in London to be near her. Matt took her straight to St Thomas's last night and they've kept her in for tests. They don't know what's the matter yet but I gather she's not at all well and everyone's very worried. Luckily she's under Matt's boss, Professor Gibson, so at least they know she's in excellent hands. I'll tell Mr Cameron you rang.'

Gervaise left appropriate messages and said he'd ring again. He knew how much had hinged on the concert the night before – Flavia's big comeback in England after a year away studying in France, on a scholarship funded by a music trust, where she'd had a terrific success. Before the concert her eldest brother Peter had confided to him that personally he thought Antoine du Fosset was an arrogant shit. It looked as if he had been right.

Gervaise looked at his watch and knew he must gird himself to face the meeting. The governing body of Winsleyhurst School was to meet in the private dining room. Since the death of his mother, Gervaise only used this room if he was entertaining, and had his breakfast and lunch with the boys, and dinner with the rest of the staff. He made a mental note that the wisteria was encroaching across the French windows and would soon block out all the light. He must get it cut back, though he feared Pamela Boynton would be bound to tell him it was the wrong time of year whenever he did it.

He was not looking forward to the day – the first time Lady Boynton would be presiding in the Chair. Though he was fond of her, she had been something of a thorn in his flesh when her sons were in the school – she had such strong ideas on everything. The fact that she was immensely kind and very practical had to be set against this, of course, but what annoyed Gervaise was that this time she was a self-inflicted wound since it was Gervaise himself who had decided to turn the school into a charitable trust, thus necessitating a governing body.

Gervaise realized that if he wanted a chairman of his own choosing he had better think of someone fast or the rest of the Governors might get too big for their boots and produce their own ideas.

He had intended Sir Lance Boynton to be Chairman, a man he deeply respected and very much liked, whose financial acumen and social connections would have made him an ideal choice; everyone always wanted Sir Lance to do things for them. He could have been relied on to give wise counsel, have the welfare of Winsleyhurst (from which both his sons had won scholarships to Orton Abbey) at heart, and yet not interfere in the day-to-day running of the school. However, Sir Lance had turned the invitation down, saying that he was too over-committed at the moment and felt it would not be fair to accept.

'I'm away from home so much at the moment – this new inquiry that the Government have let me in for is terribly time-consuming – and when I do get a weekend at home there are so many things on the estate that have to be dealt with that I feel I couldn't do justice to something so important. Ask me again when I retire from public life and I warn you I shall be tempted to say yes.' Everyone had laughed politely. It was impossible to imagine Sir Lance ever being allowed to retire. It was at this point that his wife had made the offer which none of those present had the courage to refuse.

'Look, why don't I take on the chairmanship for you?' she had asked, with the look of a conjuror producing a rabbit from a hat. 'I could always go running to Lance for his expert

opinion, so it would be almost as good as having him really.'
There was an uneasy silence, partly because nobody knew what
to say and hoped someone else would say it anyway, and partly
because none of them could imagine her actually running
anywhere, least of all in pursuit of advice. Lack of confidence
was not one of Lady Boynton's failings, though she certainly
lacked her husband's skill in keeping feathers smooth while
taking difficult decisions.

'Perhaps we should have a proposer and seconder and then
a show of hands to make it all above board – or perhaps you
don't want me?' she suggested, suddenly struck by this unlikely
idea, and looking momentarily vulnerable.

'Oh, um, yes, of course we do. I shall propose you myself.
How very good of you, Pamela.'

Gervaise had despised himself both for his lack of foresight
in allowing the situation to arise, and for his cowardice in
dealing with it now that it had. He was embarrassed to catch
the eye of Sir Lance, who had shot him an amused and not
unsympathetic glance but failed to come to his rescue. He
could cope very well with his wife himself and quite enjoyed
watching her pushing less robust characters along in front of
her like a giant snow plough on a blocked road. He thought
she might be rather good for Gervaise, for whom he combined
great affection with the occasional desire to give him a good
shake. He was also aware that, contrary to everyone else's
opinion, his wife quite often not only sought, but also acted
on, his advice.

'And I shall have great pleasure in seconding the motion,' said
sycophantic Mr Gregson, the school solicitor, who happened to
live in a rented house on the Boynton estate.

A submissive show of hands was a foregone conclusion after
that, and Gervaise wondered, not for the first time, if he had
done the right thing to forfeit the right to run everything
himself. His father would have hated it, but then he had been
every inch a dictator, whereas Gervaise found the strain of
taking all the decisions in the present financial climate an
increasing burden. Besides, though he knew himself to be a
first-class teacher, and also a good schoolmaster – by no means
necessarily the same thing – he was not a natural administrator.

As soon as everyone had arrived, Lady Boynton, amply filling the carving chair at the head of the table and looking quite capable of carving anyone up if they proved tiresome, called the meeting to order. They were to discuss whether or not Winsleyhurst should open its doors to girls in order to attract more pupils, and in response to requests from several parents who wished to have their sons and daughters educated at the same establishment. Lady Boynton was strongly in favour ('must move with the times') but Gervaise, who disliked upheaval, was more cautious, though he acknowledged the need to pay some attention to parents' wishes nowadays. The school was doing well, but the days when Gervaise's father had been able to turn down pupils simply because their parents did not immediately appeal to him were long since gone.

Someone suggested that Meg Price, the second matron, should be offered a higher salary and asked to take on the role of housemother to a special girls' wing, but others wondered if this might upset Sister, a stickler for hierarchy, and jealous about her position. If Meg were elevated to become a head of department, and therefore of similar rank, would they risk losing Sister? She and Meg did not always see eye to eye over the care of the boys: Sister's medical qualifications were superior to Meg's, but the younger woman had a knack of being right in her intuition about the children, who greatly preferred her anyway.

'There wouldn't be any of this trouble between the two of them if only you had a wife,' said Pamela Boynton. 'You really ought to think about it, Gervaise. When your mother was alive there wasn't a problem.'

'I don't think there's a real problem now,' said Gervaise mildly. The school seemed to him to be overrun by women already, who were always falling out with each other.

'Did you know that the boys have taken to calling you Gerve-the-Perv?' asked Pamela, with a laugh that was intended to show that though she considered it a rattling good schoolboy joke, not to be taken seriously of course, all the same it was unfortunate.

Gervaise was mortified. He had not heard this particular nickname, though given most small boys' passion for rhyming, he could see how it was derived. He had been affectionately known as Gerve-the-Swerve for years, owing to his over-enthusiastic driving of the green vintage Lagonda in which he roared around the countryside, but that was quite acceptable. Friends and favoured Old Boys often addressed him as Swerve and he rather liked it. It made him feel quite dashing.

He was not troubled by homosexual tendencies, and was horrified at the idea that in his particular position as headmaster of a boys' prep school anyone might even contemplate such a notion. Perhaps the time had come to demonstrate that his personal inclinations lay firmly with the opposite sex? Recently several well-meaning people had taken it upon themselves to hint that he required a wife, and Lady Boynton's revelation was the last straw.

Though Gervaise's hesitant charm and gentle courtesy made him attractive to women, especially those who felt a desire to mother him, neither grand passion nor wild temptation had been in his vocabulary of emotions and no one had yet managed to sweep him off his feet or inveigle him into serious commitment. His occasional discreet affairs had never lasted long and he had so far walked away with a whole heart after the first mild urge had worn off. He had too little personal vanity to imagine that he had broken any hearts himself, though in this he was wrong.

He would very much have disliked Lady Boynton to know that only a few days before he had had an experience which also led him to feel that a wife might be a highly desirable and bulletproof accoutrement for a headmaster.

There were far more single parents now than in his father's day, but Gervaise had not thought of this as a problem for himself, only for the children concerned, until that is, the arrival of Rowan Goldberg in the school. There seemed to be no Mr Goldberg, in fact there appeared to be no men concerned with the child's life at all. This was certainly not true of his mother, who usually had a male companion in tow when she came to visit her son, though seldom the same one twice running, and never one who showed the slightest interest in the boy.

Mrs Goldberg was hard to place, her accent being vaguely Scandinavian with cockney undertones, but she was clearly not troubled by financial worries. She had several houses and a large staff. She also had a mass of blonde hair, which in no way matched her dark complexion and which she tossed about with such verve that you constantly wondered if a hurricane had got up when you were in her company. She also had enormous breasts which she tossed about a good deal too, and Gervaise found her frankly terrifying. He liked her son, Rowan, however, an anxious intelligent child with a hunted look and a stammer, and felt deeply sorry for him, and it was this that made him accept an invitation to dine with Irina Goldberg at her house in London.

The invitation said 'Black Tie', and he had driven up to London curious to find out more about his pupil's background, expecting a good dinner, hoping for good wine since he was something of a connoisseur, but not expecting to care particularly for the other guests.

The food was certainly wonderful and the drink was Moët & Chandon champagne. The snag was that there were no other guests.

Mrs Goldberg was wearing revealing palazzo pyjamas that made Gervaise deeply uneasy to start with, but as the evening progressed he had become more and more panic-stricken. After three courses of sitting at extremely close quarters to Mrs Goldberg's threatening bosom and overpoweringly musky scent, the whites of his eyes were positively fluorescent as he tried to explain to her how early he was going to have to leave to get back to Winsleyhurst. There had been no further sign of the Filipino manservant who had answered the door to him on arrival, and when his hostess disappeared into the kitchen saying she was going to get the pudding, Gervaise, longing for a reviving glass of Alka-Seltzer, wondered how much more rich food he would be called on to manage. However, when she returned, and he saw that she had not only shed the disturbing pyjamas but was now wearing nothing more concealing than a glass bowl of chocolate profiteroles, he knew it was time to beat a very hasty retreat. The green Lagonda had never been driven faster in its life.

'And how many prospective parents ask you if you are married when they come to look round the school?' persisted Pamela after she had dropped the bombshell about his nickname.

'Well, quite a number of them do,' admitted Gervaise, 'but after all Douglas is married.'

Douglas Butler was the Senior Master, known as Spanner by the boys because of his passion for tightening everything up, especially the discipline.

'I quite often get Douglas and Betty to come and meet new parents. I don't really think my marital state is that much of an issue, you know, and I always reassure the mothers that we have plenty of feminine influence in the school.'

He did not say that he was well aware that the ambitious Douglas encouraged his droopy wife to be present as a means of getting in on the act himself. Douglas had applied for, but so far failed to get appointed to, several headmasterships and had recently hit on the idea that as Winsleyhurst was no longer privately owned by the Henderson family, he might manage to change his title from Senior Master to Deputy Headmaster, and then gradually take over the reins from Gervaise.

'Betty!' snorted Lady Boynton scornfully. 'Can't think she'd be much of a draw – more likely to put people off. A quick whirl in a spin-dryer is what she needs, and anyway you'd hardly be likely to say, "Actually, I'm a roaring poofter with a fancy for small boys!" would you?'

'As a matter of fact,' said Gervaise, 'I do happen to be thinking of getting married, but I consider it to be a completely personal matter and not one that I'm prepared to discuss with the Governors.'

He could see that he had taken them all completely by surprise and, what is more, skilfully by-passed a very embarrassing discussion, though nobody could have been more amazed than Gervaise himself at his utterance. He felt extremely pleased with himself for outwitting his Chairman in such a satisfactory manner.

Then, like St Paul on the road to Damascus, he experienced a flash of revelation, though luckily without the same physical after-effects. There *was* someone in his life who would not only make a wonderful headmaster's wife, but of whom he was genuinely fond. It was such a good idea that he marvelled that it had not occurred to him before.

It was later that he started to worry about what he might have let himself in for. Pamela was not one to allow a subject to fade away, though even she felt it would be inappropriate, even possibly counterproductive, to press further questions at the time. The Governors continued their discussion about school business, and Gervaise agreed to sound Meg out about her feelings regarding a girls' wing or boarding house, but of course nobody's attention was now on the business in hand. They were all itching with curiosity and several theories were put forward after the meeting, some of which concerned mothers of boys in the school and would have surprised Gervaise very much, though Irina Goldberg's name was not mentioned as being amongst the field of possible runners in the matrimonial stakes.

'Who on earth do you think it can be, darling?' Pamela Boynton asked her husband before they changed for dinner that night, as she lay in her bath like a whale in a tank. There was room for very little else once she was installed, which was economical on the hot water.

'Meg?' suggested Sir Lance. 'I've always thought she carried a candle for old Swerve. She's such a nice woman too, and she'd be a marvellous headmaster's wife. Ideal. Taken him long enough to notice her, though. I was afraid he never would.'

'Of course! Meg! How clever of you, Lance. Why didn't I think of it myself? I must ask them both round to Sunday supper at once to help hurry things on a bit,' and she heaved herself energetically upright via a reinforced handrail, water sloshing over the side of the bath.

'Oh I think I'd wait a bit, my love,' said Sir Lance, much amused as ever by his lady's enthusiasm and lack of subtlety. 'Why not try to let them think it's all their own doing?'

'Of course, darling, you're right as usual. I shall only take a hand if they drag their feet. Can't have that. But what a relief! It will be a pleasure to work with Meg, and I'm sure she and I will see eye to eye about everything – she's so sensible. I'm so glad that I allowed everyone to persuade me to take the Chairman's job on.'

Sir Lance gave his wife a very affectionate look as they went downstairs together for one of their rare and treasured evenings alone.

III

FLAVIA WAS CURLED up on the sofa in the old nursery at the top of the house in a state of near despair. It was getting cold but she could not summon up enough energy to throw another log on the fire.

It was three months since the disastrous concert. On bad days such as this, she wondered if she would even try to escape if the ceiling fell in. She had a vision of herself submerged in rubble, quietly allowing plaster dust to cover her until finally she was completely lost to view. After a concert in the Wigmore Hall a distinguished music critic had written of her 'intoxicating sense of vitality' and she wondered gloomily where it had gone to now. I am disappearing, thought Flavia. If I don't get a grip and do something soon I shall become invisible. A little spark of resolution flared inside her.

Antoine had not been to see her in hospital. Every day she had been convinced he would come. Once she had been diagnosed as having pericarditis, brought on by viral pneumonia, surely he could not go on blaming her?

Friends and family had flocked to visit her – Tricia had come, of course, and former students from her Guildhall days. She had been touched to receive a visit from Jim Barnard. He had brought a card signed by every member of the orchestra – they had all been deeply distressed for her and appalled at the callous way their conductor had treated her. Because Matt and Di both worked in the hospital they had been a lifeline, though they were so busy it was frightening; even friends of her parents like Gervaise Henderson and all sorts of other unlikely people had turned up. The Ward Sister, who thought they all exhausted her, said she had far too many visitors and was always driving them out of the ward, snapping at their heels like a collie in a sheepdog trial. But of the one person she longed for, there had been no sign.

'Are you sure he knows I'm still here — have you told him?' she kept asking. Maurice Fenstein, her agent, had organized a press release, and floral tributes poured in from well-wishers.

There had been several sympathetic newspaper articles about her. 'Flautist Flavia Collapses after Concert,' said one headline, and 'Brilliant Young Musician Rushed to Hospital.' Maurice, who was one of the top agents in London, said the response from the media would go a long way in damage limitation. He and his wife, Ina, adored Flavia — she was the daughter they had never had. He had been reassuring and encouraging about the future.

'When you're really well, we'll make a big splash with your comeback,' he said, but when she tried to talk to him about Antoine he had looked miserable, going to look out of the window rather than meet her eye. Antoine was exceptionally busy preparing for his American tour, said Maurice unhappily; had also unexpectedly had to return to France for a meeting — but of course he was very upset about her and would no doubt be in touch soon. Maurice Fenstein was also Antoine's agent. It was due to Antoine that he had taken Flavia on in the first place. He had been very loathe to do so: his top clients, especially conductors, were always asking him to take their particular loves-of-the-moment on his books. Usually it was a disaster and he had learnt to refuse; he knew Flavia through her famous godmother, Dulcie Norman, of course, but when he had first heard her perform he realized that she had that indefinable extra quality that makes for something special. Maurice was very angry with Antoine now, and Ina had declared that she wouldn't have him in the house.

There had been one large bouquet that had briefly given Flavia hope.

'Oh look! It's from Antoine! About time too!' said Tricia, who was with her when it was delivered. 'Best wishes for a speedy recovery. Love Antoine,' she read, holding the card up for Flavia to see.

'That's not his writing.'

'Oh well, I expect he telephoned to Interflora.'

'That's Dan's writing, the Orchestra Manager. Antoine must

have dictated it to him,' whispered Flavia. 'How could he?' and she had torn up the impersonal, chilling little card and asked Tricia to put the flowers near someone else.

She had felt so ill to start with, and was on such strong painkillers, that she had not really thought about the possible long-term effects of the illness on her career. Now she'd been at home convalescing for so many weeks, she'd had too much time to think. She had twice spoken to Antoine on the telephone since she got home – impossible, stilted calls. He had asked about her health as though she had been a mere professional acquaintance.

'But, Antoine, when am I going to *see* you?' she had asked desperately, and he had been evasive. He was off to the States to do some guest appearances, would be in touch, they'd have to see how she was.

'But you do realize I couldn't help it? Haven't you forgiven me yet?'

'Of course, of course. Unfortunate, but these things happen. You get well. I'll be in touch,' said Antoine – but he hadn't been.

Her mother was frantic for her to get back to the concert platform, though Professor Gibson had warned Flavia not to force the pace. He had assured her that there was every chance she would make a complete recovery – but it would take time. Maurice also agreed from a professional point of view that it would be a disaster to attempt a return until she was completely ready. The critics would be forgiving once, but the next concert would need to be a knockout.

Spurred on by Matt, she knew she must bring herself to have a confrontation with her mother, but how could she explain to someone who loathed Antoine as much as her mother did, that in Flavia's own mind her performing had become so intertwined with him that she could not bear to think of one without the other? It was awful to feel trapped in the home she had always adored, and by the prospect of a career for which she had been destined since she was a small girl.

Her favourite flute, a Louis Lot, lay in its case on top of the piano. Up to now it had always been her great delight; she had been described as making music with it as if she were indeed playing 'under the greenwood tree' to the accompaniment of birdsong. She longed to recapture that feeling of joy and spontaneity – two of the qualities which had brought her such acclaim.

She heard her mother's voice calling now: 'Flavia? Flavia? Are you there, darling?' and then the sound of someone running briskly up the stairs. The door was flung open and the light snapped on.

'It's absolutely freezing in here. I can't bear you moping away in the dark like this – you'd be better properly tucked up in bed. Is the pain bad again?'

'No, truly, Mum, thank you – I'm fine.'

'You can't be fine. No wonder you feel awful, just sitting here with the lights out.'

'Oh Mum, do leave me alone. Please.'

'I have left you alone but I don't suppose you've moved off that sofa since I last saw you. Did you come down for tea? Have you even taken Fudge for a walk?'

'No, no and no.' Flavia rolled her eyes upwards.

'You won't get well by freezing and starving. Now then, Gervaise is coming over for supper tonight to discuss the Common Entrance changes with your father and then play chess. Shall I bring yours up to you in bed?'

'Oh good, I adore Swerve. I'll come down. Poor Mum – you've carried more than enough trays for me.' Flavia put out a hand towards her mother to make amends.

'Now you know I don't mind – anything to get you going again. What I do mind is all this moping over things.' Hester Cameron did not refer directly to Antoine, who was a taboo subject between them. She bustled round drawing the curtains, whacking cushions and making up the fire, a super-charged little dynamo.

'Okay, okay. Sorry, Mum.' Flavia galvanized herself into action, dislodging the portly Labrador, who had been lying on top of her, off the sofa too. 'I'll take Fudge out right now,' and she whisked off downstairs, a less than enthusiastic Fudge plopping gloomily after her. The only exercise the bolster-shaped dog enjoyed was her solo morning scavenging expedition round the dustbins of the boys' boarding houses. Life in a public school was an idyllic existence for a greedy

Labrador and Fudge, on her daily bin-crawl, was a well-known Orton sight.

Hester could have screamed with vexation, and wished she had never mentioned a walk. She rushed to call down the stairs, 'Not *now*, Flavia! It's far too late *now*. You'll get cold.' But Flavia had gone.

Her mother felt at her wits' end. Flavia, her precious prodigy daughter of whom she was so proud and to whom she had always thought herself so specially close until Antoine du Fosset had come and gobbled her up, seemed not only to be frighteningly unwell still, but to be changing in a more subtle way too, becoming out of focus. There might have been a mile of mist between them. Most of the time she was as sweet-natured as ever; the little outburst of irritation a few minutes ago was not typical. Hester had always felt rather smug when other parents complained about their daughters being difficult. 'Of course I'm so lucky,' she would say. 'Flavia and I are so close – she tells me everything,' and she had actually believed it to be true.

The Professor had told her that Flavia should forget about her career for at least six months and just have fun. Fun! Doctors appeared to have no notion how important regular practice was for a musician – not something you could just lay aside like a piece of embroidery until you felt in the mood again – but Flavia seemed as incapable of having fun at the moment as she was of buckling down to serious things.

Hester had got seats for a concert at the Albert Hall a few days previously, to hear Simon Rattle conducting, thinking that if Flavia could only be got back to the atmosphere of a fine performance it might motivate her to get going. Andrew had told his wife that he thought it could only be a mistake at the moment, but she had not listened and in the end Flavia had not been well enough to go, so she had been forced to take one of the housemasters' wives rather than waste the tickets.

After her mother had left for London on that particular day, a stream of instructions pouring from her as she departed, Flavia had spent a happy evening at home doing the crossword with her father and playing Ding-Bats with Matt, who was home for a rare weekend. They had laughed inordinately at small silly things, and had cooked a fry-up which they'd eaten in front of the fire. Flavia had only realized afterwards that she had not thought about Antoine all evening. It occurred to her for the first time how little laughter had come into her relationship with him.

Now, as she grabbed the ragged sheepskin coat that was communal family property and let herself out of the door that led into the cloisters, she thought about that evening. Matt had always been her boon companion and protector, her champion in family squabbles and her closest confidant, and much as she liked Di, it had been lovely to have him to herself. Matt sailed through life with a happy nonchalance that drove their mother crazy; despite her dire warnings he had always swanned through exams or interviews without apparent effort.

'Don't let Mum get you down,' he said. 'You want to go and dance barefoot on a beach for a bit. Perhaps I'll write a paper on you, and future physicians will quote my amazing research on the Flavia Syndrome when they're faced with prodigies with overbearing mothers. You'll probably get more famous through my research than standing on a platform blowing your flute! The Prof thinks you're doing fine. Of course he's fallen in love with you.'

He did not tell Flavia that Professor Gibson, after meeting Hester Cameron had said, 'Is illness not allowed in your mother's book then?' and Matt had replied: 'Oh yes. You can be ill and she'll nurse you with total devotion – but you need to get better pretty damn quick.'

Flavia had felt enormously cheered by Matt – most people felt better for being with him. He had given her a huge hug before clanking back to London in the dilapidated old Ford that appeared to be held together by bits of wire and made a noise like a concrete mixer.

'You will get better, I promise,' he called as he departed in a swirl of exhaust, tooting the illegal horn that sounded as if a hunt were in full cry.

When she had last seen Dr Barlow, their family doctor, who was Senior Medical Consultant to Orton Abbey, she had asked him, 'Do you think I could snap out of this if I made more effort? Mum was wonderful when I was really ill, but now she thinks I'm just wimping out, though Matt keeps telling her I need time.'

'Good for Matt. He'll make an excellent doctor one day. He has a fine sense of balance.'

'Balance? Is that what makes you a good doctor?' Flavia had a vision of stout old Dr Barlow teetering across a high wire in tights and ballet shoes. He gave her an amused look over the top of his spectacles.

'Life is all about balance. Your father has it, which is why he's such a good headmaster. Your mother hasn't, though I suppose I shouldn't say so. The question is — what about you? Is your life out of balance?'

Flavia was silent, gazing out of the window.

'I do want to get well, you know.'

'Of course you do, and you will. These viruses can be the devil to shake off, but when someone of your age and ability is laid as low as you've been, I think it's worth asking if your body is telling you something. What's wrong in your life? Is it all too much? Do you need changes?'

'Perhaps.'

'All this pressure, these concerts — is that what you really want? Could you imagine a life without music?'

'Oh, not without music, no, I'd die. It's like breathing for me. I love playing chamber music, sharing together, making it fun, and I might even enjoy teaching — not Pa's daughter for nothing perhaps, but if I'm honest . . .' Her voice trailed away, and she suddenly looked so anguished that she couldn't speak.

'Go on, Flavia.'

'At the moment the thought of giving another big solo concert fills me with total panic. I've completely lost my nerve. It's not enough to be talented, you have to be dedicated, and I don't *want* it now. But Mum can't accept that. It always has to be the top for her. I don't think she gets any fun out of her own music, you know. I pity her pupils, I really do. She hates most of them.' She struggled to control her voice, while the doctor watched her face and listened in silence.

'I used to love giving a solo performance but it wasn't just the applause and everyone being pleased. You feel so in touch with yourself — able to communicate with other people at a much deeper level than by speaking to them. It's wonderful when it's like that. But after I'd won The Young Musician of the Year the pressure really started to build and Mum got the bit between her teeth. It seemed to be concert after concert, and endless competitions. Then – then Antoine du Fosset gave me my big break and life's been totally brilliant ever since.' She paused again and Dr Barlow felt he was witnessing a terrible personal struggle.

'I expect you've heard about Antoine?' she asked, her voice only just audible. 'Well, he's dropped me now. Mum thinks if I don't go back soon I never will. It's a bit like in *Alice* you know. There's always a porpoise close behind you treading on your tail. It's so hard for Mum because of her accident. She knows I can do what she was prevented from doing. I can't bear letting her down.'

'H'mm.' Dr Barlow tapped the desk with his pen. 'You can't live your mother's life for her. Because her own career as a soloist was cut short it doesn't mean that you have to be one. Live your own life, Flavia. Be yourself. If you don't want to go on with it then tell your mother so. You must. Your father will back you whatever you decide – that I do know. How's the pain in the chest?'

'Better on the whole. It only comes back if I get tired or bend forwards.' She did not say that it was the ache in her heart rather than the pain in her chest that would not heal.

Dr Barlow got up and put his arm round her thin shoulders. He was very fond of the whole family, but for Flavia he had a specially soft spot. He hated to see her looking so frail and hunted.

'Buck up,' he said. 'You're not Elizabeth Barratt Browning. Keep your sense of balance. Don't forget that.' He'd had several head-on clashes with her mother himself over the years, but he thought that if Flavia could stand up to her formidable parent, it might be the making of her. He also thought that Flavia was a much stronger character than most people, including herself, realized. She had been so sheltered in some ways, and so forced on in others that she reminded him of an over-watered pot plant, wilting from too much attention.

The cloisters smelt of damp stone and were always cool even in hot weather; now they struck chill. There was a whiff of creosote from the special preservative with which the massive oak doors were treated, and this evening there was also a pungent smell of impending autumn coming from the huge plane trees in the playing fields outside. Flavia and Fudge made their way to the tow-path that ran beside the river. In summer there would have been masters and boys on bicycles pedalling precariously along, not looking where they were going as they shouted instructions through megaphones to crews on the river, but now it was deserted. The sky was the colour of a thrush's egg, except for a faint pinkness in the west against which the twin spires of the abbey stood out, very black. There was a nip of frost which would soon bring leaves down.

She walked as far as the little wooden bridge over one of the streams which flowed into the main river. As children they had called this the 'Poohsticks Bridge' and had endless races, tossing their chosen twigs over the rail and watching them career downstream. Flavia leant over and threw a stick into the water now, but it was too dark to watch its progress and it was soon lost to view in the inky water.

I will pick my moment, she thought, and then I'll tell Mum that I am not going on as a soloist. I'll give it up. Then she said the words aloud, shouted them to the sky, and imagined that by doing so she had given power and life to her resolution, and a rush of energy seemed to flood back into her.

When she got back to the house there was a spicy smell coming from the kitchen. Hester was making tomato sauce.

'Oh good – pasta for supper.' Flavia wasn't hungry, but she thought it would please her mother to think her appetite might be returning. Hester cooked with the disciplined competence which she applied to all household tasks, and the spaghetti bolognese would be good – not sensational, but good. Culinary triumphs and disasters were not her line; she reserved all her passion for music and the achievements of her family, and stirred the cauldron of family life with alarming fervour.

Flavia, who was a good bit taller than her diminutive mother, came up behind her, rested her chin on top of her head and put her arms round her.

'Can I help, Mum?'

Hester shrugged her off. She was impossible to help, greatly preferring to wear the sackcloth of single-handed management than to feel beholden to anyone, no matter in how trivial a way.

'No thank you, I've already done everything. Gervaise has arrived but your father's not in yet, so you can go and entertain him if you like – or if you're suddenly feeling better you could go and practise for half an hour?' and she shook the frying pan briskly to stop the mince from sticking.

Flavia had meant to wait for an opportune moment before tackling her mother but was afraid if she postponed it any longer, her resolution might fail. She also hoped that the presence of Gervaise Henderson at supper might dilute a family scene.

'Mum, darling Mum,' she said, 'I have something I want to tell you.'

'Oh yes?' The tone of voice was not encouraging.

Flavia took a deep breath. 'I've been doing some thinking.'

'Well, you've certainly had time for that.'

'I've decided to give up music – as a career, I mean.'

'Don't be ridiculous, Flavia! You can't imagine that anyone would seriously let you take a decision like that.'

'I know it's awful for you. I'm truly sorry – but I've made up my mind. Please try to understand.'

'Oh I understand all right.' Hester murdered the sauce she was stirring. 'It's all that wretched man's fault. I shall never forgive him – never. I shall talk to Dr Barlow about you. He'll say you're not in a fit state to take any sort of decision yet. Do stop picking at that parsley, Flavia.'

'Dr Barlow thinks I'm right,' said Flavia through a mouthful of parsley stalks.

'Dr Barlow knows nothing about music.' Hester switched tactics.

'But he knows about me.'

'And I don't, I suppose?' snapped her mother, her small plump figure so tight with annoyance that she looked as if the stuffing might burst out of her like an over-filled pincushion.

'You've never been able to think of me doing anything else, but I might want to try other things.'

'Such as?'

'I don't know yet.' Flavia felt on weak ground here. 'I just want to see what comes up. Mum, darling Mum – please, please don't look like that.'

'What do you expect me to look like?' asked Hester. 'I've spent years trying to help you achieve what I know you can do – and the first time anything goes wrong you pack up. All right – you gave one poor performance. But you were ill. Everyone knows that now. A big talent is a sacred trust, not something you can choose to discard,' and she started to clear up the saucepans at such a speed that it seemed as if they leapt back onto the shelves by themselves in sheer terror.

Flavia knew it would be useless to prolong the discussion, and could only hope that she would have the strength to ride out her mother's furious opposition.

She walked slowly back into the hall, and found that she was shaking.

The front door opened and her father came in still wearing his gown from evening school.

'Hello, my darling, you look very bright-eyed,' he said, and then as the brightness in her eyes started to spill down her cheeks 'Hey – what's all this?'

'Oh Pa – I've just done something dreadful.'

'Oh well,' said Andrew Cameron cheerfully, 'I need to hear something dramatic. You've no idea how dull it is trying to insert information into the heads of some of those oafs in B5. Come and get a drink and tell me all about it.' He took off his gown and hung it on a hook outside his study, and held the door open for Flavia. Gervaise, who was sitting on the sofa, got up as they came in, unfurling himself like a long scroll.

'Flavia – how absolutely lovely to see you. Are you any better? Andrew, I'm afraid I've committed the awful sin of breaking into the crossword for you. I've only done one corner, though. Try this – six across: "Roast Mules are turned over;" it's ten letters.'

'Somersault,' said Flavia and her father with one breath.

'Bother,' said Gervaise. 'You're too quick, you two. So how's life, Flavia?'

'She says she's just done something dreadful,' said Andrew Cameron, going over to the table where a tray of drinks sat amongst piles of papers. 'She's going to stun us. Whisky, Swerve?'

'Umm, please – lovely. I can't imagine Flavia ever doing anything dreadful. Have you robbed a bank, seduced the Head Boy or smashed up your father's car?'

Flavia took the glass of vodka and tonic which her father held out to her, and took a large swig.

'Worse, much worse – not funny at all,' she said. 'I've just told Mum that I'm giving no more concerts. May give up music as a career altogether, anyway as a soloist.'

'Now that was really brave,' said Gervaise. 'I don't think I'd have had the courage to face Hester with that.'

'I've been expecting you to say something of the sort for weeks,' said her father. 'I think you need a break. Well done you,' and he raised his glass to her.

'Really, Pa? You don't mind?' Despite what Dr Barlow had told her, Flavia was astonished.

'Not if it's right for you. I've been thrilled by all your success but you must do what *you* want. Mum will be upset for a bit but she'll get over it.' Andrew Cameron had no intention of letting his daughter guess just how much trouble he anticipated from his wife. He bled for them both, but he had told Hester that he thought Flavia was far more likely to get over Antoine if she wasn't put under pressure.

'What do you think, Gervaise?'

'Oh, I quite agree. Must do one's own thing. I always have, but then I've never been ambitious. You'd think my parents would have been pleased that I wanted to take on the school from them, but no, they really wanted me to aim for a much higher profile at Cambridge. Instead I opted for a life I knew I'd enjoy. You can't think what trouble I sometimes have with over-ambitious parents. Some of them think I don't push their young geniuses nearly hard enough. Thank God I haven't got children of my own – it's so easy to advise other people.' He stretched out his long legs and gave her his charming, lopsided smile. He thought Flavia looked very white and strained. A sudden idea struck him.

'I suppose you wouldn't consider a bit of temporary part-time teaching, Flavia?' he asked tentatively. 'Just to keep your hand in, as it were, while you give yourself time to think? Joan Hall, our music mistress, is having to take the rest of term off because her mother's ill. A bit of extra help would be a godsend.'

'Oh Gervaise — what an amazing idea. I might love it.'

'Perhaps it's rather a nerve to ask but it would help me out of a hole.'

'Can I think about it?'

'Of course.'

Flavia flashed him the smile that so enchanted audiences and lifted her face into sudden beauty, transforming her woebegone appearance.

Andrew Cameron gave Gervaise a grateful look. He knew he must go and find his wife immediately. He intended to support his daughter to the full, but he ached for the uncomprehending disappointment that his wife would endure. He had no hope at all that she would understand.

'I'll just go and see how Mum is getting along with supper,' he said to Flavia. 'See Gervaise's glass is topped up and I shall expect you to have done at least two clues each before I come back. We can't eat until you have.'

'Don't think that I shall give in, Andrew,' Hester Cameron said, angrily shaking off his sympathetic embrace. 'I should never forgive myself if I made it easy for Flavia to drop out. If you really loved her, you'd see that too but you've always spoilt her.'

When she was in a rage it never bothered her if her accusations were untrue. She glared at her husband.

'And I think you should look carefully at your own motives for wanting her to continue, my love, as you very well know,' Andrew answered quietly. Occasionally he was capable of being extremely formidable, though it was not a side of his character that surfaced often. 'I won't have Flavia's health sacrificed to your ambition,' and he turned on his heel and left her, knowing that she was spoiling for a row which he had no intention of allowing to develop at the moment.

Supper was not the easiest of meals. There was a layer of ice over all Hester's conversation, and though both her husband and Gervaise, a friend of long-standing, did their best to ignore it, Flavia felt utterly wretched. She knew her mother intended to try to freeze her into agreement, and she could hardly wait to creep off to bed the moment they had finished eating.

'The offer to help will stay open,' said Gervaise as she went to kiss him goodnight. 'Come over and have lunch with me and look at the new music wing. You've no idea how smart we are nowadays – a far cry from the old army hut which the orchestra used when Matt was at Winsleyhurst. I'll give you a ring.' He gave her shoulder a gentle pat and whispered, 'Don't weaken,' as he kissed her cheek.

'Night, Mum – see you later?' Flavia looked questioningly at her mother, but Hester turned her face away. Normally she would have come bustling up after Flavia with offers of a hot drink, and then stayed to gossip while the men settled down to one of their chess sessions, but she certainly wasn't in the mood for offering olive branches tonight.

Later, as Flavia lay in bed listening to a tape of the Brahms Violin Concerto, feeling both exhausted and restless at the same time, there was a tap on the door and her father poked his head round. 'Can I come in?' He sat on the edge of her bed.

'I have something to tell you, Flavia,' he said. 'Perhaps it's rather disloyal to Mummy in a way, but there is something I think you should know about the accident to her hand all those years ago, long before you were born.'

Flavia's eyes filled with tears. 'That's what makes me feel so bad,' she said. 'I've always known how awful that must have been for her. I feel an absolute cow.'

'Well, you mustn't, because it wasn't really like that. The accident was in many ways a blessing – a real let-out for Mum. She plays the piano extremely well, if not to concert standard, as you know; but you see, darling, unlike you, your mother was never going to make the top grade as a soloist. She just wasn't good enough. That was the thing she couldn't come to terms with.'

Flavia stared at him. 'Pa, I can hardly believe this. All my life Mum's brought me up on the idea of her great talent and blighted hopes. Does she realize this herself?'

Her father sighed. 'Oh yes, deep down. But she's a complete perfectionist, and very proud. It has allowed her to live with herself.'

'And possibly sacrifice me?'

Andrew Cameron got up and went to the window. The moon hung over the abbey, and everything looked silver in the first frost. He might have been looking at a Christmas card. All the views from the Headmaster's House were sensational, but this was his favourite, and as always he thought how lucky he was to live in such a beautiful place.

'This is very hard for you, Flavia. Try not to feel angry. You and Mum have got different temperaments, and yours is a happier, easier one really – but don't underestimate her. She has great guts. I shall tell her that I've told you.'

'Poor Pa. If you rolled us into one we might be really good. Perhaps we're each missing a bit of the jigsaw.'

Her father smiled at her and came back to sit on the bed. 'But I love you both just as you are. I don't want either of you to change – but I do want you to be happy.'

'And Mum? I have just ruined her dream.'

'You must dream your own dream, and she must let you do it. Other people's dreams are dangerous things to tamper with. She's never found it easy to let her chicks fly the nest and escape her influence, especially you, but she'll come around.' He laughed. 'Don't look so sad, darling. She still has me to boss around, and I love her very much.'

'Don't tell her that you've told me about her hand. Let her keep the pretence. It makes it sadder in one way but in another it frees me to make my own decisions. You never know, I may come back to it all one day – but in my own time and way. Thank you for telling me, Pa.'

'You're very generous, Flavia,' said her father. 'Go on a journey of exploration and find out what *you* really want.'

After he had kissed her goodnight Flavia went straight off to sleep almost as soon as she turned her light off, and had the best night she'd had for weeks.

IV

MEG WAS SORTING socks in the linen room and had just switched on the kettle to make coffee. She always made coffee in break, real coffee, not instant, because she knew how much Gervaise enjoyed it. She bought the best beans at the excellent local delicatessen, ground them freshly every morning and made the coffee in a special jug with filter papers. Gervaise usually came upstairs to see Sister and Meg in break, to find out what the doctor had said if there were any sick boys, to discuss arrangements for boys going out or tell them who was down to play in the team if there was a match. His appearance in the sewing room at eleven o'clock was the highlight of Meg's day. She had been at Winsleyhurst for fifteen years, and had been in love with Gervaise for all of them. Everyone knew this except Gervaise himself, though it was astonishing that he did not. In such a closed community everyone knew almost all there was to know about everyone else. The details were not always exactly right, but they were never far wrong either.

Sister enjoyed the coffee too, and the fiction was kept up that Meg really made it for her. 'I must make Sister's coffee now,' she would say to Jane and Barbie, the two young under-matrons, as she sent them down to supervise the boys' milk and biscuits, but no one was deceived by this except of course for Gervaise. All the staff called him by his Christian name except for Douglas Butler, who called him Henderson, very man-to-man, and Sister who addressed him as Headmaster, and often in the third person too: 'How is the Headmaster today?' she would ask, treating him to one of her slightly toothy smiles as she crooked her little finger daintily above the handle of her cup. There was often a trace of her favourite Carmen Scarlet lipstick on her teeth no matter how carefully she blotted her mouth with a tissue, and she was apt to leave the outline of a thin bottom lip on the rim of any cup from which she drank.

In theory Sister was in charge of health, crackling about in white with a purposeful-looking petersham belt clamped round her trim waist. It was important to have her SRN qualification on the school prospectus to reassure anxious parents, but in fact Meg, who only had a Red Cross First Aid and Nursing Certificate, really ran Winsleyhurst. She always made a point of standing outside the dining room to watch the boys go in to meals, and learnt more about them just by watching them than Sister ever ascertained by questions. It was Meg who knew when Gavin-Smith was likely to have an asthma attack coming on; Meg who could spot a normally garrulous small boy being untypically silent, which might bode anything from constipation to the marital troubles of his parents at home. Meg was Gervaise's eyes and ears, his totally benevolent spy. The boys adored her.

Parents who met Meg for the first time often remarked how pretty she must have been when she was a girl; when she had been a child, friends of her mother were always saying how pretty she would be when she grew up. It sometimes seemed to her that the White Queen's rules about jam applied to her looks – pretty yesterday and tomorrow, but no one ever told her she was pretty today.

What increasingly seemed almost unbearable to Meg was the fact that Gervaise did not appear to see the thing that was so obvious to her – that they were made for each other. Lately she had started to feel a desperate urgency that was out of character for someone as calm as she was by nature; it was not that she had any great opinion of her own charms, rather the reverse, but she did have a real conviction that she could make him happy, and time was ticking on. Meg was in her late thirties – Gervaise was forty-five – and she longed for children of her own.

In her fantasies she often nursed Gervaise back to health after a serious illness; one day the scales would fall from his eyes as she held out a life-giving glass of lemon barley water. 'Oh Meg,' he would say, 'I don't know what I would do without you,' and he would gather all her rosy roundness into arms wasted by fever. The poor thin arms would then gather strength

33

with miraculous speed as he crushed her in a fervent embrace – possibly even fumbling with the bra beneath her botany wool jumper. In fact Gervaise quite often told Meg that he didn't know what he would do without her, but he would be thinking of her in connection with Winsleyhurst, and the rest of the scenario had so far been disappointingly missing. Was it her imagination that in the last few months he had been noticing her in a new way? She hardly dared to contemplate the idea. Her own family had long since ceased to expect her to marry – indeed, her present state of being free during the school holidays to help with her sister's children and her father's duties as a priest suited them all very well.

'Do I smell coffee?' asked Gervaise now, smiling at Meg. Lately he had thought a lot about how much he enjoyed her reassuring presence, and the idea that had come to him in the Governors' meeting in the summer was still fermenting gently in his mind like slow-acting yeast. Mustn't rush these things.

He had to duck his head to come through the door that led into the sewing room from the little-boys'-bathroom. It was in fact a large room with ten small old-fashioned baths with ball-and-claw feet in it, but it was where the youngest boys were always bathed. The bigger boys had showers in what the architect had called the new ablution block, but there was something infinitely cosy about the bathroom. It was a place for gossip and confidences, and for small boys who had newly left home to be babied again.

'Oh good, it'll be bubbles in the bath again tonight: we had baked beans for supper,' one of the new boys had said chattily to Meg the night before as she soaped his knees. The sewing room, which was large and sunny and had comfortable old wicker chairs in it, smelt of starch, clean laundry and toast, but the bathroom always had a faint aroma of grubby sock. Two washing machines were whirring away now, and there was a pile of muddy football shorts on the floor.

'I just came to check that John Whitbread would be able to play in the match before I let Douglas put up the team list. Is his knee all right?'

'Yes, he's fine. Sister got Dr James to have a look and he was quite happy for him to play.' Meg handed Gervaise his cup and also a plate of biscuits that she had made specially in the little kitchen off the sickroom.

'Oh, coconut – how delicious. You spoil me, Meg.'

They chatted comfortably about the school's chances against St Wilfred's, their arch rivals, that afternoon.

'I rather hope Mrs Whitbread won't come and watch again,' said Meg. 'She makes that boy so nervous. It's one thing to come and watch some matches, I approve of that, but she never misses – and all that shouting from the touchline. It's embarrassing. We haven't had such a blatantly ambitious mother since Mrs Cameron, when I first came here and Matt was in the First Eleven. Do you remember what a hassle she used to give him if he didn't play well? Not that he minded much, bless him, but Johnnie Whitbread is another cup of cocoa altogether. Very sensitive. She'll put him off if she's not careful. I tried to drop a tactful hint last time but it didn't do any good.'

'Funny you should mention the Camerons,' said Gervaise. 'I had dinner with them last night. I'm afraid Hester Cameron's pushing Flavia too hard now. She's so anxious for her to hurry up and make a comeback but it looks as if she's tipped her the other way. Flavia says she's going to pack in her concert career.'

'Oh I am sorry – she's so talented that would be a waste. I've got several of her recordings and I was very sorry to hear she'd been so ill. What was really wrong with her?'

'Pericarditis – though I'm not really quite sure what that is,' admitted Gervaise.

'It's inflammation of the membrane round the heart muscle, usually due to a severe chest infection. It can be a very nasty thing – not something to be treated lightly. Mrs Cameron would be very silly to rush her.'

'I've had a bright idea and asked Flavia to help us out with our music while Joan Hall is away for her mother's operation. Don't you think that's a brainwave?'

Meg hesitated. She had always been fond of Flavia, though she had not seen much of her lately, but an unaccountable warning bell rang in her head, which she did not even understand herself.

'Is that wise?' she asked. 'Flavia's so awfully attractive. You don't think there might be trouble with the young masters?'

Gervaise looked surprised. 'Why should Flavia cause any

more trouble than Jane and Barbie already do?' he asked. In his experience trouble of some sort between under-matrons and young male members on the teaching staff was par for the course. 'I know she has a special charm, but having been brought up in a boys' school all her life, and with two older brothers, she must be so used to the company of young men, I don't think she'd be all that interested. Besides, she's had so much admiration on the concert platform, I'm sure a bit of calf love wouldn't faze her. I don't think you need worry about her. Might cause more trouble with some of us oldies!' he added light-heartedly, causing Meg's spirits to sink. It wasn't the state of Flavia's heart that was worrying her.

'You don't need to get in any extra help,' she said. 'I was going to offer to help out with the music till the end of term. I know I'm not qualified but I could keep things ticking over and take choir practice.' Meg sometimes played the organ for chapel services if Miss Hall was not available, not particularly well, but competently enough, and she regularly sang madrigals with a local choral group.

'How like you to offer, Meg,' said Gervaise warmly, 'but you have more than enough on your plate already. What would we all do without you? Besides, I want to talk to you seriously about this idea of taking girls. There might be an important new role for you.'

He didn't mention that there might be a choice of two new roles on offer, and was surprised to see that Meg's comely face looked quite blotchy suddenly, and she mysteriously seemed as if she might be about to cry. Surely she couldn't be menopausal already? Gervaise's father had always warned him that most staff problems were caused by women's hormones and as such were to be ignored whenever possible. 'It's either a–certain-time-of-the-month or they start having the-change-of-life the minute they get here and go right on having it until they retire or die years later,' he had said cheerfully to his son. 'Not that you'd ever notice much change – they're all exactly the same. You don't want to pay any attention. I never did.' Gervaise, however, was a more sympathetic character than his father and though not very perceptive about women, liked to smooth out troubles if he could. It certainly seemed as if he had inadvertently ruffled Meg's feathers about something.

'I thought you'd jump at the chance of running the girls' side,' he said. 'You have such a way with children, it would be bound to be a success if you took it on.'

'It's the little boys that I love.'

'Well, they'd still be here too, of course.'

'But would I have so much time for them? Could I still be as involved?'

Gervaise had to admit that he didn't really know the answer to that. Meg was always so enthusiastic, so eager to help, that it came as a surprise to him that she wouldn't automatically fall in with almost any suggestion.

'I often think the school means almost as much to you as it does to me. Think about it,' he said persuasively, giving her his attractive smile. 'I know you'd do anything for Winsleyhurst.'

How could Meg tell him that much as she loved the school it was the Headmaster himself for whom she would do anything?

'Well, I'll think about it then,' she said, but she didn't sound encouraging, and somehow a light had gone out of her face as though her battery needed renewing.

Gervaise was puzzled but made a mental note to get Pamela Boynton to discuss the idea of girls with her. Talk it out with another woman – that would be the thing. He was far from sure himself that taking girls was a workable option, and was not fond of major changes anyway, but if he were to brace himself to make the enormous alteration that he was contemplating to his own easy-going way of life, then it all might fit into place.

He decided to telephone Flavia to ask her to come over and talk to Miss Hall about the music, and keep his promise to take Flavia out to lunch. Might do her good, and she always made him laugh – get her away from under her mother's skirts and take his own mind off the school for a bit. Perhaps he allowed himself to become too preoccupied with it sometimes.

'Lovely coffee, Meg, as usual, thank you so much. Hope I've left enough for Sister. You look a bit tired, though. I don't like to think you're getting overdone at this stage in the term. Do let me know if you want more time off or anything. A weekend away perhaps? And please don't think about taking on the extra music. I'll sort that out with Flavia,' he said disastrously, and sloped off, unaware that he had succeeded in laying a minefield.

V

FLAVIA ACCEPTED GERVAISE'S invitation to go over to Winsleyhurst with pleasure and relief. The atmosphere at home was still sizzling with unresolved resentment, all the more uneasy for being unspoken. She didn't know exactly what her father had said to her mother but it was clear that he had negotiated some suspension of direct hostilities, though she guessed it would almost certainly be in the nature of a temporary cease-fire rather than a permanent peace settlement. Hester Cameron treated her daughter with a brittle politeness, a determined cheerfulness and a general air of humouring someone who has temporarily lost their marbles and must be handled with discretion until they have found and gathered them up again. Any attempts to reopen discussions were dismissed with a cool smile, a pitying shake of the head and a brisk change of subject, and yet Flavia, who hated to be at odds with anyone for long, was surprised to find that she still retained the sense of relief that had come to her when she had taken the decision. It would clearly be a good thing to remove herself from the scene as much as possible, and she did feel better in herself – not right, but better.

She rang Matt, carefully choosing a moment when her mother was out, and brought him up to date with home news.

'Poor old Mum, but well done you,' he said. 'Do you feel well enough to come and spend a night or two in London? Di would love to see you too.'

Di and Matt shared a minute flat in Clapham in a street that had not yet been totally taken over by suede-clad mothers zooming about in Mercedes cars. You were unlikely to be jostled off the pavement by Swedish au pair girls exercising King Charles spaniels in Vindaloo Road, though there were signs that a few smart young professional couples were beginning to consider it as a possibility for a first home.

Flavia liked Di very much. The flat was always a cheerful tip of books, unwashed mugs, huge rubber plants belonging to the landlady, and strange African fertility figures which Di, who intended to be a gynaecologist, collected. She said she had a passion for collecting and they seemed a suitable choice of subject, though she wasn't all that keen on the objects themselves. Matt, who had a penchant for bad puns, told everyone that they were reproduction. They would probably end up in a jumble sale. Hester tolerated Di without much enthusiasm. She disapproved of Matt and Di living together for a start: she had rigid, and her children considered antediluvian, notions about such arrangements, and thought Di an opinionated career girl and slovenly to boot; she preferred her elder son, Peter's, genuinely fertile wife, Wanda, who was busy collecting real live babies, was a dab hand with a damp cloth and the Jif, and didn't argue with her mother-in-law, whom she found intimidating. Matt and Flavia called their sister-in-law Wanda-the-Baby-Wipe-Wonder, and couldn't understand what their mother saw in her. Hester's ambitions for her daughter didn't extend to careers for her daughters-in-law.

Flavia promised to go and stay with Matt and Di the following week.

'I'll be able to bring you up to date with all the Winsleyhurst gossip too. I'm having lunch with Gervaise tomorrow. He was so kind and understanding the other night. Pa says that fearsome old battleaxe Lady Boynton's putting the fear of God into him, now that she's Chairman of the Governors.'

'Oh great,' said Matt. 'Give my love to Swerve and Meg but mind Sister doesn't bite you with those fearsome teeth of hers. Be good. Take care.'

Flavia drove over to Winsleyhurst on a bright billowing morning full of scudding clouds and racing leaves. The school was about ten miles from Orton Abbey and it was a pretty drive which took her past Boynton Park, with its famous beech woods just beginning to turn colour. Her mother had insisted on ringing up Dr Barlow to ask if he thought Flavia was fit to drive the car again and had not been best pleased at his irritable reply. 'Heavens, yes – do leave that girl alone, Hester. If she doesn't feel well enough I'm sure she won't do it. It's a very good sign that she wants to drive about again and she's quite capable of deciding for herself anyway.'

'So you think she would be fit to start music again?'

'I didn't say so and that is entirely a matter for Flavia too. Look, Hester, I know this is all very difficult for you and must be distressing, and if you would like to come and see me on your own account you know I'd be only too pleased to see you. Make an appointment with my secretary if you're feeling over-stressed,' which was crafty of the old doctor because Hester took pride in being as strong as an ox, and did not wish to discuss her own health at all.

Gervaise was still in school when Flavia arrived, the bell having not yet gone for break, so she let Fudge out of the car and the dog rapidly disappeared to inspect the dustbin situation. Winsleyhurst School was a mile out of the village and stood at the top of a hill surrounded by superb grounds and gardens. Gervaise's father had been a notable gardener, and the rhodo-dendrons and azaleas were famous. Gervaise took a pride in their upkeep but was not a hands-on horticulturist himself. The house was less beautiful, and looked as if its original owner, faced with a pattern book of different styles, had been unable to choose between them and had opted for a little bit of everything. Kind people said it had character, purists shuddered, but it had the advantage that no additional extensions for classrooms, or buildings like sports halls in the grounds, could ever look out of place or make it any worse. In fact it was a great deal better inside than out, with big light rooms and a cheerful shabby feel that blended well with the inevitable kicked paintwork that betokens the presence of small boys.

Flavia wandered upstairs, looking at school photographs on the walls and finding pictures of Peter and Matt in various groups. She made her way to the sewing room and poked her head round the door.

'May I come in and join you?'

The full complement of matrons was assembled. Sister gave her an unexpected peck on the cheek, which she felt must be like being kissed by a parrot, and was thankful Matt wasn't there to make her giggle; she must remember to tell him that as it hadn't actually drawn blood she hoped not to be scarred for life. Meg on the other hand, from whom she expected a warm embrace, seemed withdrawn, and said, 'Oh hello, Flavia, nice to see you,' but turned at once to fiddling with the coffee grinder in a way that precluded any kissing.

'Och well now, Flavia,' said Sister, whose speech pronounced her an ex-patriot from Edinburgh's Morningside, 'and how are we progressing? Do we have to be careful or would a wee drop of caffeine be allowed?' Flavia, rightly interpreting this as an enquiry after her own health said we were progressing fine thanks, really on the mend at last, and yes please coffee would be lovely, Sister. She exchanged grins with the two under-matrons, always referred to by Sister as 'my gairrls'. The Janes and Barbies came and went fairly frequently and Flavia had not met this particular pair who looked fun and friendly and clearly thought Sister was an absolute scream. Flavia began to feel that a part-time job at Winsleyhurst might be just what the doctor ordered. She perched on the table next to the sewing machine, accepted a mug of coffee from Meg and prepared to enjoy herself.

When the bell rang at eleven o'clock its clang was immediately followed by a noise like a magnified flock of starlings as the chatter that had been more or less contained inside a hundred and fifty small boys burst out as they all came surging from their classrooms.

'Och – Christopher Robin!' exclaimed Sister, the only expletive she allowed herself to use on the school premises. 'Where does time go? We can't stay gossiping here all morning! Hurry up, gairrls, or the boys will be in the dining room before you've poured the milk out,' and she bustled off to her surgery to dole out antibiotics and inspect verrucas. Jane and Barbie winked at Flavia as they dashed away, giggling.

'Oh Meg – what fun this is. I'd forgotten how much I loved coming over when the boys were here. You were always so sweet to me – do you remember how you used to let me pour out the boys' orange squash on match days from that old jug? I bet it's still the same jug now – chipped yellow enamel with a black handle. I thought it was a terrific treat,' said Flavia, aware that the old rapport with Meg seemed to be missing and wanting to bring it back, but unaware that she had just succeeded in making Meg feel as vintage as the old yellow jug herself. A less generous character might have made a barbed rejoinder, but Meg could only look wistfully at Flavia sitting on the table, and wish that the engaging, but not particularly pretty child with the gap-toothed smile who used to take her hand so confidingly, had not turned into this elegant young woman whose smile now displayed a full complement of perfect teeth., Flavia would have been astonished to know that she seemed threatening to the older woman, as she sat helping herself to chocolate-chip cookies and swinging her long legs in scarlet jeans. Her dark hair was tied back from her pale face, and Meg reminded herself that Flavia had been awfully ill and must be having a difficult time. Feeling ashamed of her own reactions she forced herself to try to sound more welcoming.

'I remember it very well too,' she said. 'I used to look forward to your visits, and Matt was one of my favourites of all time. He was Head Boy when I first arrived and was so helpful. How are the brothers?'

'Oh well, Peter's a solicitor in London and he and Wanda have three small children. Matt and I think Pete's in danger of getting seriously stuffy, and Wanda can't talk about anything but potty-training, which palls after a bit, but the children are divine. Oh Meg, these biscuits are dangerous – very moreish.'

Flavia rattled happily on, crunching and chatting while Meg darned grey socks and tried not to think about Gervaise, and what it might feel like to have this gorgeous creature, something of a celebrity, around for the rest of the term; not that the Headmaster had ever shown the slightest interest in any of the young under-matrons, and Jane and Barbie both clearly thought him as old as the hills, so perhaps Flavia did too.

'I hope you're not going to devour all those biscuits, Flavia,' said Gervaise, coming in at this moment. 'Sorry to keep you waiting but I had a few notices to put up. Good morning, Meg. Have you managed to keep me any coffee?'

'Oh Gervaise – hello.' Flavia slipped off the table and went to kiss him, dusting the crumbs off her jersey.

Poor Meg's heart turned over as she watched Gervaise hold Flavia at arm's length before returning her kisses on both cheeks and saying, 'Why, I really think you look a bit better at last! One could almost imagine that you've got a little colour in your cheeks.'

A frightful retching sound from the bathroom next door interrupted this touching scene and they all three went to the doorway, Meg's professional instinct immediately taking over from her love-lorn longing as she rushed to see which of her protégés had been taken ill. But it wasn't a small boy who had been stricken; Fudge stood in the middle of the room disgorging the entire contents of the Winsleyhurst garbage bins all over the floor.

'Oh God, I'm sorry – I'd clean forgotten Fudgey,' said Flavia. 'What a bit of luck she's come up here though – she usually chooses a carpet.'

'Such a discriminating dog, Fudge. So clever of her to find the right place. We are lucky!' said Gervaise, much amused.

'We'd better wait till she's got rid of it,' said Flavia, trying not to laugh as Fudge heaved again and added to the already unbelievably large pile on the floor. 'Have you got a shovel or something and I'll scoop it all up as soon as she's finished. I'm truly sorry.'

'Oh don't worry, we're quite used to this sort of thing here,' said Gervaise, who had no intention of helping to clear it up himself. 'We have all the equipment for this kind of emergency to hand, don't we, Meg?' But Meg had already whizzed off and returned with buckets, disinfectant, shovels, mops and all the really vital equipment for life in a boys' prep school.

'Here, please let me,' said Flavia, trying to take them from her, and failing. 'Oh I do grovel. I'll never let her loose here again, I swear.'

'Better leave it to Meg – she's an expert. You might get those smart trews mucky and I'm taking you out to lunch when we've looked at the music block, don't forget. I'm not having you reeking of pigswill, it'll spoil my appetite. Bring that frightful hound and come along.' And he wafted Flavia off, leaving Meg not at all consoled at having the opportunity to serve her beloved in this particular way.

The new music block was reached through a passage linking the main house with various classrooms, and had been opened by Lady Boynton a couple of years before. Gervaise was very proud of it. On the ground floor there were several practice rooms which housed pianos of varying merits and defects. At the bottom of the stairs was a huge rack where various musical instruments were stored – cellos were always a bit of a problem – and up the stairs which led to the large music room there were colourful posters with pictures of all the different instruments that go to make up an orchestra.

'This is really marvellous, Gervaise,' said Flavia, genuinely impressed.

He introduced her to Miss Hall, who was giving a recorder lesson to a group of boys. There was a flute on top of one of the cupboards and Flavia picked it up, tuned it while Gervaise was talking to Miss Hall and then joined in the playing of an arrangement of 'Bobby Shaftoe', harmonizing with them and playing the lower part. The boys, always highly susceptible to feminine charm, were delighted, and Miss Hall beamed approval.

'G-g-gosh', said Rowan Goldberg, who learnt the flute himself, 'h-how do you get it to sound like th-that?'

'Just lots and lots of boring practice, I'm afraid,' said Flavia, laughing, 'but also making the sound beautiful in your own head before you even play a note. It all starts inside you.'

'I think I might leave you and Joan together for a bit, Flavia,' said Gervaise, thinking suddenly just how difficult Flavia's defection must be for her mother to accept, and wondering how permanent that decision would prove to be. It was impossible not to notice that when she picked the instrument up it looked as right and natural as if it were an extension of herself. 'You can discuss just what you feel you could take on till the end of term. We're going to miss Joan dreadfully. She's made our music live in the last five years. I think you'll be impressed by the choir too. I'll come back and collect you in about half an hour. Keep that dog with you, for heaven's sake.'

'Lovely,' said Flavia. 'Could I stay and join in with you till the end of your lesson, please?' she asked the boys, getting a good mark from Joan Hall for her friendliness and lack of pretention.

After the class had finished, Miss Hall, who was then free, showed her all the improvements.

'This is a super room,' said Flavia, 'so big and light.'

'Yes,' said Miss Hall. 'It's wonderful to teach here now. I can have the full choir in here, and we're building up the orchestra too.' There was a baby grand across one corner of the room and an electric organ.

'We also have three small rooms up here for teaching individual lessons,' she said. 'What would you be prepared to teach, Flavia?'

'Well, I could obviously teach flute, recorder, and piano,' said Flavia, 'and of course music theory. I wouldn't be qualified to teach any other instrument but I could certainly supervise practice for clarinet and oboe. What I'd adore to try my hand with is the choir. But you must tell me what you'd want. The only snag is that I couldn't come full time. The doctor won't let me do an entire day's work yet, but I'd love to try and keep things ticking over for you. I'm so sorry about your mother's operation. It must be ghastly for you.'

'Well, it's an anxiety at her age and I want to see her through her convalescence, but with luck I should be back at the beginning of next term. It's so like Gervaise to offer to keep my job open for me, and your help would make all the difference. Kind Meg had offered to help, but she isn't qualified at all and one or two of the parents might be awkward over that, though of course we have other teachers coming in, so specialized instruments wouldn't be a problem. I don't really think Meg ought actually to teach though.'

'Oh,' said Flavia quickly, wondering if this was the cause of the slight indefinable frost she had sensed, 'I wouldn't want to do anything to upset Meg.'

'I don't think you would – besides, she does so much already and I don't think Sister would have allowed her to take on any music for a moment. Now *she* can be really be tricky, but Meg's just a darling and never upsets anyone.'

All the same Flavia felt uneasy.

When Gervaise came back to fetch her, he found them deep in musical discussions and getting on like a house on fire. He felt very pleased with his idea, and thought how lovely it would be to have Flavia around and how tactfully and easily she would fit in with everyone, quite apart from giving her a much needed breathing space herself.

He took her to lunch at Tratts, the newly opened Italian bistro in nearby Steeple Lacey, one of the prettiest villages in Berkshire, leaving Fudge shut in Flavia's old red Polo. There was no way Gervaise was prepared to risk her being sick in his precious car. It was such a brilliant day that he put the roof down, and lent Flavia an old pink Leander scarf which she wound round her head. He thought she was lucky to be one of those people who look just as good muffled up in woolly hats as they do when dressed up for a party.

Lunch was fun for them both. Gervaise, setting out to amuse her with stories about the school, found himself telling her about the episode with Irina Goldberg, and Flavia laughed so much that she choked over her minestrone.

'Oh Gervaise, you are funny,' she said. 'Did you know Matt and I always used to fight over which of us should sit next to you when you came to stay in the holidays? I watched you casting your spell over Peter's children the other weekend and they were just the same. How the boys must adore you – we always did when we were little.'

'Well, do go on adoring me now that you're grown-up,' said Gervaise, greatly enjoying himself.

'Is Meg all right?' asked Flavia as she licked the coffee granita ice off her spoon.

'Why do you ask?'

'I don't really know, but she seemed a bit funny – not exactly unfriendly but very nearly . . . I can't quite explain. She's always been so lovely before. Perhaps she's a bit down?'

'I've noticed that too,' said Gervaise. 'She's usually so sunny – as you say, a lovely person. About the only member of staff that never causes trouble. I wonder what's the matter.'

'Oh well, I'm relieved it's not just me,' said Flavia. 'Where does Meg live? Somehow one only thinks of her in connection with Winsleyhurst. Perhaps she doesn't have enough fun?'

'I've never thought about it,' Gervaise admitted. 'Her father's a retired parson and occasionally comes down here to preach to the boys. He's nice – bit sanctimonious perhaps – and her mother always seems very sweet. They live near Salisbury. I know there's a married sister who Meg often stays with – she'd be a marvellous aunt.' He suddenly thought how very little he really knew about Meg's home life. Up to now it hadn't greatly interested him.

'I love being an aunt – well, sometimes,' said Flavia. 'But then I shall probably have rows and rows of children of my

46

own one day. Can't be so much fun *just* being an aunt if you're too old to have children of your own.'

Gervaise was amused that Meg, whom he still considered to be a young woman, should seem so ancient to Flavia.

'You ought to take her out, Gervaise. Give her a lovely lunch like this – it's a great little place. Bring her here one day and cheer her up.'

'Good idea. I want an excuse to talk to her about the new scheme about girls that Pamela Boynton is trying to bulldoze me into considering. I'll do just that.' Gervaise sent for the bill and they screamed back to Winsleyhurst in the open Lagonda with some very exciting cornering. When Gervaise kissed Flavia goodbye, exactly as he had done since she was a small girl, they were both blissfully unaware that they were being watched with great interest by several pairs of eyes. The news that Old Swerve had actually been seen snogging with a girl went round the school like a bushfire in a drought.

VI

THE FOLLOWING DAY Flavia had a relapse, a return of the pain and pressure in her chest combined with the miserable feeling of extreme fatigue, and she had to spend the day in bed. Her mother, who had not wanted her to go to Winsleyhurst, was almost triumphant and blended extra solicitude with a look of I-told-you-so, which made it hard for Flavia to be grateful for the feverish supply of tempting little dishes, iced drinks and extra plumped up pillows. However, Dr Barlow had warned her that there would be ups and downs; by the next morning she was better, and in a couple of days she was up and about again. She decided to go to stay with Matt and Di as planned.

'How can you be well enough to go to London if just one day out at Winsleyhurst exhausts you so much?' Hester Cameron objected.

'Well, after all they are both doctors – I could hardly be in better company, could I?' asked Flavia.

'Doctors they may be,' her mother snorted crossly, 'but they're also quite irresponsible.' She was afraid that Matt and Di would encourage Flavia's ridiculous ideas.

'I shall go and visit Dulcie too while I'm in London,' said Flavia.

Dulcie Norman was the distinguished but now retired concert pianist, once famous both as a performer and for her master classes, who had taught both mother and daughter and for whom Hester had a profound respect. She was Flavia's godmother.

'I thought I would ask her advice – but please don't try and nobble her first, will you, Mum?'

'I wouldn't dream of it,' said Hester huffily, who had immediately decided to do exactly that. 'But why shouldn't I have my say too?'

'You can, you have. I know what your opinion is but I want to hear Dulcie's for myself – and anyway it can only be my own decision in the end.'

Hester looked at Flavia with foreboding. Dulcie, who was capable of being an iron taskmaster herself, had always warned Hester about the dangers of putting too much pressure on her daughter. Part of her success as a teacher had been her flair for guessing just when and how hard to push her pupils, and the sensitivity to know when this was not the wisest course. Hester had a nasty feeling that Dulcie might take Flavia's part.

'Very well, darling,' she said sadly, after an inner struggle, 'I'll promise then.' But she looked so forlorn suddenly that Flavia nearly recanted, and it took all her resolution not to back down. She gave her mother a hug and this time it was returned, and mother and daughter clung to each other for a moment, a lot of unsaid things hanging between them.

It was difficult to move in Dulcie's drawing room, which was crammed with knick-knacks as well as huge ornate pieces of furniture, not to mention two Steinway grand pianos. There were some really valuable paintings and pieces of sculpture, portraits of Dulcie and gifts from admirers, but every available surface and wall space seemed to be crowded with signed photographs of royalty, celebrities, other famous musicians, and the memorabilia of her own illustrious career. It was hardly possible to see what colour the walls were, let alone find space to put anything down. Dulcie sat in her chair by an electric fire whose heat might have been expected to melt the metal of the zimmer frame which was kept beside her. Movement was very difficult for her nowadays, and to those who met her for the first time she looked not unlike a giant toad, but to Flavia, who had known and loved her since she could remember, the likeness to the dazzling young pianist of long ago, pictured wearing romantic off-the-shoulder evening dresses, was still discernible. The aura of great beauty remains like an echo long after the cruel brush of old age has tried to paint it out. Dulcie's rooms were always full of flowers, especially lilies which were her particular favourite, but lately a less pleasant odour lurked beneath their sweet heavy scent. The room was stifling. Dulcie's housekeeper, Hilda, who had looked after her for years, was now almost blind and there was a layer of dust over everything. Flavia found it profoundly sad.

'Oh my dearest child – how lovely to see you.' Dulcie's voice was as strong as ever. 'Forgive me if I don't get up. Ring the bell and Hilda will bring us some tea.'

'No, no – let me go and fetch it, then I can go and see her.' Flavia could not bear the thought of Hilda tottering in with the heavy silver tray. Hilda and Dulcie adored each other, but they took considerable trouble to disguise the fact, Hilda grumbling openly about her employer's selfish wilfulness, and Dulcie behaving with an autocratic lack of consideration that could take your breath away. Everyone dreaded the fact that one day soon one of them was likely to have to learn to live without the other.

'Oh well, do if you want to, darling, but Hilda's really getting awfully lazy,' said Dulcie now. 'She'll just be sitting in the kitchen fiddling with her beads or nattering away to one of those lesser saints she's so fond of.' Hilda was a Roman Catholic, and Dulcie always spoke as if Hilda's prayers were on a par with entertaining trades-people at the back door, while she herself dealt directly with the boss whenever she rang for him. Hilda's rosary had long been a weapon in their war: either of them were capable of hiding it – Dulcie in order to interfere with Hilda's devotions, and Hilda in order to have it miraculously found by St Anthony to bait Dulcie.

When Flavia returned with the tea, having been told in most unwelcome detail about Hilda's brother-in-law's kidney stones, and how impossible Madam was to look after, Dulcie had her eyes closed, but, on hearing Flavia, she snapped them open with all the alertness of a lizard just about to catch a fly.

'So, Flavia. What have you come to tell me?' she asked. 'Good as you are at coming to see me, I know this is not just a social visit.' And she turned her still brilliant gaze on Flavia, ready to listen with the concentrated attention that made everyone who talked to her feel special.

Flavia sat on the floor by Dulcie's chair and poured out her misery of the last few months. She knew she could talk to Dulcie about Antoine in a way she found impossible with anyone else. It was Dulcie who had introduced them in the first place.

'I was fine in the morning,' said Flavia. 'The rehearsal was probably the best I've played – Antoine can draw music out of one that's beyond one's dreams – but I started to feel very strange before I went on in the evening. I thought I must be getting flu or something, but you know how you can often step outside yourself when you're performing and completely override a headache or a pain?' Dulcie nodded. 'Well, it didn't turn out like that. I had trouble with my sound from the start, and if that's not right it's difficult to lose yourself. I just about got by with the first movement, but it was in the second that I really had trouble.' She paused to steady her voice, and went on, 'I had been looking forward to the Ibert so much – it's such a brilliant warhorse of a piece you really feel you're galloping into battle on it, and I knew I could do it well . . .'

She fought the tears, and the old lady bent forward and gently touched her cheek with a gnarled arthritic finger.

'I got through it, but, Dulcie, you know when you play really well, how you feel you and your instrument and the audience are all sort of part of each other, and the music flows through one, and then out and on for ever?'

Dulcie nodded again.

'Well, it wasn't like that at all. It's hard to explain. I felt as if I was shut *in* with the music, like being a prisoner in a kind of glass jar or something – I was trapped inside with the music and I could see outside, but I couldn't *take* it out. I couldn't take it to the audience. And the pain in my chest was awful. It was a nightmare.'

She stopped, unable to speak, and they sat in silence for a bit, the old lady gently stroking her hair.

Dulcie could not help wondering guiltily if Antoine, a past pupil who owed much to Dulcie's early championing of his career, would ever have started an affair with Flavia if she had not made the huge mistake of trying to warn him off. Antoine did not take easily to gratitude.

Flavia went on to describe the last months of illness, of the disappointment of feeling better one day only to be down again the next, and how she kept secretly testing herself out, unable either to practise properly or leave her flute alone, and all the time conscious of her mother's anxiety and gnawing ambition.

'Mum is always nagging at me to play but she has no idea

how often I secretly try and fail. And then there's Antoine,' she said sadly. 'I thought we were so close. I still can't believe he could feel so little for me as a person. I have to face the fact that perhaps he only wanted my success as a sort of extension of himself, but without him nothing means anything to me any more. So what am I to do, Dulcie?' she asked. 'Because I do think I'm beginning to get better at last, but the thought of a concert paralyses me with panic and makes me sweat and tremble. Do you think there's any chance of Antoine coming back to me?'

'Would you take him back after he's behaved so badly to you?'

'Oh yes. Yes, I'd take him back all right. He'd only have to whistle. I can't get away from the feeling that I let him down – he said I should have given in sooner and not allowed myself to go on playing so badly.'

'That's ridiculous!'

'Maybe – anyway, I know I must get on with life. I can't stop loving him, so I think I might change direction.'

'It seems that you and Music need a little break from each other,' said Dulcie. She always spoke about music as if it were a person. 'I think you should let it go for the moment, though I don't think you should drop your practice completely, but I must warn you, Flavia, that though you may try to give it up, it may not be so willing to let you go in the end. Music will be back in your life one day whether you like it or not. Meanwhile, of course, you need a lover.'

'A *lover*? How can you say that?' Flavia looked flabbergasted. 'I've just had the big love of my life. I never want to go through anything like that again. Ever.'

'What nonsense!' Dulcie looked scornful. 'You have not had a lover – you have been infatuated and you have had sex. All young women of your age have that now – it's like taking their driving test.' Dulcie had never driven a car in her life but she'd certainly had plenty of experience with lovers. 'I'm sure Antoine was a good driving instructor and you will be grateful for that one day, but he didn't love you,' said Dulcie, hating to see the anguish in Flavia's face, but thinking it was kinder to be truthful in the long run. 'When you find a real love – and you will recognize the difference only when you have found it – Music will find you again too. I feel sure of it.'

'Oh well, perhaps I'll advertise,' said Flavia, trying to hide her hurt by being flippant. 'Failed Flautist urgently requires new passionate romance.'

She could see that the old lady was getting tired, and bent to kiss her goodbye on her rouged and powdery cheek, gently holding one of the swollen and misshapen hands that had once been so strong and supple that they could produce sounds out of a piano to reduce strong men to tears of delight. Dulcie still made up her face every day as if she were giving a concert, though sometimes the pencilled eyebrows or the line of her mouth were a little bit askew.

'Tell your mother to come and talk to me,' said Dulcie. 'I have a lot of things to say to her. Not as talented as she would have liked, poor Hester, but she made up for it in determination. She should have been honest with you years ago about her career, but once she allowed this face-saving myth to build up it all became too difficult. I am very fond of her – she has always been such a little tiger. Now I must rest. Play me something before you go, child.' So Flavia went over to one of the Steinways and started to play 'Dreaming' from Schumann's *Scenes From Childhood*, which she had first played to Dulcie years ago, and as she played the tears trickled slowly down her cheeks. The old lady nodded her approval of the music, but the nods got slower, and when Flavia judged that Dulcie was really asleep she gently closed the lid of the piano, collected her coat and quietly slipped away.

There was a strong small of curry in Matt and Di's flat. They gave Flavia a terrific welcome.

'I've been to the takeaway down the road specially for you,' said Di proudly, as if this were the acme of good housekeeping. 'I thought we'd eat Indian tonight. They have the most scrummy things but I hope it won't disagree with you. I went on a pilgrimage in Dharmshala a few years ago and had the most terrible dysentery, but the old guru at whose feet I'd gone to sit, told me I ought to be thankful and welcome it as a cleansing experience, so perhaps it could be just what you need.'

'Oh great,' said Flavia. 'Dr Barlow wants me to learn balance and you want to give me the squitters – but I've had enough of shits lately, I can tell you. Dulcie's just had the gall to tell me I need a lover!'

She tried not to let Matt and Di see just how unhappy she felt and they had a good evening. The two doctors thoroughly approved of Flavia's plan to teach at Winsleyhurst.

Later as Flavia slept on their sofa surrounded by the pot-bellied fertility goddesses and the remains of the Indian supper, Matt said to Di: 'Dulcie's a shrewd old bird – about the only person apart from Dad who's got Mum sussed out for one thing. I wonder what she really thinks? Let's hope Flavia does fall for someone else soon and gets over this crush on Antoine.'

'Oh Matt, you do make me cross!' Di sounded quite put out. 'You still think of Flavia as your little sister, but she's been seriously hurt. She was wild about Antoine and she's not going to want to look at anyone else for a long time.'

'Well, I can't understand what she saw in that megalomaniac midget.'

'He's terrifically sexy,' said Di.

Matt looked appalled. 'You don't find him attractive, do you?' he asked.

'He's not my scene – but I can understand what Flavia saw in him. I only hope he doesn't come back and wreck her life again just when she starts to get over him. It's no good thinking she'd fall for any other Prince Charming in her present state.'

'Let's hope she doesn't fall for another Frog Prince anyway,' said Matt. 'Talking of which how about turning your mind to this Prince Charming for a bit?'

'Umm,' said Di. 'Why not?' and then: 'Phew! lucky I like the taste of curry.'

At Winsleyhurst, Gervaise called a staff meeting in the common room to put forward the governing body's suggestion about taking girls. Opinions were divided.

Douglas Butler was against the idea. He felt he knew how to handle boys and would still have approved a régime of cold baths and running naked round the grounds before breakfast. He liked to think of Gervaise as an ineffectual Headmaster, though somehow he never managed to get his own way with him. It irked him that Gervaise, who appeared to allow the boys any amount of rope, never had the slightest problem with keeping order; he had no problem himself, but he achieved discipline through a reign of terror. Another bone of contention was that Gervaise never let him preach in chapel, and Douglas felt himself pregnant with many a rousing sermon. He greatly regretted the passing of corporal punishment – which he had secretly found far more exciting than having intercourse with his wife, Betty, though sadly just about as quickly finished. But girls? That would be a nightmare.

Sister could not make up her mind, which was no surprise to anyone. Though she bustled around in such a businesslike way she was not a great one for decision-making until she was sure what the general opinion was going to be – except of course where her own status was concerned.

'What does the Headmaster think?' she asked, playing for time.

'Well, the point of this meeting is that I should get to know what all of you think.' Gervaise was not falling for that one. 'But I can tell you that our Chairman is all for it. I've invited her to come and join us, but I thought you might all welcome the chance to consider the question before she arrives.' Which was one way of saying skip out of the way if you don't want to be flattened by a bulldozer.

'I think it would be very good – it could have a civilizing effect to have young members of the fair sex among us. One should move with the times too. I would be in favour,' said old Mr Foster.

'That's a turn-up for the books,' muttered James Pope to Michael Stockdale. As the two youngest members of the teaching staff they had been surprised to have their opinions asked for, though it was typical of Gervaise's courteous approach to have done so.

Old Mr Foster – Fossy to generations of Winsleyhurst boys – had taught Classics for as long as anyone could remember. No one knew for sure how old he was and no one had ever heard him called by his Christian name. There were those who thought he should have been compulsorily retired years ago, but Gervaise would not hear of it. Many of the scholarships of which the school was justifiably proud were won due to his brilliant teaching, and though Gervaise now arranged things so that Mr Foster only taught the really bright boys who actually wished to learn and were less likely to take advantage of his failing eyesight and slight deafness, he was genuinely revered. Most parents realized that real intellectuals are not so easily found in prep schools as they once were, and on the whole knew how lucky the school was still to have him. His view about taking girls was a surprise, however, and just showed that you should never take anyone for granted. Gervaise thought he might be well advised to reconsider his own views for he had great respect for the old man's opinion.

'Where would the girls' accommodation be?' asked Meg. 'I think they would have to be housed in a separate building for all sorts of reasons. They could hardly share washing facilities with the boys, and what about sickrooms?'

'Good point. I'm so glad you asked me that,' said Gervaise untruthfully, scribbling away on his jotter in what he hoped was a businesslike way. He hadn't the faintest idea what the answer was.

'With great respect,' said Douglas Butler, who couldn't stand old Fossy, but had been banking on him to be anti girls and was much disappointed by his reaction, 'I should like to ask Mr Foster what makes him approve of the idea?' Everyone else wanted to know this too.

'When I was young I never met any girls,' said the old man, 'and if I had, I would have been far too shy to speak to them. I can't help thinking that life might have been easier and happier if this had been otherwise.'

There was a silence in the room. The two young masters felt abashed at hearing such an unexpected revelation and one or two people looked somewhat embarrassed. Meg gave Mr Foster her warmest smile; she thought it was a brave speech.

Gervaise said, 'Thank you very much. I think Mr Foster has just made an important and relevant contribution, one that will make us all think carefully whatever our prejudices may be.'

Spanner Butler shrugged his shoulders in mock resignation, and shot his employer an irritated look. What a lot of wets they all were. He intended to hang on to every prejudice he had.

The tension was broken by the crashing of doors, and the

approach of the Chairman of the Governors was heralded by the sound of footsteps marching briskly across the hideous tiled floor of the hall outside. The bulldozer had arrived.

'Hello, everyone,' said Pamela Boynton breezily, as she stomped in with her usual following of the Norfolk terriers which she bred, processing after her like wiry bridesmaids. 'Now then, no ceremony please. Do settle back wherever you were sitting, all of you.' And she sat herself down in the armchair that Gervaise had been occupying. He caught Meg's eye as he moved to perch on an arm of the sofa, and gave her a barely perceptible wink, which caused her heart to flutter deliciously. It did not in fact go unnoticed by Lady Boynton, who took it as a thoroughly good sign that the romance was progressing favourably and did not resent it in the least.

'Pamela, good of you to come,' said Gervaise. 'We've had some discussion and as you might expect opinions vary and some of us, including myself, have not quite made up our minds. Sister for one is not sure what she thinks.'

'Really?' Pamela Boynton couldn't imagine a situation in which she would not feel sure of what she thought. 'How's that, Sister?' she asked, sounding as if she was making an appeal at cricket.

'Not out, worse luck,' muttered James Pope to Barbie.

'Och, Lady Boynton,' said Sister, quickly deciding which side she should now back and simpering in what James Pope, Michael Stockdale and the two under-matrons afterwards agreed was a quite sickening way, 'I just wanted to point out a few possible snags, but of course the idea of having some wee gairrlies about is especially appealing to me pairsonally.' Nobody quite knew why, but everyone nodded politely.

'Must be a closet lesbian,' whispered Barbie to Jane.

'Meg?' asked the chairman. Meg hesitated, torn between her constant desire to do anything that might help Gervaise, and her fear that if she allowed herself to get embroiled in looking after girls she might see less of him.

'Well, I love the school so much as it is, and so specially love the boys that I'm a bit cautious about changing the atmosphere,' she said, 'and then the whole accommodation question might be tricky.'

'There is the possibility of the Old Stables, I suppose,' said

Gervaise. The Old Stables had been converted into a house for his parents when they retired, but since his mother's death it had been empty. There was talk of Gervaise using it as his private house during the holidays to avoid keeping the main building open, but he was so often away that he had not so far got round to doing anything about it. Pamela Boynton saw the situation in an absolute flash, as she told her husband later. It explained Meg's curious reluctance about taking on the girls. Of course! The Old Stables would be the ideal house for Meg and Gervaise when they got married, but the poor woman could hardly be expected to come right out and say so until he had got round to proposing to her. Naturally Gervaise, who was rather slow to add these things up, might not have realized yet how perfect it would be. She did hope he would get a move on.

'Let's leave the decision about where the girls will be housed till later,' she said with what she considered masterly diplomacy, 'and simply take a vote on whether we want to have them. All in favour?' and she stuck her own arm firmly in the air.

With the notable exception of Spanner, who thrust his hands deep in his pockets as if daring them to pop out and vote against his will, everyone put their hands up.

'Good. That's settled then. I think it will be at least a year before we're ready for them, but we'll sort out the details later,' said the Chairman.

'That gives us a very useful indication of the wishes of the staff. Most important, of course, but I take it you are planning to let the governing body have the final say, Pamela?' Gervaise knew very well that she'd forgotten all about the rest of the Governors.

'Oh. Well, yes. I mean, naturally. Of course.' Pamela Boynton gave Gervaise a grateful look. Had she perhaps got a little too carried away? She must ask Lance how much power she really had.

After the rest of the staff dispersed to their various duties Gervaise chatted to Pamela about one or two other matters, and then walked back to her car with her. Once outside, the terriers immediately humped their backs on the edge of the grass. 'Oh clever girls. Well done,' said their owner proudly, and Gervaise made a mental note to be careful where he walked.

Sir Lance always swore that he and his wife had once been invited to stay and shoot with some rather nouveau riche clients of his who had just acquired a smart estate in Hampshire and that when Pamela had said, 'Would it be all right if we brought the Norfolks with us?' she had been surprised and pleased when they seemed not only amenable but positively ecstatic about the idea. It was by no means the reaction she usually got from friends who knew her well, and her opinion of Sir Lance's clients with whom she had not at all wished to go and stay had gone up. However, on arrival their hosts had looked far from enchanted as the unruly pack of yapping little rat-catchers tumbled out of the car, and it transpired later that they had been expecting the Duke and Duchess and had made extensive preparations for entertaining the ducal pair. It was one of Lance's favourite stories.

'I'm a little concerned about Meg,' said Gervaise now, opening the door for his chairman. 'She's so wise as a rule but her heart doesn't seem to be in this idea and I think I'd like to talk the whole thing out with her. I thought I would take her out to lunch next week to give me a chance to discuss a few things quietly away from the school.'

'What a splendid idea,' said Lady Boynton, putting the dogs into the back of the car and then squashing herself into the driving seat before driving off with a grinding of gears that made the car-loving Gervaise wince.

'You would have been really proud of me, darling,' she said to her husband that night, when he had returned late from London and they lay in bed holding hands and telling each other about their various activities.

'I was *so* tactful you'd have been amazed, because – guess what? – I'm sure we're right about the romance between Gervaise and Meg, but I never let on for a moment that I could guess what he really had in mind.'

VII

FLAVIA BEGAN TEACHING at Winsleyhurst two weeks later. She loved it from the start. She went twice a week from ten o'clock till four, staying for lunch, and for two mornings, which Dr Barlow considered to be just about right. She also went over on Saturday mornings to take choir practice.

Miss Hall had left her notes about everything with comments about the various pupils and the standards they had reached. Flavia taught flute and recorder, and also took some of the piano pupils, and the other part-time teachers offered extra help if required. Meg played the organ in chapel and the arrangements seemed to suit nearly everyone.

The boys announced that Miss Hall could stay away for ever as far as they were concerned, and they did hope her old mother wouldn't snuff it or get better too soon, thereby releasing her to return to school before the end of term.

The two young masters said they fancied Flavia, but this was partly to stop Jane and Barbie from becoming too uppity and behaving as if they were the only fish in the sea. James and Michael thought it would be very good for them to experience some real competition, and flirted outrageously with Flavia while being unable to resist the lure of gossips with the under-matrons as well. Nobody was bothered by this, least of all Jane and Barbie, and though it gave them the chance to do a lot of hair-tossing and flouncing if they thought either of the young masters was looking, they got on very well with Flavia too and regarded her as another ally against all the stodgy old fuddy-duddies by whom they considered they were surrounded.

Flavia herself was quite unmoved by the adulation. As Gervaise had expected she was far too used to young men to take it seriously – and anyway after Antoine they seemed very juvenile to her – but she quite enjoyed the game, which was balm to her wounded self-esteem. Gervaise was delighted with the success of his idea. It gave him enormous pleasure to watch Flavia losing the look of a fine piece of silk that has been stretched too tightly over an embroidery frame and is starting to wear thin.

During her first few days he looked in on her classes to make sure that she was all right and that the boys were not playing her up, though he need not have worried on this score – she was far too professional a musician to allow any fooling about. Somehow the habit stuck with Gervaise, though, and he was always dropping in on the music block. He loved listening to her playing either flute or piano, or conducting the boys in singing or orchestra practice – loved the sound of her laughter and theirs – but he also loved watching her. Flavia was unaware that she was receiving special treatment and merely thought, as she had often done before, what a very kind person Gervaise was and how much she enjoyed his company.

She enjoyed trying to make music, which she felt so strongly should be a pleasure above all else, into a subject that the boys would regard as fun. Occasionally she would have one of her off-days, but they were getting fewer and less acute. The heartbreak settled to a dull ache.

The only thing she disliked and found daunting was the atmosphere in the common room at Winsleyhurst, and this was entirely due to Douglas Butler. Once or twice he was positively unpleasant to her and she always felt as though in some way he was trying to catch her out; at other times he was embarrassingly attentive, sometimes paying her extravagant compliments and teasing her in an unpleasantly suggestive way, but always with an undertone of hostility which she found very uncomfortable. He would waylay her during break and put her through an inquisition about the boys she had been teaching.

'How is our famous musician?' he would ask. 'You must find us all very dull after such a glamorous life-style.'

Flavia grew to loathe him and took to going up to the sewing room at break to have coffee and a gossip with the matrons as a way of avoiding him, and was unaware that Meg felt cheated of her special time with Gervaise. If Flavia had tried to monopolize Gervaise's attention, Meg would almost have preferred it because she would then have felt she had reasonable grounds for her own resentment. She knew she was being unfair and hated herself for it. Flavia was far more likely to giggle with Jane and Barbie than make advances to the Headmaster, but all the same Meg watched them closely, and did not think it was her imagination that he seemed very taken up with his protégée.

Sister, who had also noticed Gervaise's fondness for Flavia, put it down to the fact that her parents were great friends of his, but decided that it would be diplomatic to make a special fuss of the girl, and made a great show of always asking her how she was. 'Is it Sister's imagination or are we just a wee bitty weary this morning? We mustn't over do it,' she would say, to Flavia's acute embarrassment. She and Jane and Barbie could all take Sister off to a T., and found it quite difficult not to drop into a Scottish accent when Sister was actually there.

When Gervaise invited Meg out to lunch it therefore came as a pleasant surprise to her.

'There's this really quite good little Italian place in Steeple Lacey which I tried out a few weeks ago when I took Flavia there for lunch the day she came to see Joan Hall about the music,' said Gervaise to Meg. 'There are lots of things I want to discuss with you, but I thought it would be much more fun if we made a jaunt of it as we both have a free day. Would you like to come and have lunch with me there, or is there anywhere else you'd rather go?'

'Oh no, that would be lovely. I've passed it when I've been shopping and thought it looked nice. I wasn't going to do anything special this week, so it would be a huge treat.'

This was not in fact true. Meg had planned to go up to London for the day, meet an old school friend for lunch in Peter Jones, do some shopping and go to a film, but guile was not in Meg's nature, and the thought of playing hard to get never entered her head. Her friend Anne, who knew all about Gervaise, would understand. Anne had been telling Meg for years that she ought to be more forthcoming with Gervaise.

'The trouble with you, Meg,' she was fond of saying, 'is that you have no Come Hither. You're just the same with men as you are with women. If I hadn't gone after Peter and let him see I was mad about him I'd never have got him to come up to scratch.' But Meg had always felt herself incapable of such a go-getting approach. Her father, the archdeacon, would have been horrified, but the creed that virtue brings its own reward which he had inculcated so firmly into his children didn't seem to be working too well for Meg at the moment. She longed for a new and more dashing image and felt it was time she stopped measuring her own behaviour by her father's unbending standards. She didn't think the rewards for her mother's dull and blameless life of service to others were sufficiently encouraging to entice her to go jogging stodgily along in the same old harness. Meg wondered what it would feel like to kick over the traces and do a bit of galloping.

They both enjoyed lunch enormously. Gervaise had always liked Meg and found her easy company, but it is possible to see someone every day without really registering their appearance in any detail until something sparks a special attention. Looking at her across the table that day he found himself thinking that Meg was really very pretty when she was animated, and suddenly there seemed to be a new liveliness about her that was most engaging. He didn't find the aesthetic pleasure in watching Meg that he found in gazing at Flavia, but there was something infinitely cosy and restful about her that brought another kind of satisfaction. He had rather lost sight of his matrimonial resolutions lately, but being with Meg on her own gave him pause for thought again.

They had so much in common and were both so bound up in the school that they were never short of topics of conversation. They chatted happily about boys and parents, and then discussed the question of the admission of girls. Meg put forward some very sensible ideas. She had the courage to say that she would definitely prefer not to be in permanent charge of a girls' house, but might be prepared to start it off.

'I do think you should use the Old Stables for them,' she said. 'That was a very good suggestion of yours if you don't want it yourself, and it is a bit big for just a holiday house. You would rattle about in it on your own in the holidays almost as much as at the school. What I think you should do is to have a married couple over there. From a security point of view it would be a good idea to have a man about, but it would also give it a family feeling that I think parents might like.'

'Now that's an idea,' said Gervaise. 'Michael Stockdale leaves next year. He was only a temporary appointment in the first place, filling in after university, and I don't think he's cut out to be a schoolmaster – he's far too ambitious. I was thinking of looking for another young man to replace him, but I could consider a married couple.'

'The general health would come under Sister and myself,' said Meg, delighted that her suggestion had met with approval, and greatly relieved to have managed to be helpful without committing herself to long-term exile from the main school. 'But the day-to-day running of the house would be done by the wife of the couple. You could plan for at least four rooms of five girls, and give them a little sitting room as well, and there would still be plenty of space for married quarters, even if the couple had a child.'

'Brilliant,' said Gervaise. 'And should we ever need to it would be very easy to build on an extension there. You are clever, Meg. Will you promise to get it started for the first term, though? Then I know it would be a success and get off to a good start. And of course you're quite right: I wouldn't want to lose you from the main building either.'

'I promise,' said Meg, her heart singing, sunbeams dancing over her head.

'Right,' said Gervaise, 'now we'll talk about other things. Let's look at the menu again and choose a pud. What would you like?'

Meg, who usually tried to be careful over sweet things, decided to throw caution to the winds and have chocolate pavlova, and Gervaise ordered treacle tart for himself. Afterwards they sat over their coffee, feeling pleasantly in harmony, and were unaware that Pamela Boynton, who was walking down the High Street, had spied them through the window.

On the way home Meg, mindful of Anne's remarks about Come Hither, and made bolder than usual by two glasses of white wine, said, 'Oh Gervaise, thank you for that. I can't tell you how much I enjoyed it. I've been feeling a bit low lately and that has really cheered me up. I do so enjoy being with you.'

It was then that Gervaise, a modest, fair-minded man, and not one to take credit if he did not feel it was his due, made a disastrous mistake.

'Oh good,' he said. 'I am so glad; I enjoyed it too – we must do it again. I had indeed noticed that you weren't quite your usual sunny self, but I can't pretend it was my idea. Flavia thought you seemed a bit down and it was her suggestion that I should bring you here and try to cheer you up a bit.'

Meg's heart stopped singing and gave a terrible downward lurch, and the sunbeams exploded over her head like volcanoes and turned to a pile of dust and ashes. Because Gervaise was driving he did not notice her face, and mistook the ensuing silence for a companionable one until they arrived back at Winsleyhurst, and he saw to his horror that Meg was crying.

'Why, Meg,' he said in great surprise and distress, 'whatever is the matter? We've had such a happy time. What on earth has brought this on?' And Meg – beside herself with misery and mortification, longing for him to comfort her, but too proud to risk being humiliated any further – made a dreadful mistake herself as she wrenched the car door open.

'Flavia!' she almost shouted. 'I might have known it. Everything always has to be about Flavia. You're all besotted by her. Why couldn't she get on with her wonderful career without coming and upsetting the whole school as she has – and why don't you just get on with it and ask her to marry you and then we could settle back to normal and get on with our own lives?' And she banged the car door and ran into the house without a backward glance, leaving Gervaise sitting in the car in astonishment and dismay.

VIII

MEG'S FURIOUS OUTBURST left Gervaise extremely shaken and caused him to do some long overdue heart-searching, during which he discovered some unexpected things both about Meg's feelings and his own.

A few weeks later, he went over to Orton for one of his chess sessions with Andrew. Neither Flavia nor Hester was there. Hester had gone to help with the school orchestra, and Flavia was in London for the the weekend with Tricia. Though he had only seen her earlier that day Gervaise was ridiculously disappointed not to find her at home.

Both Andrew and Gervaise enjoyed pitting their wits against each other at chess, and the tally of wins and losses, kept over a number of years, was fairly even. Because Winsleyhurst sent so many boys on to Orton Abbey, the matches also gave them both a chance to discuss school affairs and the progress of various boys of mutual concern. This evening Andrew won their first game with unusual speed.

'Well, that was rather easy,' he said. 'You're not concentrating, Gervaise. It's a long time since you've given me such a quick victory. Something on your mind?'

'As a matter of fact, yes.' Gervaise got up and helped himself to another drink, but instead of sitting down again he paced restlessly round Andrew's study, picking up a copy of the *Spectator* that was out on the table and flicking through the pages without really looking at them.

'Anything I can do? I hope you're not letting Pamela Boynton make life difficult for you. Strong-minded lady, Pam, though I must say I do love her – heart of gold underneath that bossiness. Is it this new idea about taking girls?'

'No, it's not that – though that is on my mind, of course, and I'd like your views sometime. No – it's Flavia.'

'Oh dear,' said Andrew, surprised. 'I've been so relieved by the improvement in her health. It was such a good idea of yours to ask her to teach, and I've felt so grateful to you for providing her with a breathing space and a distraction – and, come to that, for giving Hester a chance to cool down a bit without too much loss of face. Isn't it working from your point of view?'

'Oh, Flavia's being marvellous – in fact I think Joan Hall will have quite a problem when she comes back. No, it's not that.' Gervaise continued roaming round the study picking things up and putting them down, and finally coming to a halt in front of the fireplace where he straightened the perfectly straight portrait of Andrew's grandfather that hung above it with great concentration. Andrew wondered what on earth was coming.

Then, 'Do you think I'm too old for Flavia?' Gervaise asked.

Andrew was extremely taken aback. 'What exactly do you mean?' he asked. 'You're surely not suggesting you've fallen for Flavia?'

'Well,' said Gervaise, 'you'll probably think I've taken leave of my senses. I think I have myself, but – actually yes. That's just what's happened. I realize of course that it's impossible,' he went on, gazing up at the image of Andrew's grandfather, resplendent in kilt, outside his baronial lair, and moving the top left corner of the picture down a few centimetres and then very carefully up again. 'I'm more than twenty years older than her. I simply don't know what to do.'

'And what does Flavia think?' asked Andrew, playing for time.

Gervaise looked rather shocked. 'Oh, I haven't mentioned it to her. Naturally.'

'Don't you think you should?'

'I wanted to know what you thought. If you were against it I wouldn't even tell her. I would never have believed I could feel like this.'

'I can't tell you what Flavia's feelings are,' said Andrew decisively. 'And I wouldn't if I could. But aren't you jumping the gun a bit? I take it you know about Antoine?'

Gervaise nodded and Andrew looked at him with a spurt of sympathy. He felt annoyed with himself for not having had the slightest inkling that this situation might occur and was surprised to find his immediate reaction was one of anxiety for his friend rather than his daughter.

There was silence in the room except for the ticking of the heavy oak clock that stood on the desk. When Andrew spoke it was as if he were carefully measuring his words with a slide-rule.

'I can't help you, Swerve. I've watched with anguish and considerable pride as Flavia has struggled to cope simultaneously with a serious illness, a ruined relationship and a major career setback – all of which hit her out of a brilliantly clear sky. I have no idea if she's ready for a new relationship, least of all with a family friend whom as far as I know she's always regarded as a sort of honorary uncle.'

Gervaise winced. 'I know how badly she's been hurt,' he said. 'I quite understand that, but I just long to smooth her path and cherish her.'

Andrew got up and smiled suddenly at Gervaise, with the smile that was so like his daughter's. 'Then you'll have to stick your neck out and take a risk. I don't know if I wish you luck or not, but don't underestimate Flavia. She's had a lot of cherishing all her life – possibly too much – but under the sensitivity she's always had a mind of her own and she'll make it up for herself, whatever we all think. Now for goodness' sake see if you can't give me a better game, even if we don't have time to finish it this evening.'

When Hester came in they both appeared deep in contemplation of what their next moves should be, and she had no idea that these were not wholly connected with chess.

After Gervaise had left, roaring away in the green Lagonda, his concentration for driving greatly impaired, Andrew decided not to tell Hester about the conversation. He was sure she would not find the idea any more suitable than he did himself, but he was also sure she would be unable to resist shoving her oar into the water – and probably catching a good many crabs in the process. He thought it was a good thing that Flavia had gone off for the weekend.

'Well, my love,' he said to Hester, 'I think bed now, don't you?'

'I wish Flavia hadn't gone to Tricia. I shan't feel happy about her until she gets safely home.'

'For God's sake, Hester, stop being such a goose.' Andrew sounded exasperated. 'Just because she's living at home again at the moment is no reason to revert to treating her like a child.'

'She's certainly not fit to live away from home yet.'

'She's very much better, and if you go on fussing over her health in this claustrophobic way while simultaneously trying to force the pace professionally you'll simply drive her away altogether.'

'Just because you're a Headmaster and play God with other people's children doesn't mean you know best about your own,' flashed Hester. 'I shall follow my instincts as a mother.'

'Then do try and be a bit more subtle, darling.' But Andrew knew his wife's weapon had always been the bludgeon rather than the rapier and went up to bed with a sinking heart.

When they had put the light out Hester felt for Andrew's hand and wept into his shoulder, but after they had gone to sleep she had a nightmare. She dreamt that Flavia was standing on top of a hill with the wind blowing through her long hair, dancing a private dance. Hester stood below her, shouting a warning that a storm was coming. She tried desperately to pant up the hill and join Flavia, but though her legs were moving frantically she remained rooted to the spot, having to run faster and faster just to stay still, like the Red Queen in *Through the Looking-Glass*. She yelled at Flavia to wait for her, but Flavia did not hear and picked up her flute and started to play. Hester could not hear the sound though she could see little black notes jumping about in the air as though they had leapt from a printed sheet of music. Then she saw Flavia go dancing out of sight with the notes chasing after her.

Hester woke pouring with sweat and panting for breath, and it took Andrew a long time to comfort her and calm her down, and both of them a long time before they were able to sleep again.

Since Flavia now appeared well enough to have a part-time job, Tricia had considered the time had come to throw a party and expose her to a burst of wildly desirable new men. Personally she found Flavia's declaration that if she couldn't have

Antoine then she wasn't interested in anyone else quite incomprehensible. She decided to pretend the party was to be a celebration of her own birthday, knowing that Flavia would almost certainly veto the venture otherwise. She bullied Roddy into telephoning Flavia to make sure she would come.

'You must say *you're* giving the party and it's all a special surprise for *me*,' she instructed him.

Roddy, not a Machiavellian type, regarded this brief with the utmost misgiving, and his worst fears were immediately realized when he rang Flavia up.

'Oh Roddy, you are sweet, but I'm not really in party mode at the moment. You can tell Trish that you tried to get me, but I couldn't come. I know she'll understand.'

'Oh no she won't,' said Roddy gloomily, 'and it will all be my fault if you say no. You can't do this to me, Flavia – it'll put me in the doghouse for weeks.'

'But I thought you said Trish didn't know anything about it?'

'Oh. Ah. Well. Umm.' Flavia could practically hear the wheels of Roddy's mind grinding desperately round and took pity on him.

'Of course I'll come. It's a lovely idea.' She imagined him mopping his brow.

Tricia worked in a prestigious art gallery specializing in macabre creations mostly made out of the skeletons of birds. Since trade was not exactly brisk in bird bone collages, she usually had plenty of time during working hours to devote to more important activities, such as trying on dresses in Fenwick's, or arranging parties. She immediately got on the telephone to skim off the cream of her enormous circle of friends and acquaintances, determined that no one at all resistible need be invited. This left a large question mark hanging over the faithful Roddy, but Tricia decided that he would be too useful with the drinks to be left out and that anyway he didn't really count – quite forgetting that he was supposed to be the host.

The party was in full swing when Flavia arrived. Music was blaring and people were already overflowing on to the stairs. Resisting a terrific temptation to creep away before she had even arrived, she fought her way through the crowd until she found Roddy. He beamed at her.

'Thank God you've come. I expect you guessed this is all in aid of you really – and someone's just turned up who specially wants to meet you. Promised I'd point you out the minute you arrived.' Roddy felt Tricia would be pleased with him.

Flavia gave him a hug. She was very fond of him, and thought his deficiency in subterfuge was more than compensated for by his extreme kindness; she suspected that Trish, who regarded infidelity as her own prerogative, would be totally devastated if he ever defected.

'So who wants to meet me then?'

'No idea – don't know who half these people are anyway. That's him. I'll take you over and then get you a drink. Think he must be a fan of yours – seemed to know all about you anyway.'

Flavia's heart sank. The last thing she felt like was a discussion about her aborted career. The young man in question hardly looked like one of Tricia's first XI of heart-throbs and she thought he would have had no trouble melting unmemorably into any crowd, but she smiled politely.

'I'm Justin Oliphant,' he said. 'I came here especially to meet you.'

'That's very flattering of you.'

'And to ask your views on the engagement?'

'Engagement?' Flavia looked quite blank, wondering if Tricia and Roddy were finally going to spring a surprise on their friends.

'Miranda Harper's. I thought you'd know all about it.'

'I'm afraid you've made a mistake. I know who she is of course.' Everyone knew about Miranda Harper, BAFTA award-winning television actress. 'But I've never met her.'

'But you do know Antoine du Fosset.'

Where before there had been a crowded hubbub, now suddenly there seemed to be silence and a space round them. Flavia felt as if all her life force were leaking away.

'Their engagement will be in the papers tomorrow. I thought you'd be bound to know, seeing that you were such a close friend of his.'

'You're press!' Flavia said. 'You've gate-crashed this party to find me!'

'So you really didn't know? Can you give me a quote?'

'Yes,' said Flavia clearly. 'Please say I hope they'll be very happy – of course I wish them joy.'

'And your own career? There were rumours that Antoine du Fosset said he wouldn't be conducting you again. Are you planning a return to the concert platform?'

And Flavia, amazed that her voice should sound so normal, heard herself answer: 'But of course. As soon as the doctors give me the go-ahead I shall make a major comeback.'

'With Antoine Du Fosset conducting?'

'Oh I can't say that – there are other conductors. Now if you'll excuse me . . .'

The next minute Mr Justin Oliphant was being frogmarched downstairs by Roddy.

Flavia got through the rest of the evening on automatic pilot; she tried to be the life and soul of the party, and several budding young stockbrokers couldn't believe that anyone apparently so frivolous could have been a serious musician, but to Tricia's disappointment Roddy's great friend Ed said, 'That chum of Trish's is really over the top. A little goes a long way.'

Next morning the gossip columnists had a field day. 'Conductor Struck by Lightning!' 'A Tempest for Miranda!' 'How to Conduct a Love Affair!' One paper said: Former girlfriend Flavia Cameron told our informant, 'I wish them joy of each other – luckily there are plenty of other conductors to choose from.'

Tricia was filled with misery that her idea had backfired so badly.

'You'd never find the right chap for Flavia,' said Roddy. 'The Hooray Henries you enjoy or dimwits like me just aren't her scene. She just wants you to be her friend. You make her laugh and she can ring you up and tell you things without it mattering. Stop match-making.' And for once Tricia thought he might know best.

It was a huge relief to Flavia to get back to Winsleyhurst on Monday morning where the only gossip of burning interest was that Rowan Goldberg had asked Sister if she knew how to say six tall pine trees in Latin, and Sister had said no, and then gone all red in the face when he told her it was *sextus pinus erectus* and everyone in the Blue Dormitory had gone around mouthing SPE at each other and falling about with giggles until Meg, who had been unaccountably grumpy lately, said they were all very silly, that was quite enough, thank you, and why are you wearing your trainers in the house anyway, Goldberg?

IX

ONE OF THE advantages of Winsleyhurst's long connection with the Boynton family was that the school was given the run of the park with its wonderful woods and even more famous rhododendrons and azaleas. It made a delightful place for the staff to walk in and was safe for the boys to bicycle in without fear of traffic. Gervaise, a competent athlete himself, had always recognized the unfairness that too great an emphasis on games can put on the unathletic during schooldays and was pleased to be able to offer an alternative. Although the front gates of Boynton Park were about three miles from the main entrance to Winsleyhurst, there was a short cut from the back drive of the school to a side entrance so there was no need to go near a main road or cross in front of the house itself – not that either Lance or Pamela would have objected. They were far too generous and hospitable.

It was on a beautiful frosty morning in late November that Gervaise and Flavia went for a walk in the grounds of Boynton.

Flavia had been taking an extra choir practice for the Carol Service. She was enormously enjoying organizing the music for it and was determined that nobody should say that this year's service was not up to scratch. To start with she felt she owed this to Joan Hall, but soon she was taking a great pride in it for herself. Where music was concerned she was a perfectionist, but because she was able to combine this with a lightness of touch the boys were unaware that she really worked them very hard. For the time being her professional standards were being vicariously satisfied by the performances she got from her pupils, and she was very grateful for this. When Gervaise decided to drop in on her lesson, as he did increasingly often, the boys were singing 'The Cowboy's Carol' from the *Malcolm Sargent Carol Book*.

'Come *on*, Atkinson,' he heard Flavia say. 'You can do better than that – let me hear that again.' And she sang the line herself. 'Let's have a bit more go about it,' she said 'You're *cowboys* – right? You sound like a lot of wimpy milkmaids, and I want those "pink-a pang, pangs" really snappy!' Then she caught sight of Gervaise.

'Oh good,' she said. 'Here's Mr Henderson. We'll co-opt him as an extra cowboy and raise the roof. Will you come and sing the bass line? I was going to ask if you would do it at the Carol Service and James Pope says he'll do the tenor part.' Gervaise was beguiled into singing the carol with them and thought how good Flavia was with the boys. He had not been joking when he told her father that he thought Miss Hall would have trouble when she returned next term.

'Sir, sir, will you really sing it with us in chapel?' 'Sir, you've no idea what a slave-driver Miss Cameron is. She's a real bully.' Atkinson rolled his eyes admiringly.

Flavia laughed. 'What, bully you lot? Fat chance. Now get your carol books together and I want them all in a pile over there. Quickly – or we'll have Mr Butler complaining I've kept you too long again.' Though they treated her almost as an equal and clamoured for her attention she clearly had them completely under control.

'Can't we sing it one more time? I really think we need more p-practice with the p-pink-a pangs.'

'You Artful Dodger, Goldberg! You just want to be late for Maths and get me into trouble. No, the bell's gone and it's as much as my life's worth to make you late. Off you go,' and Flavia shooed them out. They would clearly have been prepared to go on singing for the whole morning.

'What's this about getting into trouble with Douglas?' asked Gervaise.

Flavia pulled a face. 'Oh well, you know how complicated the music lesson timetable is. He's always checking up that I'm not teaching anyone I shouldn't during one of his classes. The other day I ran overtime with the choir, which really was my fault because I just got carried away, and he was livid and came storming in and tried to wipe the floor with me. It was no big deal.'

Gervaise looked annoyed. 'That's typical, I'm afraid, but I

won't have him upsetting you. And it's monstrous in front of the boys too. Why didn't you come to me?'

'Oh I can fight my own battles – I shall wreak a terrible revenge one day,' she said lightly. 'But I don't go a bundle on old Spanner, I must say. He really does creep for England. Matt always said old Spanner was a sadist.'

Flavia did not tell Gervaise just how unpleasant Douglas Butler had been to her, nor that he had said, 'And now I suppose you'll go running to the Headmaster for protection.' Nothing would have induced her to do so, nor did she say that while everyone else had fallen over themselves to be extra kind to her over the publicity of Antoine's engagement and her own misquotation by the press, Douglas had gone out of his way to bring it up, pretending to tease her in a heavy-handed way but actually being extremely insulting.

'Well, let me know if you have any trouble. He's a funny chap, Douglas. What are you doing now?'

'I've nothing more to do today. My next lessons have been cancelled because John Whitbread and Sam Croft are both off sick, so I'm going home – unless there's anything extra you want me to do?'

'Well, there is. I've had a cancellation too. I had some prospective parents coming round the school and they've just rung to say they can't make it. It's such a lovely morning I wondered if you'd like to come for a walk at Boynton? Then we might have a pub lunch.'

'What a lovely idea,' said Flavia. 'I'll get my coat out of the car. Pity I haven't got Fudge with me – though it might be difficult to keep her out of the black mud at the edge of the lake.' Gervaise thanked his lucky stars.

Flavia met him outside the front door, enveloped in a vast caped tweed coat of a strikingly loud check. It almost came down to her ankles and made her look like a little girl in dressing-up clothes.

'Good Lord!' said Gervaise 'Wherever did you get that? How sensible to allow so much room for growth.'

Flavia twirled round, the coat ballooning round her.

'Isn't it amazing? It belonged to my grandfather. I found it in a trunk in the attic at Duntroon and I winkled it out of Aunt Elizabeth last time we were there. It's in the old estate tweed and I think it's gorgeous. Matt had his eye on it too, but I got in first.'

Duntroon was Andrew's family home in Perthshire, now lived in by his elder brother, Colin.

'Amazing is the word,' said Gervaise. 'Hop in my car, if you can hop wearing such an extraordinary garment. I thought we'd drive to the cascade and then walk up to the folly. The view should be wonderful today.'

It only took them a couple of minutes on one of the estate roads to reach the far end of the lake which Capability Brown, another Lancelot, had designed for one of Sir Lance's ancestors over two hundred years earlier. Gervaise parked the car at the foot of the series of waterfalls which tumbled down into it, fed by a natural stream and a series of artificial ponds. A path wound up beside the stream. Lance Boynton was proud of his woods, and specially of the collection of trees, many that he had planted himself and were now in their prime – acers and liquidambars and a particularly fine specimen of the beautiful Nyssa Sylvatica which grew in a sheltered spot by one of the pools. A few weeks earlier it had worn a flame-coloured crinoline, which glowed as if it were lit from within, but now nearly all its leaves had fallen and they made a scarlet carpet underneath its delicate branches. Gervaise picked a leaf up and gave it to Flavia.

'A ruby for you,' he said, and stuck it in her buttonhole.

At the top of the path they came to the folly, an extraordinary tower that could be seen for miles away, and was a well-known local landmark.

'It's beautiful up here,' said Flavia. 'I can never make up my mind whether I like trees better with their clothes on or off.' They sat down on one of the stone seats which stood on either side of the door. 'I'd forgotten how brilliant the park looks from this viewpoint. I haven't been here for ages. Pa used to bring us sometimes on Sunday afternoons when we were children. I always loved it, though I found the folly rather scary. The boys used to make up frightful spooky stories to frighten me and I never wanted to be here alone.'

'And would you be afraid of being alone now?' asked Gervaise, looking down at her.

'Oh I shall expect you to look after me and fight off any dragons and ogres – keep me safe,' she said, laughing.

'That's just what I'd like to do,' said Gervaise.

Something in his voice took Flavia by surprise, and she got up and went and stood on the edge of the clearing looking down towards the lake.

'Flavia – what are you going to do with your life?' asked Gervaise, coming to stand beside her.

'I wish I knew,' she said. 'Oh, I wish I knew. Funny you should ask me that. I was thinking about it all last night. I couldn't sleep, but I didn't come to any conclusion. This part-time job has been wonderful for me. Great fun too.'

'I suppose you wouldn't like to consider a full-time job?' asked Gervaise, watching her face closely.

'Teaching music, you mean? When Miss Hall comes back there wouldn't really be enough for us both to do and I certainly wouldn't want to do her out of her job, if that's what you're suggesting.'

'No, I didn't mean teaching music – and yes, there would be a sort of full-time job for you – if you would consider it.'

Flavia glanced up at Gervaise and read something in his face that made her look very quickly down again. Gervaise put his arm round her. He could hardly feel her inside the huge coat. 'It may seem ridiculous to you, but an awful thing has happened. I'm afraid I've fallen in love with you, Flavia. I'm asking you to marry me, old grey-beard that I am. Please don't laugh at me.'

'Laugh?' said Flavia. 'Of course I wouldn't laugh, but goodness – a proposal! That's completely unexpected.'

'And might you ever consider it, do you think?'

'Oh, dear, darling Gervaise, I . . . I don't think so. I'm flattered to death. It's amazing of you, but you see I love someone else. I've had to accept these last few weeks what everyone seems to have known from the start – that he doesn't love me. No doubt you know about it too. Up to now I've secretly hoped we might get back together, but now he's going to marry that girl I've got to face the fact it's really over.' She gave a wobbly attempt at a laugh, but the sadness in her face smote him to the heart. 'You have caught me on the hop, haven't you?' she said.

'There must be lots of much younger men eating their hearts out for you. I wouldn't expect you to feel for me as I feel for you. Funnily enough if it hadn't been for this heartbreak of yours I don't think I could ever have plucked up courage to ask you, but now I just want the chance to look after you and be with you.'

Flavia's mind was spinning. The expression on Gervaise's face was balm to her lacerated feelings. He put his other arm round her and held her against him, rocking her to and fro and then gently bent to kiss her. She responded by snuggling into him like a loving child.

'Oh Gervaise, I'm very honoured, so touched and proud, but I know I could never feel for you or anyone a fraction of what I feel for Antoine – I don't even want to. It wouldn't be fair to you. You deserve more.'

'I'm so much older – I know you really ought to have someone more your own age, a dashing young blade – but might you just think about it?'

'Dashing young men are usually pretty boring,' said Flavia. 'There were plenty at Tricia's party the other night but I wasn't tempted. I'd certainly never be bored with you and I will think about it, but I can't truly hold out any hope.'

All the same Gervaise felt her reaction was better than he'd dared expect, and was not dissatisfied just to have planted the small seed of an idea in her mind.

'Just think,' she said suddenly laughing at him, 'I should have to become immensely stuffy and earnest and have deeply fascinating conversations about athlete's foot and bed-wetting.'

'Ah no,' said Gervaise. 'That's not what I want. I should hate you to change. Stay as you are always, darling Flavia, but do stay with me.'

They stood in silence gazing over the landscape until Gervaise suddenly worried that she might be hungry and suggested they should go and find some lunch.

'Yes, I'm starving,' she said. 'Do let's. I suppose you haven't got any Polos on you to stave off the pangs?'

'I don't usually carry Polos, I'm afraid. Perhaps I should start?'

'Oh yes, you must,' she said. 'I run on Polos. If we got married you'd have to have them on you night and day. Perhaps

I may even have one,' and she fished in her pocket and produced the stub end of a grubby packet. 'Want one?' she asked. 'I'm afraid they're a bit grey.'

'I think I'll pass on those, thank you, they look quite revolting. We'll find some proper food. Come on.'

'Let's run all the way down the hill,' she said, holding out her hand, and together they ran down the path, sending flurries of autumn leaves flying in their wake, and reached the car breathless. 'Shall I tell you something?' Flavia said, delighted. 'I haven't got a pain in my chest. That's the first time I've been able to run for months.'

'It's the first time I've run like that for years!'

'Wouldn't it be funny if Sister saw you now? She'd say, "Och, Headmaster! We shouldn't be doing that at our age. We might pull our ligaments." ' Flavia reproduced Sister's refined Scots accent and toothy smile perfectly.

'You're a very dangerous young woman, Flavia Cameron. I don't know how I dare have you at Winsleyhurst at all.'

They went to the Boynton Arms in the village, which was a pleasant pub in a rather self-conscious way, full of old beams and gleaming horse brasses, with a collection of fearsome primitive weapons displayed on the walls purporting to have been used on Boynton enemies of long ago, though some of them looking suspiciously as if they had been made in the local blacksmith's shop.

The ploughman's lunch was excellent, though Gervaise wondered how Flavia could eat so much and look so fragile. He drank coffee and watched her indulgently while she topped herself up with a lurid-looking ice cream served in a long glass. When they got back to the school he leant over and kissed her goodbye, a loving, gentle kiss.

'You would make me so proud and happy,' he said. 'Think about what I've said,' and he watched her drive away in her little car, waving her arm out of the window, no fingers visible, since her coat sleeve covered her hand.

Miss Hackett, the school secretary and Sister's arch enemy, caught him as he came into the hall.

'Oh Mr Henderson, I've been looking for you – I didn't

know you were out for lunch?' She left the query hanging in the air.

Gervaise ignored it. 'What did you want me for?'

Miss Hackett looked huffy. The making of Gervaise's appointments gave her a sense of power over the rest of the staff which was much resented in certain quarters. She hated to be in the dark about his movements, and normally this didn't bother Gervaise since he hardly ever did anything that he minded anyone knowing about. This afternoon was an exception.

'A message from Mrs Goldberg – can she have Rowan out on Sunday and she'd like a few words with you when she comes.' Gervaise groaned. 'And Meg was looking for you. She urgently wants a word with you too – I don't know what about, I'm afraid. I did ask her but she didn't say,' said Miss Hackett pointedly.

'Right then – yes, to Goldberg going out on Sunday even though it's not an exeat. Poor child, he never knows whether he's coming or going, but do try and head his mother off from seeing me if you can. Perhaps you could tell Meg I'm going to my study now so I'll be there if she wants me. I expect it's about the arrangements for the Carol Service,' said Gervaise, which didn't deceive Miss Hackett in the least.

She knew that if she told Sister that the Headmaster had come in looking very unlike himself from a private luncheon engagement and what a pity it was that he was never given a minute's peace by his staff, she could rely on this poisoned dart being shot straight back to Meg. Miss Hackett had a nose like a bloodhound for trouble and Meg's blotchy face and unusually buttoned-up expression during the last weeks had not gone unnoticed.

Meg had spent a miserable time. She knew she had made a terrible mistake and had lain awake at night going over and over every moment of her happy lunch with Gervaise and her own disastrous outburst after it. She had rung up her friend Anne who had been quite bracing.

'A very good thing, if you ask me,' said Anne. 'It will shake him up and make him think. It's good for him to know you're not always a doormat. He'll think all the more of you, you see if he doesn't. Just keep your cool and he'll come running back.'

But though Gervaise had been as pleasant as always, indeed most disturbingly extra kind and polite, he had shown no signs of coming running. Meg felt she could not leave the incident alone. It festered inside her. After much agonizing she decided the only thing to do was to apologize, and then to offer to commit herself definitely to looking after the girls' house. Perhaps then he would be pleased with her again, see how much she really cared for him and for the school. She couldn't help knowing that for all too short a time during their ill-fated lunch Gervaise had suddenly seen her as a new person.

When Meg knocked at his study door Gervaise was correcting exercise books, and his heart sank.

'Hello, Meg, lovely to see you, do come in. What can I do for you?' He tried to sound casual and normal and hoped very much that she was not going to refer to the scene she had made, though he knew quite well that she was.

'I've come to apologize,' said Meg bravely, looking straight at him.

'There's no need I assure you, that's perfectly all right. I expect you were over-tired or perhaps the vino was stronger than we thought,' said Gervaise, hoping to make a joke of it while being uncomfortably aware that to Meg it was no jesting matter.

'It's not perfectly all right. I was not only very rude and ungrateful . . . I was very unfair as well. To you and to Flavia.' Having decided to apologize, Meg now had a desire to immolate herself. 'I am truly, truly sorry.' Might he come and kiss her, tell her he loved her, tell her he needed her – that her suspicions about Flavia were quite unfounded?

'Dear Meg,' he said. 'Please don't think any more about it. I promise you I shan't. It is all forgotten.'

But this was the last thing Meg wanted to hear. All forgotten? It gave her a cold feeling inside.

'I want to say something else,' she went on. 'I have thought it over carefully and I want to tell you that I have decided I will take on the girls' house for you. At least to start with. That's a promise.'

Now surely there would be a response? She was offering him

a real sacrifice. Gervaise was well aware of it but felt helpless to do the right thing. To turn down her offer seemed churlish, to accept it might be to do so under false pretences.

'Thank you, Meg,' he said. 'How very like you to offer and what a wonderful help it will be, if that is what we eventually decide to do. I can't tell you how much I appreciate it. I'll keep you well informed of all the decisions that are taken.'

There was a long uncomfortable silence and then Meg said in a tight little voice, 'I have to go and supervise the boys' tea now, but thank you for seeing me. I'm glad you're pleased,' and she turned and walked out, closing the door with exaggerated quietness.

She did not go to the boys' dining-room. She told Jane that she had a splitting headache, Meg who was never unwell, and then went to her room and cried and cried as though she would never stop.

Gervaise tried to concentrate on the work he was correcting, but somehow could not do so. He doodled a diagram in red pen on his blotter of a circle surrounded by arrows all pointing in the same direction. Round it ran pin figures, each of them in pursuit of the figure in front, but none of them wanting the one that was trying to catch them. Then he marked the sixth form English books with unusual severity.

X

WHEN FLAVIA GOT back home it was already after three o'clock and the shine had gone out of the day. She went upstairs to the old nursery to inspect her feelings about Gervaise's most unexpected suggestion. She settled herself on the wide window seat, hugging her knees, her back leaning against the shutters that were in every room of the old house, and gazed out of the window.

The nursery was immensely cosy, and everything in it spoke of her happy, sheltered childhood. The huge squashy sofa had a rug thrown over it to hide the stain where Peter had once upset a whole bottle of red ink on its faded cover years before, and the linings of the William Morris curtains were torn and threadbare. An array of battered soft toys, looking like the survivors of a defeated army, were lined up on top of the old white-painted toy cupboard, many an empty eye-socket, missing limb and bald patch marking them as veterans of years of nursery campaigning. They were undergoing an Indian summer nowadays and were greatly beloved by Peter and Wanda's three small children when they came to stay.

This was where Flavia gravitated when she needed to be alone, a place in which she could safely retreat into her inner space. She had liked to retire to the nursery to think about a performance and get herself attuned to whatever message she wished to be able to convey through the music. Outwardly the most gregarious creature, she had always needed periods of solitude to dream her secret dreams and fly into her private fantasy world. Her father perfectly understood and respected this side of her character – he had a similar need himself – but to her mother the part of Flavia that withdrew into an inaccessible snail-shell was disturbing and she hated the feeling of being shut out by her daughter.

Flavia tried to analyse her feelings for Gervaise. Could she marry him? She remembered Dulcie's certainty that her music would come back to her when she had a lover, but she could not think of Gervaise as a lover – just as someone she loved. She always felt happy in his company, shared his sense of humour and many of his tastes. She thought life with Gervaise might bring her the care that her mother had always lavished on her, but without the pressure to achieve all the time that Hester placed on her, together with the happy companionship that she enjoyed with her father. Was this enough?

She could not possibly discuss it with Hester though she ached with pity for her. Every time she tried to let her mother come close, as they had been when she was a child, she felt overwhelmed by Hester's iron will and restless ambition, and would put up the shutters of self-protection and wound her mother all over again.

She had meant it when she told Gervaise that she found most young men boring. Antoine's sophisticated glamour had whirled her into a different dimension of existence, but the scars of her great romantic passion, which she had thought was fully requited, had left her so damaged she could not believe the wound would ever heal. Neither sex nor romance was what she was looking for now – but love and security were very attractive. She felt she had swarmed too quickly up the tallest ladder on the board to a square beyond her wildest dreams, and then a toss of the dice had sent her down a terrible elongated snake. Perhaps it was greedy to want too much?

Marriage suddenly seemed a possibility. She had a vision of herself and Gervaise walking together in the sunshine at Winsleyhurst – Gervaise had a little boy on his shoulders and they were both holding the hands of a small girl in a blue smock.

Then what about Gervaise's feelings? He had paid her an enormous compliment, but could she make him happy with the half-loaf which was all she had to offer? Flavia rested her chin on her knees and looked out at the abbey. Perhaps she should pray about it? Her father had told her once that a prayer for help never goes unanswered, though the help might not be what one had in mind. A few weeks earlier he had told her that she must dream her own dream, but she no longer felt she knew what that was. Help was certainly needed.

She heard the front door bang downstairs, and went to see who it was.

'Hi, Mum,' she called. 'Shall I come down and put the kettle on? Shall we have tea?' She ran downstairs. Her mother was putting some music sheets away in the cupboard.

'I was expecting you home for lunch.'

'Oh Mum, I am sorry – didn't you get my message on the answering machine?'

'Yes, I got it. But I came in specially at one o'clock to be with you, and you didn't even say where you were going. Very friendly.' The moment she uttered the words Hester Cameron could have bitten her tongue out.

Don't rise, don't rise, thought Flavia to herself. Aloud she said, 'Well, I'm sorry, Mum, but I keep begging you not to change anything you're doing because of me. Gervaise asked me out unexpectedly and it was such a lovely day that we had a heavenly walk up to the old folly and then went to lunch at the pub.'

Hester felt a dreadful twinge of jealousy. 'You seem terribly wrapped up in Winsleyhurst,' she said unwisely. 'And I do feel you're wasting your time there. It's not helping you back to your proper course one bit. I'm fond of Gervaise, of course, and I dare say he meant to be kind, though it seems to me that the advantage is all on his side. I've always thought him a bit ineffectual, but your father thinks he's wonderful so I suppose you feel you have to be grateful.'

'Of course I'm grateful, Mum,' said Flavia in a dangerously quiet voice. 'But not just because of the job or because he's a friend of Pa's. Gervaise asked me to marry him this morning – and I think I'm going to accept. I may be out for dinner tonight. Please don't wait up for me,' and she was gone through the front door before Hester could catch her breath.

As soon as she was out of the door Flavia leant against the wall of the house, taking slow breaths to quieten the agitated thumping of her heart, and feeling again the pain and pressure in her chest that had been so much better lately. She thought for a moment that she might faint, and crouched down with her head between her knees until the drumming in her ears subsided and the cold sweaty feeling started to wear off, but leaning forward still hurt. I'd be miles off giving a performance yet, she thought, even as part of an ensemble. I'd be terrified of letting the others down. She would have liked to go back inside and creep up to bed but pride would not let her. She decided to use the portable telephone in her car that Andrew had given her in case of emergencies.

The car was parked in the courtyard at the back. She wondered who would answer the telephone at Winsleyhurst as she punched in the school number with a shaking finger.

It rang for some time. There was often a hiatus around this time when Miss Hackett had gone home, the boys were having high tea and everyone thought it was someone else's job to answer the telephone. She was just about to give up when to her great relief she heard Gervaise's voice.

'Hello, Winsleyhurst School. Gervaise Henderson speaking.'

'Gervaise? It's me, Flavia. Can I come over?'

'Flavia, darling!' Gervaise was so surprised that he forgot that someone else might have answered on another telephone and be listening in. 'Are you all right? Where are you? You don't sound like yourself.'

'I'm okay — sort of. Are you very busy or could I possibly come and see you?'

'Of course you can,' Gervaise did a bit of quick thinking. 'Look, I'm supposed to be teaching after tea, but I'll get James or Michael to take my school. Come in at the front door and go up to my study. I'll be there — and, Flavia? Do drive carefully,' said Gervaise, not liking the sound of her voice at all. He had an awful feeling that she must be coming to tell him that his suggestion was absurd and had upset her — that she didn't even want to go on helping till the end of term. He knew he was going to mind unbearably and wished he had not been so precipitant.

'See you in about half an hour,' she said.

Gervaise went in search of one of the young masters, and found Michael, who was not best pleased at being given extra duties at short notice. He was supposed to be supervising the fourth form prep, but had planned to leave a monitor in charge and sneak off to the pub where there was a very pretty new barmaid.

87

Gervaise went to find Sister to ask her to answer the telephone for the next hour or so. Normally this request was extremely well received as it gave Sister a chance to hint to Miss Hackett next morning that she, Sister, was in possession of some riveting information not generally available, but Meg's sudden absence meant that she would have to help Jane put the small boys to bed, as it was Jane's day off. Unlike Meg, Sister had little affinity with her young charges. She only really liked them if they fell off the roof, or had roaring temperatures. She adored bandaging legs, was a whiz at hospital corners on sickroom beds and had a snappy way of shaking down a thermometer, but from the inconsequential flow of chatter that pours from small boys she derived no enjoyment. She had banked on spending the next hour in what she called 'my sairrgery', telephoning to her friend and planning their Christmas holiday. 'My friend from Amersham' featured largely in any conversation with Sister, though no one had ever met her. Jane and Barbie had a theory that she didn't actually exist, since no one could possibly want to spend time with Sister voluntarily.

'Well, Headmaster,' said Sister now, 'I will of course do my best, but with Meg off sick I am very busy.'

'Meg off sick? I only saw her a short time ago.'

'She was taken ever so poorly just after she'd been down to see you,' said Sister beadily. 'She so rarely ails, I'm sure I don't know what can be the matter with her.' Which was not very honest of Sister who had very clear ideas about what she thought was the matter with Meg.

Gervaise, however, had learned a trick or two about dealing with Sister over the years. 'Oh well, I expect she'll be better soon,' he said outwardly easily, though his heart smote him. 'And don't think twice about the telephone if you're too pushed. I'll ask Jane, I'm sure she won't mind.'

This did not suit Sister at all, as Gervaise knew very well, so she smiled a martyred smile, top teeth indenting bottom lip, and said there was nothing she wouldn't do to help and the Headmaster knew he could always rely on her.

Having made suitably appreciative noises, Gervaise beat a hasty retreat. He felt tortured about Meg, but since he had ruled out the only remedy that could help, he had no idea what to do about it. The misery of inflicting such pain on someone else's feelings was a new and distressing experience for him. He was beginning to wonder if he had ever been aware of a good many things that had been under his nose for years.

When she arrived at the school, Flavia sat in the car for a minute or two confronting the enormity of what she was about to do, and was half minded to turn round and drive away again, but when she tapped uncertainly on the study door and Gervaise opened it and held out his arms, she flew into them and was enfolded in his comforting embrace. He had the presence of mind to push the door shut again with his foot in case any interested spectator happened to be passing, before turning his full attention to the shaking girl.

'What's all this about?' he asked gently. 'What's happened to my bright companion of this morning?'

'I've come to say I think I'd like to marry you,' said Flavia and burst into tears.

'Oh,' said Gervaise, enchanted and concerned at the same time. 'What a lovely cheerful way of breaking the news to me!' and he produced a handkerchief from his pocket. 'Could you mop up a bit and tell me more?' He led her to the sofa and sat with his arm round her and waited while she blew her nose and apologized into his handkerchief and explained about her hasty exit from home.

'Darling Flavia,' said Gervaise, 'I can accept that you can't love me as I love you, but I don't think I want to marry you just because you've had a row with Hester.'

'Oh no, no, of course not − it's not like that at all,' said Flavia, horrified that she had sounded so unflattering. 'That just sort of precipitated it. I was sitting in the old nursery thinking what an amazing idea it could be to be married to you, when Mum came in and − well, you know how she can get one all worked up, and now I've said it to you all wrong.'

She looked so tragic that Gervaise laughed. He kissed and comforted her, told her how wonderful she was in his eyes, and how much he wanted to save her from just these sorts of pressures.

Flavia thought how understanding he was and how delightful it would be to bask in this warmth. She switched off the nagging litany of doubts that had been droning through her head because she did not want to hear the response. At that moment she told herself they could be truly happy, and she returned his kiss with enthusiasm and then sat rubbing her cheek against his faded green corduroy jacket that had seen better days – though not much better. Gervaise was not a natty dresser.

Meanwhile in the Headmaster's House at Orton Abbey, Andrew Cameron had come in to find his wife in a state of near hysteria. It was not a good moment for him to be waylaid at home. The end of the Michaelmas term was always hectic, he had just taken a confirmation class, a task he shared with the school chaplain, and was due to attend a meeting of the Debating Society at which the boys proposed to discuss the crucial motion 'Should unmarried fathers in the Armed Forces be eligible for compensation if they are dismissed for taking paternity leave?'

Hester poured out a jumbled torrent of misery, from which he gathered that Flavia was ungrateful and wilful and must learn by her own mistakes; was Hester's most special, gifted little daughter who must not be allowed to waste her talent, but at the same time was not well enough to be away from Hester's loving care. Gervaise was a cradle snatcher, but at the same time despicably missing in drive, enterprise and all the qualities that Hester admired in a man. Andrew listened to this tirade with a sinking heart and as much patience as he could muster, and made a quick decision that the unmarried fathers must be jettisoned in favour of the crisis on the home front. He knew from long experience that when Hester was in this sort of state, it was quicker in the long run to let her have her say and spill everything out.

The awful thing was that he felt deeply concerned himself. He administered a strong measure of brandy to his distraught wife and had just managed, by dint of putting on what his family called 'Pa's headmaster act', to calm her sufficiently to make some sense of her account of what Flavia had said when the telephone rang. Hester rushed to answer it, but Andrew was quicker.

'Why hello, darling,' she heard him say, and then, 'Yes of

course you can – how lovely. I'm sure that will be all right. I'll tell Mum. See you later then.'

Hester made frantic signs that she wanted to speak, but Andrew put the telephone down and rang off.

'That was Flavia,' he said unnecessarily. 'She wants to bring Gervaise over for late supper. They have something to tell us.' And he took his wife in his arms and held her in much the same way as his daughter had just been comforted by Gervaise.

'Oh Andrew,' said Hester, 'I don't think I can bear it – can't you do something? I know you think I'm obsessed about Flavia but I really don't think this would be right for her, and it's such a waste – such a wicked, dreadful waste. She might listen to you. Can't you stop it?'

'No,' said Andrew, 'no, my darling, I don't think I can. If it's any comfort to you I don't feel happy about it either – though she couldn't possibly marry a nicer chap and it just might be a brilliant success.'

He didn't add that he felt his wife must be responsible for the suddenness of Flavia's decision to rush into marriage on such an obvious rebound. Knowing his tender-hearted daughter he also knew that if she ever caused Gervaise to be hurt, then she herself would suffer greatly too.

'Gervaise came and asked me what I thought about the idea the other evening,' he said.

Hester was astounded. 'Surely you told him it was out of the question?'

'No, Hester, I didn't. I told him what I'm telling you – it is their decision and no one else's. You have to let her go, my love. She's very gifted, yes, but she's not your little daughter any more. She's a grown woman. It worries me far more that she's not got over Antoine than whether or not she becomes an international flautist – though God knows, if she'd married him that would have been certain disaster. Now go and wash your face and take a pull on yourself. I shall put a bottle of champagne in the fridge.'

When Gervaise and Flavia walked in they found her parents in the drawing room, her father reading the paper and her mother doing needlepoint. If Hester's eyes were a little red, that was safely hidden by her glasses. Gervaise and Flavia stood in the doorway and Flavia shot an anguished look of enquiry at her father. He gave her a reassuring little nod and Flavia rushed to her mother and nearly squeezed the life out of her. Then she went to kiss her father, beaming up at him and looking happier than she had done for ages. Andrew hoped that he had misread the situation.

'You've guessed, of course!' said Flavia. 'Isn't it brilliant? Gervaise has asked me to marry him and I've said yes. Say you're pleased.'

'Oh Flavia, you've stolen all my limelight,' said Gervaise, laughing. 'But I expect I'd better get used to that. I was going to make a choicely worded formal speech asking for her hand, but as usual I wasn't quick enough!' He went to kiss Hester who was now holding Flavia again.

'I do know what she means to you,' he said, 'and I don't want to take her away from either you or her music. I'll do my very best to make her happy. I'm incredibly lucky.'

They drank champagne and then had soup and omelettes, and drank more champagne, and Hester achieved a brittle brightness which made her husband very proud of her, her daughter immeasurably grateful, and cost her a huge effort. It was decided not to announce the engagement officially till the end of term, which would give them time to speak to all the people who would be mortally offended if they read it in the papers before being told.

'After my sister – and God knows what Flavia will make of her, she gets dottier by the week – the first person I must tell is Pamela,' said Gervaise. 'I'll ring up and ask if we can go over for a drink. I think she'll be terrifically surprised. I won't tell her – just ask if I can bring a friend to see them. As soon as we've told the Boyntons we can tell everyone else at the school. They're all going to be absolutely thrilled.'

'Except for horrible old Spanner,' said Flavia. 'He's not going to be one little bit thrilled, I can tell you!'

She walked out to the car with Gervaise and twined her arms round his neck for a goodnight kiss.

'Darling Gervaise,' she said, 'wasn't Mum wonderful – such a relief – and of course I knew Pa couldn't help but be thrilled. I do love you, you know. Differently from how I loved Antoine, but it will get better and better, and I'm going to try and make you really happy. You'll be amazed!'

Gervaise drove home feeling the old green car might easily become airborne and arrive at Winsleyhurst as the crow flies instead of lurching round the twisty corners.

Luckily there was very little traffic about.

XI

FLAVIA WAS RELIEVED that the following morning was not one of her days for going to the school, so no dissembling would be required from her at Winsleyhurst.

A great deal of telephoning went on. She had to leave a message for Matt and Di, but luckily they were coming down for Saturday night anyway. She was not at all sure what their reactions would be. Tricia was another matter. Flavia dreaded ringing her up and her reaction was totally predictable. She was appalled.

'Flavia! You absolutely can't! He's geriatric.'

'You said that about Antoine who's thirty-four.'

'Well, at least he was an absolute dish. I could understand you longing to leap into bed with him.'

'I shall never long to leap like that with anyone else. Anyway, I've always adored Gervaise and this will be something completely different.'

'Certainly will,' said Tricia gloomily. 'I should think you'll be lucky if he can even get it up.' For once Flavia couldn't wait to get her off the telephone.

She rang Dulcie in some trepidation, but Dulcie was far too clever to give a verdict, and simply made her promise to bring Gervaise to meet her as soon as possible.

Andrew got on to his brother, Colin, at Duntroon, which was very much a second home to the whole family and where they always went for Christmas. Colin suggested that Gervaise might like to come up and join them for the New Year. Flavia was delighted.

'That's brilliant of Uncle Col – I'd adore to show it all to Gervaise. I'm so glad they're pleased,' she said.

Her barrister brother, Peter, was out but Wanda announced that he would be ecstatic, which sounded very unlikely. Peter, who possessed much of his mother's ambition and was hotly tipped to become a judge one day, was not given to hyperbole, except in court. His wife on the other hand was entranced.

'Oh it's so lovely.' Wanda adored weddings. 'Just think how lucky that Peregrine and Daisy are the perfect age to be your page and bridesmaid! We might have to pop a nappy on Daisy for the big day – she's a bit of a late developer in that respect, you know.'

This was an major understatement. Daisy's floods were legendary and she had learned that standing with her legs wide apart and producing an ocean was a guaranteed way of getting attention. 'What a pity Toby's walking is still so unsteady. I wonder if we dare risk it?' went on Wanda. 'Anyway, perhaps he could wear a little matching outfit. Wouldn't that be heaven?'

'Heaven,' agreed Flavia, trying not to laugh, and making a mental note to tell Matt and Di about these latest Baby-Wipe-Wandaisms.

'Anyone would think we'd got engaged entirely for her children's benefit,' she told Gervaise later. 'I'm certainly not having Toby crawling down the aisle after me. It would be quite in character for Wanda to suggest that you and I should all go on all fours to keep him company. Now that would be original.'

Gervaise rang up his sister, a lady of alarming enthusiasms who lived in Gloucester and spent much of her time popping in to the Cathedral to be fortified by a quick pray, rather as other people might pop into a pub. Though she had never been married, she was usually wedded to a cause. Her divorce rate however was high and she seldom stayed with the same one for long. Recently she had got herself on to a rota for cleaning the Cathedral which gave her a splendid opportunity to lobby God with lists of requirements for her charity-of-the-month. At the moment she was deeply concerned about the animal kingdom, which left her little time or inclination to be bothered by the problems of her fellow humans. She was mildly surprised by her brother's news but not particularly interested as her mind was too full of a scheme to interest Prince Charles in sponsoring an exhibition of watercolours by chimpanzees. She felt sure that this would be a venture after HRH's own heart if only she could get direct access to him by telephone or in person, something which she had so far inexplicably failed to achieve.

Gervaise felt he had done his family duty by informing her of his engagement, and secretly hoped she would be too busy chaining herself to a jump at Cheltenham racecourse, or lying down in front of a lorry-load of livestock (if so, almost certainly the wrong lorry) to attend his wedding. Monica Henderson was ten years his senior and they had never been close, but though she had always bordered on the eccentric, recently her behaviour had occasionally been positively bizarre. Gervaise dreaded her visits to Winsleyhurst and the idea of letting her loose on a captive audience of wedding guests made his mouth go dry.

His next call was to the chairman of the school's governing body. He was relieved to find the Boyntons not only at home when he rang, but also free on Saturday evening. Pamela was triumphant. She felt she had engineered a brilliant coup and went to tell Lance that Gervaise would be bringing Meg for a drink.

'It's really rather sweet and touching,' she announced. 'He said he had an exciting bit of news for us and could he bring someone to see us. They'll be coming over separately about six, which seems funny, but he obviously thinks we've no idea who it is, so I played along with him.'

'It might not be Meg,' teased Lance. 'Gervaise may have misinterpreted your intentions for him. Perhaps it's Sister or Miss Hackett or that dreadful mother of the nice little boy with the stammer. Rumour has it that Gervaise dives into the broom cupboard when he sees the woman coming, but perhaps she's managed to trap him in there with exciting consequences.'

'Don't be silly, darling,' said Pamela fondly, slopping milk on the floor as she gave the Norfolks their morning snack of Doggibrek. 'No one could get into any of the broom cupboards at Winsleyhurst. I keep meaning to organize a proper clear-out – toothless old brushes seem to breed in them. There wouldn't be room for Gervaise and the Goldberg woman. Of course it's Meg – there's no one else it could be. I wonder what they'd like for a wedding present? I expect Meg's father will want to take the service, but retired archdeacons don't have parishes of their own, you know, so I've just had rather a good thought: wouldn't it be lovely if they had the wedding in Winsleyhurst chapel and then we could let them have the reception here? Clergy houses are always so poky and I don't expect they have much money, poor things. I've always wanted to organize a wedding.'

'Doesn't Meg have a mother then?' asked Lance, who remembered all too well Pamela's astonished disappointment that the parents of their daughters-in-law had all seemed perfectly capable of running their own weddings.

'I've no idea!' Pamela was much struck by this unwelcome thought, but ever an optimist added, 'I've never heard her talk about a mother. Naturally there won't have been a divorce. Perhaps she's died?'

'Well, that would indeed be a bit of luck,' said Lance. 'Still, I think I'd wait till the engagement is actually announced before ringing up the caterers and fixing the day.'

'Lance! You're laughing at me again!'

'Now what in the world makes you think that, my love?' and Sir Lance, who was going shooting, kissed his wife, promised to be back in good time to toast the happy pair and went off to collect his guns and dogs whistling 'Here Comes the Bride'.

Flavia was rather daunted at the thought of breaking the news to Lady Boynton. 'Will you meet me at Boynton about six then?' asked Gervaise. 'If you come over here first someone is sure to get suspicious and I want to announce our lovely news before it becomes a rumour.'

'Well, mind you arrive first. I'd die if I had to go in and you weren't there. What shall I wear?' asked Flavia.

'Wear?' Gervaise had yet to learn that there is no right response to this all-important and recurring question. 'Oh any old thing – you always look lovely anyway. It won't matter at all,' he said, meaning to be helpful and giving the most unhelpful answer of all.

'I'll ask Di,' said Flavia. 'They'll be here by then and I can always nick something of hers.' Gervaise, who liked and was amused by Di but thought her clothes were quite extraordinary, couldn't help feeling this might be a mistake but didn't like to say so.

Gervaise managed to arrive before Flavia and was greeted with much enthusiasm by his chairman. She took him through to the library, which she and Lance used when they were on their own in preference to the rather grand and formal drawing room. She felt Meg would be more at ease in these cosier surroundings.

The library was indeed cosy – a splendid jumble of the beautiful and the frankly hideous. Pamela had recently gone through a period of backing her own taste, and buying contemporary works of dubious artistic merit. Her husband bore them with equanimity, but intended to banish them the minute she was safely off on a new tack, rather as one might in due course remove something made at school by a spectacularly untalented child. Luckily Pamela had not so far come across the gallery where Tricia worked.

It would not have taken Sherlock Holmes long to guess the interests of the occupants of the library. Old numbers of the *Field*, endless gardening catalogues and copies of the Atlantic Salmon Trust Blue Books were stacked in piles; parish magazines, minutes of WI meetings and copies of the *Financial Times* jostled for space, and family photographs vied with pictures of Norfolk terriers and prize Hereford bulls. A large jigsaw puzzle was laid out on what had once been a beautiful mahogany side table, now much scratched, and a priceless *famille verte* bowl was full of plant labels, stubs of marker pencils and members' badges for various racecourses. Despite several dog beds of doubtful cleanliness, the room smelt deliciously of the pots of gardenias which had been brought in from the greenhouses, and of wood ash from the log fire blazing away in the fireplace.

Lance, in his shooting plus fours, but wearing an ancient red cardigan in place of his jacket, stood with his back to the fire, a large glass of whisky in his hand.

'Swerve, my dear chap – how good to see you. I gather you're going to stun us with some news,' he said, twinkling at Gervaise. At that moment several dogs erupted, barking furiously.

'Oh good, the front door,' said Pamela. It was impossible for mere humans to hear the bell, which rang miles away, but luckily there was never any shortage of canine attendants to give the alarm. 'I'll go and answer it – that will be Meg,' and she charged off, happily unaware of having let out a cat that would have been much better left in its bag.

'Meg?' said Gervaise in dismay. 'I didn't know Pam had asked her for a drink this evening. That's really rather awkward.'

'Oh my God!' Lance gave a shout of laughter. 'My darling wife! I'm so sorry, Gervaise, I rather think she's just made another complete Horlicks. She hasn't really invited Meg, she's just put one and one together and made the wrong couple.'

Gervaise, torn between amusement at Pamela and foreboding for Flavia, knew his lovely surprise had backfired and wished he'd told them the identity of his bride-to-be in the first place.

Pamela, having tugged open the heavy door and flung her arms wide ready for a huge welcoming embrace, was astonished to see Flavia standing at the top of the imposing flight of stone steps that led up to the front door of Boynton. She reined in her welcome as though it were a runaway horse. This was really a bit of a bore.

'Why hello, Flavia, my dear,' she said kindly, hospitable as ever, no warning bell ringing. 'What a surprise, but how nice to see you. We were just expecting Meg Price for a drink so I thought it must be her, but do come in too. What can I do for you?'

A terrible realization overwhelmed Flavia as she recognized in a dreadful flash the cause of Meg's unaccountable lack of friendliness, and at the thought of the hurt they must now be going to inflict on her all the colour drained from her cheeks. She made no attempt to come in, just stood in the cold and dark, wanting to run back down the stone steps, leap into her little car and drive away.

Belatedly, realization dawned on Pamela too.

'Oh dear,' she said painfully. 'Oh my dear Flavia, I do believe I've just been quite incredibly stupid and tactless. Please, please come in.'

'I can't,' said Flavia in a strangled voice. 'I'm so sorry, Lady Boynton, but I really won't. Could you possibly just tell Gervaise that I've gone home?'

At this moment Lance arrived to rescue them both, taking in the situation at a glance, sweeping Flavia into a great bear hug and propelling her into the house.

'Gervaise has just told me your wonderful news – don't stand there getting cold, come along in and celebrate. It's the best news I've heard for ages. God, what a lucky man! We knew it would take someone very cunning or very special to tempt such a confirmed old bachelor to the altar but I never thought he'd be this lucky,' and, keeping his arm round Flavia and not giving her a chance to utter a word, he swept her along to the library on a tidal wave of goodwill. A mortified Pamela followed behind, sending up a prayer of thanks for her husband, as indeed she did every day of her life.

A glance at Flavia's face told Gervaise what had happened, and Pamela didn't look much better. Lance positively shoved Flavia into Gervaise's arms.

'There,' he said, realizing that it would be no use pretending. 'Don't let's allow any silly misunderstanding to spoil this happy occasion or I'm going to have such a miserable wife tonight that I simply shan't be able to cope with her. I'm going to fetch the champagne. It's on ice but we didn't think it would be tactful to have it out on the tray, but tact not being our strongest suit I think we should drink some now.'

Gervaise gave Flavia's shoulder a reassuring little squeeze but she felt as tense as a coiled spring and did not respond.

'I . . . I think I'd rather not, if you don't mind,' she said, and Gervaise, though distressed on her behalf, suddenly felt absolutely terrified of losing her.

'I can't bear it,' said Pamela. 'Flavia, I'm the clumsiest, stupidest old woman in the world. I just made a wrong guess and blundered on in my usual way. Lance will tell you I'm sort of disabled – I was born without antennae. One look at Gervaise's face when he saw you come into the room makes me realize how wrong I was. It's wonderful news. Please, please say you'll forgive me?'

'Oh Lady Boynton, there's nothing to forgive,' said Flavia quickly, but her eyes were full of unshed tears. 'It's not your fault at all. It's just that you've shown me something about Meg that I should have seen for myself weeks ago. She must hate me. I can't do this to her.'

'Hang on a minute, you two,' said Gervaise, thinking it was time a lighter note was introduced. 'I come into this too, you know! There's never been any question of me marrying Meg and I don't flatter myself for a moment that she would want to.' But he was uncomfortably aware that neither statement was quite true. 'Flavia darling, don't look quite so reluctant or Lance and Pamela will think I've kidnapped you.' Flavia managed a watery smile but shook her head. Lance coming back with a couple of bottles of Krug '82 and falling over a terrier created a much needed diversion.

'Oh my God,' he said laughing, and collapsing safely on the sofa with both bottles miraculously unharmed. 'Damned animals under foot as usual.' He levered himself up, opened one of the bottles and poured out four glasses. 'Come on. This is a celebration. Can't have you all looking as if you're going to a funeral! It's weddings we're thinking about now and here's to a very exciting one. Flavia and Gervaise – your very good health and many, many blessings,' and he raised his glass to them.

Flavia tried to pull herself together and enter into the spirit of the occasion, but a small piece of enamel had chipped off from her new coating of happiness.

After Gervaise and Flavia had left, Pamela stood beside her husband and rubbed her weathered cheek against his sleeve. She had been very pretty in her youth and in her husband's eyes she always would be.

'Oh Lance, what do you think?'

'Hmm. Not sure,' said Lance. 'Seems no time since Flavia was a funny little girl rather too much under Hester's powerful thumb and now she's burst out of her chrysalis and grown into a spectacular butterfly. I quite see that old Swerve is knocked for six by her, but charming as he is, one does rather wonder why she's marrying him. Thought she was supposed to be having an affair with some musician. Isn't she a bit of a star with a trumpet or something?'

'Yes, I believe she's exceptional, and it's a flute actually. But she's been ill and is helping out with teaching till the end of term, so she must have exploded on Gervaise like a firework. But oh Lance! Poor Meg! For all I made such a fool of myself I know I wasn't wrong about *her* feelings. It would be an absolute disaster for the school to lose her. What do you think I should do now?'

'Nothing,' said Lance firmly. 'I can see there may be trouble, but there really isn't anything you can do, darling. You'll just have to wait and see, and don't you let it upset you either. Now what about a bit of dinner for a poor starving chap?'

Gervaise and Flavia walked out to their respective cars. He tried to put his arm through hers but she pulled away.

'Oh Gervaise,' she said, 'how could you?'

'I'm dreadfully sorry, darling, but it's not entirely my fault. Look, we can't go our separate ways after that,' said Gervaise. 'I'll telephone school and say I won't be in for dinner after all. Shall we go to the Boynton Arms again and have something there and talk about things?'

'Mum's expecting me for supper and Matt and Di are home. I'd rather just go back, if you don't mind,' said Flavia, polite but distant.

'No, that's ridiculous, Flavia.' Gervaise sounded as if he were talking to one of the boys. 'I'm really not prepared to let you go home and leave us both miserable. You're being very unfair – Pamela is a silly old meddler but her heart's in the right place.'

'What about Meg's heart?' asked Flavia passionately. 'Haven't you thought about that? Did you know? I think you did. If you'd told me I'd never have said yes.'

'And what about my heart?' asked Gervaise gently. 'I'm not just a parcel that can be readdressed, you know.'

Flavia's head started to ache. She longed to be at home, alone with her flute and no complications. All her life she had turned to music when she needed to escape, though lately it seemed to have deserted her.

'It was all so happy and now it's spoilt,' she said childishly, but a child was something Gervaise could deal with – it was women he was less sure about.

'You're very tired and what we both need is food,' he said firmly. 'I shall ring up Hester and ask myself to supper. Besides, I have something to show you. I wish we hadn't got two cars. Are you fit to drive?'

'Yes, of course. Oh Gervaise, I'm sorry. I need to think.'

'Of course you do, and you shall,' he said soothingly, and kissed her cold face and held her against him, and after a moment or two she allowed herself to melt a little. But even as he whispered that it would all be all right, that he loved her and nothing else mattered, a part of him was thinking of the difficulties that might be lying in store for them at the school.

By the time Flavia, after a huge welcome from Matt and Di, had regaled everyone with the story of her disastrous arrival at Boynton she had recovered her sense of humour; at least Pamela's part in the evening started to seem funny and Matt and Di thought the whole episode utterly hilarious. When Gervaise got there half an hour later he was greatly relieved to see the colour back in his bride's cheeks and hear her infectious laugh again. After supper the family left them alone, saying that newly engaged couples were excused the washing up, but not to bank on this special concession lasting.

'I have something for you, my darling,' said Gervaise. 'Are you feeling a bit better now?' Flavia came and perched on the arm of his chair.

'Sort of,' she said. 'I suppose I over-reacted, but oh, Gervaise, I think Lady Boynton is right about Meg and I do feel awful about it. What are we going to do?'

'I think the sooner we tell everyone the better. I had meant to announce our engagement at the Carol Service, but I think now I'll try and see everyone who matters tomorrow – old Fossy, and Douglas, and Sister – and of course Meg. I'll talk to her myself. Don't you worry your head about a thing. It will all be fine,' said Gervaise with far more optimism than he felt. All his life he had done his best to avoid unpleasant confrontations and to remain uninvolved emotionally and now he dreaded the thought of facing Meg.

He felt in his pocket and produced a small blue leather box. 'This belonged to my grandmother,' he said. 'I was specially fond of her and she was very musical, which makes it seem right. There are other choices among my mother's things, or you might prefer something new and think this is too old-fashioned but I think it's a pretty setting and I want you to have it if you like it.'

In the box was an antique half-hoop ring of diamonds and emeralds set in gold. Flavia hesitated for a fraction of a moment before meeting Gervaise's eyes, and then rather slowly held out her left hand and Gervaise slid the ring onto her fourth finger. Amazingly it fitted.

'I think it's wonderful – quite beautiful. Oh thank you, darling Gervaise,' and she flung her arms round him and kissed him, before rushing off to show the ring to the others. Andrew and Matt and Di exclaimed and enthused and there was much kissing and hugging.

'Don't you think it's stunning, Mum?' asked Flavia, hoping for Gervaise's sake to trip her mother into admiration.

'Lovely, darling – very pretty, though somehow I've always thought a sapphire would be right for you,' said Hester, qualified approval being very much her forte.

Gervaise felt greatly relieved that a crisis had been averted but after he had driven back to Winsleyhurst and they had all gone to bed, Flavia lay awake for a long, long time.

XII

BEFORE ANNOUNCING HIS engagement to the whole school at lunch on Sunday, Gervaise made a point of seeing all the key personnel privately first. There were no surprises about individual reactions.

Miss Hackett, who did not come in at weekends, was unfortunately away from home, and though Gervaise left a message on her answering machine he knew a black mark would inevitably be chalked up for this piece of bad luck. Miss Hackett was an umbrage junkie.

Sister simpered sickeningly and said a wee bird had been whispering rumours in her ear for some time, and she had always had a feeling in her bones. In reality she was far from pleased as she had always considered herself First Lady at Winsleyhurst.

The two young masters had always liked and respected Gervaise but the news sent him even higher in their estimation – though they were surprised that Flavia could possibly prefer Old Swerve to themselves, and Michael thought himself heartbroken for at least half an hour. Old Fossy was touchingly delighted and nearly wrung Gervaise's hand off before driving to the local garage to buy a slightly weary bunch of carnations and gypsophila for Flavia, the first time he had ever given flowers to a woman. In fact nearly everyone was genuinely pleased and could hardly wait to rush off and discuss this riveting piece of information and speculate about every aspect of the romance.

Douglas Butler, however, who was on duty for the weekend, could hardly conceal his dismay and annoyance. For one thing the browbeaten Betty would no longer be required to see prospective parents, and then he had found Flavia's nubile presence in the school extremely titillating and had greatly enjoyed trying to embarrass her. He was confident that he had a way with women and would dearly have liked to have it with Flavia. The thought of the pleasures in store for Gervaise Henderson made him sick with jealousy and fuelled his existing resentment to alarming proportions.

'It seems I should wish you joy then, Henderson,' he said, gazing in an insinuating way at the flies of Gervaise's trousers. 'And let's hope your young bride finds it too.' He resolved to make life as difficult as possible for both of them, and went home to criticize the Christmas decorations which Betty had spent all day putting up.

Gervaise resolved that somehow he had to get rid of Douglas, and felt sullied by the encounter.

He had managed to tell Meg before he told any of the others. He caught her after breakfast on her way to chapel to practise the organ for the service.

'Meg, dear Meg,' said Gervaise, walking beside her, his face creased with anxiety, 'I have a piece of news that I would like to share with you and I want you to be the first person at Winsleyhurst to know it,' and Meg feeling as if the bottom was dropping out of her world, but loving Gervaise too much to make it difficult for him, had tried to smile at him.

'I think I know,' she said, her voice almost steady. 'You are going to marry Flavia. I know I haven't been very welcoming to her but she is quite exceptional and very nice and I wish you both all the happiness in the world.'

'Thank you, Meg,' said Gervaise, feeling humbled by her dignity and honesty. 'Yes, you're right. Flavia and I hope to get married in the spring. I'm going to tell the staff after chapel, but you are such a very close and dear friend that we both wanted you to know first.' They had reached the chapel and stood in the porch. Gervaise could have wept at the pain in her face. He felt an urge to take her in his arms, kiss her rosy face and tell her he understood how hard this was for her and how honoured he was by her feelings, but wisely resisted.

'Would you think it might be a good idea if you looked for someone to replace me?' asked Meg, feeling as though she might be writing her own death warrant.

'No one could ever replace you,' he said. 'I would very much dislike to have to do that. If you feel you must leave then of course I shall accept what you think is best for you, but do please stay if you can.'

They stood in silence while Meg wrestled with herself, then: 'I would hate to leave Winsleyhurst,' she said. 'And I gave you my promise to start the girls' side off if you wanted. I have never gone back on my word yet. Now if you'll forgive me I think I must practise the psalm,' and she walked swiftly into chapel and closed the door, longing for Gervaise to come after her but knowing that he would not do so.

In her heart she was aware that she had used her promise over the girls' house as an excuse to stay on, because however agonizing it would be to see Gervaise married to another woman, she knew very clearly that the pain of deciding to cut herself off from him completely was more than she could bear. She was also uncomfortably aware that her father, the archdeacon, would have roundly condemned her decision, but deep inside her a tiny pilot light of illicit hope still flickered faintly, and she had no intention of turning it off.

Gervaise told the boys at the beginning of lunch as soon as he had said grace and they had all sat down with much scraping of chairs. Wild cheering immediately broke out as soon as he said, 'Now you may talk,' and there was great drumming of feet and banging of spoons, partly because Gervaise was much liked by his flock, and those who had come into contact with Flavia thought she was *wild*, incredibly cool, but partly because any excuse to let out the maximum volume of noise is welcome to small boys.

Those who were being taught by Flavia naturally gave themselves great airs and pretended to be a mine of information about the matrimonial affairs of their headmaster, and those who could lay no such claims to inside knowledge naturally had to say chill out and try to look bored. The question of sex however was another matter, something in which all were united in fascination. Luckily Rowan Goldberg's unpredictable parent had not turned up to take him out after all. He was generally regarded as the school expert on matters pertaining to sex and sometimes smuggled extraordinarily interesting magazines into school which he nicked from his mother's lovers. He was temporarily forgiven for shooting an own goal in the

Under Eleven match against St Wilfred's, and invited to give his views on what he thought Swerve and Flavia actually *did*.

'D'you suppose he gives her Chinese burns or French kisses?' asked Gavin-Smith.

'F-french kisses,' said Goldberg authoritatively, 'Chinese burns are just for b-babies.'

'Imagine having old Swerve pop his tongue in your mouth! Yu-uk, that would be really gross.' They laughed so much that Whitbread minor choked on a Brussels sprout and Mr Pope sent him out.

Altogether a good time was had by nearly everyone.

The end of term at Winsleyhurst brought the usual tide of excitement and irritability with it. Suitcases were brought down from the attic, and had much the same effect on the boys as the sight of a lead does on an energetic dog needing a walk. Sister rushed about looking frantic and countermanding her own orders while Barbie and Jane did all the packing; Garry, the school chef, who would have been furious if he had been denied the chance to show off his skill with a piping-bag, as usual behaved like a prima donna, and Meg had to use all her tact to coax him into icing the Christmas cake, a task he adored. He eventually said that he would only do it as a special favour so as not to disappoint the Headmaster's future wife.

Flavia felt nervous at appearing in the school for the first time after Gervaise had made their engagement known, but was warmed and touched at the boys' enthusiastic response. Everyone gathered round her and admired her ring. She had dreaded meeting Meg, but luckily Meg was extremely busy. For the first time in all her years at Winsleyhurst she longed for the holidays to start.

Flavia threw herself into rehearsals for the Carol Service. Rowan Goldberg, the only boy in the school who was not looking forward to the holidays, was to sing the solo verse in 'Once in Royal David's City' as the choir processed in to chapel. He put his heart and soul into practising it, but Flavia found him weeping behind a door in the big music room when she went back for some books she had forgotten one morning.

'Rowan – whatever is the matter? I was so pleased with you this morning. Don't you want to sing on your own?'

'Yes, oh yes.'

'Then what is it? Have you had a quarrel?'

He shook his head.

'Is your mother not coming to the service then?' asked Flavia. She had not met Irina Goldberg yet and was full of curiosity.

'I th-think so. She promised she would come.'

'Then whatever is it?'

'I d-don't want her to come. She might laugh, and I couldn't bear it.'

Flavia was truly shocked. 'Of course she won't laugh,' she said fiercely. 'She'll have me to answer to if she does. I'm very proud of you.'

She was full of indignation when she told Gervaise about the episode. 'She must be a monster,' she said. 'Imagine not wanting your mother to come and hear you sing!'

'That makes two of us who don't want her to come near Winsleyhurst then,' said Gervaise.

In the event neither Rowan Goldberg nor Gervaise need have worried. The stammer which plagued the boy's speech was always absent when he sang and his clear voice dropped onto the top notes as accurately and easily as a bird landing on its chosen twig. He brought a pleasurable lump into many parental throats, but not that of his own mother. Though she so often arrived unannounced, as usual when she had actually said she was coming Irina Goldberg simply didn't turn up. Since the boys were all taken home for the holidays after the service, Meg had to arrange for Rowan to be given a lift to London, having first ascertained that the Filipino couple who ran his mother's house would be in, though they had no idea where Mrs Goldberg was herself nor when she was expected home.

The Carol Service was a great success. The orchestra played a medley of Christmas music arranged by Flavia, including 'Walking in the Air' from *The Snowman*. Douglas Butler told Flavia he thought some of the tunes were unsuitable for chapel, but everyone else loved it; all the soloists sang well and everyone congratulated Flavia on both the music and her engagement. She stood beside Gervaise in a glow of pleasure. Miss Hall, who had managed to leave her convalescent mother for the afternoon, could not help being aware that Flavia had drawn some quality out of the boys' performance that she had never quite achieved herself. She thanked Flavia profusely for standing in for her and wondered how difficult it would be to take over again next term.

Watching her daughter's face as she conducted the orchestra and the choir, and especially when she accompanied them on the flute while they sang 'King Jesus Hath a Garden', Hester Cameron took some comfort. She felt it was impossible for Flavia to get and to give so much pleasure and not eventually be drawn back into her own world of music.

Except for anxieties over Meg, Flavia thought she would be entering an existence of much quiet happiness at Winsleyhurst and tried hard to put thoughts of Antoine out of her head.

XIII

GERVAISE WAS DUE to spend Christmas with his sister and
some dull but worthy cousins, who felt that by having Monica
to stay once a year they must surely earn considerable immunity
from hellfire.

Monica's dottiness often amused Gervaise when they were
not actually together, but after five days of her company he
knew he would be as near screaming point as anyone of his
easy-going temperament could be, and looked forward to
spending the New Year in the entertaining company of the
Cameron family, not to mention being reunited with Flavia.
He could hardly bear to let her go.

'Will you miss me too?' he asked.

'Of course I will. I wish you were spending Christmas with
us,' she said. 'You can't think what fun we always have. Still, at
least you'll be there for the New Year and the Arbuthnots' reel
party. That's always wonderful.'

'Darling Flavia, I'm afraid I can't dance.'

'Oh don't worry, we'll teach you the reels. You'll pick them
up in no time.' But Gervaise had no intention of dancing reels
or anything else. He did not wish to confess to her yet that he
had a long-standing and deeply rooted inhibition and never,
under any circumstances, took the floor.

'Will you take your flute with you?' he asked, to turn the
conversation.

She looked surprised. 'Oh I never go anywhere without it.
I expect we'll have music at some stage – Mum always plays
and Pa might even scrape away on his cello. And Matt's a
brilliant piper – did you know? He can't practise in London or
the neighbours go mad, so he keeps his pipes at Duntroon.
The bag usually gets dried out and has to be lubricated with
golden syrup. Matt nicks it from the kitchen and makes every-

thing sticky and Aunt Elizabeth complains she can only make gingerbread for the shoot before he arrives because he uses it all up.'

Gervaise thought how wonderful it was to see Flavia getting back to her bubbly self again, and how much he would enjoy sharing the family life she loved so much – but he also wondered if he would live up to some of her expectations.

Duntroon was a vast monstrosity in Victorian baronial style which escaped being gloomy because its miles of stone passages usually echoed with the sound of laughter rather than ghostly footsteps.

Flavia arrived a few days earlier than the rest of the family to help her aunt, to whom she had always been specially close, with the preparations. Together they decorated the enormously tall Christmas tree, which came from the estate, and put holly wreaths on the suits of armour which stood round the vaulted entrance hall, giving them an inebriated look as though they had already been at the festive punch.

Elizabeth Cameron would dearly have loved a daughter of her own and Flavia often confided things to her which she would have hesitated to tell her own mother, though both were aware that the steel trap of Hester's potential jealousy was dreadfully easy to spring. Now, as they hung baubles, sprayed trails of ivy with gold, and draped tinsel, it gave them a chance to talk.

'And Antoine – you've really got over him? I was stunned when I read about his engagement.' Elizabeth held the bottom of the ladder while Flavia teetered on the highest rung, struggling to fix the angel on the top.

'Not half as stunned as I was. He never even bothered to tell me. I don't think I'll ever quite get over him, but I've come to terms with it, yes. I feel I can be happy with Gervaise and make a new life.'

'Is that going to be enough for you, darling, and enough for him too? And what about the music?'

'I've been absolutely open with him – he swears he doesn't mind. He's such a special person I don't think he knows how to be jealous – and I do love him. As for being a soloist – I really don't know myself. It had become rather a treadmill before Antoine. Then after he took me up and we got together, it was so blissfully tied up with him, I can't separate it in my head yet. I've totally lost my nerve at the moment, but I suppose I haven't ruled it out for ever. Please don't tell Mum though, or she'd never leave me alone.'

'No, of course I won't.' Elizabeth handed Flavia a reel of fuse wire, not very reassured by her words. 'Anyway it's heaven to have you here, and we're all dying to meet Gervaise – such a pity Malcolm's the only one at home and the others will have to wait till the wedding.'

Colin and Elizabeth had three sons, but the elder two were married and spending Christmas with their respective in-laws this year. Flavia enjoyed the privileged position among the cousins of being not only much the youngest, but also the only girl, and though her brothers and cousins reserved the right to tease her unmercifully, she could twine the lot of them round her little finger.

Elizabeth stood back to survey their handiwork. 'The poor angel doesn't exactly look bursting with glad tidings, more like someone with a slipped disc in need of a surgical corset,' she said. 'Can you give him a tweak to the right and brace him up a bit?'

Despite the absence of Gervaise and the missing family members, Christmas was wonderful. By the time various relations who lived in the neighbourhood had turned up, they still sat down eighteen for lunch, and all the usual hoops were jumped through. Peter and Wanda's children woke everyone at five in the morning, having found the bulging stockings at the ends of their beds, and there was the usual rush to get ready to drive up the glen to the little church, which was packed to bursting. During the first part of the service Daisy succeeded in eating a whole packet of Smarties, which unbeknown to her mother, Father Christmas had slipped into her stocking; she had craftily hidden it up her knickers and then announced loudly that she was going to be sick. Wanda rushed her out in the middle of the service with maximum disruption, whereupon she recovered immediately and ran wild over all the graves, shrieking with excitement. Poor Wanda walked an agonizing tightrope between her inclination to give in to her children's every desire and her conviction that a grain of sugar passing their lips might do them irreparable harm. In the gaps between verses of 'Hark the Herald Angels Sing' her plaintive voice could be heard trying to reason with her daughter – a triumph of hope over experience.

'Just a little foretaste of your wedding,' whispered Matt to Flavia.

The rest of the day was devoted to opening presents, listening to the Queen, and for some, a long walk to counteract the effects of too much brandy butter.

The Boxing Day shoot was a great success, and Fudge, who usually disgraced herself by eating pheasants and beagling through the woods ahead of the beaters, was firmly secured to Flavia by a rope and voted a reformed character.

Peregrine and Daisy rode their Christmas present tricycles up and down the passages and everyone cursed Matt for giving them hooters to screw on the handlebars. Toby's walking improved so much it confirmed his mother's opinion that she had given birth to a genius and made her hopeful that he might qualify as a page for Flavia's wedding after all. Away from the law courts Peter forgot to be pompous and became quite fun again.

Hester poured out her anxieties to her sister-in-law and felt better for getting so much off her chest, and as she never waited to hear Elizabeth's opinions there was no chance of disagreement building into resentment. Andrew fitted back into his childhood home as though he had put on a comfortable old shoe. He and Colin were devoted to each other, though their wives complained they reverted to behaving as if they were small boys when they got together. The learned Headmaster of Orton Abbey was actually seen to flip a butter pat at his host during dinner.

On the day before New Year's Eve, Gervaise, having broken his journey in the Borders, arrived in a snow storm in time for lunch. Flavia, who had been watching for him, rushed out.

'Oh how heavenly – and snow to greet you too! It usually comes after Christmas and I've been praying for it specially for you. I so want you to see Duntroon at its beautiful best,' and she flung her arms round his neck, huge white flakes settling on her hair and sticking to her blue Guernsey sweater. Gervaise, whose Christmas had been no better than expected, felt as though he were wheeling along in overdrive after grinding up a hill in low gear.

'Uncle Col, Aunt Liz – look who's here!' shouted Flavia, tugging Gervaise along by the hand. The introductions over, he was instantly absorbed into the family party. In the afternoon, the snow having temporarily stopped falling, they went tobogganing. Gervaise had always been a pied piper with children and Flavia laughingly complained that she couldn't get a look-in when Peregrine and Daisy were with him. They became thoroughly out of hand, shrieking with excitement, and when Paula, the Australian girl who helped Wanda with the children, came to get them for bed, Daisy attached herself to Gervaise's leg and went off into one of her best tin-whistle screams. Paula, who was built on Wagnerian lines, nearly toppled Gervaise over as she prized the furious little limpet off, and Daisy, true to form, retaliated by wetting herself, the carpet and Gervaise's shoes.

More snow fell in the night but in the morning the sun came out, making the surrounding countryside as dramatic and beautiful as any Alpine postcard. The small loch below the house had frozen over and ancient skating boots were dug out for ice hockey. Some extremely dirty play went on amid much laughter and the players came in ravenous for a huge Scottish tea.

Flavia had forgotten that she had meant to organize a reel practice for Gervaise's benefit and he did not remind her.

After tea there was much discussion about which cars to take to the Arbuthnots' in the evening. A general veto was placed on Gervaise's car, and it was decided that only vehicles with four-wheel drive would make it. They all dispersed to change, and as usual the hot water ran out before everyone had managed to get a bath.

The invitation was for black tie, but Gervaise felt like an old crow in his dinner jacket beside the rest of the men in their kilts and doublets, and thought how drab English formal dress is compared with the glamorous Highland version, though normally he never gave much thought to his appearance. Flavia wore an ankle-length dress in vivid kingfisher-blue silk, and looked radiant. She adored dancing and was greatly looking forward to the evening. She was also conscious of being well: the long weeks of creeping about feeling constantly below par almost seemed worth it, so delightful was the contrast now.

'Just look at Flavia,' remarked Colin Cameron to Gervaise as she came downstairs. 'I haven't seen her so stunning since before that ill-fated concert. Being engaged must suit her. You're a lucky man, Gervaise.'

'I am indeed. I tell myself so every day and wonder what I've done to deserve her.'

The Duntroon contingent were by no means the first arrivals at the party and already a good many people were drinking champagne and balancing plates of food when they appeared. Flavia and Matt seemed to know everyone, and there were shrieks of welcome. Flavia was kept busy introducing Gervaise to friends of all ages, very few of whom he had any hope of remembering. Food at the Arbuthnots' was always delicious and the atmosphere welcoming and relaxed. Soon most of the older members of the party gravitated to the far end of the drawing room while the younger members on the whole stayed in the hall.

'You and Gervaise go and sit on the stairs and keep places for us, and Matt and I'll get some food for us all,' said Malcolm to Flavia.

'I'll come too and help,' protested Gervaise, but they wouldn't hear of it, and he suddenly felt conscious of the difference in age between himself and the two young men. It seemed odd that he should be aware of it at this particular party, for there was a lovely mix of all ages present, ranging from nine to ninety. If Flavia noticed it too, she gave no sign, only patted the stair for him to sit beside her.

When the young men returned, doing a wonderful job of balancing plates, they had two girls in tow.

'Di would be livid,' whispered Flavia. 'The fair one's Matt's ex-girlfriend – I think she's trying to get her talons back in, don't you?' The girl in question, very groomed and glamorous, could hardly have been less like Di, but there was no denying that she was very pretty. Poor Di, who had also been invited for New Year, was on duty at the hospital.

'Don't tell Di,' whispered Matt to Flavia, rolling his eyes as he gave her a plate piled high with food. 'She can't stand Catriona, but I couldn't shake her off.' Flavia laughed. He didn't seem to be trying very hard.

After supper the parquet floor in the vast dining room was cleared for action and Flavia and Gervaise joined the rest of the party from Duntroon. A large blackboard had been put at the end of the room with the order of dances chalked up on it and the band, which was composed of one of the Arbuthnot sons and several schoolfriends, started playing the Dashing White Sergeant to get everyone going.

'Oh good,' said Flavia. 'This is lovely and easy for you to start with. Come on, Pa, do it with me and Gervaise, and he'll soon pick it up.'

'Not me, I'm afraid,' said Gervaise, smiling fondly down at her. 'I'm just going to watch, which I promise you will give me the greatest pleasure.'

'Oh but you must dance – please, Gervaise. This is the best possible one for you to start with,' but he shook his head as she stood clasping her father's hand and holding out her other one to him. Luckily Colin came to the rescue, while Matt and Malcolm grabbed Catriona. There was no time to argue so Flavia blew a kiss to Gervaise as the reel began and danced happily away between her father and uncle. Gervaise walked over to Elizabeth, who was talking to their hostess.

'I think I may need your help,' he said. 'I most particularly don't want Flavia to feel she can't dance because I won't.'

'Oh but how very silly of Flavia,' said Elizabeth. 'We could so easily have taught you one or two.'

Gervaise laughed. 'That's what I was afraid of! I never dance. Not even Flavia could persuade me onto the floor. But I couldn't bear to spoil her fun.'

Elizabeth felt a frisson of anxiety for them both, but, 'Don't worry,' said Lady Arbuthnot kindly. 'As a matter of fact it might be very helpful to me, because we've got someone staying with us who says he won't dance this evening either, but unlike you he's actually a superb dancer and I have every intention of dragging him onto the floor. Let me get you a drink and let's go and sit over here where we can see all that's going on, and I can keep my eyes open in case there should be a child without a partner.' She was a wonderful hostess, and no one ever felt left out at her parties; very soon, seeing a small girl not dancing, she went off to rescue her, leaving Gervaise and Elizabeth Cameron to chat.

'I'm sure you must take much of the credit for Flavia looking so much better at last,' she said, liking Gervaise very much, but privately thinking it a pity that Flavia, so completely wrapped up in music at a stage when most girls were more interested in meeting friends, and then plunging immediately into a passionate and ill-fated relationship, should be marrying someone so much older than herself so soon. However, as they chatted together Elizabeth began to see that his gentle charm must be very appealing to Flavia – and very safe.

The Dashing White Sergeant was to be followed by the Reel of the 51st. Flavia came back to join Gervaise and perched on the arm of his chair, and Colin came to claim his wife for the dance.

'This is one of my special favourites,' said Flavia. 'It's so romantic. Did you know that it was invented by officers of the Fifty-First Highland Division while they were in a prisoner of war camp? Be brave, try it?'

Gervaise was saved from replying by the arrival of Matt.

'Come on, Flavia, you've got to do this with me because I've told Catriona I've already booked you. Thought I'd better extricate myself from her clutches so I said I had to do my duty by my little sister. You don't mind, do you, Swerve?'

'Not at all.' Gervaise laughed at him. 'Listening to those bloodcurdling war cries you've been making I wouldn't dare deny you anything. You go and dance with your rowdy brother, Flavia. I hadn't realized reel parties were like clan warfare – unnerving for poor sassenachs like me. I shall feel much safer in this comfortable chair.'

'All right – just this one and I'll be back to bully you,' and Flavia allowed herself to be led by Matt to the top of the set. 'Come on then, Bonnie Prince Charlie,' she said. 'We'll show everyone how it should be done.'

Matt, whose wild dark locks annoyed his mother so much, really did look rather romantic in his kilt, tartan stockings and the otter-head sporran that had been made for his grandfather in the days when otters were still plentiful and conservation unheard of.

As the music started, they cast off the top two couples and Matt presented her to the first man. Flavia thought she knew everyone at the party, but she had never met him before. He had very blue eyes but such a blank expression that it gave him the look of someone wearing the kind of dark glasses which enable the wearer to see out, while preventing anyone from seeing in. As she curtsied briefly before setting to him, she gave him her usual friendly smile but he did not smile back.

'Let's make this an Aberdonian,' whispered Matt as they reached the end of their own set, so they whirled on through the next sets to the end of the long line of dancers, rather to the disapproval of one or two of the stuffier members of the older generation who did not approve of such excess of enthusiasm.

'Thank you, Matt, that was terrific. Now I'll release you to Catriona, but I shall be on to Di if you step out of line! I'm going to persuade Gervaise to try and do an eightsome. I'm sure he can dance better than he pretends,' and Flavia, still doing reel steps, danced her way back to where Gervaise was sitting, and collapsed onto a chair beside him.

'That was such fun! But it was mean of me to neglect you like that. Am I forgiven?'

'Darling, there's nothing to forgive. I was very happy. Watching you was like watching a humming bird, hovering and darting, and so colourful in your lovely dress.'

She beamed at him. 'You do say the nicest things. I shall become swollen-headed if you go on like this. Now it's your turn. We'll dance together and you'll see why I've been such a brilliant teacher to your little boys.'

Gervaise felt a pang as he looked at her bright face, and knew he was going to disappoint.

'Darling Flavia, I'm truly sorry but I meant it when I said I wouldn't dance. I'd do almost anything else for you – sit up and beg, jump through a hoop – but reels, no.' He could not bring himself to try to explain a humiliation of years before that literally paralysed his legs in any ballroom – it seemed so feeble, even to himself.

She gave him a puzzled look, but quickly said, 'It doesn't matter. I'll be happy to stay with you. Don't think about it.'

But a little stab of dismay went through her, which she told herself was both selfish and petty. It is, however, difficult to have a relaxed conversation in close proximity to a band and a room full of people doing the eightsome, not to mention the hoots and war cries which Gervaise had teased Matt about, so after a bit they sat in what was meant to be companionable silence, Flavia trying her best to look as if she were having a marvellous time, not only through the eightsome but during the foursome that followed it.

They had just decided to go and get a drink when the eldest Arbuthnot son, a contemporary of Flavia's, came up to them.

'Flavia! How marvellous to see you! If I'd known you were coming I'd have hung all the flags out.'

'Sandy, how are you?' Flavia jumped up and kissed him and then said, 'I don't think you know Gervaise, do you?'

'How do you do, sir?' Sandy's polite greeting made Gervaise feel about a hundred. 'Come and do the next one with me, Flave.'

'Did you know I was engaged, Sandy?' she asked.

'Engaged? You? What a porky! You know you're not allowed to get engaged to anyone but me – we agreed that when we were six. Introduce me and I'll shoot him!'

'I just have, you ape,' she said, laughing.

The look on Sandy's face as he took in her engagement ring and the fact that Gervaise had put his arm round her was one of ludicrous disbelief.

'Oh my Lord, what a clanger! I apologize.'

'Don't worry,' said Gervaise. 'I've snatched her from under everyone's nose. Let's all get a drink.'

It was a relief to join the rest of the family, who as so often happened had all congregated together. Peter had been dancing with the youngest Arbuthnot daughter, aged thirteen, who had scorned what she considered the horrendous dress her mother had wanted her to wear and felt herself the acme of sophistication as she galumphed about the floor in the briefest of black Lycra miniskirts and huge Doc Marten shoes.

'I've never before felt frightened of being trampled to death by a schoolgirl!' Peter told them, when his partner had gone off to tell her best friend that she'd only been dancing with the old man out of duty, Peter being all of thirty-four.

'I can't understand Lady Arbuthnot letting her wear those clothes.' Wanda looked as shocked as if she'd noticed a stain on a tea-towel. 'I'd never let Daisy appear like that.'

'Oh I don't know, Wanda.' Matt could never resist baiting his sister-in-law: 'You told me yesterday that it was so important to understand the child's point of view. You must let her express her personality through her clothes.'

'Oh shut up, Matt,' said Peter, fearing his wife might genuinely think this a serious point for discussion. 'Come on, darling, let's go and dance.'

'Do stop getting at her, Matt.' Hester stuck up for Wanda, but Andrew, who found his daughter-in-law irritating to a degree, winked at the others.

There was an interval while the band revived themselves before playing again; the next dance was to be the Duke of Perth and they needed all their energies for that. Flavia refused her cousin Malcolm's invitation to partner him and suggested to Gervaise that they might go and sit out on the stairs where they could hear each other speak. She didn't think she would be able to watch the Duke of Perth without her face betraying the fact that she was itching to join in. Gervaise willingly agreed. She slipped her hand in his and they walked towards the hall together, but were intercepted by Lady Arbuthnot. She gave Gervaise a conspiratorial smile.

'Flavia, you're the very person I've been looking for. I gather Gervaise doesn't do reels so I'm sure he'll forgive me if I borrow you. We have a cousin staying who's had a very bad time lately and says he can't face dancing either, but I'm sure it would be good for him. I got him to do one reel with Catriona, but she looked as if she was going to eat him alive and he took fright. You're just what I need – may I take her, Gervaise?'

'With my blessing. I'll come and applaud.'

Gervaise gave his hostess a grateful look, and she bore Flavia off to the dining room. The band was tuning up again. There was no time for introductions. Lady Arbuthnot grabbed the green velvet sleeve of a man who had been just about to leave the room and pushed Flavia towards him.

'I told you I wouldn't let you escape,' she said to him. 'Here's Flavia Cameron and she needs a partner. Buck up or you'll be too late,' and she left them to it.

It was the man with the blank eyes whom she had briefly danced with in the Reel of the 51st. He looked no more friendly now – almost hostile. She opened her mouth to excuse herself but without a word he drew her into the top set just as the reel started. Flavia was used to dancing with experts, but this man was the best dancer she had ever known. As they whirled down the set she felt as if her feet hardly touched the ground and as the band played faster and faster she was positively airborne. She forget all about Gervaise and gave herself up entirely to the moment, with the joyful suspension of time she so often experienced when she was totally absorbed in playing her flute. The young members of the band were full of flair and innovation and changed the tune from 'Broon's Reel' to 'Captain Pugwash', and from 'Captain Pugwash' to the theme music from *Dallas*, playing at a breakneck speed that was more reminiscent of the Cresta Run than a ballroom.

When the reel finally came to an end everyone was too out of breath to speak for a minute, then it was as though a spell had been broken.

'Oh thank you so much. That was quite fantastic. I haven't enjoyed anything so much for ages!' Flavia's face was pink from exertion. She had never looked prettier. Her partner looked at her, and made a stiff little bow.

'Thank you too,' he said but before she had time to think what to say next there was a deafening droning noise as Matt appeared with his pipes and joined the band in playing 'Auld Lang Syne' on the stroke of midnight. Everyone grabbed the person nearest to them and they all joined hands and sang, and then there was much hugging and kissing and cries of 'Happy New Year'.

So it was that Flavia's first kiss of this New Year came not from Gervaise, but from a stranger – but it was not a stranger's kiss. She emerged from it gasping as if she had been underwater, and their eyes locked. His blank look had lifted and they stood there gazing at each other. Then, 'That was a quite unpardonable thing for me to do,' he said, and without giving her a chance to reply he turned and walked away, leaving her shaken to the core.

She continued to stand there oblivious of all the convivial buzz around her. She felt first overwhelmed and then suddenly furiously angry – no one except Antoine was allowed to make her feel like that. No one.

'Flavia? Where's your partner gone? You look like Cinderella. Don't I get a New Year greeting?' Gervaise had made his way over.

She gave a start. 'Oh! Of course you do. I was just coming to look for you. I didn't know where you were.'

'I couldn't get to you in time, but very happy New Year, my darling – our first year together.' Gervaise kissed her upturned face and thought she looked white and pinched, as she had not done for some time.

'Perhaps you shouldn't have done that. I've never seen anything so energetic. You look tired out.'

'No, no. I'm fine, honestly.' But Flavia still seemed rooted to the spot.

'Let's go and find the others.' Gervaise took her arm and together they walked over to where her parents were standing. There were more New Year greetings and though Flavia tried to pull herself together Hester immediately noticed her pale face and started to fuss.

'I think we should take you back now. This is a good moment to break away.'

'Oh Mum, I'm fine. I was just out of breath. It was great.'

Matt coming up to join them seized her in a bear hug. 'Happy New Year!' he said, lifting her up and swinging her round. 'Goodness, you look like a melting snowflake.'

At that moment Colin Cameron came to say he had just looked out of the front door and it had started to blizzard really hard.

'If we don't want to spend the night on the Arbuthnots' floor,' he said, 'I think we'd all better head for home sharpish before we get stuck.'

Several other people had also looked outside, and suddenly the party came to an end, with much laughter and thanks, and hurried farewells as most of the guests piled into their cars to make a hasty getaway, so in the end there was no question of Flavia being whisked away ahead of the rest of the family – or of dancing again either.

The snow appeared to be coming from all directions as they drove home, and they made slow progress, keeping awake and talking for the sake of Malcolm who was driving and holding an enjoyable post mortem on everyone at the party. Flavia did not join in. She closed her eyes and leant against Gervaise – but her ears were still ringing with the music of the Duke of Perth.

=====

XIV

NEW YEAR'S DAY was something of an anticlimax after the excitements of Christmas and the Arbuthnots' party. The children were cross and grizzly and Wanda, consumed with anxiety lest they might be starting colds, refused to let them go out to play in the snow, which made them even crosser. Hester nagged Flavia into having a day in bed.

'Not much to choose between Mum and Baby-Wipe when it comes to fussing about their chicks. I feel as if I was five years old too,' Flavia said to Matt when he came to say goodbye to her early the following morning. The snow had stopped falling, but more was forecast so he had decided to leave a day earlier than originally planned. He sat on her bed.

'Are you all right, Flave? Nothing wrong is there?'

'Don't you start on me too – I had Mum and Gervaise asking the same question all yesterday. I probably had a hangover like everyone else but it doesn't mean the dancing was too much for me – I adored it. I wish you hadn't got to go, though. It's so lovely having you here. It'll be sad without you.'

Matt gave her a troubled look. 'I'm so longing to be with Di, you see. I couldn't risk not getting back to her. She's had a rotten Christmas.'

'Not tempted by Catriona then?'

'Lord no! I'd forgotten how juicy she is till I saw her again, but I'd also forgotten just how dumb she is – she can't even see my jokes! Di's the one for me. I feel I'm half a person when she's missing. If she could have been here too I wouldn't want to go back at all.'

'Do you remember how we used to dread the end of the holidays? I still hate leaving Duntroon too. I might ask if I could stay on for a bit – I'm sure Aunt Liz wouldn't mind. There's really no hurry for me to go back now that I haven't got any concerts booked and won't be teaching at Winsleyhurst. I shall miss that, but Gervaise thinks I ought not to get in Miss Hall's hair at the beginning of term, and I'd hate to cause trouble.'

'But you'll be living there full time soon and there's your wedding to plan.'

Flavia pleated her top sheet into little folds.

'Umm, I suppose so. Matt?'

'Yes?'

'Oh nothing,' Flavia looked as if she had wanted to say something but then changed her mind. She smiled brilliantly at him. 'Give Di the biggest hug from me. Drive carefully.'

The moment for a confidence was gone, but her eyes were full of tears as she kissed him goodbye.

In fact a few days later it was Elizabeth herself who suggested that Flavia might stay on at Duntroon. She had not recovered her energy and Gervaise, who felt anxious about her, pressed her to accept. Flavia found herself both longing to stay on and at the same time half wishing Gervaise would persuade her to go back with him.

'Are you sure you don't mind?' she asked him, the day before he was due to return south, but he only smiled at her and shook his head.

'The one thing that matters to me is that you're well and happy. The beginning of term is always hectic and I shall love to think of you recovering here. I do think Elizabeth is one of the nicest people I've met.'

'She is, isn't she? I knew you'd get on.' Flavia was pleased. 'But don't think I don't know how generous you are yourself, Gervaise, because I do – and I have a very clear yardstick about kindness nowadays. You're very sweet to me. I do appreciate you.'

Though Gervaise was touched by her words, it was an unwelcome reminder to him of how deeply wounded Flavia still was. Originally this was something he had thought he could cope with easily; now the more he loved her the less sure he felt about it.

Hester was less keen for her to stay, but made it plain that if she did it would be a wonderful chance for her to work on a new piece of music. Something challenging.

Flavia stood with her aunt and uncle on the steps and waved everyone goodbye. After they had gone Elizabeth Cameron said, 'I have something I want to show you. Do you feel like a trip to the attic?'

'Just what I need. I adore the attics.'

'Come with me then, but I hope you're well rugged up because it's freezing up there.' She led the way upstairs and then up again via a spiral staircase in one of the bogus turrets which made the house look so romantic from the outside.

'You know where we found that coat that I let you have?' 'Well, it started me looking through other old trunks and I came across something else you might like – now which one was it in?'

There were several old trunks and boxes, some huge tin chests and piles of furniture under dustsheets. A strong smell of mothballs hung in the air. Elizabeth opened the lids of several trunks.

'Ah, here we are. Now, Flavia, you must promise to say if you don't like it. It may not be your sort of thing at all, but we just wanted you to look at it before you made up your mind about anything else.' She removed several layers of yellowing tissue paper, then carefully lifted out a dress and held it up.

'Oh Aunt Liz! It's a wedding dress! Whose was it?'

'We don't know for sure, but it looks Edwardian so Col thinks it may have been your great-grandmother's. It's in wonderful condition.'

The dress was of heavy ivory silk. The skirt, cut straight in front, fell at the back from several deep folds into an enormous train.

'Can I try it on?'

'Of course – not here though, for heaven's sake, you'd die of exposure.' Elizabeth laughed at Flavia, who had already started to rip off her thick sweater. 'We'll take it down to my bedroom and turn the fire on and you can preen yourself in front of the long mirror. Of course it may not fit.'

'Oh it will – it must. I know it'll be perfect.'

They carried the dress carefully downstairs, Elizabeth holding the top and Flavia supporting the heavy train. It was quite tricky negotiating the narrow turret steps. When Flavia had flung her clothes on the huge four-poster bed in her aunt and uncle's room, Elizabeth held the dress out and Flavia stepped carefully into it.

'Can you zip it up?' she asked anxiously.

'Zip? They didn't have zips then, you goose – there are masses of tiny covered buttons down the back. It'd take ages to fasten them all so I'll just do up a few. Goodness, you are thin, Flavia – just as well because I expect your great-grandmother would have been laced in at the waist.'

'Dare I breathe?'

'Breathe away. In fact it's slightly too big, but nothing that couldn't easily be altered. There – have a look at yourself.'

Flavia gazed at her reflection. The sleeves of the dress were tiered in a series of large tucks down to the tight wrist bands; above the bodice, which was heavily darted at the waist, rose a boned stand-up collar in beautiful old lace with a narrow frill at the top.

'Could I really wear it? It's absolutely amazing.'

Elizabeth sat back on her heels and gazed too. The dress might have been designed for Flavia, so well did it suit her.

'Oh Flavia! You look like a water lily!' she said, pleased to see a sparkle back in Flavia's eye at last.

Colin was called for to come and admire, which he duly did. 'But you don't have to have it if it's not what you want. Nobody'd be hurt,' he said, and Flavia thought it was typical of them both to offer her something so lovely and yet make it so easy to refuse if she didn't like it. In fact she was entranced with the dress.

When her parents rang up that evening to say they had arrived home safely, despite some hazardous road conditions, she was bursting to regale Hester with a detailed description of the dress. Hester sounded huffy. She thought her sister-in-law could have looked out the dress while she was still at Duntroon, and was not best pleased.

'I'll save my opinion until later,' was all she said.

'Oh dear, I think I've been a bit tactless with Mum.' Flavia looked crestfallen, and Elizabeth, uncomfortably aware that she had purposely not produced the dress until Hester had departed because she knew how very quick Hester could be to veto any suggestion that was not entirely her own, felt guilty.

'Be a bit guileful, darling,' she suggested. 'Don't let her feel you've decided yet. I quite see how she feels – but she simply won't be able to resist when she sees it on you. Nobody could.'

Flavia stayed on at Duntroon for another two weeks, by which time both Orton Abbey and Winsleyhurst were well into term. She went for long walks round the estate with her uncle, enjoyed accompanying her aunt wherever she was going, and seemed perfectly happy to practise her flute for hours or curl up with a book. In fact she behaved exactly as she always had done on visits in the past and though Colin and Elizabeth loved having her with them, they began to feel a little uneasy that she showed no anxiety to return south. Gervaise rang her up every evening. She was always pleased and chatted happily away to him, but that extreme urgency to communicate with the beloved at all hours of the day that afflicts most engaged couples was missing.

Sometimes Elizabeth thought she caught a wistful look on Flavia's face, but it was always quickly banished, and Flavia never referred to Antoine again as she had when they were decorating the tree, or showed any further inclination to discuss her engagement.

Colin and Elizabeth were beginning to wonder if they should ask what her plans were, when she announced that Hester had said that if she was better she really ought to go home soon as they must get the wedding organized.

'I'd forgotten I was even supposed to be convalescing,' admitted Flavia. 'There's nothing wrong with me now – it's just been so lovely being with you here.'

They drove her down to Perth to put her on a train, with the dress carefully packed in a huge cardboard box, and felt very sad to see her go.

XV

MEG'S CHRISTMAS FOLLOWED an all-too-familiar pattern. Archdeacon and Mrs Price had married late in life and had now both turned seventy, and though they were quite fit and active it was impossible to imagine either of them ever having been young. Meg's mother was generally regarded as a sweet person, bordering on the saintly, whose mission in life was to minister to her husband's comfort. She felt perfectly comfortable in a hair shirt herself and saw no reason why other people shouldn't wear one too. It was taken for granted that Meg would do the cooking and take on a good many other duties from her mother when she came home. Meg's arrival in the house was the signal for Mrs Price to down tools.

It wasn't that Meg didn't like cooking; she did – it was the assumption made by the whole family that she was an ever-willing horse that was beginning to irk her. Her sister, Isobel, expected her to take charge of her three small sons for at least a week out of every school holiday, so that she and her husband, Martin, could enjoy a break, but it never seemed to occur to them that Meg might need a break from small boys herself.

She was well aware that if anything happened to either of her parents, Martin and Isobel would expect her to give up her job and devote herself to them.

'I simply couldn't cope, what with Martin and the boys, and after all you have no one else to think of,' as Isobel so kindly put it, Isobel being one of those fortunate people born with the conviction that too much should not be expected of them, whereas Meg was a born coper.

She cooked Christmas dinner for them all, after attending two services, and then took her nephews out for a walk to get them from under the archdeacon's feet, the house being small and his level of Christian tolerance low. She was genuinely fond of the children, and they behaved far better for her than for their parents, but this year a spirit of rebellion was fermenting in Meg. She had a vision of what her future might be if she did not begin to stand up for herself, and it was not enticing.

She helped her mother organize a sherry party for the old people in the village – most of whom would much rather have stayed in to watch the television but were no match for Mrs Price in her deceptive velvet gloves – and she drove her father to a good many meetings. Though he had officially retired he complained that he was busier than ever, filling in during interregnums and sitting on endless committees, all of which he adored. 'Isn't your father absolutely splendid?' people said to Meg as she turned out yet again to collect him from some parish hall at ten o'clock at night.

The only thing that was different about this particular holiday was that instead of looking forward to the Lent term with unallayed enthusiasm Meg was dreading the return to Winsley-hurst. Would everything be different now?

It was nice to find Miss Hall had returned to teach music; Jane and Barbie, brown and bouncing from skiing, were pleased to see her, and Sister had been on a wonderful package tour to Marbella with 'my friend from Amersham' for a wee winter break. The hotel had been an absolute gem, they had made ever such lovely friends who had insisted, positively insisted, on looking at all Sister's snapshots of other gem-like holidays. Miss Hackett said that personally she wouldn't dream of going on a package tour because you never knew what class of person you might have to rub shoulders with, and some people could be so pushy, to which Sister replied that it was sad when people were too nairrvous to be adventurous, but we couldn't all be enterprising, could we?

It was all reassuringly familiar to Meg, but the biggest relief of all was that Flavia was not present. Meg knew that if she'd been engaged to Gervaise nothing would have prevented her from standing at his side on the first day of term and meeting the boys and parents as they arrived.

Meanwhile Gervaise had greeted Meg with his usual friendliness and she was more than happy to help him get everyone happily settled in, as she had done for so many years.

Gervaise went up to London to meet Flavia's train when she returned from Duntroon and she gave him an enthusiastic greeting. It seemed that whatever Scottish mist had descended on her spirits at the New Year had dispersed.

Arrangements for the wedding caused much discussion. That the service should take place in Orton Abbey was a foregone conclusion. Flavia had set her heart on having both the choir from Winsleyhurst and the Orton choir to sing at the service, which of course would be difficult during the holidays, when the wedding seemed most convenient, so with Pamela Boynton's encouragement, Gervaise allowed himself to be persuaded that he could go away before the end of term and leave Douglas Butler in charge for the last week, a plan Douglas managed to revel in and disapprove of at the same time.

Hester threw herself into planning every detail of the wedding with all her competent energy and the Headmaster's House became swamped with lists written in her neat strong handwriting. Andrew complained that wedding arrangements had completely taken over. There were fraught discussions about how to reduce the number of guests without giving mortal offence, and the usual discovery was made that someone really vital had nearly been forgotten. Gervaise had a terrible time deciding which of the Winsleyhurst parents to invite.

Pamela Boynton, practical as always, raised the question of where Gervaise and Flavia should actually live and wondered if changes needed to be made. The Old Stables had now been earmarked for girls in about a year's time, so Flavia agreed to move into Gervaise's existing quarters, though they were not exactly self-contained and some prospective brides might have demanded a greater degree of privacy. It was decided that while they were away the big bedroom which Gervaise occupied, and which had once been his parents', should be completely redecorated.

Flavia went up to London and spent happy hours choosing wallpaper and a dashing chintz for new curtains with Tricia, whose lunch hours seemed infinitely elastic, and they shopped for clothes for both of them.

'It's only the bride who's supposed to have the trousseau,' complained Flavia as they staggered down the King's Road, weighed down with carrier bags, more than half of which were Tricia's. 'We have gone rather over the top, haven't we?'

'Oh well, we can always return things if we don't like them when we get home, and I'm feeling flush at the moment,' said Trish comfortably. She had just received a fat commission for selling a dead bat mounted on synthetic cobwebs, a work of art guaranteed to attract dust like a magnet.

'Talking of over the top,' she went on, 'my stomach's beginning to look like the Hanging Baskets of Babylon.'

'Don't you mean Gardens?'

'Same thing – definitely one of the seven wonders of the world, anyway. I'm *really* going to have to go on a diet soon.'

Tricia's optimism always led her to buy clothes at least one size too small for her luscious curves, and her attempts to diet were as frequent and short-lived as her efforts to kick the Roddy habit.

She was dying to discuss every aspect of Flavia's forthcoming marriage, but as she made no bones about the fact that she thought her friend was making a ghastly mistake, Flavia felt she couldn't talk about any flickering worries without being disloyal.

'And you haven't even slept together yet?' Tricia was astounded; she was a great one for having goods on approval herself.

'We're not all sex maniacs like you,' said Flavia crossly.

'You weren't exactly reluctant with Antoine yourself.'

But Flavia clammed up at that. She couldn't explain to Tricia how grateful she felt to Gervaise for his understanding forbearance.

They switched to less dangerous ground and discussed the Bride's Book list in Peter Jones.

Flavia had enjoyed herself so much at Winsleyhurst the previous term that it was disconcerting to feel slightly out of things now that she was no longer teaching. The music wing drew her like a magnet, but if she went there the boys made such a beeline for her it was embarrassing with Miss Hall. She told herself it would all be different once she was married and had a definite role to play. In the meantime she took up her father's suggestion that she should teach a few special pupils at Orton, and these moments in her week became as thirst-quenching as an oasis in a desert.

Gervaise took Flavia to Gloucester to meet Monica and Flavia took Gervaise up to London to meet Dulcie. Neither visit was entirely satisfactory. Monica was on a sponsored fast in aid of donkeys, so she couldn't offer them anything to eat as there was no food in her flat. She seemed vaguely pleased to see them, and they told her about the arrangements for the wedding but she clearly wasn't very interested.

'Is she specially fond of animals?' asked Flavia on their way home.

Gervaise roared with laughter. 'Lord, no. She's never even owned a cat herself, but she likes the idea of rescuing things. She'd stop on the motorway to try and give the kiss of life to a squashed adder, but she wouldn't be a bit pleased if someone gave her a real live animal to look after. It's the campaigns she likes – it doesn't matter what the causes are.'

Dulcie, on the other hand, greeted them with every appearance of pleasure, plied them with delicious food, or rather caused Hilda to do so, and wanted to hear every detail about their plans, but all the same Flavia was far more bothered by her reception than by that of her future sister-in-law. Gervaise knew the old lady's opinion was of great importance to Flavia, but though Dulcie directed her charm on him like a searchlight, he was pretty sure the marriage did not meet with her approval.

'Do you remember how you told me that when I found a lover my music would find me again?' asked Flavia, trying to coax a reaction out of Dulcie when Gervaise had gone to collect the car from a parking meter.

'I remember.'

'So do you think it will come back to me now?'

'Who knows?' Dulcie looked enigmatic. 'It will certainly come back sometime,' and she would not be drawn further. She made it plain that the interview was now over by closing her eyes, though Flavia did not think that she was genuinely exhausted.

Wedding presents started to arrive, some of which were infinitely touching in their generosity, though the offering from one of Winsleyhurst's wealthiest parents still had a red price label with 'Reduced' on it.

XVI

GERVAISE AND FLAVIA were married on a bright, breezy day at the end of March. The air was full of the sound of bells as volunteers from the Orton Campanology Society rang joyful peals to announce the wedding of the Headmaster's daughter, and the sky was full of wings as flocks of the pigeons which roosted all round the cloisters wheeled over the abbey in an impromptu fly-past.

Tricia came to stay and helped Flavia to dress; she also greatly helped mother and daughter to stay on a reasonably calm and light-hearted note, for which both were grateful. Tricia vowed to herself that now that the decision was irrevocable, she would get to know Gervaise better and try to see him with new eyes.

Old Mr Foster, wearing a morning coat with a greenish sheen to it, acted as Gervaise's best man and beamed shyly at everyone. He had been deeply touched and most surprised to be asked to fill this post of honour. Contrary to expectations Flavia's retinue of small bridesmaids and pages all behaved perfectly, and Daisy looked as if she had stepped out of the pages of a Kate Greenaway book. The music was as beautiful as everyone had known it would be. Both choirs surpassed themselves singing William Walton's 'Set me as a seal upon thine heart', and everyone felt a pricking in their eyes when Rowan Goldberg and the Winsleyhurst choir sang 'I would be true for there are those who trust me' to David Andrews' arrangement of the Londonderry Air. The bride and groom left the abbey to the thundering sound of Widor's 'Toccata' and walked across the school courtyard in brilliant sunshine, between lines of cheering Orton Abbey boys, to the old refectory for the reception.

The guests managed to display an amazing variety of wedding finery from the chic to the dowdy, from the ultra conventional to the frankly freakish. Sister was almost unrecognizable under a beige tulle mushroom of giant proportions which would not have looked out of place growing from the bole of a tree, and Pamela Boynton looked surprisingly smart in delphinium-blue silk and socking great diamonds except for the fact that she'd forgotten to change out of her old driving shoes. Despite her membership of the RSPB, the bridegroom's sister appeared to have half a dead seagull on her head.

'The gallery'd go wild for Monica's hat – shall I make an offer for it?' whispered Tricia as she slipped into her reserved place beside Roddy, who had been one of Flavia's ushers.

Meg drank rather more champagne than she was used to at the reception, which accounted for her face looking somewhat blotchy, and her being more than usually animated, but very few people could have guessed that her heart felt as if it had been shattered into splinters.

Even plain girls often manage to surprise by taking on an aura of beauty on their wedding day but Flavia took everyone's breath away as she came down the aisle on Gervaise's arm, wearing her great-grandmother's dress. Andrew and Hester were filled with pride at having produced this beautiful young woman, but in common with most parents, a part of them ached a little for the child they were losing and trembled a little for her future out of the nest they had hitherto provided.

Flavia tossed her wedding bouquet of freesias and lilies of the valley to Tricia, who made a spectacular catch, which gave Roddy hope, and Matt piped the bride and groom off after the reception to 'The Skye Boat Song' as they drove away in the green Lagonda which had been given a tremendous spring clean by the Winsleyhurst monitors. Hester said a painful private goodbye to years of musical ambitions for her daughter and then waved her away with a brilliant public smile.

Gervaise took Flavia to Italy for their honeymoon. They spent the first week in Venice and then hired a car and drove to Tuscany. It was a wonderfully happy time for both of them. The anxieties and uncertainties that had gnawed at Flavia's peace of mind during their engagement seemed to have disappeared and she found Gervaise as amusing and companionable as a husband as she had when he was only a family friend. If his gentle and considerate love-making lit no unexpected fires, that was quite acceptable to her: it suited her present state of mind perfectly if their song together was more like the music of Hush-a-bye Baby than the love duet from *La Traviata*.

For his part Gervaise felt he had recovered the enchanting companion who had beguiled him when she was teaching at Winsleyhurst, but who had seemed worryingly elusive during most of their engagement. Thoughts about Meg, about Flavia's role in the school, about her musical future – all these anxieties were put on hold by both of them. They greatly enjoyed each other's sense of the ridiculous, Flavia adored everything about Italy, which she had never visited before, and Gervaise felt he was experiencing the impact of its special magic all over again through her eyes.

To watch her face became his great pleasure, whether she was spellbound in front of a Bellini Madonna, amused and delighted by the strip-cartoon charm of the Carpaccios in the little Scuola San Giorgio or simply soaking up the atmosphere as they wandered by the canals and over the numerous little bridges of Venice. He marvelled at her capacity to down *bomboloni* and *gelati*.

'Doesn't culture make one ravenous? I'm absolutely *starving!*' she would say, laughing at him. Gervaise was a wonderful guide, and Flavia, who had spent so much of her life responding to aural delights, was entranced to have a window flung open on to a world of painting and architecture.

They went to hear Vivaldi's music being performed in his own city and were lucky to find opera on at The Teatro La Fenice where Donizetti's *L'Elisir D'Amore* made the perfect production for a honeymoon couple to attend. Then their roles were reversed and she became the one to give Gervaise small special insights into music that he had not had before.

Flavia could hardly bear to leave Venice, but nightingales sang for them in the hills round Florence and the smell of wisteria filled the bedroom of their little hotel in Fiesole. Gervaise watched her hold her breath in the white serenity of the San Marco, almost afraid of stirring the air in front of Fra Angelico's frescos and oblivious to the other tourists pushing and shoving round her; she anguished over Michelangelo's *Prisoners* emerging half finished from their marble in the Accademia

– and then insisted on searching for Vivoli's among the twisting little streets round Santa Croce for a restoring ice cream to bring her back to earth. Gervaise, who had always hated shopping, even enjoyed watching her try on tempting Italian shoes.

'Thank you for such a wonderful time – don't let's go back,' said Flavia on their last day. 'Let's freeze time and stay here for ever,' and Gervaise saw there were tears in her eyes. He stroked her hair.

'We'll come here again.'

'But it won't be the same.'

'No, it won't be the same – you can never have a first time twice, but it may get even better. We'll visit other places and do other lovely things. We have all the rest of our lives to be together. This is only a beginning. Darling, you're shivering – are you all right?'

'We won't ever let anything come between us, will we?' she whispered, and then: 'Hold me,' she said, 'hold me tight.'

XVII

THIS TIME, ON the first day of term, Flavia was with Gervaise to greet the boys and their parents, feeling very much like a new girl herself and nervous of being asked questions to which she might not know the answer. Luckily there were no new boys as the big intake was now always in the autumn to fit in with the current policy of the public schools. Having met so many parents at the Carol Service she was afraid they might expect her to remember them.

'Don't worry about anything,' said Gervaise when she confided these anxieties to him. 'Of course they realize that you can't possibly remember them all. They'll all fall under your spell – nobody could help it.' But Flavia was all too aware that two people on the staff had certainly managed it.

'If there's a query, pass it on to Meg,' went on Gervaise, with less than brilliant perception. 'She's been coping with the first day of term for years – and of course there's always Sister,' he added as an afterthought.

Cars started to arrive between six and seven o'clock, disgorging boys, suitcases, cricket paraphernalia, tennis racquets and musical instruments in front of the house. There seemed an endless stream of people coming and going, and a general din of mainly cheerful greetings; most of the boys started ragging the minute they saw each other, though inevitably there were also some sad farewells and a few tearful faces.

The front door was hooked back and summery smells of newly mown grass from the grounds wafted in together with the scent of wallflowers from the beds in front of the house. Flavia felt like a wallflower herself. The daffodils were going over but Meg had put a large vase of Pheasant's Eye narcissi mixed with young beech leaves and early yellow azaleas on the highly polished gate-legged oak table that stood in the middle of the large entrance hall. It all looked very welcoming.

'I usually do the hall flowers,' she had said to Flavia in a neutral sort of voice, 'but perhaps you will want to do them now?'

'Oh no, no. You'll do them much better than me – do please go on doing them,' Flavia said quickly, and then immediately regretted it. She loved arranging flowers herself.

She was thrilled with the reception that those boys she already knew gave her, rushing up to tell her about their holidays and clamouring to introduce her to their mothers. Most of the parents were extremely friendly, but she felt rather lost when all but a few latecomers had departed and Gervaise disappeared to keep an appointment with a couple wanting to discuss their son's chances for Common Entrance. Everyone seemed busy but she was not sure what she ought to do to help.

She went upstairs, intending to say goodnight to the youngest boys, some of whom she was sure would be feeling homesick, and hoping to help cheer them up. Meg was putting them to bed in the large bedroom known as the junior dormitory and Flavia stood in the doorway listening to her easy, cheerful flow of chat, and watching how the children responded to her confident cosiness. She would have liked to join in, but did not want to interrupt, and after several minutes of standing there unnoticed, went back downstairs feeling useless.

She was however quite wrong in thinking that Meg had not noticed her.

Had it not been for her fear of upsetting anyone, Meg and Miss Hall in particular, Flavia would have enjoyed her new life. The trouble was that she found herself living in a household in which she seemed to be the only person to have no particular niche, and feeling very much like a visitor in what was now her own home. She regretted not sticking out for moving into the Old Stables and thinking of alternative accommodation for a girls' house. Living in the school, there wasn't even any cooking to be done, since there was no kitchen other than the big school one, where Garry, the chef, produced all the meals for the staff as well as the boys. It couldn't be said that Flavia was domesticated but cooking would at least have been a natural ploy for a newly married young woman with no job of her own. She had been surprised and puzzled to discover that the double bed, which she and Gervaise had bought, was turned down for them every evening, since none of the domestic staff except Garry was resident.

'Oh that'll be Meg,' Gervaise said easily when she asked him about it. 'She's always done it for me though it's never been part of her duties, of course. How lovely that she still wants to do it for you. I expect it's her way of showing that she's completely accepted you.' Flavia did not think this was at all the message it was intended to convey but could not bring herself to say so to Gervaise, still less mention it to Meg. She hated the feeling that even her bedroom was not sacred to her and Gervaise alone.

Douglas Butler buttonholed her the day after the boys came back.

'So how is the blushing bride after her honeymoon?' he asked.

'Very well thank you.' Flavia was not at all unnerved by Spanner, she just loathed him, an easier emotion to handle. 'We had a wonderful time.'

'I'm sure Gervaise did anyway.' Douglas eyed her up and down. 'I wanted to speak to you because Betty wants to know what you wish her to do now that we have a real headmaster's wife in charge of us all.'

'What does she usually do?'

'Well, Gervaise has relied on her pretty heavily in all his dealings with the mothers,' lied Spanner. 'Discussing the boys' health, showing prospective parents round and all that. Betty will be delighted either to be with you and put you in the way of how things are done – or else, of course, to go on doing it herself.' Betty, who loathed coming up to the school, had been looking forward to Flavia's arrival as a heaven-sent excuse to get out of all the things that Douglas insisted she did and which were really an agony to her. But Flavia had no intention of being manipulated by Douglas.

'That's very sweet of her. I'll talk it over with Gervaise and find out what he wants me to do, and then I'll go and discuss it with Betty myself.'

Douglas felt he had lost the first round in what he fully intended should be an on-going power struggle.

'Betty will be helpful in warning you about all sorts of pitfalls,' he said. 'But just one word of fatherly advice from me – I should be a bit careful about Meg if I were you. It's fairly common knowledge that she and Gervaise were courting before you came on the scene. She could be easily upset and it would be a great pity for the school if she felt she had to leave.' And he saw by the look on Flavia's face that he had scored a bull's-eye.

So it was that Flavia, though surrounded by people, began to feel lonely and isolated. When she was actually with Gervaise everything seemed all right, but more desperately in love every day and terribly afraid his young wife might find her new life dull or get over-tired and suffer a relapse, Gervaise was so anxious to smooth her path that he actually succeeded in making things more difficult. When she tried to get him to tell her what she could do in the school, he only told her not to worry, he didn't want her to feel she had to play the role of a headmaster's wife, he just wanted her to be happy; as far as he was concerned she could do no wrong. He had no idea how long the days sometimes seemed to her.

She still enjoyed gossips and giggles with Jane and Barbie, but because of Meg found the atmosphere in the sewing room increasingly strained; they did not come to seek her out because Sister, obsessed about pecking order, told them that they must not presume to treat Flavia as they had done before.

'It would be awkward for her, gairrls, if you kept dropping in uninvited to her side of the house,' said Sister, who considered that dealings with a headmaster's wife should be entirely her prerogative.

'I expect she thinks we should catch old Swerve and Flavia *in flagrante*,' muttered Jane to Barbie, but they were slightly hurt that Flavia came to the sewing room so seldom now. Because of this, a little barrier also built up between Flavia and the two young masters. She had been on such easy terms with them all before Christmas and very much missed the fun and light-hearted banter they had shared.

Gervaise continued to have his mid-morning coffee with the matrons because he had to go to find out how all the boys were anyway. He suggested that Flavia should come with him but, conscious that her presence would spoil his visit for Meg, she often declined and Gervaise did not press it.

Another difficulty was that the so-called private side of the house was in reality anything but private. The school had grown over the years, and rooms once occupied by Gervaise and Monica as children had long since been turned into staff bedrooms or classrooms, and the whole house was now a jumble. The drawing room, still decorated as it had been years before by Gervaise's mother, was a pleasant enough room, but it was not only next door to the office, where Miss Hackett reigned supreme like the spider in her parlour, but it opened off the hall and its huge windows overlooked the front of the house. During the day it was therefore very public and Flavia felt as if she lived in a goldfish bowl.

Miss Hackett, source of all information, kindly felt it to be her duty to pass on to Flavia Joan Hall's awareness that the boys had preferred Flavia's teaching of music to her own.

'Of course you must do what you think best, Mrs Henderson,' said Miss Hackett, who had always called her Flavia before, 'but I just thought you'd like to know that Joan feels nervous about you dropping in to the music wing,' and she treated Flavia to a sugary smile. 'She begged me not to tell you but I knew you'd want me to drop you a little hint about it.'

'Oh dear – well, thank you. I'll try and keep away then,' said Flavia, which of course gave Miss Hackett the chance to report back to Miss Hall that Mrs Henderson was not at all keen to visit the music wing now that she was no longer in charge. Joan Hall was too nice a character to take umbrage but it certainly prevented her from taking the initiative over inviting Flavia to join in any music making.

An unexpected person came to her rescue. Looking into the drawing room one day in search of Gervaise old Mr Foster surprised Flavia reading. She leapt up guiltily when he put his head round the door and instinctively hid the book behind her back, for all the world like a schoolgirl caught reading pornography.

'Oh Mr Foster, it's only you,' she said in a voice of relief, putting the book down on the sofa. 'I thought it might be Miss Hackett or Sister. Do come in.' He picked the book up.

'Ah,' he said, '*Mansfield Park* – an old friend. Are you a Janeite too or is this the first time you've read her?'

'Oh no – I've read them all several times. I know lots of people get irritated by Fanny Price, but I feel I understand her. I wish she'd fallen in love with Henry Crawford though, instead of that priggish Edmund.'

'And you obviously love reading?'

'Well, yes I do – only of course I wouldn't normally be reading in the middle of the morning.'

'I can't think why not. It's delightful to find someone who likes books.' The old man smiled at her kindly, her look of vulnerability over-riding his habitual shyness.

'Everyone else is so busy you see,' she said, twisting her fingers, 'and I thought I'd been caught slobbing out when I ought to be doing something useful.' She gave a little giggle. 'Och my! What are we thinking about – indulging in a book, and in the morning too?'

Mr Foster laughed at her perfect reproduction of Sister's mincing manner.

'Don't let it get you down,' he said. 'It's always difficult beginning somewhere new. If your husband was a lawyer or a stockbroker no one would expect you to start your marriage living in his office, and it must feel like that – especially when your own career is in abeyance.' Old Fossy was a far shrewder observer of what went on than most people realized.

'Would you come and have tea with me one day?' he asked diffidently. 'I'm not much good at entertaining but it would be a rare treat for me to show you my books.'

'Oh I'd love to. When can I come?'

It was the beginning of a firm friendship between them and one that gave great pleasure to both. She took to having tea with him quite often, and sometimes played for him and gave him private little concerts. He bought her horrendous sticky cakes at the local bakery which she munched her way through rather than hurt his feelings. Gervaise was delighted and hoped it was a sign that Flavia was becoming settled at Winsleyhurst. Douglas Butler noticed too, with displeasure and total incomprehension. What could she see in such a desiccated old fool?

Her teaching sessions at Orton became more and more important to Flavia, and she got in the habit of going over to play with the school orchestra whenever possible. She and Gervaise often went to dine with Andrew and Hester but Flavia tried to hide her growing unhappiness from her parents. She toyed with the idea of returning to her career. She knew Gervaise would not mind and her mother would certainly be overjoyed. It would solve the problem of what she should do at the school but the thought of a concert, even as part of a group, still made her sweat with anxiety; she was convinced that she would get a fatal tremor in her hands that would be death to a performance. She spent more and more time practising. Technically her playing had never been better, but it was lacking in joy and inspiration. What Dulcie would have called the *decòro* was there but the *sprezzatura* was missing, let alone the *grazia*, and she knew she was not ready to make a comeback. Sometimes she went up to London to see Dulcie or visit Maurice and Ina Fenstein. Maurice was biding his time. He knew it would be a mistake to press Flavia about her future too soon.

Of course, it was not all bad. She loved the boys and enjoyed taking prospective parents round the school with Gervaise. The grounds were lovely in May, with drifts of bluebells growing under the banks of flame-coloured azaleas and the species rhododendrons that Gervaise's father had planted. Matt and Di came down for a weekend and Flavia discovered what fun it could be to act as hostess.

Matt was worried by his sister and was not deceived by her pretence that all was well. He took Di up to meet Meg, whom he greeted with a terrific hug.

'Look after my sister, won't you?' he said to her when they left. 'I think she's finding life here unexpectedly tough – seems worse to be a new girl than a new boy, but then we always had you to turn to when we were miserable and that made all the difference.'

Meg was well aware what this coded message meant. In her misery she felt locked in with a part of herself she had not known existed, and was horrified to find she was capable of deliberate bitchiness – but it only made her resent Flavia more. She carried her jealousy round with her all the time, as if it were a hidden flask out of which she constantly felt impelled to take wicked little sips to feed her addiction like a secret alcoholic.

Matt took his sister to task about the music, though.

'You really ought to get together more with Miss Hall. It's such a waste for everyone if you don't. You may make her feel like a billiard table, flaunting your luscious legs round the place, but you can neither of you help that, and she's very nice. Why don't you ask for her help? Everyone likes that. Tell her you're starved of music and ask her to let you teach a few pupils just to keep your hand in? I think you're being a bit feeble.' Flavia was rather put out, but it made her think.

Pamela Boynton, who was always popping up to the school on one pretext or another – 'keeping my finger on the pulse' was how she explained it to herself – was also aware that all was not well and felt much inclined to tackle all those concerned, bang their heads together, and give the problem a thorough airing, but Lance, who had seen the results of Pamela's efforts to clear the air all too often over the years, managed to persuade her that such drastic measures might make matters worse.

'Give it time,' he advised. 'They'll all shake down together soon. Flavia is very young, but she'd never have got where she did in the music world without great determination and she's no wimp. She'll start defending herself soon – you see.'

Pamela asked Gervaise and Flavia for Sunday supper. Flavia, who had not been looking forward to going to Boynton after her last disastrous visit there, pulled a face when Gervaise told her he'd accepted the invitation, but it turned out to be a happy evening and she enjoyed herself very much. Both the Boyntons went out of their way to be nice to her, and most people felt better for basking in the warmth of Lance's genuine interest in them.

Lance was tying flies in the library when they arrived. He was seated at a battered old card table, which was littered with a curious assortment of garish feathers, reels of wire and mouldy old bits of fur. Flavia went to admire his handiwork.

'Dad ties his own too, but only salmon flies. These look much more delicate. Which fly are you making now?'

'Special dry fly for a chalk stream. I'm sure your father would know it. It's made with wool of a very erotic appeal – no trout is going to be able to resist. It's called a Tup's Indispensable,' he said, twinkling at her. 'Originally invented by a clergyman, would you believe it? Trust a parson to think that up. I have high hopes of this one.'

Flavia laughed. It was all very easy and friendly.

'Oh by the way, Swerve,' said Lance, piling Flavia's plate with egg mousse when they'd sat down to supper, 'might you be able to fit an extra boy in at short notice if required?'

'Probably – if I wanted to. We none of us like to admit it, but very few schools are actually bursting at the seams at the moment. Still, we're not desperate for boys either, thank God, and I can afford to have a slight margin. Of course I'd always try and do anything for a friend. Why do you ask?'

'Rather a sad case really. Young man called Alistair Forbes that I've had dealings with recently – he's a distant cousin of mine – rather a one-off sort of chap but I like him very much. Brilliant at his job. He used to be in the Special Services and was very well thought of. Did something pretty brave and was decorated for it, and now he's a consultant for a firm of security advisors that we have occasion to use sometimes. It's all to do with special protection. His wife died of cancer last year. Very tragic, she was only in her early thirties and they had one little boy. I gather he's been at a day school in London and there was a splendid old nanny who coped. Trouble is that the father's job entails a lot of trips abroad, often at a moment's notice, and now the old nanny's packed up and he's got to try and find a boarding place for the boy. I mentioned Pam's connection with Winsleyhurst and said I'd ask what the form was. He sounds pretty desperate.'

'He'd better come and see me,' said Gervaise 'Tell him to give me a ring. Remind me to tell Kathleen Hackett to put him straight through to me if he rings up, darling.'

'Oh yes I will – poor them. I can't bear it.' Flavia's eyes were wide with pity.

'Well, what do you think of our Headmaster and his wife?' asked Pamela later as she and Lance had their usual post mortem on the day's events.

'I'll tell you one thing about them,' said Lance. 'Gerve-the-Swerve is like a cross between a lovesick boy and an old mother hen. He simply can't take his eyes off his wife. I do hope she won't get irritated with him fussing over her all the time – almost worse than Hester. I must say she's a very winning number, but I can't help feeling that behind all that froth and bubble she's finding living in the school pretty heavy going in spite of having been brought up in one. Smaller world in a prep school, though. It must be awful for Meg too, if she's as keen on Swerve as you've always thought. Can't be good for those two women to be cooped up together – one of them's bound to explode. It's only a question of which one.'

XVIII

AT SIR LANCE'S suggestion Alistair Forbes telephoned Winsley-hurst the next day and spoke to Gervaise.

'I've said he can come down on Wednesday about five,' Gervaise told Flavia. 'It's not very convenient because I must go and watch the First XI play an away match at St Wilfred's, but he sounded rather desperate so I felt we ought to try and help. I warned him I might be late, though I'll try not to be. Will you hold the fort if I get held up?'

'What shall I say?' asked Flavia.

'Oh, you don't need to go into the vacancy question or anything like that. Just talk to him and find out what the problem is. Show him round. Take him to look at the Second XI match if you like – Sister and Meg will probably be there and you could introduce them. I could ask Douglas and Betty if you don't want to do it.'

'Of course I'll do it,' said Flavia. 'I'm not asking that horrid old Spanner for any favours. He'd gloat over me for weeks.'

In fact Miss Hackett came in search of Flavia earlier than expected. Flavia was practising a new piece and was upstairs in Gervaise's study. She greatly preferred hiding away in there or in their big bedroom to the more public drawing room downstairs.

'Mr Forbes is here. I've shown him into the drawing room and asked him to wait.'

'Oh thank you so much. I'll come down.'

'I could easily take him round for you if you're too busy.' Miss Hackett hovered about like a queen wasp.

'That's very kind but I promised Gervaise I would see him myself,' said Flavia firmly, swatting her. She was beginning to get the measure of Miss Hackett. 'There's no need to wait. I'll be down in a few minutes.'

Miss Hackett stumped off, her walk clearly managing to convey her doubt about Flavia's ability to stand in for her husband.

The drawing room door was ajar and the man who was standing at the far end of the room obviously did not hear Flavia come in. He was gazing out of the French window that opened on to the garden and looked deep in thought. He was wearing a pair of dark red moleskins and his hands were thrust into the pockets of a well-cut but rather ancient tweed jacket. Flavia stood in the doorway, uncertain how to attract his attention, and suddenly felt very unsure of what to say to someone who had recently suffered such a terrible bereavement. Did one mention it or not? Then she thought of her own father's unfailing warmth and kindness, and how good he always was at putting people at their ease. 'Shyness can be a form of selfishness,' he had said to her once when she had been agonizing about going to some party. 'Try thinking of the other person and not yourself all the time.'

'Hello,' she said. 'I'm so sorry you've been kept waiting.'

He swung round. Flavia gazed at him in astonishment. It was the man with the blank eyes with whom she had danced so wildly at the Arbuthnots' party, and whose New Year kiss had so disturbed her equilibrium. At the memory of it, and even more of her own response, a deep flush crept up her neck and into her cheeks.

'Oh!' was all she could think of to say.

Once again their eyes locked, but this time with mutual astonishment and instead of the expressionless face, he looked stunned.

'How quite extraordinary!' he said. Then he pulled himself together. 'I believe I owe you an apology.'

'You most certainly do.' Anger flared in Flavia. 'You took a monstrous liberty with me and then just walked off. What a nerve!'

'Oh,' he said, looking momentarily amused, 'was it the liberty or the walking away that made you so cross?'

'Both,' she flashed. 'One was inexcusable and the other just plain rude.'

'What are you doing here?' he asked, not moving. 'Do you work here or are you a daughter of the house?'

'I'm Gervaise Henderson's wife,' she said coldly.

'His wife? Good God!' This time he looked thunderstruck. 'I can't expect you to excuse me.' He sounded almost irritable. 'Why should you? I behaved very badly, but I assure you I don't make a habit of doing that sort of thing. Now it seems I owe you yet another apology. I didn't know Mr Henderson was married, and I thought your name was Cameron.'

'It was. We only got married in March.' Flavia was torn by her wish to punish the ill-mannered and arrogant man of New Year's Eve, and the sudden memory of the personal tragedy that had brought him so unexpectedly to Winsleyhurst.

'I have an appointment with Mr Henderson, but I'm afraid I'm early.'

'I know,' she said. 'He asked me to look after you until he comes in. He's had to go and watch a match at another school.'

They stood like two protagonists weighing each other up. Compassion won: 'I'm dreadfully sorry about your wife,' she blurted out, picking at the skin round her thumb with her middle fingernail. 'Won't you come and sit down?'

'Thank you.' He had retreated behind his mask again. He was not much above average height, not as tall as Gervaise, but he had a stillness about him that made you instantly aware of his presence. It was as though he filled the room with a barely suppressed energy that might break out at any moment. A muscle in his cheek flickered occasionally and Flavia thought that if he had been an animal, a tiger, for instance, it would have corresponded to the slight warning twitch at the end of its tail.

'Can I get you anything – would you like a cup of tea?' She tried to sound cool but polite.

He came and sat on the sofa. 'No thank you. So you're the Headmaster's wife. I must say you're not what I would have expected at all.'

'I don't seem to be what anyone expects,' she said.

He laughed suddenly and it altered his face completely. 'Well, lucky Winsleyhurst boys, that's all I can say! What fun for them to have you around. The Headmaster's wife at my prep school was an awful old dragon – we were scared stiff of her. What a turn up for the books you must have been when you arrived. Do you enjoy it?'

'Well – I love the boys, and most of the parents have been very kind so far. Tell me about your son, though. You haven't got him with you, have you?' She felt that they must stick to the subject that had brought him to the school.

'No, I didn't bring Ben today. Thought I'd better do a recce first, and I wanted to talk about him anyway. I've got some difficult decisions to take and I need help.'

'Would you like me to take you round the school? I may be new at being the Headmaster's wife but I do know the building inside out. Both my brothers were here and I taught music last autumn as a stopgap when the present music mistress was away.'

'Music!' he said. 'That's it, of course. When Helen Arbuthnot bullied you into dancing with me I recognized your face immediately but I couldn't place you. Julie and I followed your progress on television in The Young Musician competition. Then we heard you play at the Wigmore Hall about a year ago. We both thought you were wonderful. I hope you still play? I seem to remember hearing that you were a child prodigy or something?'

' "Or something" is about it,' she said, unaware how forlorn she sounded. 'No, I've given up now. I wasn't much cop as a prodigy so I got married instead.'

'And are you more cop as a Headmaster's wife?'

She was saved from replying by the arrival of Gervaise.

'So sorry not to be here to greet you,' he said, shaking hands, 'but I'm sure Flavia will have looked after you. I'm deeply sorry to hear from Lance Boynton about your troubles. I gather that you need to send your son away to school. Would you like to tell us all about it? Then if you want to, you can have a look at things and we'll take it from there. How old is your son?'

'Ben is just ten and he's an only child. He's at a good day school in London. He doesn't like it much but normally I wouldn't think of moving him. Only I do a rather unusual job – perhaps Lance told you?' Gervaise nodded. 'Well, I often have to go away at a moment's notice to almost anywhere in the world. When I'm at home I'm usually on call, and while I'm away I'm occasionally incommunicado and never sure when I'll be back. It's not the sort of job where you can say, "Sorry – we're out to dinner tonight so I can't come," because sometimes people's lives are involved. Really, it's a difficult job for a married man and Julie – my wife – hated it. After she got ill it was a nightmare. I tried to be at home when she was having treatments, but it often didn't work out and I didn't dare take the risk of chucking my job in. Illness can be very expensive and I thought we might need all the money I could earn.' He got up and paced round the room for a minute and then sat down again.

'What is difficult now,' he said, his voice completely controlled but the little tic in his cheek twitching, 'is that Julie's old nanny, who helped her with Ben when he was tiny and came to live with us permanently when she got ill, has had a stroke. I think she may make a partial recovery but she'll never be able to take charge any more, and it's plunged Ben's world into complete chaos again. It was a bit of an anxiety anyway because she's pretty ancient and had never learnt to drive or anything – and she was quite possessive of Ben – but he loved her and felt safe. People have been very good to us over school runs and things, and at the moment Ben stays with various different boys from his school, but it's a very temporary measure and weekends are a difficulty if I'm away. He's not happy – and I feel it's bad for him to be passed from pillar to post, never knowing when he can be at home or who he's going to be with. I think boarding school is the answer, but there's a snag.' He paused. 'Am I taking up too much of your time?'

'Of course not,' said Gervaise. 'It's what I'm here for.'

'Well, Julie was desperately against boarding schools. She was terribly homesick at one herself and swore she would never let any child of hers go away. We had some disagreements about it. After she got cancer the doctors were hopeful to start with – said the prognosis was excellent – but she was convinced she was going to die from the first moment she knew what she'd got. Some old gypsy had told her she would die young, or some such rubbish, and she just turned her face to the wall. It was very odd because she adored Ben – absolutely lived for him. I often wonder if the outcome might have been different if she had put up more fight. I think the medics felt that too . . .' His voice trailed away. Then he went on briskly, 'Anyway, she died nearly a year ago. Some people think I let Ben be too involved with her illness, but he and Julie were close and I felt she should have him with her as much as she wanted. It was all I could do for her.' He shrugged his shoulders. 'You have to cope as best you can. But she wouldn't have liked him to go away to school – I do know that, and Ben was aware of her views. I never made her an actual promise, but in a way I feel I'm breaking a trust.'

'What does Ben want? That seems rather important,' said Gervaise. 'Have you asked him?'

'He sees the problem; he's very adult in some ways. I think he'd rather board than go on as things are. He's an uncompromising child – always has very definite ideas about people – and he's taken against one family who've been very helpful to me, which is awkward. Home is pretty bleak for him without either Julie or Nanny. I do my best but it's not the same. I'd like to give him some say in the decision because he'd be more likely to co-operate.'

'Any grandparents?'

'No. We're short of close family. That's another snag – he's a great companion but I don't want him to become too dependent on me either. I have a special aunt who more or less brought me up but she's pretty eccentric. Spends most of her time on an island in Scotland when she's not off on some expedition to far-flung places searching for rare plants and then painting and writing about them. We're a nomadic lot. Ben's dream would be to go and live with her but of course that's out of the question. He's bright. I don't think work would be a problem – and he's quite musical too,' he added, looking at Flavia.

'Let's go round the school,' said Gervaise, getting up and smiling at him. 'I think you should have a good look at everything before we get any further with discussions. Do you want to come too, darling?'

'No,' said Flavia. 'You go together. I'll have a drink waiting for you when you come back.'

She went to fetch ice for the drinks tray and was glad to have time to collect her thoughts. She felt very shaken by this unexpected encounter.

When the two men returned Gervaise poured out drinks for them all. 'Well now,' he said, 'you'd better go home and think it over. If you decide you want to send Ben to us I imagine you'd want him to start next term, and of course I will offer him a place. We'd like to help, wouldn't we, Flavia?'

She nodded. She was touched at the way Gervaise tried so hard to make her feel part of any decisions concerning the school.

'I go to Argentina in ten days,' said Alistair. 'I suppose . . .' he paused, 'I suppose you couldn't take him straight away?'

Gervaise considered. 'We don't normally do that. It would be very unusual, but it wouldn't be impossible. Half term starts on Friday and the boys go away till Thursday. I don't think he should arrive the night they get back. What about on the Sunday after – that's Sunday week? It would give me time to make arrangements and it would mean I wasn't too busy the day he arrived. It may not be easy for him, you know.'

It was left that Alistair should go home and talk to Ben and ring up with a decision the following day. Gervaise felt that if he were to have any chance of settling down it should at least be established that the boy was not coming to boarding school against his will.

After Alistair had driven away Gervaise said, 'My goodness, I do feel sorry for him. He's really got problems – but what a nice chap.'

He put his arm round Flavia and kissed the top of her head. 'I always find one of the great satisfactions of schoolmastering is that one can occasionally do something really helpful – and thank you for helping me too, my darling. It's so wonderful to have you to share it all with. I felt so proud to have you with me, and it wasn't so bad coping alone till I came back was it? Are you beginning to feel more confident?'

She nodded uncertainly. Gervaise clearly hadn't recognized Alistair. It occurred to her that neither she nor Alistair had made any mention of the previous meeting in front of him.

That night Gervaise and Flavia made love. Unusually for them, it was at her instigation. Though she was often spontaneously affectionate, it was the first time she had made an explicitly sexual overture to him. She felt a desperate need to show Gervaise that she loved him and he was surprised and pleased. Afterwards he fell asleep immediately, but Flavia lay awake feeling restless and unsatisfied, trying to banish from her

mind some most unwelcome questions that snaked around
her brain and would not go away.

XIX

THE LONG WEEKEND was a relief to Flavia. She and Gervaise went to stay at Orton, which was also on long leave, so Andrew and Hester were free. Matt and Di had been able to come down for a couple of nights and they played a lot of light-hearted tennis. The only shadow was that Hester's chronic jealousy made her prickly with Gervaise and Flavia felt very defensive of him. However, the men had gone off to play golf on Saturday and Flavia had laughed and gossiped with Di and felt as though she could relax into being her real self after weeks of keeping up a sort of pretence. When it was time to return to Winsleyhurst she was ashamed to find herself on the verge of tears, almost as if she were going back to boarding school herself, and not going home with her husband.

Alistair Forbes brought Ben down to Winsleyhurst on the Sunday afternoon after the school had reassembled.

Gervaise had talked to the staff about the difficulty of taking a pupil in the middle of the term, stressing that it was at the special request of the Chairman of the Governors and explain-ing the exceptionally difficult circumstances that the boy's father found himself in. He also talked to the boys, telling them how hard it was going to be for Ben, and making it plain that he expected them to go out of their way to be kind and friendly. With one exception everyone was very keen to help and agreed that Gervaise was doing the right thing.

'I'm sure we can make him happy,' said Meg. 'It's the sort of challenge I really like.'

'Poor wee motherless mite,' said Sister. 'It's plenty of extra cuddles he'll be wanting.' Nobody had ever seen Sister cuddling anyone.

'What a grisly fate. God help the poor little bugger – I'd

rather be cuddled by a python,' said Michael Stockdale when Barbie regaled him with this latest Sisterism.

'I have to say I think you're making a mistake,' said Douglas Butler, put out that he had not been consulted before the rest of the staff. 'The circumstances may be tragic, but I think that's clouded your judgement. It sounds as if he's thoroughly spoilt at home and personally I think he's unlikely to settle. I feel you should at least have insisted on him starting at the beginning of next term.'

Gervaise thought, as he often did, that it would have been easier to get rid of Douglas if only he'd been an ineffective teacher, but he achieved good exam results. The boys laughed at him behind his back but many of them were also afraid of him.

Gervaise and Flavia, who had been on the lookout for father and son to arrive, walked out to greet them as soon as the car pulled up outside the front door.

The 'wee mite' turned out to be a tall, self-contained boy, polite but aloof. He had straight reddish hair, and except that he had his father's piercingly blue eyes there was nothing particularly remarkable about his appearance. His manner certainly did not encourage uninvited cuddles, and he gave the impression of being older than his ten years. They shook hands.

'Shall we get his kit – what there is of it – out straight away?' asked Alistair.

'Oh yes, but we'll just dump it in the hall for now. I think we should walk round and show Ben everything first. He might not like the look of us,' said Gervaise, smiling at Ben. 'Then we'll go and visit Meg and she'll see what you need in the way of clothes.' Among all the many other things she was in charge of, Meg organized a second-hand service for school uniform and had promised to try to fix Ben up with all the main things he would need. It was perhaps fortunate that Sister had the afternoon off.

'I'm sure your dog would like a run, wouldn't he?' Flavia looked at the large animal of questionable parentage who was taking up most of the back seat. 'What's he called, Ben?'

'Wellington.'

'Boot or Duke of?'

'Duke,' said Ben.

'He looked so battle-scarred when we first got him I thought we ought to call him after a great soldier. No need to let him out – we stopped and gave him a run on the way here,' said Alistair.

But something in the way father and son looked at each other, a sort of resigned acknowledgement of hopelessness made Flavia ask, 'What's going to happen to Wellington when you have to go away?'

There was a pause. 'I'm afraid the old boy's got to go into kennels for a bit. I'm taking him on the way home,' said Alistair. 'Then we'll see. We may have to find a home for him, but we're not going to face that yet, are we, Ben? It would be a last resort.'

Ben scuffed the gravel with his shoe and said nothing.

'Why not let him come round the grounds with us now?' suggested Flavia. 'I'd like to meet him. You can't consider yourself properly introduced through a car window.'

Ben looked questioningly at his father, who hesitated and then nodded. Wellington bounded out of the car and responded to Flavia's overtures with extreme enthusiasm. He really was enormous. He looked as if he might easily have a dash of Shetland pony in his breeding.

They set off on a tour of the grounds. It being a Sunday there were no organized games, though some boys had made up informal cricket sides. Others were tending their gardens or building tree houses and a good many were tearing about in groups playing a game of Attack and Rescue, the rules of which had been handed down by generations of Winsleyhurst boys but were quite incomprehensible to the uninitiated.

Ben was very reserved, speaking only when asked a direct question but volunteering nothing. He was not exactly antagonistic, but nor by any stretch of the imagination could he be described as friendly. He had something of the shuttered look that Flavia remembered so clearly on his father's face when she had danced with him on New Year's Eve. Obviously hearts were not stitched on sleeves in this family. It was a lovely day and eventually they walked down to the swimming pool. It would have been easy to locate it from miles away because of the racket of happy shouts and yells that filled the air and which any contact with water seems to extract from children. Meg, who was helping James Pope supervise the boys in the pool, was sitting on a seat nearby chatting away with several boys who had already swum, and were now towelling themselves dry. It all looked very friendly and relaxed. Gervaise introduced everyone.

'Why not let Atkinson and Goldberg show Ben round the buildings?' suggested Meg. 'They've just finished swimming and I've put Ben in the same dormitory as both of them. Then they can bring him up to me in the sewing room and we'll sort out the clothes. How very nice to have you with us, Ben. You're taller than I expected,' she said, smiling at him, 'but I think I have a jacket that will just fit you nicely.'

'Take Wellington with you,' said Flavia, thinking this might help to break the ice. Ben whistled and the huge black dog went bounding after the boys.

'Good idea, Meg,' said Gervaise, approvingly. 'We'll meet you up at the house. Much better for him to get to know the others straight away. I thought we might make Goldberg into Ben's shepherd anyway. Judging from the report they sent me from Ben's school I think they're likely to be in the same form. Anyway, that's where I propose to start him off.'

They stayed and chatted for a few minutes and Alistair was impressed by the easy way in which the boys appeared to treat their headmaster and his wife. As they walked back towards the house he said, 'You already have my home address but I'm so often away I'll give you my office number too. There's always an answer night and day and if there was ever any real emergency Lance and Pam have kindly said they'd help, but I think I'd have to ask you to act *in loco parentis*.'

'Of course.' Gervaise nodded. 'What about leaves out? Is there anyone other than yourself who could take him? I imagine you may not always be able to.'

Alistair looked doubtful. 'Julie's only sister lives abroad. My aunt might come, I suppose. I think I mentioned her to you. If she does turn up Ben will be thrilled. She's quite his favourite person, but she's highly unpredictable. I've left you a list of godparents but none of them lives close. I do hope Ben won't be difficult. He knows this is the only workable option and has agreed to try. He usually gets on well with other children, but he's a bit of a loner in some ways.' He hesitated and then said,

'I have to say he does occasionally get up against certain people and can be obstinate. He has a very strong sense of justice. I'm always trying to impress on him that life isn't fair and the sooner one faces that the better, but – ' He stopped and looked as if he would have said something else but at that moment the three boys returned.

'Don't worry too much,' said Gervaise, easily. 'We'll face any difficulties as and when they come. Now then, Ben, you'd better put your military attendant in the car and I'll take you up to Meg.' Wellington was duly disposed of and Gervaise took the boys upstairs, leaving Flavia and Alistair in the drawing room.

Flavia had chatted away easily enough to him while Gervaise was there, but now she felt suddenly awkward and inadequate. She thought Meg would have known exactly how to reassure him about his son. He walked over to the window and stood looking out with his back to her as he had done when she had come in and found him there a few days before.

'This must be so hard for you,' she ventured at last, wanting to break the silence, 'so very difficult. I – I wish I could be of more help. I will make a special effort to find out how he's getting on, and Meg – who you've just met – she's really brilliant with the boys. They all absolutely love her.'

'Yes, I thought she was extremely nice, but I should think they all love you too,' he said. 'Did you say you taught music here?'

'I did at Christmas but I haven't done since then, no, though I would quite like to. You said Ben is musical. Would you like me to try and teach him?'

He turned round. 'Would that be difficult?'

'No,' she said. 'No, I don't think it would. If I'm honest I'm dying for an excuse to do it, but I don't want to pinch any of Miss Hall's regular pupils. I could suggest it – if you think Ben might like it, that is. What does he play?'

'Only piano at the moment – but I think he'd love to learn an instrument.'

'Do you think he'll be very homesick?'

'Probably, but I don't think he'll show it. I'm more afraid of him alienating people by appearing unresponsive. I think it would be great if you would teach him music. He might respond to you. You hit the right note immediately about Wellington. He adores that animal – he belongs to him, you see. His mother gave him to Ben for his seventh birthday. We got him from the Battersea Dogs' Home and he and Ben have been inseparable ever since. I'm terribly bothered what to do about Wellington. Now that Nanny's gone, the dog is more important than ever.'

'Does Ben talk about his mother much?'

'No,' said Alistair. 'That's another difficulty. He'll mention her to me sometimes, not very often, just if something crops up. Nanny used to try and talk to him – after all, she was Julie's nanny too – but he clams up with other people. They couldn't get a word out of him about her at school.'

'Did he know she was going to die?'

'He knew she was seriously ill. I tried to prepare him a bit, but you can't ever say you've got these things right. I decided to send him up to Scotland when it became obvious that the end was very near. My aunt came down to fetch him, and I took him to say what I knew would be his last goodbye to Julie, though I didn't spell it out to him. I'll never ever, as long as I live, forget it. He sat on the bed and put his hands on her face and kept feeling it – he just kept on touching it and feeling it all over and stroking the shape of it like a blind person might. It was as though he were trying to imprint it on his memory. Then he said, "Goodbye, Mum," and walked away without looking back. Aunt Moy said he didn't cry when she told him Julie'd died three days later. He just said, "I know," and walked away by himself up the hill with the dog and didn't come back for hours.'

Flavia's eyes brimmed with tears. She felt she had been given a rare confidence and that it was somehow very important that she reacted to it in the right way, though she was not at all sure what that was. She said nothing for a bit, and then, 'I will try to respect his obvious feeling for privacy,' she began hesitantly, 'but you know I do think music might help him. He might be able to let his feelings out that way and still feel safe. I know I do that. I will try and teach him myself, either flute or piano. Whatever happens I promise you that.'

Alistair sat down opposite her, hands thrust in his pockets again and legs stretched out.

'I'm off on Wednesday, as you know,' he said. 'Can I ring when I get back and find out how things are?'

'Of course,' she said. 'Any time. I know Gervaise would want you to. Ring tonight as well.'

'I shan't hang about now,' he said. 'As soon as your husband comes back I think I'll push off smartish. Long drawn out farewells are awful. I don't think we could either of us take it.'

They heard Gervaise's voice and he and the boy came in together.

'All kitted up with clothes,' he said, 'and we've seen where he's sleeping and which his form room is. Rowan Goldberg's going to look after him, so I think, Ben, if you would like to say goodbye to your father this might be the right moment. Shall we leave you on your own for a few minutes?'

Alistair got up and put his arm round his son's shoulders. 'We'll just walk out to the car together. I expect Ben would like to say goodbye to Wellington as well as me.'

'Why not let Wellington stay too?' said Flavia on a sudden impulse, unable to bear the white controlled faces of both father and son. 'You said you were taking him straight to kennels, but I could look after him for you here. I'd love it.' She turned to Gervaise and put her hand on his arm. 'Gervaise darling? Please? You know how much I miss having a dog. Couldn't Wellington be a boarder too? Then he and Ben could both be new boys?'

The look of gratitude in the child's eyes would have lit a forest fire. Alistair looked very taken aback.

'I couldn't possibly ask you to do that. You've both been more than kind as it is,' he protested, glancing from Flavia to Gervaise and then at the face of his son.

'But you're not asking,' said Flavia. 'I'm suggesting it – and I'd love it for myself. I adore dogs. I'd thought of asking my parents if I could have our old Labrador here, only I think they'd miss her too much. Wouldn't this be brilliant, darling?'

Gervaise threw up his hands in a gesture of resignation and laughed. 'Absolutely anything would be better than that frightful Fudge,' he said. 'I've been holding my breath in case we got landed with her. Still, on your head be it, darling. Don't think I'm in on this deal. And he'd have to be on probation. Is he boy-proof? It wouldn't be very popular if he sank his teeth into someone's child.'

'Oh he's never bitten anyone – any person that is.' Ben looked as if he had been offered a reprieve from a life sentence; his face had suddenly coming alive. 'He does have the occasional spat with other dogs but only if they start it first. And he's very obedient, isn't he, Dad?'

'Surprisingly, yes.'

'You can't refuse,' said Flavia. 'If it doesn't work I promise I'll tell you next time you come, but do let's try. Gervaise, tell him he must.'

'I always do what my wife tells me,' said Gervaise laughing. 'All right, darling. It looks as if we've got two new boys then – and they're both on trial.'

Flavia beamed at him. 'I knew you'd say yes.'

Ben was sent to fetch Wellington's enormous beanbag from the car and also a lead and whistle. After a swift goodbye to his father he followed Goldberg back into the school for tea.

Alistair leant out of the car window before he drove off. 'I really don't know how to thank you both,' he said. 'You can't imagine what a load you've taken off my mind. I think Ben may co-operate now. He damned well should, anyway.'

Flavia watched the car disappear, and wondered what it would be like for Alistair returning to an empty house with neither wife nor son to keep him company. She made up her mind to try to keep up the contact she felt she had made with the boy. Gervaise took her by the shoulders and shook her very gently before bending to kiss her.

'You look absolutely miles away,' he said. 'Come back from wherever you are, you tender-hearted creature,' and he took her arm and led her into the house. 'I do hope you haven't let yourself in for more than you realize. Now let's go and have some tea together and forget about the school and boys and dogs and everyone else's troubles for a bit. I think I want my wife to myself.'

XX

LATER THAT EVENING Flavia did something she had been longing to do since her abortive attempt on the first night of term, but which she had not dared to try since. She went upstairs to visit the dormitories and say goodnight to the boys. At Gervaise's instigation she had tentatively suggested it to Meg a few weeks before, but had been so daunted by the obvious lack of enthusiasm for the idea, that she had lacked the courage to put it into practice. She let Gervaise assume that she did not want to go. He had not pressed it, though she felt he was surprised and a little disappointed. Tonight, however, she decided she would neither ask first nor wait to be noticed – she would just go.

Meg was coming out of the junior dormitory and because it was such a hot evening and she knew the little boys would never settle down to sleep, she had just put on a Dick Francis tape for them to listen to.

'Oh Meg, I'm just going to see Ben Forbes and say goodnight if that's all right?' said Flavia, hoping she sounded confident and breezy. 'I've brought his dog with me.'

Meg, full of good intentions since her conversation with Matt, had in fact been thinking of asking Flavia if she would like to do exactly that, and had been on her way to issue the suggestion. She very much disliked the scratchy, grudging person she felt she was becoming, and had thought that this would be a good way of offering an olive branch to the younger woman. She was conscious that she was making Flavia extremely unhappy and deliberately preventing her from developing the easy, friendly relationship with the boys that would have been both natural to Flavia and very helpful to Gervaise into the bargain, but, 'Do you think that's wise?' she asked now. 'It might look very like favouritism.' The words were out before she could stop them. She could have bitten her tongue out, but it was too late. Flavia froze. It had cost her a struggle to come into what had been plainly marked out to her as Meg's territory.

They stood on the landing confronting each other, and a sudden spurt of defiance sparked in Flavia. It shouldn't have to be like this.

'Oh I don't think so.' Her voice was very quiet but spiked with icicles. 'What could be more normal than for a headmaster's wife to see a new boy on his first night? However, if that's the way you feel about it, then I'll go and say goodnight to *all* the other boys that have come up to bed as well.'

Meg stood between her and the dormitory door. 'I'm afraid I have just settled the little boys down,' she said, not moving.

'Then I will go and unsettle them,' flashed Flavia, and clicking her fingers to the dog she brushed past Meg and opened the door. 'Hello, you lot,' she said brightly, hoping they would not notice the tremor in her voice, 'I've brought someone to say goodnight to you.'

Wellington, hoping for Ben, but clearly very well disposed to all small boys, bounded in, leapt onto the first bed he came to and landed on top of the occupant, nearly crushing him to death and sending the bed skidding across the floor with the weight of his impact. There were squeals of delight.

'Let him come on my bed!'

'No, no, please make him come to me.'

'Is he yours? Is he Mr Henderson's?'

'What's his name?'

'Oh wick-ed!'

Dick Francis's gripping tale was forgotten, as they all tumbled out of bed and surged round Wellington. Flavia put her hands over her ears, laughing.

'What a lot of questions! Now if you all get back into bed, quick-sticks, I'll bring him round to see each one of you. No, he doesn't belong to us, but he's going to stay with us. He's my visitor but he really belongs to Ben Forbes – the new boy you've been told about.'

Meg stood in the doorway, having switched off the cassette player. The whole scene was exactly what she herself would normally have both encouraged and enjoyed, but this evening the taste of it was very sour. She watched Flavia take the huge dog round to each bed in turn, making sure that everyone was back in bed and properly tucked in. The boys were enchanted and most unwilling to let her go. They wanted to show her the photographs of their families, their beloved teddies or their special possessions, for which there was a wooden box provided under each bed, known as a treasure chest. These were full of the amazing clobber that small boys like to squirrel away – anything from pebbles and marbles to old golf balls and bits of string; things they had made in carpentry, including, though strictly forbidden, attempts at catapults concocted out of forked sticks and discarded garters.

There were cries of, 'Look at this, look at this!' – to attract her attention.

'There now, I really must go. Goodnight all of you and sleep tight – and don't dare make any noise or Meg will never let me come and bring Wellington to see you again.' She walked out onto the landing, forcing herself not to hurry, but conscious that her heart was thudding against her ribs and her throat felt tight. Meg followed her, closing the dormitory door sharply behind her. Flavia's immediate instinct was to rush and give her a hug and say she was sorry, couldn't they deal better with each other than this? But fear of a rebuff – and of the consequences to both of them if one were delivered – was too strong. She hesitated just too long, lost her nerve and the chance was gone. Instead she said, 'I hope I haven't over-excited them. I'll go upstairs to all the others now. Don't bother to come up with me, I'll see that they're shut down afterwards.'

Meg watched the slight figure in the absurdly short miniskirt go up the next flight of stairs, her head held high but at the slight angle which was characteristic of her and had the effect of making her look as if she was listening with peculiar intensity when you were talking to her. Flavia walked with the unself-conscious grace of a ballet dancer. Meg watched her and felt like a carthorse.

Ben was sitting up in bed. He was in a bedroom with Goldberg and Atkinson, both of whom Flavia had taught in the choir, and two other boys of the same age. Meg was brilliant at trying to put together those whom she thought would get on well, or who had some special link in common. She took enormous trouble over the 'sleeping list', and tried as far as possible to fall in with the wishes of the children, though she was ruthless at moving them into different rooms if she felt their behaviour didn't warrant such consideration. All Flavia's pleasure in the visit had vanished and she longed to rush back to the safety of her bedroom and hide herself away from everything to do with the school, but she was not going back on her decision now. She had promised Alistair Forbes that she would keep a special eye on his son and she intended to do so. The look on Ben's face as he caught sight of the dog was reward enough. Wellington went wild. The boy clutched him round the neck and buried his face in the hair of his long black coat. Flavia guessed this was to hide the tears that she had seen well up in the child's eyes and which she was very sure that he would hate anyone to see.

She chatted away to the other boys, bouncing on their beds to test the springs, which they thought was enormously funny, and generally trying to give Ben time to collect himself.

'It's much b-better bouncing standing up. Do it like this, Mrs Henderson. Watch me – I can jolly nearly hit the c-ceiling.'

'Rowan Goldberg, you'll break the bed and then I'll be in awful trouble. Stop, stop! Whatever have I started?'

'Why haven't you been to hear us sing this term?' asked Atkinson.

'Well, it's funny you should say that because I was thinking of asking Miss Hall if I could come and listen one day. But you must promise to be extra good for her and not let me upset things.'

'Oh we will. We'll be b-brilliant, I promise,' Goldberg assured her.

Flavia sat on Ben's bed. 'You have no idea what trouble I had with this gang last Christmas,' she told him. 'I had to try and make them stop talking for more than a minute at a time. You can't think how difficult that was. Now I need to consult you about this great hairy mountain of yours. He's wolfed down some dog food I had over from having my parents' dog for a weekend, but tell me what he really likes to eat – a whole ox?'

She chatted away to them for a bit and then patted she beclothes on top of Ben's knees.

'Goodnight, Ben,' she said. 'I know just how strange it can feel being new, but it's lovely to have you with us, and everyone here is going to look after you specially well – aren't you?' There were choruses of yes, yes, yes. She blew them all a kiss and went off to say goodnight to the next-door boys, some of her courage having returned.

It was the first time she had really enjoyed the company of the children since the Christmas term, and she felt very cross with Meg and Miss Hackett for preventing her from involving herself with the school and the music. But perhaps Matt had been right. Perhaps she had been rather feeble. She decided to consult old Fossy.

At the top of the stairs she looked nervously down to the landing below. She had no wish to encounter Meg again and was relieved to see no sign of her. She could not know that the feeling was entirely mutual and that Meg, standing just inside the sewing-room door, had seen her and whisked quickly out of sight.

It had done nothing at all for Meg's self-esteem to note Flavia's anxious face, and to know that she was the cause of it. That Gervaise was in love with Flavia was anguish enough, but the one area in which Meg had always had total self-confidence was in her dealings with the young. She might have no faith in her own power as a siren, but Meg was used to being universally loved at Winsleyhurst, and it was this quality of loveability which Flavia also possessed in such abundance that seemed to her to be the last straw in unfairness.

Flavia and Wellington made their way through to Gervaise's study on the other side of the house. Flavia felt a terrific urge to ring her mother up, but a combination of loyalty to Gervaise and her own pride prevented her. Hester could always pick it up from her voice if something was wrong; also the telephone at Winsleyhurst was anything but private. Anyone might pick up one of the numerous extensions. During the day Miss Hackett was in charge of the antiquated switchboard in her office, and in theory could put through a confidential call to Gervaise and switch off the other lines, but it was well-known that she listened in herself at every possible opportunity. Gervaise was always meaning to get a more sophisticated system installed but never quite got round to doing it. He was not in his study and Flavia guessed he was probably taking prayers.

At that moment the telephone started to ring, and she saw that Gervaise had forgotten to take his mobile telephone with him. She hated answering it in case the caller was a parent she had not yet met or did not remember, asking her something about a boy she did not yet know. She let it ring as long as possible, but after a bit she picked it up. She had developed what she hoped was an unidentifiable voice to allow herself time to think.

'Winsleyhurst. Um – er, hello? Wh-who is that?' she asked cautiously. It came out rather quavery.

'Can I speak to Mrs Henderson?'

'You are.' Her heart most unreasonably started to thump again, though not this time with the feeling of dread that she had felt during her little altercation with Meg.

'Oh Flavia, it's Alistair Forbes. I'm afraid I didn't recognize your voice.'

'Oh good. I had my antiparent device switched on – that shows it's working.'

He laughed. 'It certainly was. I thought I'd got through to an old people's home or something. You said I could ring up about Ben.'

'I've just this moment come down from seeing him.'

'How is he?'

'Rather stony-faced on the surface but a bit wobbly underneath, I think. He perked up like anything with Wellington. He's in with some boys who are pals of mine and I think they'll be nice to him. They'll be in trouble if they're not.'

'You're a star,' he said, 'but then I think you know that.'

'Why don't you ring him up yourself and talk to him as soon as you get back?'

'Yes,' he said. 'Yes, I'd very much like to do that. If I were able to come down, could I see him even if it wasn't an official exeat weekend – or am I asking you something you don't know?'

'Well yes and no – but I'm sure the answer would be yes to

seeing him. I'll ask Gervaise. Would you like to speak to him? He should be free any minute.'

'Don't bother him specially. Just thank you both more than I can say and I'll ring as soon as I'm back. And Flavia? Will you tell Ben I rang?'

'Of course I will. And I promise I'll look after him. I feel very new as well so trying to help him will help me too in a way,' she said honestly.

'Bless you,' he said and rang off.

She was still standing in the middle of the room with the receiver in her hand when Gervaise came in two minutes later.

XXI

THE ARRIVAL OF Ben at Winsleyhurst marked a turning point in Flavia's life at the school.

The following morning she went over to the music wing during break. She timed her visit carefully so as to catch Miss Hall before she went down to the staff room for her cup of coffee, but after the boys would all have gone stampeding off to get milk and biscuits and let off some of their pent-up energy. She particularly wished to avoid the enthusiastic greeting she knew she would get from any members of the choir.

She poked her head round the door of the big music room. Miss Hall was sorting sheets of music into piles.

'Are you too busy or could I come in for a moment?'

'Why Flavia, how nice. Of course you can come in. What can I do for you?'

Flavia perched on the window sill and looked out. She could see small figures tearing around the grounds and hear the sound, familiar since her childhood, of bat on ball: some of the boys were having cricket practice in the nets. She found it difficult to know how to start what she wanted to say. It did not take any great powers of perception to notice the anxiety on her face. Miss Hall, who was not only very fond of Meg but had recently been sipping from Miss Hackett's poisoned chalice, remembered how much she had liked Flavia when they had first met in the autumn term. She thought now that Flavia looked very young to be a headmaster's wife and it occurred to her for the first time that Meg might not be the only person needing sympathy.

'I've come to ask you a favour,' said Flavia

'I hope I can help then, and it's good to see you anyway.' Miss Hall smiled at her kindly. 'There are so many things about the music that I'd like to share with you and consult you about. I'm glad you've come.' She was rewarded for this generosity by Flavia's vivid smile.

'Oh Miss Hall – what a lovely thing to say. I've been so anxious not to intrude after I'd enjoying doing your teaching so much. You see, Miss Hackett said . . .' She paused, and started to draw notes of music in the chalk dust on the window sill.

'Kathleen Hackett says a good many things we should all do better not to hear. I don't know why any of us listen to her – but somehow we do. Now what's this favour?'

Flavia found herself telling Miss Hall how much she needed to be of use in the school and how spare she felt while everyone else was so busy, how terrified she was of treading on anyone's toes, though she did not mention names. Then she admitted how much she also longed to be involved with the music again, and told Miss Hall about her promise to try to teach Ben.

Miss Hall said that would suit her very well; she had too many pupils anyway, and suggested that Flavia might like to take on a few more – she thought it would be awkward if Flavia only had one pupil.

'Might you ever like to come and play some chamber music in the evenings?' asked Miss Hall. 'Several of the part-time music staff and I get together once a week. You'd be in a different class, I know –'

'Oh I'd absolutely love to. I feel starved.'

The two were still deep in conversation when the bell rang and the boys came clattering up the stairs again. Several of them rushed up to Flavia like enthusiastic puppies. She looked rather nervously at Miss Hall, who nodded reassuringly and did not appear to mind, and Flavia went off feeling happier than she had since the first day of term.

She looked forward to telling Gervaise what they had decided and thought he would be pleased. She felt she had at last done something positive and regained a little self-respect. She paused halfway down the stairs to listen. From one of the small practice rooms she could hear someone playing 'Annie's Song' on a flute – not perhaps quite like James Galway, but not too badly either. She guessed it might be Rowan Goldberg, and went off humming to collect Wellington for a walk. She would make a special point of seeing Ben at lunch-time.

During the next few weeks Flavia found Ben rather baffling.

Some of the staff thought he was deliberately subversive. She had secretly expected to have an instant rapport with him, but though he was polite enough, she felt she was not getting through to him. She was a little hurt that her quixotic gesture in offering to house his dog had not opened an instant door through his reserve. She confided her disappointment to Old Fossy; somehow she didn't want to talk to Gervaise about Ben.

'Don't expect so much so soon. He must be a very angry little boy.'

'At being sent away to school?'

'No, at his mother dying.'

'But that's not anyone's fault. It's because of her I'm trying to help him.'

'Children don't think like that. He's lost the one person he could always rely on to love him and be there for him. Don't you think that might make you a bit cautious of allowing yourself to trust anyone else?'

'I hadn't thought of it like that.'

'Don't rush him. Let him come to you. Just teach him music, and expect proper standards. Children feel safer if they're not allowed to get away with things. Don't suck up to him.'

It was food for thought. Flavia was guiltily aware that she felt competitive about Ben Forbes. She wanted him to like her better than he liked Meg.

Ben had reached Grade Three in his piano playing and had obviously been well taught. She did not think he would be a flyer, not a child that made you think that music would become a serious consideration for his future, but when he chose to, he played with an instinctive feeling that made her very sure that he could indeed express himself through it.

'You haven't practised, Ben,' she said one day.

'I don't want to play the piano any more. I want to play the trumpet.'

'Perhaps next term you can.'

'Dad said I could learn this term if I wanted.'

'Well, I say not,' said Flavia. 'For one thing there isn't a space in the timetable, and for another you're not starting a new instrument if you don't bother with the one you're learning now. If you're prepared to try for the rest of the term I'll talk to Miss Hall about the trumpet for the autumn. But I don't waste my time teaching people who don't practise.' There was a long pause.

'Sorry,' said Ben gruffly, looking at his feet.

'Was your mother musical?' Flavia tried to sound casual, wondering if the shutters would come down. She felt it important to test the ground if she was to help this child, as she so badly wished to do, but he answered easily enough.

'No, Mum never played, though she loved listening to music. It's Dad who plays. He's brill – really cool. He can just sit down and play anything by ear. He's wonderful at jazz. You ought to hear him – you'd love it.'

After this she started to look forward to her sessions with Ben. She felt grateful to Old Fossy for his insight and thought what a wise old schoolmaster he was.

The dog accompanied her everywhere she went.

Not everyone at Winsleyhurst found either Ben or Wellington quite so much to their taste as Flavia did. Sister, for one, found the child unapproachable and the dog disastrously over-friendly. There was something in the way the boy looked at her that made her feel she might just have said something rather foolish, and there was something about the way the dog came bounding towards her that made her feel distinctly threatened, fearful of laddered tights and slobber marks on her white overall. The very thought of dogs made Sister want to wash her hands. The other member of staff who shared her feelings was Douglas Butler. He took Ben for Maths but his heavy joviality did not seem to strike an appreciative chord from Ben, who looked at him with a deadpan face and did not laugh at his jokes. Douglas was used to having his witty sallies greeted with polite titters, though few of the boys considered him at all funny, or certainly not in the way he intended. There was no denying that the Forbes boy was bright, and especially quick with figures; he worked hard, the other boys appeared to accept him, and though it would have been hard to fault his outward display of manners – indeed they were more punctilious than average – Douglas, like Sister, felt uncomfortable under his blue gaze. He started to make jokes at Ben's expense, especially little digs about Wellington. Ben remained expressionless.

'Like Queen Victoria, you are not amused, Forbes?'

'No, sir.'

'Oh dear, I shall have to be more careful what I say in future. We like people here who can take a joke against themselves. Do I understand that you can't take jokes about your dog?'

Ben smiled politely. 'It all depends who makes them – sir,' he said.

There were stifled giggles and the rest of the form looked at the new boy with admiration. Anyone who could outface Spanner was someone to be reckoned with. Douglas went purple in the face.

'If you were not so new here I would be tempted to give you an order mark for insolence, Forbes.'

'Yes, sir.'

It was not a good start.

'Do you like Mr Butler?' Ben asked Flavia during their next piano lesson.

'Oh Ben, I don't think you should ask me that.'

'Then you don't like him. I hate him – I hate him and he hates me.'

'Has he been unkind to you?'

Ben shrugged his shoulders and looked scornful. 'I don't mind. I don't care what he thinks of me. I only mind about people I like. But he's awful to Goldberg. He makes fun of his stammer and asks him things about his mother. He likes oily little creeps like Waring who suck up to him all the time.'

Flavia had come across Billy Waring when she was taking chapel practice last autumn. He was one of those boys who always seemed to be in the foreground, a sharp, cocky child with an answer for everything. She had asked Gervaise about him.

'Umm, Waring,' Gervaise had said, considering. 'Not a likeable child. Big hearty mother and a shifty little father who's made a lot of money. The slightest criticism of their child has them up in arms. He's never actually done anything wrong – not that I can pin down – but I wouldn't trust him further than I could kick him. He's bright and good at games, but I have to struggle to be fair to Waring.'

Flavia remembered this conversation now.

'Waring is a suck, and Mr Butler,' said Ben, 'is a fuckwit.'

177

Flavia's heart sank. Having wanted to win his confidence, she was not sure how to cope with this.

'Look, Ben,' she said, 'I can't discuss members of the staff with you and I don't think you should use that word to me, but if anything makes you really unhappy – if . . . if things got bad, I'd like you to feel that you could come to me for help.'

Ben considered. 'Help for me and for Goldberg too?'

'Yes of course. Help for Goldberg too.'

'Well, I might. If you promise to tell me something.'

'What's that?

'Whether you like Mr Butler.'

Flavia looked at the boy. 'No,' she said slowly, 'no, I don't like Mr Butler very much either, but that's a private and personal feeling and he's supposed to be a brilliant teacher.'

She thought that Ben had opened the door of his trust a little way for her, and felt honoured.

Meg spent a morning with Lady Boynton at the Old Stables discussing the architect's proposals for altering it into a girls' boarding house.

Pamela had suggested to the rest of the Governors that she should co-opt a sub-committee to deal with all the necessary organization. She was a great believer in small sub-committees, the smaller the better, ideally of course just herself, though she reluctantly accepted that this was not usually considered very democratic. In this case, however, she had been happy to invite Meg to join her. She knew they would work well together, and that Meg could stand her ground if she felt strongly about something. Despite her natural bossiness Pamela was always ready to listen to sensible suggestions.

'Do we need anyone else?' she had asked Meg.

'Oh I don't think so. Between us we should be able to think of most things, and it will take so much less time with just the two of us. Then we can report back to Gervaise.'

'My own feelings exactly.'

It had not occurred to either of them to ask the Headmaster's wife to join them.

They had spread plans out over the floor, made lists of points which they felt the architect had overlooked, and had in fact thoroughly enjoyed themselves – two highly competent women who liked good organization and enjoyed running things.

'I think we've done pretty well. It will make a jolly nice house.' Pamela scooped up the architect's drawings, which were now covered with bold amendments in red pen. 'Men are so impractical, but I knew we could improve on these suggestions between us. Oh – just one more thought: I know they'll only be little girls but they all seem to mature so young nowadays. Surely there ought to be some sort of provision for disposing of sanitary towels or Tampax or whatever? A machine to gobble everything up. We don't want all the drains getting blocked all the time – such a waste of everyone's time,' said Pamela.

Meg groaned. 'Of course you're right. I'll make a note; I should have thought of that. Planning is fun but, oh dear, I do rather wish I hadn't let myself in for starting it off. Boys are so much more straightforward. I can cope with boys.'

'Your heart isn't really in this venture, is it? What made you agree to take it on?'

'Gervaise seemed so anxious for me to do it and I wanted to help him out.'

'And now?'

'Now I shall of course stick to my word – but once it's got going and Gervaise has found a suitable married couple to run it I shall go back to looking after the boys with great relief.'

It was on the tip of Pamela's tongue to ask Meg if she really intended to stay on at Winsleyhurst at all. Now that Gervaise was married, presumably all her hopes were dashed, but she couldn't think of a tactful way of phrasing the question. It was most out of character for her to allow such a trifling difficulty to inhibit her, but amazingly she remained silent. There was something about Meg's expression, a sort of defiant, mulish look, that Pamela had not seen before and which did not encourage any probing. She had always thought of Meg as very easy-going, a smoother of ruffled feathers, rather a pliable sort of person; now she wondered if she really knew her.

Nowadays Meg wondered if she really knew herself.

At half term she had gone to stay with her friend Anne in London. She had meant to go down to her parents, but in her present state of mind had felt she could not face a weekend spent being a dutiful daughter and a convenient baby-sitting sister and aunt. Her sister had been very aggrieved.

Meg had poured out her misery to Anne, who gave it as her opinion that Meg should leave Winsleyhurst and make a fresh start. 'Unless of course,' she had added, 'you don't think the marriage will last anyway. From what you say they sound very ill-suited.' Fatal words, but music to Meg's ears.

Another thing that had jolted Meg out of her habitual view of herself had been the sudden attention that she was receiving from Douglas Butler. She had never much cared for the Butlers, disapproving of his tendency to make favourites of certain boys and thinking him unreasonably harsh on others, though it was difficult either to like or dislike Betty. Suddenly, however, Douglas had taken to paying Meg compliments and seeking out her company. Against all her better judgement she couldn't help feeling flattered, and his admiration was balm to her low self-esteem, though he kept the compliments just within the bounds of what was acceptable from a married man. He invited her to supper with Betty and himself. She had accepted and enjoyed quite a pleasant evening.

'Betty and I always feel you are very under-valued,' said Douglas, pouring Meg a very strong dry martini. 'We've never understood why Gervaise hasn't got rid of Sister and made you Head Matron years ago. We've often said so, haven't we, dear?'

Betty nodded dutifully. It was the first she'd heard of it.

'As for this thing about the girls' house – well, you'd just be wasted doing that. I was rather against the idea originally as you know; not that I disapprove of co-education, it's just that I think it's more difficult in a boarding school. Still, I bow to superior judgements. In fact, Betty and I would be perfectly willing to take charge of the girls' house ourselves.'

Betty's limp jaw didn't do anything so positive as to drop – it just sagged a little.

Douglas had offered to run Meg home, but she insisted the walk would do her good. She felt distinctly light-headed. They both kissed her goodbye, Betty offering a pallid cheek and not really making physical contact, and Douglas giving her three smacking kisses on her very rosy cheeks, and her arms a con-spiratorial squeeze that might equally have been intended to convey sympathy or something a little more intimate. He smelt powerfully of bracingly tangy aftershave.

Meg had walked back through the school grounds in a haze of alcohol, thinking that there was no place on earth as dear to her as Winsleyhurst. Every tree and blade of grass seemed to be imbued with special significance for her, to be part of her very being. There was a huge oak known as the Leavers' Tree, whose low-growing branches made it ideal for climbing, and on whose vast trunk generations of boys had carved their initials before going on to public school. Meg felt a sudden urge to gouge her own name into its rough bark, though not as an indication that she was about to move on somewhere else. Gervaise's name was on the tree, carved when he was a child, and he, after all, was still very much a part of the place. She knew that she would rather live here than anywhere else in the world.

As she walked across the cricket field she automatically picked up several odd batting gloves, a discarded tennis racquet and a grubby handkerchief that were lying in her path. She had the rare ability to be extremely tidy herself without being in the least irritated by other people's chaos. Whatever advice anyone might give her about what she should or should not do, Winsleyhurst was home to Meg.

XXII

'OH BY THE way,' said Gervaise to Flavia at breakfast a few days later, 'Alistair Forbes is back. He rang yesterday evening to find out how Ben was.'

'Oh Gervaise, you might have told me.'

Gervaise looked surprised. 'But I am telling you. I told him I thought all was going well on the whole, and I got Meg to find Ben and let him have a word with his father. You'd gone to take Wellington for a walk.'

'I might have liked to tell him about Ben myself.'

'But you don't usually want to talk to parents – you're always telling me you hate answering the telephone.'

'Ben's different. I feel involved.'

Gervaise smiled his sweet sleepy smile at her. 'Of course, and I'm so pleased about that, it's lovely. I know he's the first new boy of your own too, but it can lead to difficulties if one becomes too wrapped up in only one boy, you know.'

'I'm not wrapped up in him,' snapped Flavia – but she knew she was.

Gervaise privately thought Flavia was being a bit difficult, but never one to have a confrontation if it could possibly be avoided he said soothingly: 'I wasn't criticizing you, darling, that's the last thing I'd ever do. Apparently Lance has asked Alistair Forbes to take Ben to stay at Boynton for the next exeat. Christopher and Jane Boynton are there for the weekend with their little girls and Pamela has suggested that we might like to go over for dinner on Saturday to meet them all, but I said I thought we'd be going over to Orton. Was that right?'

'I think we ought to accept if Lady Boynton's asked us. We can go to Mum and Pa any time. I'll ring and say we can manage it after all.'

Gervaise gave her a worried look. He knew she was on edge,

and couldn't help feeling occasionally that there was no pleasing her. Perhaps this teaching wasn't such a good idea after all. He was terrified she might be ill again. He had forgotten that his original object in inviting her to teach at Winsleyhurst last autumn had been to get her away from the stifling effects of over-protection.

On the two exeat weekends, either side of half term, boys were allowed to be collected at lunch-time on Friday. Gervaise liked the teaching staff to be available in case there were any points parents might wish to raise about their child's progress in any particular subject. Douglas Butler was much in evidence, exuding muscular Christianity and wearing a suit. Flavia watched him make a bee line for the enormous Range Rover in which Mrs Waring, mother of the oily creep, had just driven up. Her laugh could be heard from miles away and she had the terrifying look of someone who might slap you on the back without warning. Gervaise always stood well clear, but Douglas was made of sterner stuff and went in close to exchange a crushing handshake which left him feeling most invigorated.

'This chap of yours is doing really well,' he said, flashing his bathroom tiles smile at her, and putting a heavy hand on Billy Waring's shoulder. 'He's mad keen, never misses a net and tries like a tiger at his maths.'

'Good! Great to see you, Mr Butler. Billy's always telling me what a brilliant cricket coach you are. Must get you over in the hols. Hop in, kids, we've got an action-packed weekend ahead,' and the Waring family departed with a confident crunch of gravel.

Flavia, who had just come out, caught Ben's eye and tried not to laugh as he jerked his head towards the Warings and silently mouthed 'Creep' at her. He was waiting expectantly beside his overnight bag, and Flavia had brought Wellington's bed and a supply of food to put beside it.

She had telephoned Pamela Boynton, who had been delighted to hear that she and Gervaise could come to dinner.

'Alistair told Lance that you'd both been quite wonderful. It was an inspiration to have that dog and I'm so pleased you're beginning to be interested in the boys, Flavia. I thought it would be nice for you all to meet away from the school – and more fun for you than just seeing Lance and me.'

'But I loved it the other Sunday too,' said Flavia truthfully. 'And, Lady Boynton? What shall I do about Wellington at the weekend?'

'Send him too. One dog more or less doesn't make any difference here. It'll be a good ice-breaker – and, my dear, do try and call me Pam.'

When Alistair drove up Flavia had just been buttonholed by Atkinson's mother, who was pretty, friendly and fun, and wanted to make a date for the Hendersons to come to dinner one night. Gervaise, seeing them talking out of the corner of his eye, was pleased. Sarah Atkinson couldn't have been much more than thirty, and Gervaise thought of her as a particularly young mother who might make a nice friend for his wife, though to Flavia all the boys' parents seemed like another generation. Normally she would have been pleased too, grateful for the chance to get to know more parents, but this morning she had been telling herself that she must have a word with Alistair, and had been keeping an eye open for his arrival. When she realized that she had missed him and that he had scooped up Ben and Wellington without seeing her she felt absurdly put out.

After the last boy had gone Gervaise came to find her.

'How wonderful,' he said. 'Now we can just be our two selves. Isn't that a treat?' And she had smiled and nodded and made an effort to appear as pleased at the prospect as she knew she ought to be.

There was quite a large gathering assembled in the drawing room at Boynton. Pamela, match-making instincts ticking away, had also invited her daughter-in-law, Jane's, glamorous sister, Claire, who had recently been divorced and had a boy a bit younger than Ben. Claire was standing at the far end of the room talking to Alistair when Gervaise and Flavia arrived. The little Boynton girls, who were in their dressing gowns, were supposed to be saying goodnight, but Lance was tossing them up in the air and getting them thoroughly over-excited. They squealed, and rampaged round and round the sofa.

The two boys were sitting on the floor playing cards. Flavia went over to talk to them.

'Have you had a lovely time?' she asked. 'Has Wellington been good?'

Pamela came to give them an affectionate greeting.

'You both know everyone except Claire Palmer and her son, Johnnie,' she said, introducing them.

Claire shook hands with cool disinterest and turned back to Alistair who said, 'Hello. Good to see you both,' but a quick glance at his face showed Flavia that his shutters were in place again and she felt disconcerted. Gervaise went over and joined easily in their conversation, but Flavia hung back and stayed talking to the two boys until Lance, a granddaughter hanging on each arm, came to join her.

'Ah, here's the most beautiful headmaster's wife in England,' he said, kissing her. 'Has Ben told you what he did yesterday evening?'

She shook her head and looked enquiringly at Ben.

'Just caught the trout I've been trying to catch for weeks, that's all. He casts as well as I do, damn the boy.' Ben went pink with pleasure.

'Could the erotic fly have had anything to do with it?' asked Flavia, laughing.

Jane Boynton came up to remove the little girls.

'Flavia – haven't seen you since your wedding. It was all so lovely. Christopher's been positively boring about how stunning you looked. Now I must try and get these little monsters to go to bed – fat chance now. Lance has a terrible effect on them.' Lance threw them in the air again to the accompaniment of more excited squeals.

'Grandpa just can't stop frowing up,' the youngest was heard to say as Jane dragged them both out of the drawing room.

'We don't really need a *placement* for such a family party,' said Pamela as she shepherded them into the dining-room, and then proceeded to tell everyone exactly where to sit. A practised hostess, she had actually thought it all out most carefully: remembering how important school outings are, and how agonizing grown-up meals can be to the young, she had arranged the table with a special eye to what would be easy for the two boys. Flavia found herself between her host and Ben, and Johnnie Palmer had been put between his Aunt Jane and Gervaise. Claire Palmer sat on the other side of Alistair. She was wearing a cropped Lycra top and a minute white linen skirt which displayed the maximum amount of bare brown midriff and long brown legs to perfection. Flavia, who had a good line in long brown legs herself, bitterly regretted that she had given way to Gervaise's alarmed look of doubt and opted for a droopy cotton skirt that reached her ankles, instead of the zinging orange miniskirt that had been her first choice.

They had roast turkey with all the trimmings – 'Just like Christmas,' said Ben to Flavia – followed by ice-cream with hot fudge sauce and fruit salad. Ben, who seemed much more relaxed than she had ever seen him, chatted happily away to Flavia, telling her how Wellington had wallowed in the lake when they'd all gone boating that morning, and how Lady Boynton hadn't minded a bit when he shook himself all over her. As for catching the monster trout it had been amazing, wicked. Lance, who had noticed how reserved Ben could be, was impressed that Flavia had managed to establish an easy relationship so quickly with the boy, who treated her more like an elder sister than a headmaster's wife.

As soon as they'd finished their pudding, it was suggested that the boys might like to watch a video before going to bed while the grown-ups had cheese and coffee. The boys' chairs were put back against the wall, everyone moved up and Flavia found herself sitting next to Alistair.

'How do you find Ben?' she asked.

'Thanks to you, much better than I expected. Being Ben he's already formed some strong likes and dislikes. I knew he would. You're one of the likes.'

'Oh good,' said Flavia, pleased out of all proportion, 'I like him too.'

'So what's it like being in charge of all these characters I've been hearing about? Spanner, who's absolutely *gross*, and Old Fossy, who's a bit scary but okay really, and Sister and Meg, and grotty Mr Stockdale, who fancies Barbie, and Goldberg, whose mother is stinking rich but knows all about sex, and Waring, who's a suck and greases up? You see I know all about everyone now.'

'My goodness, you do – only I'm certainly not in charge. They all run rings round me. I'm either scared witless by them or think they're utterly hilarious. You'd be amazed what goings on there are. Sister and Miss Hackett – she's Gervaise's secretary – are like the ugly sisters in Cinderella. Barbie and Jane swear they each nip into the loo and take the loo paper out when they think the other one's going in. Beat that for pettiness!'

'No!' he said, laughing at her. 'Tell me more.' So she regaled him with snippets of school gossip. How one of the washing-up ladies from the village, long suspected of being light-fingered, had smuggled a catering pack of Cheddar cheese up her knickers the week before, but the elastic, always under considerable strain, had burst and the cheese fell out as she was walking down the drive. 'Just like a chicken laying an egg,' said Flavia. She told him about Sister's friend from Amersham, and how Miss Hackett would have been a brilliant spy. She also told him how much she enjoyed teaching music, and about her slight altercation with Ben about the trumpet.

'Good for you,' said Alistair. 'I'm glad you've got his measure.'

She was beginning to find him easy and enjoy herself until Claire from his other side said, 'Don't you think we ought to get our sons to bed, Alistair? I'm going to see what mine is up to. Are you coming too?' And he excused himself and got up and went off with her. Flavia felt young and silly and wished she hadn't prattled on in such a childish way.

They went back to the drawing room, and Christopher Boynton came to sit by her and gossiped about her brothers until Claire came back.

'God! Children!' she said, collapsing on the sofa. 'Could someone get me a large drink? Thank heaven for boarding schools. I couldn't survive otherwise. I can't think how you stick seeing so much of yours, Jane.'

Flavia disliked her very much. She and Gervaise were just about to make a move when Alistair came back too.

'A special request,' he said, going over to Flavia. 'Will Mrs Henderson please come up and say goodnight?'

'Oh I'd love to.' She was very surprised. 'All right, darling? I won't be a minute.'

'Of course.' Gervaise looked delighted. 'Half the school are in love with my wife,' she heard him say as she followed Alistair out. 'I have a lot of rivals, but as far as I know they're all under thirteen.'

Ben was sitting up in bed covered in Wellington, who thumped his tail enthusiastically at Flavia.

'Hello, you frightful old sinner,' she said to the dog. 'What's all this about swimming in the lake?' Then without stopping to think she bent down to kiss Ben good night. He put his arms round her neck in a stranglehold and hugged her.

'Night,' he whispered into her hair.

'Good night, Ben,' she said, greatly touched. 'Sleep tight.'

Alistair was standing at the end of the bed. She glanced up at his face and caught him at a moment when the shutters were wide open. He looked devastated, and she guessed he must be thinking of his wife. Flavia instinctively put out a hand towards him and then lost her nerve and withdrew it. He held the door open for her and she went slowly downstairs. By the time he had said goodnight to Ben and joined her in the hall his face was quite expressionless again except for the little muscle ticking in his cheek.

Flavia ached for him so much that it was a physical pain. She would have given anything to have the chance to make him laugh again as she had during dinner.

XXIII

FLAVIA CAME HOME from the Boyntons' dinner party in a turmoil.

Turmoil would have been too powerful a word for Gervaise's emotions, but he felt uneasy. He had got through life without feeling strongly enough about most personal issues to have suffered from jealousy, but he had watched Flavia sparkling away at dinner and felt a pang of something very like it. He was dismally aware that he seemed unable to strike such a bright light from her himself. On the way home in the car he tried to tell her how much marriage had transformed his life, how he had never believed himself capable of feeling for anyone half of what he now felt for her. She had thanked him in a subdued voice, but made no reciprocal declaration and he couldn't help feeling hurt.

When they got home she went quickly upstairs while he pottered about downstairs, locking up and checking on the numerous doors into the school. He never appeared to be in a hurry over anything.

Flavia undressed quickly, flinging the Indian cotton skirt over a chair and got into bed. When Gervaise eventually climbed in beside her he put out a tentative hand towards her but she did not respond. He ran his finger down her arm and gently touched her breast. For the first time in their marriage she withheld herself from him. She felt like a stone and knew that tonight she could not bear the restlessness and disappointment that had started to come over her after he made love to her. She had not felt this acute sense of let-down to begin with, so the quality of their love-making had not mattered. Now, suddenly it seemed to matter very much.

'I'm a bit tired, darling,' she whispered. 'Not tonight.'

Gervaise, the most unselfish and least demanding of lovers, was immediately all concern.

'Of course not. How thoughtless of me. Are you all right? Not feeling ill?'

'No, no, only tired, I'm sorry, Gervaise, just a headache,' she murmured, falling back on the age-old excuse.

He kissed her gently, turned over and in a very short space of time his even breathing told her he was asleep. She was simultaneously both relieved and dissatisfied. She got cautiously out of bed and crept into Gervaise's study across the landing so that she could read without disturbing him, but somehow the biography of Marcel Moyse, the famous French flautist, in which she had been engrossed earlier on, failed to hold her attention. Eventually her head really started to ache. It seemed like just retribution for her thoughts, and she was almost glad.

Flavia was not at Winsleyhurst when the boys came back on Sunday evening. She had driven over to see her parents. She was toying with the idea of discussing with Hester – very cautiously, no promises – what steps she would need to take if she decided to try to go back to performing chamber music the following term. She had also rung up Dulcie and asked if she could pay her a visit.

At the school, Alistair went upstairs with Ben and handed him over to Meg, who could not have been nicer or cosier and at once took charge and led Ben off to find Goldberg; after a swift goodbye Alistair went down to find Gervaise and deliver Wellington. Father and son had both been disappointed not to find Flavia.

'Come and have a drink,' invited Gervaise. 'Flavia's gone off to see her parents, she'll be sorry to have missed you.'

'I much enjoyed seeing you both last night. I'm so grateful for what you're doing for us. I can't tell you what a relief it is that Ben has settled so well. Does Flavia really want to be burdened with this hound again?'

'Oh Lord, yes. She loves him. I have to tell you that having both your dog and your son have been very helpful to Flavia. They've given her a purpose. It's me that should really be grateful to you,' said Gervaise, feeling generous. He had been relieved when Flavia had announced her intention of going to

Orton, and now felt his secret suspicions had been petty and unworthy.

'How are you fixed for the holidays?' he asked Alistair.

'All right I hope, fingers crossed in case I have a drama. We're going to be in London for a bit, and various friends will help me out, and then I'm taking Ben up to Scotland. I'll have a couple of weeks with him and then I'll leave him at Ardvrechan with my aunt. We can manage Wellington for the holidays.'

'Well, don't hesitate to let us know if we can help. I really mean it. It wouldn't be the first time I've looked after boys whose parents are abroad in the holidays and I know Flavia would always welcome Ben's company. We're going to be in Scotland part of the time too. Anyway, talk to her about the dog on Parents' Day.'

Winsleyhurst Parents' Day was held on the last day of term so that the boys could be taken home after it was over. The school provided a tremendous tea for everyone, but parents brought a picnic lunch which they could eat in the grounds if fine, or anywhere on the school premises if wet. As most of the activities very much depended on fine weather, anxiety was always acute, and there seemed to be someone listening to the weather forecast at every possible opportunity for days beforehand.

This year there were no worries on that score: the hot spell looked set to last. The only real anxiety was that Monica Henderson had announced that she wished to come to stay.

'She hardly ever comes down. I can't think why she wants to choose this moment,' grumbled Gervaise.

'Can't we just say no?' asked Flavia, but Gervaise felt that Winsleyhurst had once been Monica's home too, and though she never showed the least interest in the school, he was conscious that he had benefitted from it more than she had, and felt obliged to let her come whenever she wanted.

The grounds had been marked out for sports, the form rooms were full of projects that the boys had done and all their exercise books were on show. The term's marks, good and bad were on display, a source of anxiety for some and satisfaction for others, partly dependent on ability, but also on widely differing parental attitudes.

It had been Flavia's idea, which had delighted Miss Hall, that the orchestra should have two short slots in the day and play popular selections of music.

'Not formal like at the school concert, more like a band playing at a fair or something so it won't matter if people are wandering about, and not for too long or nobody will listen.' She had offered to play with them if Miss Hall conducted, and they had roped in various members of the staff who could play an instrument to add a bit of volume as well. The boys were thrilled, and it had given Flavia something extra to do which in no way encroached on anyone else's preserves.

Monica arrived the day before the big event, and because they were all so busy, no one took much notice of her. Flavia had tried to talk to her, to ask her about her childhood in the school and make her feel welcome, but Monica seemed preoccupied and not much inclined to talk. Flavia was always amazed by the fact that Gervaise's sister, so different from him as a person, should look so like him, a sort of walking caricature; but features that are attractive in the male are not always so kind to the female. Monica looked like Gervaise in drag.

'Goodness,' said Flavia to Tricia, who had rung up for a gossip, 'but she is one very strange lady. She goes round in the same dismal old dress and a pair of gym shoes, and though she's only come for the weekend, her suitcase weighed an absolute ton. Gervaise could hardly lug it up stairs. When he asked her what on earth she'd got in it she just said, "Personal possessions and mind your own business." '

'Perhaps she's got a bomb,' suggested Tricia.

'Could well have – more likely to be loads of bibles I should think. She's frighteningly fervent. Anyway, I'm beginning to think she's not just eccentric but totally noisettes. Hope it's not hereditary.'

On Saturday morning the sky was as blue, and the sun as blazingly confident, as everyone had hoped. The school looked amazingly orderly and the boys unnaturally tidy. Gervaise decided that it would be safe to have tea out and a task force was appointed to carry trestle tables into the garden. Winsleyhurst was *en fête*.

Cars started to arrive early, most parents being fearful of

letting their sons down by being caught in a traffic jam, though there were always the rogue few – fortunately very few – who didn't give a jot about such a trifling consideration. Irina Goldberg, whom Flavia had been dying to meet, was certainly considered to be in this category and had not even answered the invitation. However, to everyone's astonishment, not least her son's, she was one of the first arrivals. She was accompanied by two Afghan hounds on scarlet leads and a lugubrious-looking American gentleman, not on a lead, whom she introduced as Luther, and who was, she told everyone, an absolute angel.

Gervaise, rather unwillingly, introduced Flavia. Irina gave her a surprisingly friendly smile.

'You must have something I haven't got,' she said with great good humour. 'Your husband's a very remarkable man. I made a pass at him and he turned me down! What's your secret?'

'Perhaps I play hard to get.'

'I've certainly never tried that.' Irina looked genuinely amused and gave a husky laugh which sounded as if her throat were full of hot ashes; Flavia quite expected her to breathe fire from her nostrils like a dragon. She felt she might rather like Mrs Goldberg, though she could see that she would be impossible as a parent.

'You'll find Rowan down on the cricket ground. I must say, I love your son – but I think he wants lots of encouragement.'

'Oh well, you go right ahead then, da-a-rrling – boys always need lots of encouragement in my view.' And Mrs Goldberg gave a sexy wink and wafted off with angelic Luther and the Afghans, leaving a strong smell of Femme lingering on the innocent July air.

The action-packed day started smoothly. It had to be admitted that Spanner came into his own at organizing the timing of all the events: no easy task when a boy who was in the first tennis pair and due to play a sudden-death set against two of the beefiest Mothers, might also be due to run in the senior hurdles race at the same time. Even his greatest detractors had to admit that Spanner was a wizard with a timetable. When he wasn't striding about with a stopwatch, looking keen and indispensable, he seemed to have latched on to the Goldberg party.

The members of the orchestra gave a lively performance, and

their turn was considered a good innovation, though Pamela Boynton complained that she couldn't recognize any of the tunes. As the Norfolks sighted a squirrel just as the band struck up, and yapped wildly when it shot up a tree, this was perhaps hardly surprising. In any case, Lance told Flavia that his wife only knew two tunes: the National Anthem and the 'Eton Boating Song', but as people generally stood up for one and quick-waltzed to the other this was a bit of a cheat.

At lunchtime everyone sat about in the sunshine drinking Pimm's or Coke and tucking into picnic lunches of varying degrees of sophistication, though sausages, chicken and strawberries featured largely on most menus. A few parents produced tables and chairs, proper plates and cut-glass tumblers, but most people had a motley assortment of picnic equipment and lay about on rugs. Much to Gervaise's disapproval the Warings had excelled themselves by hiring a mini marquee for the occasion, from which they dispensed loud hospitality. Small brothers and sisters dashed about shrieking with excitement, and there was a plentiful supply of doting grannies who made half-hearted attempts to help control them. Parents yelled themselves hoarse as their offspring panted, scarlet-faced, to the winning post, and some ancient rivalries were revived between fathers who were also old boys. Gervaise was relieved to get the visitors' races over without anyone having a coronary or breaking a leg, but there was an anxious moment when Mrs Digby, the wife of a well-known racehorse trainer who had recently been in trouble with the Jockey Club, collapsed at the start of the Mothers' Race. Sister, in the unlikely role of stable-lad, had to lead her away to the sickroom – supposedly to have a plaster applied but actually to sleep off the effects of too much champagne from the Warings' private tent. Michael Stockdale, a keen racing man, who was unfortunately standing too near the loudspeaker at the time, was heard to say, 'Poor old Digby – up before the Stewards again.'

After lunch everyone settled down to watch the First XI play the Fathers. Flavia went and joined the Boyntons on rugs under the shade of the Leavers' Tree. Quite soon Alistair and Ben came over. Alistair collapsed beside Flavia on the grass.

'Oh dear, we've nearly had a rape. For heaven's sake, take Wellington for a run somewhere, Ben, and make him let off a bit of steam away from other dogs.' Ben shot off, grinning. 'Ben wanted me to meet his friend Goldberg's mother, but Wellington got wildly interested in one of Goldberg's mother's dogs. I can't say I agreed with his taste. I thought we'd better beat a strategic retreat.'

'Were you actually on the run from the dogs or from Mrs Goldberg?' asked Flavia.

'Good question. What a dame! By the way, who's the dotty old trout marching up and down wearing sandwich boards?'

'Only sandwich boards?' asked Lance.

'Perhaps it was Mrs Goldberg demonstrating for heterosexual rights?' suggested Flavia.

'This one was demonstrating against blood sports in the car park.'

Flavia clapped a hand to her mouth. 'Oh my God!' she said. 'Monica! It couldn't be! Oh poor Gervaise.'

Lance Boynton gave a shout of laughter. 'Flavia, you haven't got that old crackpot here, have you? What can have possessed Gervaise to invite her? She might do anything.'

'She invited herself.' Flavia was torn between giggles and concern. 'What a nightmare – what shall I do?'

'Let's go and recce the car park for a start.' Alistair got to his feet as Ben and Wellington reappeared. 'Come on, Ben, keep Wellington on the lead. We have espionage work to do.'

'I'll come too,' said Flavia, thankful that Gervaise was umpiring the cricket. She knew he would be mortified.

When they reached the car park, Monica was no longer wearing sandwich boards, which lay discarded by the hedge. She was standing on the bonnet of a large Discovery, busily writing 'Down with Blood Sports' in foam across the windscreen with an aerosol can of Christmas snow. One glance at the rest of the cars showed that it was by no means the first vehicle to be given the treatment.

Flavia was convulsed with laughter. 'It's no good me going to reason with her,' she said. 'She wouldn't pay the slightest attention. I might make her worse.'

'Right then – guile,' said Alistair, who was clearly enjoying himself enormously. 'Which upstairs room in the house, apart from a loo, has a key?'

'I think there's one in Gervaise's study.'

'You'd better stay clear. Go back to the Boyntons and keep hold of Wellington. Ben and I'll see what we can do.'

Flavia lingered behind a bush and watched Ben go up to Monica and engage her in conversation. Monica started pointing. Ben appeared distraught, he looked as if he was in tears. After a few moments Monica climbed down from the bonnet and they went off together in the direction of the house. Flavia, who inevitably got waylaid by several lots of parents en route, had only just got back to Lance and Pamela and was describing the state of the car park to them when Alistair and Ben turned up looking very smug. Alistair handed Flavia a key.

'Right,' he said. 'Over to you now. We've locked her in your husband's study. She's kicking the door a bit, but I don't think she can get out.'

'How did you get her there?'

'Easy. Ben pretended he'd been sent to get something by Gervaise and spun her a tale about being new, and not knowing the way and please, please would she go with him. I just followed. He pretended to hunt about in the desk while I got the key out of the lock, then he whipped out and we locked her in. She's got quite a vocabulary, your sister-in-law, I must say. I had no idea Parents' Day could be such fun.'

'Nor did I,' said Flavia. 'Ben, you're a hero.'

'You give that key to me,' said Pamela. 'I shall deal with Monica. I've been longing to have a go at her for years. I shall have her on a train back to Gloucester before she knows what's hit her. You'd better consult Meg about cleaning up the cars.' And she strode off, the little dogs tearing noisily along behind her.

'God help poor Monica,' said her husband, wiping tears of laughter from his eyes. 'I wouldn't be in her shoes now.'

Flavia went to search for Meg, who was amused and horrified, but instantly agreed that they must get the cars cleaned up before Gervaise heard about it, or the parents started to go home. It was the first time she and Flavia had really been in accord. 'We'll need very strong detergent,' she said, years of Christmas decorating at schools and church bazaars behind her. 'It's awful stuff to get off windows but thank goodness she didn't use paint. I'll get Jane and Barbie to help.'

Monica had obviously targeted those cars with British Field

Sports stickers on, of which there were a considerable number, but luckily hadn't got very far with her scheme. By the time the match was over the cars were clean and the self-appointed car park attendants were very wet. Flavia had to change into another dress before reluctantly going back to playing the part of hostess.

A good many people had seen the dotty woman marching about at lunchtime covered in slogans, so Gervaise, who was appalled to discover what had been going on, decided to announce that they had been visited by a campaigner, tiresome but harmless, who had been escorted off the premises and any traces of vandalism had been cleaned up. He did not announce the identity of the culprit though he had no doubt that word would get around in due course, and quickly went on to make a few announcements, thanked everyone for coming and passed the microphone over to Pamela to say a few words in her capacity as Chairman of the Governors.

Pamela had returned from putting Monica, her suitcase now light as a feather without the campaign equipment, into a taxi to the station.

'Luckily it was old Mr Turner who I've known for years, so I tipped him well and he promised he wouldn't leave till the train had actually pulled out of the station,' she told them.

'My goodness I did enjoy seeing her off. I really put the fear of God into Monica.'

'Oh, I shouldn't think so,' said Gervaise gloomily. 'She always thinks God's on her side. She'll be popping into church tonight to register a complaint. She'll expect Him to send at least a plague of boils or locusts.'

As the parents girded their loins at the prospect of having their children at home for the next eight weeks, and gathered up their various offspring, Flavia stood beside Gervaise saying endless goodbyes and wishing everyone happy holidays. When it was Alistair and Ben's, turn she hugged the boy and the dog, and then hesitated. Alistair hesitated too, and then gave her an amused look.

'Have I earned a kiss this time?' he asked lightly, and kissed her quickly on the cheek before piling all Ben's luggage and accumulated clobber into his car.

She stood watching them drive away. The school suddenly seemed very large and bleak and empty.

XXIV

HESTER WAS ELATED when Flavia had asked her, with a casualness that did not deceive, what she thought she could do to keep the door ajar in case she might want to get back to the concert platform.

Though it was Hester's dearest wish that Flavia should do this, she did not feel it spoke well of Flavia's present happiness. This time Hester intended to learn from her previous mistakes and knew that she must try not to force the issue. Besides, she had to face the fact that her daughter had shown herself more than capable of making her own decisions, however difficult these might be. She was terrified to probe too much in case Flavia retreated behind her electric fence again. Andrew, on the other hand, was afraid to question Flavia because he did not wish to open emotional floodgates which might afterwards prove too difficult to close.

'I don't suppose you've practised much lately?' Hester asked cautiously.

'Oh yes. I've actually played almost every day and I've always done my Taffanel and Gaubert exercises as a warm-up.'

'What about lessons?'

'No, I haven't had a lesson. Do you think I should give the Prof a ring? I don't want to waste his time.'

'Nothing wrong with asking for a lesson and seeing what he thinks about your playing now. I think he'd be only too pleased, and you know you'd get a very honest opinion.'

No more was said, but Flavia rang Alfred Tatham, her flute teacher, and made a date for a lesson with him.

'I've been waiting for you to get in touch,' he said. After speaking to her he made an off-the-record call to Maurice Fenstein. They had talked about Flavia several times over the last year if they happened to meet. Maurice had a great deal of clout, but despite his affection for Flavia, Alfred Tatham knew Maurice would need to be convinced that she was not only serious in her intention to return, but capable of sustaining the pressures that would be involved in an attempt to climb the ladder again after such a painful fall. He promised he would let Maurice have his opinion after he had heard Flavia play.

Gervaise was very busy the first week of the holidays writing reports and dealing with the numerous small decisions about the running of the school that tended to get put on hold till after the end of term. Her father was similarly occupied at Orton so Flavia spent quite a lot of time with her mother. They went up to London to an exhibition at the Tate, did some shopping, and then went to a concert at the Barbican to hear a brilliant Indian flautist, and both came away lit up by the magic of his playing. Flavia could hardly bear it when the concert ended: it gave her some new insights and stirred old ambitions from their hibernation. Mother and daughter hadn't enjoyed each other's company so much for ages. They drove back to Orton afterwards and Flavia spent the night in her old bedroom. It felt strange. Last time she had slept there, home had begun to feel like a prison; now it made her feel free.

What have I done, thought Flavia – what have I gone and done?

A school without its pupils is like a deflated balloon. For the first few days, key members of the staff were still there, making uneasy conversation at meals. The common threads that bound them together in the term-time, albeit sometimes uncomfortably closely, had been temporarily loosened, and they were like an ill-assorted bunch of travellers whose coach has temporarily broken down. It was a relief when everyone went off.

Flavia visited old Mr Foster in his little house in the grounds. He gave her tea and she played the piano for him.

She missed having Wellington to take for walks and couldn't wait to get up to Duntroon, where she and Gervaise had been asked to stay for as long as they liked during the holidays.

She had received a letter from Ben.

'Dear Mrs Henderson,' she read. 'Thank you very much for having Wellington. I loved my music lessons. Dad and I wanted to play tennis today on the courts near us but thousands of mice had been eating our balls since last summer so we weren't much good. I am having a super time. Love from Ben xxx.'

This interesting epistle came with some Interflora flowers, and was enclosed with another card which read: 'For Flavia, with love and thanks from Wellington, Ben and Alistair.' She kept the letter and card long after the flowers were dead. It was the first time she had seen Alistair's writing.

She thought a great deal about whether she should write back and thank them for the flowers, themselves in the nature of a thank you, fearful of saying too much, but fearful too — shamefully fearful — of saying nothing. In the end she found what she thought was the right answer. Elizabeth Cameron had sent Gervaise a postcard when Flavia had stayed on at Duntroon after the New Year, of Sir John Everett Millais's picture called *Bright Eyes*. On the back Aunt Elizabeth had written, 'Who does this remind you of?' It was the portrait of a girl in a red caped coat, with a white chiffon scarf tied round her neck in a bow. She was standing, as Flavia so often stood, with her head ever so slightly tilted, her hands in her pockets and her long dark hair loose over her shoulders. She had a sensitive, vulnerable face with a surprisingly sensuous mouth. She was looking expectantly into the future, but she stood against a background of grey clouds. Over her head were two sprigs of mistletoe. Gervaise had been so delighted with it that Elizabeth had bought several more from the Aberdeen Art Gallery next time she was there, and had sent them to Flavia. She took one now and addressed it to 'Messrs A. B. and W. Forbes', and wrote: 'The flowers are *lovely.* Bad luck about the mice, how unfortunate for you both! Thinking of you all and hope you have a wonderful time together. Love, Flavia.'

She stamped it, and put it out on the hall table for whoever went to the post first, and by this openness, by leaving it there for all to see, most especially for Gervaise to see, tried to convince herself that her motive for sending it was perfectly innocuous, no more nor less than friendship demanded.

Duntroon worked its usual magic. Members of the family came and went. There were picnics and expeditions; hills to be climbed and the river to be fished; in August there were long armed walks after elusive grouse. Best of all from Flavia's point of view there was much carefree laughter, and often music in the evenings. Everybody loved Gervaise. He was the ideal guest, one of those people who are invaluable in any house party, fitting in with all ages and getting on with everyone. Elizabeth was pleased to see how much Gervaise and Flavia amused each other and wondered why she did not feel entirely easy about their relationship all the same. Flavia was loving and demonstrative to her husband but Elizabeth thought she was trying too hard for it to be completely natural.

'What do you think about the newly-weds?' she asked Colin one evening.

'Gervaise is like a cat on hot bricks,' said Colin. 'He watches Flavia's every move – but she does look well again at last.'

Elizabeth also wondered what Flavia's feelings about Antoine were now.

One day Flavia dared to ask herself the same question, a question that she had tried to keep shut away in a secret drawer of her mind. She was sitting in the kitchen shelling broad beans for the deep freeze when her eye was caught by a photograph in the newspaper on which she was putting the pods. It was of Antoine and his wife, Miranda, and above it was the heading: 'New Arrival Expected Soon.' Flavia was reading the article when Gervaise came in.

'Budge up,' he said. 'I'll give you a hand with the beans – you don't seem to be getting on very fast. Why is it last week's papers always seem so interesting?'

'This one is interesting.' She pointed to the picture. 'Antoine with a baby!' she said. 'I simply can't imagine it.'

'Oh Flavia,' Gervaise looked extremely anxious, 'Is this very painful for you?'

'No,' she said. 'No – it most wonderfully isn't. It's like having had a ghastly sick bug, and when you can think of sausages again without feeling queasy, you know you're cured.'

Two months earlier these words would have been music in Gervaise's ears.

Sometimes there would be paying guests, to whom Elizabeth and Colin opened the doors of Duntroon in the summer, and then there would be a four-line whip for the family to be on time for meals, and to sing for their own supper by chatting up the visitors. The money brought in by this venture was a drop in the ocean as far as paying towards the upkeep of the house was concerned, but it enabled Elizabeth to have the help without which life in such an unwieldy home would have become a tyranny. Most of the visitors were charming, fun, and best of all, out for the day; but occasionally there would be those who put a strain on everyone's endurance and whom nobody wanted to sit next to in the dining room. Then it became a sort of game to see who had fared worst and to compare notes afterwards.

'You'll never guess what Arnold Hagen does,' said Flavia to Colin. 'He runs a clothes counselling service.'

'You mean he tells people what to wear? Good Lord, what a horrendous thought. I know what I'd tell him to do with his own tartan waistcoat.'

'No, no, it's more like bereavement counselling. It's not to tell them what they ought to wear. He says it's for people who've had "bad wardrobe experiences" – to help them come to terms with the trauma of the clothes they've already worn. Old Arnie says there's a hugely lucrative future in it. Do you think I could start it at Winsleyhurst for all those horsy mothers? Perhaps it would help Mum and me bear the mortification of Dad's frightful old cardigan and Gervaise's corduroy jacket?'

Nobody wanted either Gervaise or Flavia to leave Duntroon, least of all themselves, but Gervaise had to go to a conference before the end of the holidays. He suggested that Flavia might like to stay on without him for a few days, as she had in the New Year, but to his pleasure and relief she wouldn't hear of it. She decided to stay with Matt and Di in London the nights he was away, as she had made her date for a flute lesson with Mr Tatham then.

They went back to Winsleyhurst for a couple of days first. The school seemed very uncosy and echoing, and Flavia suffered severe Duntroon withdrawal symptoms which she tried hard to disguise from Gervaise. The Council had turned down the first application for the building work on to the Old Stables, and she walked over to deliver some revised plans to Pamela Boynton, and was greeted with great warmth.

'Flavia, how lovely that you're back! You're just the person who might help me. I've had an SOS from Alistair Forbes. He's had an urgent call to fly to Bangkok the day after tomorrow and Ben's arriving back from Scotland tomorrow night. It seems his aunt, Moyra Forbes, is off on her travels again and can't keep Ben till the end of the holidays. Extraordinary woman – I can't think why she wants to go jaunting off to outlandish places at her age. I got all that out of my system when I was a girl,' said Pamela, who had been to a finishing school in Paris for three months when she was seventeen. She hated accompanying Lance on business trips abroad.

'Alistair asked if we could possibly have Ben for a few days. I've said yes, and he can certainly come here, but it won't be much fun for him. Lance is away and I'm tied up most of this week organizing a big fund-raising event for the NSPCC. I wonder if by any chance you could help entertain him?'

'Oh please, let him come to us. I'd adore to have him. Gervaise is busy too and it would be company for me. I'm actually going up to London for a couple of nights. I could bring him back with me.'

'Well, that would be marvellous. You can take him fishing here or go on the lake or do anything you like. I'll leave it to you to liaise with Alistair yourself. I suggested Claire Palmer, but Alistair says he knows she's in Corfu.'

A little shadow that had no right to be there, crossed the sun. How did Alistair know that Claire was in Corfu?

Gervaise was delighted. He did not feel at all threatened by Ben, and thought he would be company for Flavia.

'I told Alistair not to hesitate to use us anyway. That will be fun for you, darling.'

Flavia rang Alistair on his office number.

'How absolutely wonderful. Ben would much prefer that. I did think of asking you but I didn't want to impose on you in the holidays.'

'I could meet his train if you like. Matt and Di are both working and once I've been for my lesson I've got nothing special to do.'

'Well, I've promised Ben I'll meet him myself so I'll be working at home tomorrow morning. I suppose – I suppose you wouldn't like to come and have a late scratch lunch with me here and then come and meet the train with me?'

'I'd love to,' said Flavia, deliberately ignoring the warning bells in her head. A lunch date with Tricia could easily be postponed.

The Forbeses lived near Wandsworth Common, not really very far from Matt and Di, but in a much smarter area. Flavia was curious to see what the house was like inside. She stood on the doorstep for a minute or two before plucking up courage to ring the bell, though it was after half-past one before she got there.

Her lesson had gone well. Alfred Tatham, her professor of flute, had said to her, 'Well, Flavia, I think you could be back on course. Your sound is fine and your long notes are very good. Flexibility leaves a bit to be desired, but we'll work on that. Your playing has always been musical and your sight-reading exceptional but I think your interpretation has matured. There is more depth, more colour. Perhaps this enforced break has been a good thing. We all knew you had the capability if you wanted it. That *if* is the thing,' and he had looked at her searchingly. 'You must expect a battle to get back, you know. There is a lot of talent out there fighting for recognition. You had it within your grasp, but you let it go. I know it wasn't your fault, but you'd need real determination now. Why don't I let it be known to various youth and college orchestras that you might do a concerto with them if the opportunity cropped up? It might be a good road back if the chance came – and you wanted it.'

She had felt both cheered and challenged.

When Alistair opened the door, Flavia's heart did a disconcerting somersault, and she wondered if coming to lunch was such a good idea after all.

'Kiss or no kiss?' he asked, laughing at her, reading the look of uncertainty on her face.

'Kiss,' she said, laughing back and holding her face up, the constraint suddenly gone.

'So how was the lesson?'

'Amazing. Just what I needed. Can I dump my flute here? I never dare leave it in the car.'

'Bring it through with you, then no one can trip over it. What a responsibility.' He led the way from the narrow hall into a big sunny kitchen where he had obviously been working. The far end of the table was littered with papers.

'Sorry about the mess. Ben and I tend to live in here nowadays. What would you like to drink? There's some white wine in the fridge.'

'Could I have it as a spritzer – or would that be insulting? Is the wine too good for that?'

'Certainly isn't. I'll have the same. Shall we eat straight away? It's all Marks and Sparks – the single man's caterer.'

'Quite often the married woman's caterer too. Lovely. I'm starving.'

He had made salad and bought coronation chicken and cold ham, and there was cheese and fruit. They talked about Duntroon, and Ardvrechan – the island belonging to his aunt where he and Ben had spent a blissful fortnight together before Alistair had had to come back to London. She felt she had known him for years, and time flew by.

When they had finished, they put the plates in the dishwasher and he made coffee.

'Let's take it through to the drawing room and be civilized. I so rarely use it now – it's nice to have an excuse.'

It was a pretty room, rather conventional, very much a woman's room, Flavia thought: the pink chintz curtains had pretty tiebacks and pelmets; there were pink silk cushions, a low table with books on it. It did not feel lived in, nor did it give much clue to what the woman who had chosen it might have been like. It lacked a sharp dash of some other colour, an unexpected object or unusual arrangement of pictures, to pull it into a sharper focus. It had obviously once been two rooms which had been knocked into one, and up the far end there was a baby grand piano covered with photographs.

'Your wife?' she asked, looking at a picture of a surprisingly stout small Ben sitting on the lap of a fair-haired girl. She was pretty, like the room, but also like the room not particularly remarkable. You would not feel confident of your ability to recognize her from the photograph, if you were just about to meet her.

'Yes,' he said. 'Yes, that's Julie.'

'It must be awful without her.'

'I wish it were worse,' he said unexpectedly. 'Oh God, but I wish it were worse.'

'Tell me,' she said, slightly puzzled, thinking he looked very unhappy already.

He leant against the fireplace, running his fingers through his very dark brown hair, which must once have been reddish like Ben's.

'I can't find her. She has evaporated. I loved her – I think I did anyway, though she was always a bit elusive. I was in the army when we first married and we both had lots of friends, or again I thought she did too, though several quite surprising people have told me since that they felt they never really knew her. She didn't like me being away such a lot, though she'd never come with me even when it was possible; yet when I came home there often seemed to be a space between us – a sort of mist-filled space.'

Flavia sat on the floor, her hands round the mug of coffee, not drinking it. She remembered her impression when he had first turned up at Winsleyhurst that he was like a wild animal. She had just that feeling now – a false or sudden move on her part and he would be off into the jungle. She didn't think he was really aware of her; it didn't matter – he needed to talk, and she was there. She was content with that.

'Did you ever read *The Lord of the Rings*?' he asked suddenly.

'Yes, lots of times. When I was at school I used to read it practically every year.'

'I read it aloud to Ben. Do you remember at the end how Bilbo Baggins faded? It was the price he paid for having touched the ring? He grew dimmer. People couldn't see him properly.'

'I remember.'

'It was like that. It *is* like that. I try to bring her back into focus and I can't. I am not even sure what she was like.'

'When Ben hugged me goodnight at the Boyntons', you remembered her then,' she said gently.

'No,' he said sadly, 'no, it just reminded me of Ben kissing her good night, and I could have wept for him that it should have been so long since he gave anyone that kind of hug. I almost envied him, because he does know what she was like. But I didn't see Julie then – I only saw . . .' he turned to look at her but didn't finish his sentence.

Flavia got up and stood awkwardly holding her unfinished

mug of coffee, and a weight of unsaid words hung between them.

He turned back to the fireplace.

'Glad you liked the flowers and that you enjoyed Ben's letter,' he said. 'And I enjoyed the picture of you.' The postcard of Millais's girl in the red coat was propped up on the shelf together with several invitations.

'Aunt Elizabeth and Gervaise think it's like me.'

'Yes,' he said, 'it is like you in a way – very like – but there's one big difference. This is the portrait of a very young girl.'

She laughed uncertainly, trying for a lighter note. 'And I look so old?'

'No,' he said, 'of course you don't, but you don't look like a young girl either. You look like a woman.'

It was lucky that the telephone rang at that moment. Lucky too that when he had dealt with the call he looked at his watch because they had both lost all idea of time during the afternoon.

'Oh my God! Ben's train – and it's rush hour now. Come on, we'll just about make it.'

XXV

BEN HAD SPENT most of the journey in the guard's van, keeping Wellington company, in between lots of trips to the buffet car to buy snacks for them both. Wellington had developed a taste for soggy bacon sandwiches. They were both overjoyed to see Alistair and Flavia. Wellington relieved himself copiously and embarrassingly against every available surface as they made their way back to the car.

Ben hardly drew breath on the way home, giving his father an update on everything that had happened at Ardvrechan in the two weeks since Alistair had left: sightings of otters, the boat needing repairs, the tally of trout caught and the preparations for Aunt Moy's latest expedition. Flavia got the picture of a magic place and a special person, both of supreme importance to father and son.

Ben seemed quite happy at the prospect of going to stay with Gervaise and Flavia while his father was away. 'So long as we don't have to see that awful old Spanner,' he said.

'He isn't there in the holidays. If we see him coming we'll hide.'

'Poor old Rowan Goldberg. Gross for him having to see Spanner in the holidays.'

'Why on earth does Rowan have to see him in the holidays?' Flavia was surprised. Ben gave her an inscrutable look.

'It's *supposed* to be for maths coaching.'

Flavia opened her mouth to ask more and then shut it again. She thought she would enquire about this from Gervaise first.

'We haven't made a plan about tomorrow,' she said, standing on the doorstep when they arrived back at the house. 'I can come for him as early as you like but I want to go and visit my old godmother in the morning. Ben's welcome to come too, though it might be a bit boring for him. What time do you want me to pick him up?'

'Aren't you coming in now?' asked Ben.

'No – I'm going to Matt and Di.'

'Will they be there?' asked Alistair, watching her face.

'I have a key.'

'I asked you if they'd be there.'

To her annoyance she felt herself flushing, horribly aware of what she would like to do, conscious that Matt and Di had said they would both be working late and would not be back before ten o'clock at the earliest, but knowing she might be on the brink of sailing into very dangerous waters.

'They have funny hours. You never quite know, but I think I ought to be getting back.'

'Why can't you have supper with me and Dad?'

'You've got to come in anyhow,' said Alistair. 'I rather think you left your flute in the kitchen.'

'Please come to supper with us. The crisps I ate seem to have worn off now. I'm dying of hunger,' said Ben.

'Oh well,' she said, 'all right. I don't need supper but I'll come in just for a little bit and see your pebbles – that would be lovely.'

Ben, who collected stones, had wanted to show her his latest finds from the beaches at Ardvrechan. Alistair groaned.

'This house is getting like a bloody gravel pit,' he complained. 'Thank God I'll be in Bangkok for the next few days and won't hear that infernal gadget of yours clunking away all the time.'

Ben showed Flavia his polishing machine, filled it up with water and switched it on, and the stones churned round noisily.

'You'll see,' he said. 'In three weeks they'll look really beautiful – all shiny and the colour will show even when they're not in water.'

While Flavia helped Ben sort out the clothes he might want for the next few days Alistair went out and bought fish and chips which they ate off the paper, and then they found some ice cream in the deep freeze.

'Do play for Flavia, Dad,' said Ben. 'I've told her how cool you are.'

Alistair went to the piano in the drawing room and sat down

and started to play. After a moment Flavia disappeared to the kitchen and came back with her flute.

'I'll busk along,' she said. 'I used to play jazz at college.'

Alistair gave her an A, watching her while she tuned the flute, and then beginning to play again very softly until she started to join in.

She felt quite intoxicated. Sometimes he led and she followed, sometimes she went off into wild flights of invention while he played along with her. When they stopped, Flavia was breathless – but not from playing the flute. Neither of them said anything at all.

'Wick-ed,' said Ben.

'I must go. I'll be here about twelve, Ben. See you tomorrow.' Flavia almost fled out of the house. She had no recollection of driving to Vindaloo Road. When she got there she sat in her car for a long time, before going up to Matt and Di's flat.

Nothing much had changed at Dulcie's. Perhaps the layer of dust was a little thicker, perhaps Hilda was a little more bent when she opened the door.

'How are you both?' asked Flavia.

'Failing,' said Hilda. 'We're both failing,' but then she always said that. Flavia knew she would mind intolerably when the final change really came.

Dulcie was very pleased to see her. Flavia prattled on, telling her all the news of the family, talking about the school, biding her time before she broached the subject she had come to talk about. In the end it was Dulcie who brought it up.

'So,' she said, 'what are you not telling me, Flavia?'

Flavia tried to sound casual as she told her about her lesson the day before, about the possibility that she might after all decide to go back to her music.

'Alfred was very encouraging. He thinks it will be tough, but he thinks I should try for a comeback,' she said. 'I love the school and I love the boys, and my bit of teaching helps, but there isn't really enough for me to do. There are so many people already to do all the things that a headmaster's wife might want to do. I could easily follow a career as well.'

'And?'

'And I think perhaps music has found me again. You said it might.'

'Ah,' said the old lady, 'and something else has found you too. I know. I looked at your face and I knew.'

'What shall I do, Dulcie? Whatever shall I do?'

'About the music?'

'No, not about the music.' Flavia's voice was a whisper.

'That is not so easy. Life is full of pain and joy – and choices,' said Dulcie. 'You have to make your own choices, Flavia.'

'And if the choice might hurt another person, someone I really love too, and hurt them quite terribly, what then?'

'Still you have to make your own decision. Often we are faced with the fact that someone will be hurt whatever we do.'

'But that's so hard.'

'Life is very hard,' said Dulcie inexorably.

'And lonely – making choices is so lonely.'

'That too.'

'I am appalled at myself,' said Flavia, her eyes wide. 'Appalled. And you were right about Antoine too; this is something quite different. Oh Dulcie, have you no advice? Can't you give me any help?'

'Well,' said the old lady, 'you may not think it very comforting. I have made many decisions in my life, some good, some not so good. Many, God forgive me, that have wounded other people, but I don't think any experiences, even our mistakes, are ever wasted – not if you learn by them. Sometimes we have to make sacrifices, but beware! Be very sure if you make a huge gesture, a big sacrifice, that you can live up to it afterwards, otherwise in the end everyone is a loser.'

Flavia came and buried her face in Dulcie's lap.

'Don't rush it, Flavia. Take your time. Something may happen which will make it obvious. In the end an answer will come.'

'Do you pray, Dulcie?'

'Some people might not call it that, but yes, in my own way I pray. I pray through my music; I pray when the blackbird sings outside my window; I offer a grudging prayer through my stiff joints and loss of beauty; I pray when I laugh – and I pray for help, for myself and the people I love, but I don't pray for a particular outcome any more. That now seems to me to be impertinent. You have grown up, Flavia,' she said. 'Your music will be the richer for it. That sheltered childhood that perhaps went on longer than most – too long – is over. You are a woman now.'

As Flavia went out into the street she reflected that it was the second time in two days that someone had told her that. It seemed a terrible responsibility.

Flavia and Ben arrived back at Winsleyhurst soon after Gervaise got back from his conference.

'What a waste of time,' he said. 'What a lot of hot air people talk at these gatherings. They're all so earnest – it has very little to do with schoolmastering as I see it. Mounds of papers, endless committees, the ghastly acronyms they make up for everything. If it weren't for the fact that I know Douglas is always itching to go in my place I simply wouldn't ever turn up at any of them.'

As always he was enchanted to see her again. Every moment spent away from her seemed to be a terrible waste. He wanted to know how her lesson had gone.

'Really well. I'm going to go for several more. If a chance came up to test the water about playing again, how would you feel about it?'

If Gervaise had a suspicion that one of the reasons that Flavia had married him was to get away from the pressure of a musical career, but that now she seemed to be contemplating getting away from marriage by returning to her career, he thrust the thought aside. He looked at her fondly and said anything she did would be all right by him – absolutely anything.

It was fun for both of them having Ben. Gervaise, unlike some prep school masters, was not a frustrated public schoolmaster at heart. He genuinely enjoyed the company of children and liked doing all the things they liked. He was wonderful at producing ploys and was a walking encyclopaedia of card games. Flavia thought, not for the first time, what a marvellous father he would make.

He played tennis with Ben, who was fiercely competitive on a one-to-one basis. Douglas Butler had described him on his report as lacking in team spirit, which was certainly true as far as any team run by Douglas was concerned. Meg had decided that he was one of the very few boys to whom she could not relate, but in the relaxed and uncritical company of Gervaise and Flavia Ben came across as a different person from the aloof, scornful boy that he had seemed to be in term time.

'I must say I do like Ben,' said Gervaise. 'He's a splendid child – different. Alistair's done a good job in bringing him up.' Flavia felt absurdly pleased.

She and Ben bicycled over to the folly at Boynton, taking the long way round, leaving their bicycles at the bottom of the hill and scrambling up at the back. Ben was enchanted.

'What a great place – can we go inside?'

'I think it's locked. I haven't been in for years.'

'I bet there's a key somewhere.'

He prowled round while Flavia flopped down on the grass and lay there thinking about the last time she had been here, nearly a year ago, and of all that had happened in the intervening months. She brooded about her life, turning over a host of new thoughts in her mind. After about a quarter of an hour Ben reappeared covered with cobwebs, with a look of triumph and a huge rusty old key.

'One of the windows wasn't properly shut, but there are quite good footholds where bricks have fallen out and I managed to climb up and stand on that sort of ridge. I got it open and squeezed in. It was quite a drop down inside, though. There was a key hanging by the door at the back and I've got that open too now, so you can come in as well.'

He led her in proudly and they climbed up a narrow oak staircase, rather rickety in places, to the first floor.

'Gosh. A proper room. What would it have been used for?' asked Ben.

'It's a hunting tower. Sometimes they were just made for ornament and fun – literally follies – but I believe this one is really old, much older than the present house is. You must ask Sir Lance. See what a wonderful view you get from all four corners? You can see in all directions.' There were four round turrets stuck onto the corners of the square tower, each with windows giving a wide view. 'It might have been used for spotting deer, or for the ladies to come and watch the hunt if they didn't want to partake themselves, or for rather grand banquety sort of picnics. I expect it was used as a secret meeting place for lovers too.'

'It'd make a smashing place for a secret HQ.'

They went on upstairs to another room, and finally up again to a tiny lookout at the top where you could see the countryside rolling on for miles round.

'Wonderful place to watch for your enemies, waiting to pour the boiling oil on them,' said Ben.

'Or to watch for your lover coming for a secret meeting by moonlight,' said Flavia, leaning on the dusty sill, looking dreamily out of the leaded window, and she quoted Alfred Noyes: ' "Look for me by moonlight; Watch for me by moonlight; I'll come to thee by moonlight, though hell should bar the way!" '

'Could we come here at night?'

'I don't see why not. We could have a moonlight supper picnic, and have candles not torches.'

Later, when Gervaise came in search of them, they were busy damming the stream. He stood and watched them as they waded about above the cascade for several minutes before they saw him. Flavia, in denim shorts and an old T-shirt, her hair tied back in a pony tail, looked about fourteen. Gervaise looked at her with love and relief. There had been many moments lately when he feared that she might be growing beyond him – searching for something he felt incapable of giving her – and it filled him with foreboding. Climbing a hill at Duntroon one day she had astonished and unnerved him by suddenly saying, 'Let's go wild and make love here in the heather,' and he had felt quite unable to oblige her – it was just not the sort of thing Gervaise did. He did not at all want his Mary Rose to grow up.

Ben asked if they could have the moonlight supper picnic the evening when Alistair was coming down to fetch him, and invite him to a feast in the folly. Flavia was enchanted but Gervaise had looked a bit doubtful and said they would have to ask the Boyntons first.

'Oh no, that would spoil everything,' Flavia said. 'Pamela would want to come too and have practical ideas like Thermoses and Calor Gas, and let's all get cracking and give the place a jolly good clean.'

'But, darling, I don't think we can trespass.'

'We wouldn't be trespassing. Pamela said if we had Ben to stay to help her out, we could have the run of the whole place. Anyway,' she added illogically, 'trespassing is half the fun.'

Gervaise salved his conscience by saying casually to Pamela that he hoped it was all right if Flavia took Ben for a picnic at the folly, and Pamela, whose mind was running on a burning scent as to whether a girls' boarding house should have bidets in the lavatories, had said yes, yes, yes, of course, but have you rung the plumber yet? Gervaise listened with happy indulgence while Ben and Flavia discussed the rival merits of cold venison and chicken legs – 'we ought to be able to gnaw things and toss a few bones about' – and decided to have both.

'Ice-cream?' suggested Ben hopefully.

'Not a chance. Where's your sense of history?' In the end they compromised with having blackberry fool and calling it syllabub, and Ben being given a special dispensation to drink Coke while the grown-ups drank wine. They pottered about together in the huge school kitchen, making an awful mess. Luckily Garry was still away on holiday.

The feast was a great success, though the candles, stuck in wine bottles, seemed to attract rather a lot of moths and mosquitos, and there was a bad moment when a bat emerged from nowhere, and the hostess fled screaming from the banqueting chamber, and could only be persuaded to return when it was finally captured in the tablecloth and put outside.

'I expect in the olden days they had huge sexual orgies after feasts,' said Ben.

'Are sexual orgies included in the history or the biology curriculum at Winsleyhurst, Gervaise?' asked Alistair.

Ben looked withering. 'We don't need to be taught it in school – we have Goldberg to tell us everything.'

'There may be things even Goldberg doesn't know.'

'Not much. Bet he knows more than you. It isn't just his mother – he listens to this old lady doctor who answers questions on the radio. Did you know that when you're really old you do it in each other's armpits?'

'Don't be ridiculous, Ben.'

'No, really, she said so. Goldberg heard her. This old man rang in and said his wife was dry – I suppose he meant she

216

didn't drink – and this lady doctor said it would solve the problem to do it in her armpit. She said it was a very erotic position.'

'Poor old lady,' said Flavia, wailing with laughter. 'What do you suppose she got out of it except a wet armpit?'

After they had finished the feast with cheese and grapes, Flavia produced her flute and played while the other three sang – anything from Hebridean love lilts to old Beatles numbers, from hymns to the latest pop songs. It seemed the perfect ending.

Before they left, it really was moonlight. Ben went ahead with Gervaise to help carry the picnic baskets down the grassy slope to the car, and Flavia and Alistair were left to make sure there was no trace of litter left behind. They stood facing each other in the pale shadowy light among the cobwebs and the silence and Flavia felt herself move towards him like a pin to a magnet. For one electrifying moment she was in his arms – and the New Year's kiss had nothing on this one. Then he thrust her roughly away, looked at her for a moment with a sort of despairing hopelessness, and they almost fell down the rickety stairs, out into the unsympathetic moonlight, and ran down to the car.

Before Alistair drove Ben back to London, he gave Gervaise a bottle of claret, a Château La Lagune 1982, which he had brought as a token of thanks for having Ben to stay, and he gave Flavia a book of music and a cassette that went with it.

'It's the *Twenty-Four Jazz Etudes* by Bill Holcombe with trio backing,' he explained. 'It's for you to busk along to.'

'For when you're not there to play for me?' she asked softly.

'Yes,' he said, very sadly, 'for when I'm not there.'

Ben went to sleep almost immediately in the car, and Alistair drove up to London in a state of terrible despair. He felt as if he had been given a glimpse of heaven, and then seen it blacked out. He had presented Gervaise with the claret as a token of thanks for all his kindness – what sort of gratitude would it show if he now tried to steal his wife?

Later that night Gervaise woke to find Flavia missing. He shot out of bed. When he opened the bedroom door and listened intently he could hear muffled sobs coming from his study. Flavia was weeping hopelessly, silently, into the cushions of the sofa.

'Darling, what's the matter? We had such a happy evening. I know it's not very exciting for you here with just me – are you afraid you'll miss Ben?'

She was quite incoherent, quite unable to tell him what was troubling her. He took her in his arms and tried to comfort her, as one would comfort a small child. He tried to tell himself that she was not completely well yet and was in any case such a finely tuned and sensitive being that she was more easily upset than most. He must take extra care of her, and see she did not get so over-tired – but he knew he was deluding himself.

Sitting on the sofa gently rocking her, Gervaise felt a helpless anguish both for himself and his young wife.

Flavia, lying in the arms of this man of whom she was so deeply fond, but yearning desperately for someone else, felt her heart might break.

XXVI

MEG'S SUMMER HOLIDAY had not gone well. Isobel and Martin had asked her to go to Spain, and though she was well aware that it was an unspoken condition of the invitation that she would act as resident baby-sitter in the villa they had taken, she was greatly looking forward to it. She had always adored the sea, was a strong swimmer, and knew she badly needed a change of scene. Her friend Anne had said there was always the chance that in a resort she might meet some wonderful man who would take her mind off Gervaise – a widower, perhaps, with a young family, suggested Anne, someone who needed help with his children, and would appreciate her home-making talents. 'But you must remember to wear total sunblock all the time,' warned Anne, 'otherwise you'll only go blotchy and he'd be put off.' Meg did not think it sounded an enticing scenario.

She'd seen a lot of the Butlers during the latter part of the term, and when, the week before Meg was due to go to Spain, Betty told her she was going into hospital for twenty-four hours for a minor gynaecological operation she had agreed, against her better judgement, to go and spend the night and look after Douglas. It was Betty who asked her, and Meg told herself that she owed her a favour after so many suppers *chez* Butler, though she knew the idea would not have come from Betty. If Spanner's wife still had ideas of her own, she had long since given up voicing them.

Meg drove the familiar route to Winsleyhurst, wondering if Gervaise and Flavia were still there and what they were doing. Douglas was extremely attentive; he laid the table, something he never did for his wife, while she cooked supper for them both, chatted to her in the kitchen and plied her with gin and tonic. He exuded admiration and managed to make Meg feel deliciously feminine – both cherished and cherishing.

They drank Sainsbury's claret with their lamb cutlets and he wouldn't let her clear away or wash up. He gave her a hefty tumbler of iced crème de menthe, put a selection of romantic music on the record player and they settled down together on the sofa. When he eventually put his arm along the back and started to fondle her shoulder, she did not pull away, and made suddenly reckless by novelty and sticky green liqueur, had allowed him to start kissing her. For several minutes she responded, blissfully substituting Gervaise for Douglas in her mind, and it was not until he suddenly gave one of her nipples a vicious pinch while getting his other hand between her legs that reality set in.

'No!' she said sharply, trying to wrench herself away.

Douglas, however, relished a struggle and had it not been for a violent lurch that sent the sofa skidding, upset a table and spread crème de menthe and broken glass all over the floor, Meg might not have managed to shake him off.

'Leave me alone! Get away from me,' she panted, seizing the fire tongs from the coal scuttle.

Douglas couldn't believe it. 'You bitch!' he shouted, shaking and purple with rage and frustration. 'You absolute bitch. You led me on.'

And Meg, utterly mortified, knew it was partly true.

She grabbed her overnight bag, which was still in the hall, and fled to her car. As she wove down the road at a very uncharacteristic speed she turned on the windscreen wipers – but it was tears, not rain, that made it so hard to see. Waves of shame and misery overwhelmed her. She knew she was quite unfit to drive and would certainly be well over the limit should she be stopped and breathalysed. She longed to have a bath in disinfectant to wash away the memory of her own behaviour.

When she got home it was to find an ambulance outside the front door. Her father had had a stroke and was being taken to hospital on a stretcher.

The archdeacon was home in a few days. The stroke was very minor: a warning shot across the bows; slow up for a bit, said the doctors; take things quietly; let that family of yours look after you for a change. It went without saying that Meg did not go to Spain, though, as Isobel pointed out, it would have been unfair on Martin and the children if the rest of them had stayed behind too. However, at the end of the school holidays Isobel found her sister unyielding. Their father was better and there was no way Meg was going to give up her job at Winsleyhurst. As Isobel said to her mother, some people could be surprisingly selfish.

The start of the autumn term was always busy. There was a large intake of new boys. Flavia presided at the traditional tea party for the new arrivals and their parents.

'What a grisly performance,' she said to Gervaise afterwards. 'Everyone hating it, including us.'

'Perhaps there isn't a right way of saying goodbye to your eight-year-old child.'

'Then why do we do it? Anyway, let's not try to pretend a few cakes can make it better by having a tea party next time.'

She went up to say good night to them all – Meg or no Meg. The Goldberg chauffeur, who had brought Ben back to school with Rowan, had kindly delivered Wellington too. Flavia felt the dog was a link with Alistair and was doubly pleased to have him back. She took him upstairs with her, and found it hard not to treat Ben as her special property when she saw him.

Meg ground through the first few days like an automaton, and dreaded meeting Spanner. When she did, he behaved as if she were an unwelcome stranger for which she was profoundly thankful. But she knew she had made an enemy for life.

Flavia waited till after half term to tell Gervaise she was pregnant. He greeted the news with astonishment, delight – and concern.

'That's wonderful, incredibly exciting, but, darling, I had no idea. I thought we agreed, I thought the doctors said . . .?'

Because of the virus the doctors had suggested that Flavia should wait at least a year before starting a baby, just to be on the safe side.

'I know,' she said, 'they did, but these things sometimes just happen – and it has, so there we are. Are you pleased?'

'Pleased?' Gervaise was ecstatic. He hardly knew what to do

with himself. She must be so careful, nothing, nothing must be allowed to upset her. Flavia could have screamed. She did not tell him she had deliberately thrown away her contraceptive pills.

The day after the feast she had returned to the folly by herself to think, to take stock of her marriage, and try to do some of the hard and lonely deciding that she had talked about to Dulcie. She could no longer disguise from herself that she was deeply in love with Alistair – and she thought, was afraid, and yet at the same time couldn't help hoping that he felt the same about her. The spark between them was in danger of becoming a blaze, and she knew that the slightest fanning of the fire would be too much for her and she would simply burst into flames like a bit of dry kindling. For the second time in her life she was in the grip of an overwhelming physical attraction. Am I hopelessly fickle or over-sexed? she asked herself, but this time she knew it was more than that. She wanted to step inside Alistair's mind and heart, and share her whole being with him. The words of the marriage service came back to haunt her – 'for better for worse, for richer for poorer'. How willingly she would say them to Alistair now if she had not already said them to another man. Alistair was free, but she most certainly was not.

Sitting on the rocks below the folly, at the top of the cascade, she had pondered on Dulcie's warning about the necessity to carry a sacrifice through if you decided to make it. She felt very doubtful of her own ability to do this, and yet how could she not at least try? How could she hurt Gervaise, whom she genuinely loved, and who she knew loved her even more. She had deliberately settled for what he had to offer, and used his congenial kindness as an easy let-out, rather than face difficulties in her own life. There was no easy way out now. She felt bitterly ashamed of herself, and at the same time most unfairly resentful of Gervaise.

What would make me able to resist this awful longing? she asked herself. And suddenly the answer had come to her. There was one thing that might make it impossible for her to contemplate deserting Gervaise – and she had gone home and thrown the pills away, popping them out of their packs and flushing them down the loo.

Some weeks later, as she sat alone on her bathroom floor with the pregnancy testing kit, already quite certain in her own mind what the result would be, her feelings were extremely mixed. If it is positive, she told herself, then there is no going back: I stay with Gervaise. But if it is negative – what then?

The result had been indubitably positive. She watched the blue line appear in the little window and a sense of inevitability had come over her. She had consulted her private equivalent of the Delphic Oracle, and had been given a verdict.

Alistair, undergoing similar misery and self-searching, had accepted Mrs Goldberg's offer of a lift for Ben at the beginning of term. He decided that for everyone's sake he must try to have as little contact as possible with the wife of his son's headmaster. He thought it would be useful to send Ben to and fro on the school coach or with Goldberg.

He longed to explain how he felt to Flavia, just to tell her that he loved her, but he knew this would be fatal. He must try to cut her out of his thoughts as well as his sight – easier said than done with Ben at Winsleyhurst. The fact that Ben was continually talking about Flavia made it even more difficult. Alistair had always imagined that if he ever wanted to marry again, Ben would find it hard to accept and possibly make life extremely difficult for a prospective stepmother. What a bloody waste it was. Alistair could hardly bear it – they all three seemed made for each other.

Flavia and Gervaise decided to tell the family but keep the news of the baby private from everyone at Winsleyhurst for as long as possible, no easy task in a small community and with Sister and Miss Hackett nosing about their private lives like sniffer dogs scenting drugs. Hester and Andrew were overjoyed and did not voice their niggling anxieties about Flavia's health. Old Dr Barlow had been brisk and reassuring.

'Waiting was the council of caution, yes, but I think it's quite right for Flavia to crack on with a family,' he said. 'Good for her.' He thought to himself that the father's age was a strong argument for doing this.

Matt and Di were thrilled; Peter and Wanda, once they got over their initial surprise that anyone other than themselves should be capable of breeding, expressed pleasure that Peregrine, Daisy and Toby would have a little cousin. 'As usual one would think it was all in aid of them,' said Flavia. Wanda immediately became so full of advice and information on every aspect of child-bearing that Flavia said to Di, 'If old Baby-Wipe gives me one more book to read about birthing pools or nipple care I'm going to be sick.'

Gervaise was surprised to find Flavia determined to go on with her flute lessons, preparing to make a musical comeback.

'But, darling, is it the right moment now? Even if a fantastic chance came up you wouldn't be able to take it up. That really does seem a bit silly.'

'Having babies doesn't stop you playing a flute. Other people do it. Opera singers are always giving performances when they're practically popping.'

She seemed more decided about her career now than at any time since her illness. Gervaise decided to humour her, but it worried him. Everything she did worried him. The doctor had been driven to saying, 'Pregnancy's not an illness – don't fuss over her so much,' but Gervaise's famous laid-back attitudes seemed to have gone smartly into reverse.

Tricia and Roddy came down for a weekend. Roddy, who thought Gervaise was wonderful, an amazingly congenial man, was immediately absorbed into prep school life, joining in football practice and playing fives with the boys. Tricia lay on the drawing-room sofa glued to the latest bestselling bonk-buster, an open box of chocolates at the ready.

Flavia looked at the lurid cover. 'Oh, I read that at Duntroon. I thought it was screamingly funny – everyone crawling about on the stairs lapping up seminal fluid.'

'Umm,' said Tricia, popping in a coffee cream. 'Great stuff – all loins and huge throbbing members. Raffik has just brought Sandra yet another peak of delight.'

'Sounds like a pack of little Chinese dogs.'

Later that afternoon Sister, as tight–lipped as it was possible for her to be, given her enormous teeth, asked to have a wee word with Flavia.

'I don't want to be critical, Flavia dear,' said Sister, who only used terms of endearment before serving an ace, 'and goodness knows I'm not one to make trouble, but I do think bathing

Wellington in my bathroom is *too much*.' She swung, dangerously stiff-legged, from foot to foot.

'But I haven't.' Flavia was astonished.

'Then how is it,' asked Sister, ripe with incriminating evidence, 'that the bathroom is awash, there's a soaked towel on the floor and the bath is full of *black hairs*?'

Tricia gave a yelp of laughter. 'Oh I'm afraid that'll be Roddy,' she said. 'He's hopeless. I heard Gervaise telling him to use that bathroom after he played fives. But cheer up – with any luck it means he's washed his hair. I've been nagging him for days.'

Sister clearly found this bit of optimism far from consoling. After much apologizing by Flavia she eventually stumped off, her starched white overall crackling with resentment.

'Goodness,' said Tricia, 'who'd be a headmaster's wife? Rather you than me. What an old Gorgon. I'll give Roddy hell.'

Gervaise was highly entertained by Tricia and regaled her with stories about Monica that made them all shriek with laughter. He told her how she had once picked up a swallow, temporarily stunned by flying into the window, and insisted on sleeping with it between her breasts. In the morning when she had released it from the window she was convinced it had come back to life through a miraculous healing.

'Of course it went off like the clappers,' said Gervaise. 'Thankful to get away, poor little thing.'

'Imagine spending the night squashed in between Monica's wrinkled boobs,' wailed Flavia. 'Pretty miraculous to survive that.'

'I've revised my opinion on Gerve-the-Swerve,' Tricia told Roddy. 'I used to think he was pretty boring but he's a great deal more fun than I imagined.'

'Hope for me yet, perhaps,' said Roddy.

Flavia loved having them both to stay and their visit was a great success. She longed to confide in Tricia about the baby, and Alistair, but it seemed disloyal. Every time she was on the point of doing so, she thought better of it.

One morning, during his visit to the sewing room, Meg said to Gervaise: 'Oh dear, I have a nasty feeling that things are disappearing. You know how hard it is to be sure – boys are always so careless, so quick to say that someone has pinched something, and all the time it's in their locker and they just haven't looked properly. But I've been checking very carefully on the sweet cupboard and the petty cash lately and I'm fairly sure things are going missing. Now Carver has lost his watch.'

Gervaise groaned. It happened from time to time of course in all schools, but it was always unpleasant and difficult to deal with – always produced a lot of false suspicions and an unpleasant atmosphere. Gervaise had his own ideas, but wanted to be very sure of his ground. He supposed he would have to alert the staff, and brought it up at the next staff meeting. It seemed that Meg was not the only person to have noticed things going missing. James Pope said uncomfortably that he had once or twice thought he had more change in his coat pocket than was there at the end of the day. Jane and Barbie, who were always leaving their bags lying about upstairs, much to Sister's annoyance, both admitted that they thought they had lost small amounts.

'Perhaps the first line of questioning should be to ask ourselves when this was first noticed and who is new in the school since it started,' said Douglas Butler blandly.

'It would be unusual for a really little boy to start anything on this scale – petty taking of tuck from other boys in their form perhaps, but not usually from the sweet cupboard which is locked, and which means finding and taking the key, and not money from the staff. I think it looks like an older boy,' said Meg unhappily.

'But we did of course have a new boy last term too,' persisted Douglas. 'One who is older and quite capable of planning something. I know he's a particular favourite of Flavia's, so this might be difficult for you, Henderson, but personally I've never trusted Forbes.'

'It's also quite well known that for some reason you particularly dislike him,' said Michael Stockdale. He didn't really care one way or the other about Forbes but he loathed Spanner.

'That is a very insulting insinuation.'

'Stop, stop, everyone please,' said Gervaise. 'It's not going to help if we all start flinging accusations about. These matters are unpleasant enough without adding our personal feelings to them. I have to ask you all to keep your eyes open. Please don't leave money lying about, and if you miss anything or know of any boy who has done so, please come straight to me. I don't want any of you – any of you – ' he repeated, 'taking it upon yourselves to deal with it. Is that understood?'

Flavia was furious when he told her about the conversation.

'How dare Spanner try and throw suspicion on Ben! He'd never do anything like that. Never.'

'Darling, I don't think so either, but I have to keep an open mind about everyone,' he said, and then added rashly: 'Of course we don't really know very much about Ben yet.'

'*I* do. I know for certain he wouldn't steal.'

'Nearly all children are capable of stealing or lying at some stage, and if they do they'll probably grow out of it, but one can't rule anyone out just like that.'

Flavia looked mulish. 'You can rule Ben out.'

'You know very well that I can't. Try and be a little more dispassionate, darling.'

'I'm not a dispassionate person – and I know Ben wouldn't do it.' She banged out of the room.

Gervaise sighed. He decided it would be better not to talk too much to Flavia about it. Were all pregnant women so temperamental? He would rely on Meg's level-headed and wise judgement as he had so often in the past.

Flavia started to feel very sick, but she insisted on dragging herself up to London for lessons and did not tell Alfred Tatham she was expecting a baby. When, just before Christmas, a chance came up to appear as a soloist at a performance in Cambridge of Mozart's Andante in C with the Mozart Chamber Players, she accepted. By tremendous willpower she got through the rehearsal and performance without anyone guessing how dizzy she felt and created a very favourable impression. Unlike the effect that the virus had on her playing, her pregnancy gave no problem with her sound. Gervaise was beside himself with anxiety, but had come up against an obdurate streak in Flavia that he had not known was there.

Hester had gone to lunch with Dulcie to take Christmas presents for her and Hilda, and tried to discuss Flavia, but Dulcie had been uncommunicative. Nobody could play emotional poker better than Dulcie. It was a game at which she not only excelled but greatly enjoyed. Hester, who always laid all her cards face up on the table, was quite outclassed. Dulcie did not tell Hester that she had discussed with Maurice the fact that Flavia was once more dipping her toes in the musical ocean.

The arrival of the end of term was a relief. Gervaise and Flavia were going up to Duntroon again. Colin and Elizabeth had generously offered to have Monica too, but everyone was highly relieved when she declined. The idea of his sister at the Boxing Day shoot would have made Gervaise sick with apprehension. In fact Monica was moving away from concerns with field sports and was now into UFOs. She was going off with a group of potential spotters to a remote village in the Pyrenees where there were reports of fascinating sightings and where she had every confidence of being made the recipient of important messages for mankind.

Ben told Flavia that he and Alistair were going skiing.

'How wonderful,' said Flavia brightly.

'I wish you and Mr Henderson were coming too. I wish it wasn't with the grotty Palmers. Johnnie Palmer's a weed and I don't like Mrs Palmer.'

'What's wrong with her?' Flavia knew she shouldn't ask.

'She's always ringing Dad up and suggesting we do things together, but then she wants to shove me and grotty Johnnie off to do something else. She sucks up to me but I know she doesn't care about me really. She doesn't even like Johnnie much either – she's always telling him to get lost and not be a bore.'

Flavia went and lay on her bed and stared at the ceiling.

To start with she had felt numb about the baby, but as the weeks passed she thought about it more and more, sometimes envisaging a little moppet of a girl in a smocked gingham dress, and sometimes a little boy in blue dungarees. The only snag about the boy image was that he always had red hair. She had private conversations with the baby, telling it that even if her motive for conceiving it, though well-intentioned, might not have been quite what it deserved, nevertheless she was going to love it to bits – did already love it passionately. Often she sang to it, old nursery songs which Hester had sung in her childhood, and when she played the flute or the piano she dedicated her playing to the baby. She had read somewhere that babies could respond to music even in the womb. This baby was going to be surrounded by beautiful sounds and endless chat. She felt no clash between her music and the child – on the contrary they seemed deeply connected. The ache for Alistair was as strong as ever, much worse than anything she had felt for Antoine so that sometimes she thought it might overwhelm her. But the love for the baby grew and grew.

XXVII

CHRISTMAS AT DUNTROON had all the usual ingredients, but this year they failed to work their alchemy on Flavia. A year ago she had been pining for Antoine; a year ago she had been engaged to Gervaise – a year ago she had first met Alistair Forbes. A year of changes, but whatever the future held she knew that it was this last event that had changed her for ever. She refused to go to the Arbuthnots' annual New Year reel party. Everyone except Gervaise tried to persuade her to change her mind.

'Do come, darling,' said Elizabeth. 'We'll all miss you so much and I think it would do you good.' But Flavia was adamant. Gervaise was extremely relieved.

The thought of the baby was a joy; she tried hard to be happy with Gervaise, but the atmosphere at Duntroon increased her longing for Alistair unbearably. She would have given anything to have him and Ben there too. For the first time in her life she was almost pleased to leave.

Everyone at Winsleyhurst professed themselves delighted about the baby, and for most people this was true, though Douglas Butler, childless himself for which he had always blamed Betty, was certainly not pleased; Miss Hackett was only concerned in case Sister had known first; Sister, predictably, had said that of course she had already guessed they were to have a stranger in their midst, and – och my! – wouldn't it be a joy to have a wee bairn to look after?

'She's not going to look after my baby,' said Flavia. 'She'd probably cast a spell on it like the bad fairy.'

Meg had managed to give Flavia a very convincing substitute for a genuinely delighted hug, had looked at her steadily and said, 'I'm so pleased for you both, that's lovely news,' and had managed not to cry until she was alone in bed at night.

The boys were enchanted. 'How many d'you think you'll have?' one small boy had asked, eyeing her speculatively up and down. 'Our spaniel had ten.' When Flavia said she thought probably just one, he clearly considered her pretty feeble by comparison.

Ben had been genuinely pleased, but had been puzzled by the look on his father's face when he reported this piece of news at home.

Goldberg, such a mine of information about the activities that could create babies, and a good many equally extraordinary activities that certainly couldn't, was rather disappointing on the actual process of birth. His mother had found once quite enough, but not surprisingly he couldn't remember much about that incident. He told his fascinated audience with as much authority as he could muster that Flavia would almost certainly have it underwater. As she loved swimming this caused much interested speculation every time she went near the indoor pool.

The beginning of the Lent term is always gloomy. The excitements of Christmas are over, the weather is usually foul, spring seems a long way off and everyone is at their lowest ebb. This one was no exception.

Almost immediately there was a flu epidemic. It was not serious, as many of the boys had been inoculated, but those that went down with it were miserable. One or two members of the staff got it, which meant that everyone else was short-handed, and tempers got frayed at times. Sister did a lot of scurrying about, especially if anyone was watching, but as always it was Meg, at her very best in a crisis, who kept calm and cheerful and did most of the work. Gervaise was very anxious about Flavia. In the end he was the one who succumbed.

'You must be so worried about him,' said Meg, trying to sound sympathetic. Flavia was surprised. She felt sorry for him, yes, but it had not occurred to her to be worried.

'It's only flu like everyone else has.'

'I mean about his chest, of course,'

'What's wrong with his chest?'

'Gervaise has always had a weak chest,' said Meg reproachfully.

Secretly Flavia found Gervaise as an invalid irritating in the extreme, though she felt ashamed of her feelings when he developed pleurisy. She thought he wallowed in Sister and Meg's ministrations, and particularly loved having his temperature taken, the more often the better. He was always checking on it himself. Flavia found it impossible to pretend that she found this of absorbing interest, though Meg clearly did. While not having any desire to nurse him herself, Flavia nevertheless disliked being made to feel not only superfluous, but positively in the way.

It was suggested that she should move out of their bedroom, ostensibly to lessen the risk of infection for herself, but actually she felt sure, to allow the professionals to commandeer both patient and sickroom. It was only after she had grumpily spent a first night in the spare room that it occurred to her that it might have been Gervaise who moved out. Sister and Meg now seemed to be in charge of her bedroom as well as her husband. She never knew when she was going to find one or other of them in there, making the bed, putting Gervaise into fresh pyjamas, carrying pretty little trays of tempting homemade soup which Meg had whipped up in her little kitchen, or even, in the case of Meg, sitting on the edge of the bed bringing him up to date with information about the school.

Needing to change before going up to London for a lesson one day, Flavia was outraged to find a notice hanging on her bedroom door with 'Please do not disturb' on it. She ripped it off angrily. Gervaise was asleep and did not wake up. She tiptoed round, half hoping he would wake, bursting with suppressed resentment but feeling guilty for her uncharitable thoughts as she rummaged for clothes and tried not to bang the doors of the wardrobe. She tore the notice up and left it on the bed.

Meg was not the only person to make the most of Gervaise's illness. Douglas Butler took over the running of the school. The stealing started again.

Ben had a new watch.

'Christmas present I suppose, Forbes?' asked Douglas.

'No, sir.' Ben made a point of never saying a word more to Spanner than was absolutely necessary.

'So where did it come from?'

'I bought it.'

'Some of us are lucky to have so much money at our disposal.'

'Mr Butler thinks I'm a thief,' Ben told Flavia during a piano lesson. He had been allowed to start learning the trumpet, but one of the part-time music teachers took him for that.

'Oh Ben, I'm sure he doesn't really.'

'I bought my watch with Christmas money but I wasn't going to tell him that. He can think what he jolly well likes – but he lets everyone else know that he thinks it's me and that's not fair.'

'Do you know who's doing the pinching?' asked Flavia, curious.

'Of course.' But she could get nothing more out of him. He buttoned his face up in a look she knew well, and his mouth shut in an obstinate line.

Flavia longed to ring up Alistair and talk to him about Ben, but this she knew she could not do. Ben had told her a good deal about the skiing holiday. The party had consisted of Christopher and Jane Boynton with their children and a nanny, Claire and Johnnie Palmer and another couple.

'Claire wanted me and Johnnie to go to ski school every day,' said Ben, 'but I've always skied with Dad. She didn't like that. She wanted to ski with him by herself.' It was very clear to Flavia that Claire was making a serious play for Alistair, an impression reinforced by Pamela Boynton telling her happily that she had high hopes that her little match-making idea might come to fruition.

'It would be so ideal – both lonely, and with boys so near in age, and I gather from Jane that they share lots of interests. Alistair used to ski for the army, of course, and apparently Claire's a beautiful skier too. We must keep our fingers crossed.'

Flavia spread her own fingers as wide apart as possible and wished Claire could have broken both her legs. She had a sickening vision of Claire swooping gracefully down through perfect powder snow in Alistair's wake, following where he led, turning where he turned.

The friendship that had started last term between Ben and Rowan Goldberg flourished. They were both well-liked by the other boys, though neither of them was really natural schoolboy material; Rowan's whole upbringing had been so different from most other boys', and Ben was too individualistic, not clubbable enough. Rowan was no sort of athlete, always a disadvantage at school however little it may matter in later life, and though Ben could have played most games well, he only really liked those in which he was a solo performer.

One day Ben asked Flavia if he could take Goldberg to the folly one weekend.

'Yes, I'm sure you could. I'll mention it to Gervaise.'

The next thing she heard was that Ben and Goldberg were in detention for being out of bounds. She went seething off to find Douglas Butler.

'Rowan and Ben were not out of bounds.'

'It is a school rule that boys can only go to Boynton Park if they ask permission. I gave neither of them leave to go.'

'But they asked me. I gave it.'

'I am afraid that while Gervaise is indisposed I run this school,' said Douglas silkily.

Gervaise was sitting up in a chair in their bedroom, a rug over his knees, having reached a convalescent stage.

'Well, it's rather petty of him but I suppose he's within his rights, darling. It's unfortunate, and typically officious, but perhaps it might have been more tactful of you to tell him first?'

'I never thought you'd take Spanner's side against me. I hate him as much as the boys do. If you ever get ill again don't ask me to stay here if he's in charge,' said Flavia stormily.

Gervaise felt very unhappy. He told Meg about it and she was most sympathetic. His temperature was up again that night, and Meg blamed Flavia and Spanner equally.

Soon after this incident Flavia went away for a week. She had played in a wind quintet while she was at the Guildhall, but had given it up when she went to study in France. The flautist who had taken her place was ill, and there was a chance for Flavia to fill in for two concerts, one in Bath and one in London. She had stopped feeling sick lately, and it was huge fun playing with the group. She realized how much she had missed the cheerful comradeship of her contemporaries. Both concerts were a great success. They played the *Petite suite* by Debussy, Hindemith's *Kleine Kammermusik* and one of Haydn's Divertimentos. As an encore they brought the house down with an arrangement by Guy Wolfenden of Roald Dahl's poem 'The Dentist and the Crocodile'. She hoped the baby was enjoying it.

Next morning Flavia woke early with a niggling pain. It wasn't severe, but she lay sweating with sudden fear until it went off; when she got up to go to the bathroom there were slight signs of bleeding – not much but enough to send her in to Matt and Di in an absolute panic. They were immediately both comforting and concerned.

'Get straight back into bed and stay put,' said Di. 'I'll bring you a cup of tea. You probably need twenty-four hours in bed and you'll be fine.'

Flavia rang Dr Barlow who said exactly the same. 'Ring me at once if there's any change, otherwise give me another ring tomorrow morning.'

She spent a wretched day, while Matt and Di were at work, willing the baby to be all right, tormenting herself in case the concerts had been too much, though the doctor had encouraged her to do them. Wanda came over to bring lunch for her, all beautifully done up in perfect little screw-top jars with paper napkins and proper silver and china. She clearly thought food eaten off any of Matt and Di's miscellaneous collection of chipped plates would be guaranteed to give anyone food poisoning, and looked round their kitchen with distaste. She was very sweet and solicitous but would keep talking about the miscarriages that various friends had suffered, always ending with, 'But I'm sure it won't be like that for you.'

Flavia longed for her to go, and couldn't wait for Matt's return. He and Di sat on the bed and managed to make her laugh.

Next morning nothing alarming had happened but she still had a slight show of blood. She felt no more pain which she was sure was a good sign but Dr Barlow rang her gynaecologist who said she must have a scan. Hester came up by car and took her to the hospital. Flavia felt Gervaise should have come himself, while not really wanting him to. Goodness, I am becoming nasty, she thought sadly. She had been longing for her first scan, now she was full of apprehension.

'Is it there? Can you see the baby?' she kept asking.

'Yes, it's there,' but the radiographer seemed very cagey.

Eventually her gynaecologist came in, and put his hand gently on her arm.

'The foetus is still there, but I'm afraid there is no heartbeat,' he said.

'What do you mean? What's happened to it? Can't you make it start again?' she asked wildly

'I'm afraid the baby's dead, Flavia. You should be fifteen weeks pregnant but this is a twelve-week foetus. It's been dead for some time. You've had what's called a failed abortion. I'm sorry.'

'But I've been talking to it – it can't be dead. It can't.' She was incoherent. Then because she had been made to drink so much water beforehand she had to rush to the lavatory, and suddenly there was a terrible flood and the blood seemed to be everywhere.

Everyone was very kind, very calm, but it was a nightmare day. Eventually Hester got her home to Orton and to bed. They told her she would have to go back into hospital in a couple of days to have a D and C. 'To clear away the last little bits of the poor baby, I suppose,' said Flavia in horror. She couldn't cry. She just lay in bed in a state of utter misery.

'I've rung Gervaise, darling. He's coming straight over.'

'Tell him not to come,' said Flavia.

'Darling, of course he's coming. He says he's all right now. He just wants to be with you.'

'I don't want to see him, Mum.'

Hester and Andrew looked at each other in dismay.

'It's just the shock,' said Hester in an undertone. 'You go down and wait for him, Andrew, and bring him up as soon as he gets here. I'll sit with her.'

Flavia felt she couldn't face Gervaise yet. She just wanted to be left alone like an injured animal to lick her wounds in private. She wished her mother would go away too.

When Gervaise arrived, still not looking well himself, his face was so creased with concern, that she tried to pull herself together and make some response. She put out her hand.

'I'm so sorry, Gervaise.' Her voice was a thread.

'Darling, if you're all right that's all that matters to me,' he said, holding her hand and gently stroking it with his thumb. 'It's terribly disappointing for us both. Our little baby – but at least we know we can make one now. We'll have other children together.'

How could she tell him that it was this particular baby she so passionately wanted, this baby she had felt such love for – this baby that was going to save their marriage? How could she admit that she had secretly always thought of it as her baby rather than his baby, and that the idea of trying for another with him was not one that she could cope with at the moment.

'Shall I stay with you?' he asked, miserably aware that he was not striking the right note but at a loss to know how to comfort her. He thought she looked terrible.

She shook her head. 'No thank you,' she whispered. 'Don't worry, I'll be all right soon. I expect I need to sleep.'

He looked at her uncertainly, and left, closing the door very quietly and went downstairs with a heavy heart.

Andrew thrust a glass of whisky into his hand.

'Bad luck,' he said with brisk sympathy, 'but maybe it was too soon after that damned virus after all. These things happen. Better luck next time. She'll be all right in a week or two.'

'I'm very worried about Flavia, Andrew. I have to tell you that it's not just the baby. I'm not making her happy any more.'

'The first year of marriage is often difficult and Flavia had a lot of growing up to do.'

'She has grown up – that's part of the problem for us both,' said Gervaise heavily. 'But it's worse than that. I think – I'm sure really – that she has fallen very heavily for someone else.' And as he said aloud the words that he had been desperate not to admit, he felt the awful ring of their truth.

'Oh God. Oh dear, that's the last thing I wanted to hear. You're not trying to tell me it wasn't your baby?'

'Oh no, I'm pretty sure it was mine – but I'm equally sure she wishes it hadn't been.'

Andrew's heart sank. He had no idea what to say. Cheap words of false comfort seemed out of place.

'Do you think I should ask Hester's advice about what to do?' asked Gervaise.

But Andrew was very sure that would be disastrous. Hester was incapable of perceiving any shades of grey, and her outlook on marriage was as black and white as all her other views. She would hate Flavia's unhappiness, but she would be absolutely certain what Flavia should do. In theory Andrew agreed with her, but in practice as he grew older he often found himself unable to share her uncompromising attitudes.

'Leave it for now, Gervaise,' he said. 'Now is not the time to cope with this. Let Flavia recover first. Give yourselves time. She may come about.' But he rather doubted it, and his heart bled for them both.

Upstairs Flavia was unable either to sleep or cry. 'Where are you now?' she asked the baby. 'Wherever are you now?' But there was no answer.

XXVIII

FLAVIA WAS ONLY in hospital for one night, and returned to Winsleyhurst the next day. It was perhaps unfortunate that Gervaise had a long-standing appointment with some parents from abroad, who were only in England for a short time and whom he felt unable to put off, so he could neither come to fetch her nor was he free to greet her when she arrived. Flavia, feeling quite unable to meet anyone, whisked straight upstairs to her bedroom, praying not to bump into anyone on the way. Soon there was a tentative knock at the door.

'Come in,' she said, though she longed to say 'Keep out'.

Meg's face peered round the door. She was the last person Flavia wanted to see. Meg hesitated for a moment then came quickly across the room and put her arms round the younger woman.

'Oh Flavia,' she said, and her face was full of genuine distress. 'Oh Flavia, you may not believe me, but I am just so sorry.'

For the first time since the miscarriage Flavia felt her eyes brimming with tears. She had been quite unable to weep to Hester, though she would have liked to be able to do so, miserably aware that her mother was longing to comfort her, to hold her, to kiss her better, while Flavia was only able to react to her with a chilling reserve that made them both wretched. Now in front of Meg, before whom she would so much rather not have cried, the tears came.

Meg was conscious of a huge sense of relief that she still had it in her to mind for Flavia; it was as though a hard shell which had enclosed her for months had cracked. They sat together on the bed, clutching each other's hands, each crying for themselves, but each able to cry, at least a little bit, for the other.

'Can I get you anything?' asked Meg after a bit. 'Would you like some tea?'

'Tea would be a life-saver. Thank you, Meg.'

'You hop into bed, then there won't be any need to get caught by anyone and I'll bring you up a tray.'

Meg bustled off, safe and comfortable in a ministering role.

The moment of intimacy was gone, not to return, but not to be forgotten either.

During the next weeks Flavia buried herself in her music. She was sure she appeared quite normal on the surface, was surprised to find she still found things funny, could laugh and joke and be amused, but she felt as though she had been switched on to autopilot: she did not feel as though her real self was any more present in her body than the baby was. Gervaise hovered hopelessly round her like a large gentle moth, unable to leave a light. She longed to be able to drop a tumbler over him and put him out of the window.

Gervaise tried to keep busy with the absorbing day-to-day business of the school, at which he knew himself to be both useful and successful. He felt safe and at home in this familiar pool in which he could swim length after length with even, confident strokes. In the turbulent waters and rough seas of Flavia's emotions and passions he was doubtful of keeping his own head above water, let alone practising life-saving techniques to prevent her from drowning.

As so often in Flavia's life, Colin and Elizabeth Cameron came to the rescue. Elizabeth had paid a rare visit to London and come down to spend a day at Orton. One look at Flavia, who had come over for lunch, told her that all was far from well, and she suggested that Flavia should go back to Duntroon for a period of convalescence. As usual Hester felt both thankful to her sister-in-law and deeply resentful, but Flavia and Gervaise accepted this offer with undiluted gratitude. It would have been hard to say which of them was the more relieved to have a little space from the other.

The stealing continued. Unwillingly Gervaise called the school together. He told the boys that unless it stopped the police would have to be called in and all leave out would be stopped. He said that if the culprit would like to come to see him he would be sympathetically dealt with.

It was easy for Gervaise to see any boy alone without arousing comment, since each week he looked at their individual books of good and bad conduct marks. He impressed on them now that no one else need know if any boy wanted to tell him something privately, either about himself or possibly about someone else. For everybody's sake the present unpleasant situation must be cleared up. Nothing happened.

Then Douglas Butler found an anonymous note on his desk one morning. It was printed and read: 'THE THIEF IS FORBES.'

Douglas took the note to Gervaise in triumph.

'I always told you it was Forbes.'

'This accusation doesn't prove anything,' said Gervaise. 'It would be a very easy way for the thief to avert suspicion from himself, but thank you for bringing this to me. Please say nothing to anyone and I will deal with it.'

'I might have known you would try and protect the boy.'

'I shall not protect him if he is guilty, but neither should you jump to conclusions.'

Douglas gave Gervaise a scornful look, shrugged and walked off. He had his own reasons for wishing to be rid of the Forbes boy.

Gervaise spoke to the boys again: 'An accusation has been made. Someone has written a note to Mr Butler. Will whoever wrote that note please come and see me. Anything you say will be completely confidential.'

No one came.

Gervaise didn't dare tell Flavia on the telephone about the accusation. He knew she would be hotly defensive of Ben and very angry. He tried to ring Alistair up, but he was out of the country. His office said they could get an urgent message to him, but they could not say how long he would be away. Gervaise decided there was no point in worrying Alistair unless, or until, the accusation was proved. The only people he felt he could discuss it with were Mr Foster and Meg.

'I know that Ben is going to Goldberg for half term,' said Meg. 'Mr Forbes rang up and said he might not be back and the Goldbergs had kindly offered to have Ben. I think it suits Mrs Goldberg because if Rowan has a friend to keep him amused then she doesn't have to bother about entertaining him – not that she ever puts herself out anyway. That nice Filipino couple always seem to look after him. He'd be lost without them.'

'It's very unpleasant,' said old Fossy, 'but you will have to set a trap. It's the only way – you must have proof.'

Very reluctantly, before the half term weekend, Gervaise did just that.

He marked some five-pound notes and left them in a coat pocket hanging over the back of the master's chair in Douglas Butler's classroom.

After dinner that evening when all the boys were in bed, he went to look. One of the notes was missing. Miserably Gervaise went upstairs to the sewing room. Sister, Meg and the two under-matrons were having mugs of coffee. Jane and Barbie got up and made their excuses and said they were just about to go off duty, but Sister favoured him with a toothy simper.

'Has the lonely husband come to have a wee nog with us then?'

'A wee snog is what she'd really like,' muttered Jane, as she and Barbie walked downstairs. Luckily the telephone rang at this moment, saving Gervaise from having to drink Sister's fearsomely sweet sherry at such an hour, and also from the dread of getting hooked up in her daintily crooked little finger as she clinked glasses with a roguish gleam in her eye. The caller turned out to be Sister's friend from Amersham wanting to tell Sister how hopeless the new president of the Women's Institute was proving to be – not a patch on Sister's friend who had just resigned *on a matter of principle*. A long chat was guaranteed, and much to Gervaise's relief Sister crackled off to send supportive waves of outrage down the wires. She would certainly be gone for at least half an hour. He did not at all want to discuss the affair in front of Sister.

Meg was as practical as ever.

'Oh dear,' she said. 'But perhaps we'll get it all cleared up now. For a start we'd better go and search all the boys' lockers.' They went downstairs.

'We might as well start with Ben Forbes,' said Meg briskly, seeing Gervaise's look of uncertainty. 'Perhaps this will clear his name.'

She opened the locker. On one side there was a pile of

money, including the marked five-pound note. There was also a watch – Carver's missing watch. His initials were clearly engraved on the back.

They looked at each other with dismay.

'Oh Gervaise, I'm so sorry,' said Meg. 'I know this makes things very difficult for you.'

'I suppose I ought not to mind it being one boy more than another,' he said. 'But you know how close Flavia has got to Ben, and I do feel extremely sorry for him. He's had awful problems at home. I suppose that wretched Douglas was right all the time – we don't know much about him, and this may all be some form of protest about being at boarding school.'

'Or it could be the excitement and the risk,' suggested Meg thoughtfully. 'Wasn't his father in the SAS or something, and doesn't he do rather a secret sort of job now?'

'Something of the sort. Yes, I suppose it all adds up – I just didn't want to see it. Oh well, I'll have to talk to him in the morning but I wish his father wasn't away. Let's keep this to ourselves for the time being, Meg, and we'll have to decide what to do about it when I've actually seen the boy. Thank goodness it's half term. It gives us a bit of time.'

Meg couldn't help a little glow of pleasure that they were back to discussing a problem together, as they had so often done in the past, though she felt genuinely upset for Gervaise and knew he would take it very much to heart.

'Shall you tell Flavia?' she asked.

Gervaise groaned. 'I don't think just yet. She'll be so upset, and she's had enough lately without this. Thank you, Meg. I don't know what we should do without you,' said Gervaise as he went off to the other side of the house. As usual the bed was turned down, his pyjamas were laid out and the electric blanket had been switched on, but the bedroom seemed a very sad place without Flavia's presence.

Gervaise, who had always had the ability to fall asleep the minute his head touched the pillow, lay awake dreading the interview with Ben and wondering what on earth to do about his wife. If he had never felt as happy in his life as he had done in the first days of his marriage, neither had he ever felt anything approaching the unhappiness and anxiety he now felt.

He sent for Ben first thing the next morning.

'Sit down, Ben. I need to talk to you. First, have you anything that you want to say to me?'

'No, sir.' Ben looked first surprised, and then acutely anxious. There was no mistaking the wary, cautious look that crept over his face. Gervaise sighed. It wasn't going to be easy.

'I think I must tell you that someone has made an allegation about you.'

Ben looked scornful. 'Who?'

'I don't know who, never mind that now, but someone has suggested that you might be responsible for all the things that have been disappearing, so of course I wanted to ask you about it myself.'

Ben said nothing.

'Did you take those things, Ben?'

'Of course I didn't.'

'You are quite sure? There might be reasons if you did – you could tell me, you know.' Ben stared at him, his face a complete blank. Flavia would have recognized the look.

'I'll ask you once more, Ben. I know this is extremely difficult. Think very hard. Did you do it?'

'No.'

'Then how is it,' asked Gervaise sadly, 'that these things were found in your locker?' And he put on his desk the pile of money and the watch.

'Those aren't mine.'

'I know they're not yours, Ben – but they were in your locker last night. Can you explain it to me?'

Ben's face was very white but his eyes blazed. 'If I had taken them, I wouldn't have left them in my locker for any fool to find,' he said with blistering scorn in his voice, 'I can tell you that.'

'Then how do you think they got there?'

The child shrugged his shoulders. 'No idea.'

'Do you think someone else put them there?'

'I don't know.'

'Ben, I want to help you. Have you no suggestions to make? No explanation that you can think of?'

'No.'

Gervaise sighed again. 'Look, Ben, nobody knows about this

except Meg and myself at the moment, and I have no intention of telling anyone until your father is back. You have a long weekend to think about this. When you return I want you to come and see me. If you have decided to say anything more then I will listen to whatever you have to tell me. In the meantime I suggest we both keep quiet and do some thinking.' He went to put his arm round the boy's shoulder, but Ben shrugged him off.

'Does Flavia know?' he asked.

Gervaise hesitated. 'No, I haven't told Flavia. You know she's up at Duntroon for a bit because she hasn't been well.'

'When is she coming back?'

'I don't know yet, Ben. Not till she's better, but I'm afraid that has nothing to do with it.'

'Except,' said Ben, 'except that she would know I hadn't done it,' and he turned and walked out of the study without either asking permission to go or giving a backward glance.

Gervaise had been undecided whether to fly up to Scotland for half term to be with Flavia or not. He both longed to see her and dreaded the sense of inadequacy that their meeting might bring him. She did not sound keen to return to Winsleyhurst yet. In the end he decided to go. He felt it would be better to tell her about the dramas at the school in person rather than on the telephone.

She greeted him affectionately, appeared pleased to see him, but slipped quickly out of his embrace. She was perfectly nice to him – made almost hectically bright conversation – but she was as brittle as a wine glass. Gervaise felt as though a clumsy move on his part might cause her stem to snap off.

'How are you really, my darling?' he asked tenderly.

'Fine,' said Flavia, 'I'm absolutely fine now, thanks.'

She had been sleeping in the small single room she had occupied ever since she was little, but when Gervaise arrived Elizabeth had insisted that she move into one of the double spare rooms.

'Oh it's not worth moving just for the weekend – Gervaise won't mind,' Flavia had said.

'Then he should – and so should you,' her aunt had replied with unusual crispness, and Flavia had been abashed.

They lay in the twin beds only a hand's stretch apart but Gervaise thought he might still have been five hundred miles away, the gap between them felt so great. However, when he told her about Ben, her reaction was as furiously positive as he had feared it would be.

'Of course it wasn't Ben. How could you even suspect him?'

Gervaise, not at all happy about the situation either, longing for a little support and sympathy himself, thought she was being most unfair. Flavia announced that she would come back to Winsleyhurst with him after all. In the end it was Gervaise himself who refused to let her come. He did not want his wife to return to Winsleyhurst simply to champion Ben Forbes.

Elizabeth Cameron also counselled delaying Flavia's return; she felt it could only precipitate trouble at the moment. She had arranged a big charity concert at Duntroon in April at which Flavia, among others, was to take part; with Dulcie's connivance she had got hold of an excellent pianist to accompany her.

There was a ballroom at Duntroon which was much in demand for charity events, and concerts had often been held there. Elizabeth had managed to get a very high-powered committee together and Sotheby's had agreed to sponsor the evening. Rehearsing for this provided a perfect excuse for Flavia to stay up north for a bit longer without arousing speculation either about the state of her health or the state of her marriage. It was the latter that bothered Elizabeth Cameron most. Physically she thought Flavia had made a good recovery.

As for Flavia, despite the one or two professional engagements that had come her way lately she was still very bothered about a big performance. The fear that her nerves might let her down and lead to another disastrous public humiliation haunted her. But she was determined to go through with it all the same.

The school reassembled after half term on Wednesday evening. Rowan Goldberg and Ben were due to return from London on the school coach and Gervaise was dreading his interview with Ben. He very much hoped the boy would decide to be more forthcoming, and wished that Ben had spent the weekend with his father and not in the unpredictable Goldberg ménage.

He didn't know whether to be relieved or sorry when Meg came to tell him that Ben had developed a sore throat and temperature and Goldberg had come on his own. Mrs Goldberg's Filipino chauffeur would drive Ben back as soon as he was better, probably on Friday or Saturday.

On Friday morning Meg came to see Gervaise with a very troubled face.

'Something very bothering has happened. Barbie left her overall hanging up in the bathroom with some money in the pocket. It was very stupid of her – Sister and I are always telling those girls how careless they are – but it seems Michael Stockdale gave her some money he owed her and she shoved it in her pocket and forgot all about it. It's gone.'

'Do you mean it was there before half term?'

'No,' said Meg. 'He only gave it her this morning.'

Meg and Gervaise looked at each other soberly: the implication of this was obvious.

'So you think it may not have been Ben after all?'

'May I act on a hunch?' asked Meg.

'Of course. I have the greatest respect for your hunches.'

'Then let's go and look in Ben's locker again. I think someone may be trying to frame him who has not noticed that he hasn't come back to school yet.'

They went to the locker room together. In Ben's locker, at the front, there was a neat pile of coins.

'This is really unpleasant,' said Gervaise. 'This is not only dishonest, this is spite.'

'Poor Ben,' said Meg. 'I'm not surprised he got ill, the stress of being wrongly accused must have lowered his resistance. I was going to ring up Mrs Goldberg this evening anyway to ask how he is. Shall I do it now? I have a feeling he will get better much quicker if he knows we don't suspect him any more.'

'Yes, go and do that – better you than me. See if you can speak to him. Tell him I'll talk to him as soon as he's well.'

Meg was not gone very long. When she came back her normally rosy face was pale. She looked distraught.

'Whatever is it, Meg? Is the boy really ill?'

'I don't know,' said Meg wildly, 'because what's the matter is that he isn't there. He hasn't been there all weekend. Mrs

Goldberg had no idea what I was talking about.' They looked at each other in horror.

Gervaise went out onto the landing and called the nearest boy to him.

'Go and find Goldberg,' he said, 'and send him to me in my study immediately.'

XXIX

AFTER GERVAISE HAD left Duntroon on the Wednesday morning to fly back south, Flavia went for a long walk. She took the dogs, including Wellington, who found life at Duntroon very much to his taste, especially the loch. After a swim in its freezing waters he liked to share his pleasure by giving anyone within range a refreshing shower. Luckily Duntroon was well supplied with kennels for soaking dogs to dry in, not to mention the gun room where the dogs always slept, and where there was always a slight odour of damp fur mingling with the smell of gun oil and old waterproofs.

It was a wonderful day, an Alpine day, all snow-capped hills and brilliant sky; a day to lift the heart. High over Beinn Chavoch Flavia watched an eagle wheeling, rising ever higher on thermal currents of air. Through the binoculars, without which no member of the Cameron family ever went for a walk, she could see the primary feathers of its great wings splayed out like open fingers. She wished she could take wing herself.

She had fully intended to make a success of her reunion with Gervaise, and knew she had failed dismally. The anger she felt about the accusations against Ben had been almost a relief – any emotion was better than the slight but crawling irritation which Gervaise's presence now produced in her; it was like having wicked little insects under the skin. Then she would look at the misery on his kind and charming face, at the devotion in his eyes, and would ache with sadness for them both. One thing she was certain about: she must now go all out for her career. Though Alfred Tatham still warned her that it would be a hard slog back and she must not expect everyone to fall at her feet, she sensed that he was optimistic about her chances. She was aware of the awful irony that she had first fled to Gervaise as an escape from her career, and now wished to use it to get away from her married life. Perhaps the challenge to fight her way back to the concert platform would help to make the marriage possible again – not happy or easy, but possible? She thought of the song from *Me and My Girl*. I must pick myself up, dust myself down, and start all over again, thought Flavia drearily.

When she got back to the house, Elizabeth said there had been a telephone call for her.

'It sounded like a child – a boy. He wouldn't say who it was or leave a message but he sounded rather desperate. I told him you would be in later if he wanted to try and ring back.'

'Ben!' said Flavia. 'I bet it's Ben. Gervaise said he's at the Goldbergs. He must be dreading going back to school this evening. Can I try and ring them?'

There was no reply from the Goldberg number, but she thought they might well be away somewhere and have taken Ben with them. She decided not to mention the call to Gervaise when he rang Duntroon that evening. It might only spark off another disagreement between them.

On Friday morning, early, there was another call for Flavia. She was still asleep but her aunt came and woke her up.

'Quick, Flavia – I think it's Ben again.'

She rushed to the telephone by her aunt's bed. 'Ben?'

'Oh Flavia.' The voice wobbled and there was a gulp. 'I'm so glad you're there now. I – I don't know what to do.'

'Are you ringing from Winsleyhurst?'

'No – I've run away. I was going to go to Ardvrechan – only Aunt Moy's not there.'

'Who's with you?'

'No one. I haven't got much money left but it's okay about the telephone. I've got my BT chargecard.' The line went quiet and there was silence.

'Ben! Ben, are you still there?' asked Flavia frantically.

There was a small sob. 'Yes. Sorry. I'll be all right in a minute. It's just nice to talk to someone.'

Flavia did some quick thinking. Detailed questions could come later.

'Wherever you are I'm coming. Don't worry. Just take a pull on yourself and tell me how to get to you.' She realized that she had no idea where Ardvrechan was, or how to find the way; she only knew that it was on an island, and access had to be by boat. 'Now take a deep breath and tell me exactly where you are. Are you ringing from Ardvrechan?'

'No. If I tell you exactly where I am, will you promise not to take me back to Winsleyhurst? Not to tell anyone till Dad gets back?'

'I'll promise not to do anything until we've talked together, but I must let Gervaise know where you are.'

'Then I won't tell you.'

'Ben, they must be worried sick. Give me your number and I'll ring you back.'

'Not till you promise. They think I'm ill at the Goldbergs'. Rowan's covering up for me for as long as he can.' Flavia took a quick decision.

'I must at least tell them I'm with you. I won't say where you are, just that we're together and you're all right. Please Ben – please. Surely you can trust me?'

'Mr Henderson didn't trust me,' said Ben. 'Promise you won't tell – and that you'll come back to Ardvrechan with me?' Of course she promised.

Ben's instructions were extremely competent. Flavia grabbed a pencil from beside the bed and scribbled them down. He told her which roads to take, and eventually where to turn off up a gated track which wound steeply uphill for five or six miles. The gates would all be padlocked but he told her exactly where to find the keys hidden in the stone walls. When she reached the top, he said, she would see the loch below her and could follow the track down hill again. He wouldn't say where he was now, but he would be on the jetty in about two hours – it sounded like the back of beyond. He refused to give her the telephone number from which he was ringing, but promised faithfully that he would be all right and would not run off again.

'You will come alone, won't you? And could you possibly bring some food?'

Colin and Elizabeth, greeted with this tale, felt strongly that Flavia should ring Gervaise immediately.

'I can't. I've absolutely sworn – he'd never trust me again,' Flavia said, but she agreed that after she'd left they could ring Gervaise and explain what had happened so long as they promised to stop him calling in the police. Ben had been very insistent about that. She assured them she would get in touch as soon as she could. Elizabeth looked very worried, but Colin grinned at his niece.

'I think you're enjoying the prospect of an adventure,' he said. 'I'd come with you, but I have an important meeting. I'd like to meet this Ben – he sounds a boy after my own heart. I have a shrewd idea where you're going too – it has to be Ardvrechan. All right, all right, you didn't tell me, it's a guess – but all the same I'm going to show you exactly where Loch Vrech is on the map, and I'll give you my large-scale map of the area too. I've been there many times in the past. It's a sea loch really, but access from the sea is extremely difficult even for an expert, so you have to get to it from the inland end and go up the loch by boat. The island's about five miles up. Moyra Forbes is a real eccentric, but she's a remarkable person – she used to be a dancing partner of mine way back. She was very beautiful and I rather fancied her once but don't tell your aunt I said so. Most women would hate to live there alone, but she's just different. You'd better take a Land Rover – the ground's probably still frozen but it might be boggy and anyway it's pretty vertical in places. You need four-wheel drive – you wouldn't have a hope in hell of making it in an ordinary car.'

'Uncle Col, you're a darling. He's special to me, this boy – and I owe it to Gervaise too,' she added hastily. Colin raised an eyebrow at her but said no more.

Elizabeth was not at all happy about Flavia going alone and offered to come too, but Flavia wouldn't hear of it. She was convinced that Ben would bolt again if she had anyone with her. Elizabeth had to content herself with producing boxes of provisions which she put in the Land Rover. After all, if Ben had managed to ring Flavia, then there must be a telephone somewhere. She knew the mobile wouldn't work in the area. Flavia flung an overnight bag in the back together with some old jerseys and waterproof clothing that had belonged to her cousins. She had no idea what, if anything, Ben might have with him. Finally she whistled up Wellington for company, and put her flute in for good measure.

'You can't possibly want that, Flavia,' said Elizabeth, but Flavia said she never moved without it. 'It's not my best one anyway. I'll pipe to the seals – they're supposed to like music,' and with a wave of her hand she rattled off down the drive.

'Oh Col,' said Elizabeth, as they stood on the steps of Duntroon watching till she was out of sight. 'Poor Flavia but, oh – poor, poor Gervaise too. That little boy is more important to her than he is.'

'Yes,' said Colin. 'Poor both of them, but poor him anyway.'

It took Flavia over two hours to reach the track to Kinlochvrechan. Already she had driven miles without seeing another car. She missed the turning the first time, and had to retrace her route. Had it not been for Ben's description of a little bridge about a mile short of two particular birch trees, which stood together at a bend in the road like a pair of lovers holding hands, she thought she would never have found it. She sent grateful thoughts to her uncle for lending her the Land Rover. Luckily she had been driving it round the estate at Duntroon since she was about fourteen, but even so it crossed her mind to wonder what would happen if she turned it over.

She was relieved when she came to the first gate and found the key exactly where Ben had described. At least she was in the right place. The bracken was quite flattened after its sleep under a winter blanket and there were still deep patches of snow in the hollows near the track. The numerous little burns were all in spate and the high tops were completely white.

When she finally came over the hill she stopped and got out. She thought she had never been anywhere more beautiful in her life. The air was fresh rather than cold as though, even this far north, Scotland was having a flirtation with spring. Mixed with the smell of moss and peat there was the unlikely scent of coconuts that always comes from places where gorse flourishes. The track fell away sharply and at the bottom was the loch – a stretch of blue and silver in the early March sunshine. She could see a couple of boats and a ramshackle jetty. There was no sign of any human being.

'Please God, let him be there,' prayed Flavia.

She climbed back into the Land Rover, started the engine again and carefully began the descent. She thought it was almost more hairy driving down than going up hill. When she reached

the bottom there was quite a wide flat parking spot that had
been concreted over. She could see no sign of Ben. She tooted
the horn several times. It seemed an act of desecration in such
a wild and silent place. The sound echoed and re-echoed. She
got out and walked over to the jetty, suddenly extremely anxious, and stood there for a good five minutes. Then there was
frantic barking, and looking round she could see Wellington
going mad inside the car; then someone let him out of the
back, and he was leaping wildly round the figure of a boy.

Flavia and Ben rushed together and clutched each other, and
all the pent-up unhappiness and worry burst out. Ben cried
and cried with relief, soaking the front of Flavia's Puffa, and
tears rolled down her own cheeks onto the top of his tousled
red hair.

'Ben, oh thank God – oh you horror, you absolute fiend.
You dreadful, dreadful boy. What a fright you've given me.'

He leant against her and rubbed his head to and fro across
her jacket. Then he stood up, gave himself a little shake and
wiped his nose with the back of his hand.

'Got any choc?' he asked and Flavia knew he was all right.

They sat in the March sunshine on the edge of the jetty
munching chocolate and bananas and drinking Coke out of the
can, while Ben told her his side of the story. He had always
guessed that Waring was the thief, but it hadn't occurred to
him that he would try to put the blame on anyone else and
play such a horrible spiteful trick.

'You see he was always top in maths till I came along, and
then I took his place in the under-eleven match,' explained
Ben. 'Also he's Spanner's great favourite – I told you Waring
was a real suck – and he hates me. Spanner hates me too
because you see I know something secret about him. He'd be
thrilled if I got sacked. When Mr Henderson sent for me I got
an awful fright because I thought he'd discovered something
quite different.'

'Like what?'

'Like my running away things. Like my secret diary. I always
knew I might need to run away – specially without you there.
At the beginning of term I took the rest of my Christmas
money and various useful things like my *SAS Survival Handbook*

and some food, and me and Goldberg hid them in the folly. With all that money being nicked I didn't dare hide anything at school because I knew if anyone found it they'd think I'd pinched it. It was good fun – Goldberg thought the folly was great. That's what we did when we biked over. The night after Mr Henderson told me he'd found the stolen stuff in my locker and wouldn't believe I hadn't done it, I knew I had to go. I guessed Waring would go on pinching and I thought if I wasn't there everyone would see it wasn't me. I got out through the little window in the master's bog and went over to the folly to collect my provisions.'

'You mean you went there alone at night?' Flavia was stunned.

'I had a torch and there was a light on the bike, but it was pretty creepy at the folly all alone, I can tell you. Not like when you and Dad were there too.'

In the end he hadn't needed the money for his train fare. Rowan Goldberg had just told the Filipino couple that Ben was to go up to Scotland to stay with his aunt and they'd bought him a ticket to Inverness and taken him to the train. It was as simple as that. All Rowan had to do on his return to school was to tell Meg that his mother had forgotten to write a note saying Ben was ill, but that was no surprise to anyone – his mother never wrote notes. In fact Mrs Goldberg hadn't been there at all.

'What did you do at Inverness?'

'Went to the bus station. That's where my Christmas money came in useful, and I bought some more biscuits and things. I got the bus for Ullapool and got off at Buchantilly. Wee Duncan – that's Big Duncan's grandson – works at the garage there. He's a bit loopy, so I knew he wouldn't ask me questions but he's awfully kind and he ran me up to the turning for Kinlochvrechan – where you've just been. He lives on up the glen himself.'

It was at this point that Ben's streak of luck had started to run out. Big Duncan was Moyra Forbes' stalker, boatman and general factotum; he was also the beloved and devoted friend of all the family. Ben knew there was a chance that his aunt might be away, but if so, that Big Duncan would look after him – he was always there, a part of Ardvrechan, as constant in Ben's experience as the waters of the loch itself. However, as the laconic Wee Duncan, a hulk of six foot three, was driving off, his grey cells had suddenly gone into overdrive and he had vouchsafed the information that his grandfather had been taken into hospital.

'He's awa to the Infirmary. You'll no' find him at Ardvrechan,' he had said as he'd rattled off in his battered old van. Ben had been left staring after him, feeling really worried for the first time. The thought of Ardvrechan without Duncan put a very different complexion on things. He prayed fervently that Aunt Moy would be at home. He had walked the six miles up the track and the adventure had suddenly seemed not quite such a brilliant idea after all. Big Duncan's croft was at the top of the hill, but just out of sight from the track. Ben had been able to get in because he knew where Duncan hid the key on the rare occasions that he locked the house. It was very cold. There was a telephone in the croft, and it was here that Ben had come to ring Flavia, here that he had watched for her coming, staying out of sight until he was sure it was her and that she was alone.

'I rang home and left a message on the answering machine for when Dad gets back saying what I'd done and why and where I am. I kept thinking he'd come. I still think he will, but it gets sort of lonely on your own after a bit. I hope you didn't mind me ringing. I just wanted to talk to you – so badly.'

Flavia felt a lump in her throat. Ben looked very thin and bedraggled; there were dark lines under his eyes which showed up very black against his white, freckled skin.

The sun had gone behind a cloud and a chilly little breeze got up, feathering the still waters of the loch. Where it had looked blue before, now it was a rather ominous grey.

'We ought to go,' said Ben. 'It's flat calm now, but the wind might get up. Things can change very quickly, and of course it's tidal a good way up.'

'Isn't there a telephone at Ardvrechan?' asked Flavia.

Ben looked shocked. 'Of course not. Aunt Moy has a radio link with Big Duncan – but he's not there, so of course it's not working now. That's what panicked me a bit.'

'Can I go into the croft and ring Duntroon and leave a message to say I've found you, that we're both all right and nobody needs to fuss? Gervaise will be worried about me if I don't, and that would be unkind.'

'Okay. I've left it unlocked. If we unload the stuff, I'll start to carry it down to the boat, but I think we should hurry,' said Ben, looking anxiously at the sky. 'Take the car and leave it behind Duncan's house, then no one will know we're here.'

Flavia couldn't feel such secrecy was necessary in this deserted place, but did so to oblige him. She thought that for a boy of ten he had shown remarkable powers of organization. She imagined Alistair must have been very like him at the same age. Ben's conviction that Alistair would come in search of him was not a thought that she dared let her mind dwell on.

She left a reassuring message at Duntroon, and when she came back Ben and Wellington were already in the boat with the engine running. Ben held out a hand to her as she dropped over the side. He had put on a life jacket, and passed one to her, handling the boat with the ease of someone who has been doing it all his life. It was a solid rather ungainly craft; a pair of oars were stored down one side. Ben told her proudly that it was a Q17, not very new, but easy to start and drive, and because it had a cathedral hull it was very stable in rough weather; he said he was not allowed to drive the other one.

'There have to be two boats – one's usually up at the house and one's down here,' he explained.

The loch was narrow to start with, but as they came round a headland it opened out and became much wider, and the water started to be quite choppy.

'How much longer, Ben?' Flavia felt a little uneasy. She wondered if it was utterly irresponsible of her to be doing this, if she should have insisted on bundling Ben into the Land Rover and heading straight back to Duntroon. Then she thought of her promises, of the faith he put in her, and knew she could not have broken his trust.

'About three more miles.'

'Do we have to be so far out?' she asked. She thought the shoreline looked too far away for comfort.

'This bit we do. It's too rocky close in along here.' He grinned at her. 'I promise I've done this lots of times before. Dad's always very fierce about safety rules.'

'Well, thank goodness for that!' Flavia laughed back at him.

There were birch trees along the shore, still with bare winter branches, but there was the faintest purple tinge to the larches, as though pink smoke had been puffed through them; seaweed made strong black and yellow patches of colour at the water's edge. She leant over and dipped a hand in the water. It was icy and when she put her hand to her mouth to blow some warmth back into her fingers she could taste the salt.

'There – look. Ardvrechan,' said Ben. Ahead of them, quite close to the shore, was an island and on it was a long low house, part grey stone, part whitewashed. It was larger than she had expected.

Ben slowed down, and made for a little stone jetty.

'But it's got a huge and wonderful garden!' exclaimed Flavia in surprise. She had not expected to find lawns and white garden seats, flowerbeds and banks of rhododendrons and azaleas in this remote setting. 'It must be sensational later in the spring.'

Ben looked pleased. 'You ought to see the daffodils in April. And when the azaleas are out the loch looks all yellow and pink and orange too. It's got lots of rare things in it. Aunt Moy's a famous gardener – she knows everything about plants and birds. I think she might be in Nepal now, perhaps collecting things, perhaps painting.'

Ben dropped anchor as they came in, and Wellington leapt out and plunged straight into the water, while Flavia climbed out, glad she had her boots on.

'Wellie loves it here,' said Ben.

'I bet. Oh God, you foul animal, I might have known,' said Flavia as Wellington shook all over her and gambolled wildly round like a lost soul readmitted to paradise.

She helped Ben pull the boat in as far as they could and he tied it up.

'Brilliant here, isn't it?' he asked. 'I've been dying for you to see it.'

The house was full of surprises. Going in at the back door it was much what Flavia had expected, the walls panelled with dark brown pine boards, and studded with coat pegs. There were more pegs to lay fishing rods across, and several moth-eaten stags' heads with old hats hanging from their antlers gazed down with baleful amber glass eyes. 'That one's a fifteen pointer,' said Ben. There were drying rooms and a pantry with old-fashioned wooden plate racks, but a light spacious kitchen with a Rayburn which was actually hot, was a pleasant surprise. At least there was one oasis of warmth. The house felt freezing otherwise and their breath hung in the air like puffs of mist. Ben explained that the stove, the fridge and the overhead lights downstairs, which had chains hanging down to turn them on and off, were run off gas. Huge great cylinders had to come up by boat. There were also oil lamps, more Calor Gas lamps and candles. There was no electricity.

The real surprise came when Ben led her through a door to the front of the house, which was much more spacious than she had expected – more like a beautiful and original home and less like a typical sporting lodge. The walls were white throughout, but all round the hall and up the stairs were hung wonderful glowing paintings of every conceivable flower, animal and bird, so that the effect was of brilliant colour like Fabergé enamel work. There was a dining room with graceful Regency chairs and a long mahogany table, and though the old pink carpet was threadbare in places and the velvet curtains patched, it had a peaceful elegance like a gracefully ageing woman who has once been beautiful and well-dressed, and has the self-confidence neither to have her face lifted nor strive for the latest fashion.

'Oh but this is quite lovely,' said Flavia. Ben in his self-appointed role of host looked very pleased.

'Here's the drawing room.' Lovely furniture, more paintings – delicate watercolours this time – and books, piles and piles of books: the room overflowed with them. At the far end was a large Steinway grand. Flavia sat down and started to play. 'Pretty well in tune too,' she said in amazement. 'How on earth does your great-aunt get a piano tuner out here, for heaven's sake?'

'I don't know but people just do things for Aunt Moy,' said Ben simply. 'Dad says she's that kind of person.'

Best of all were the views. Being on an island you could see a bit of the loch from every window. In fact there was a bridge which joined the island to the mainland in one place, though Ben said it was such a gimcrack-looking contrivance that some visitors preferred to go in the rowing boat. There was also Aunt

Moy's studio in the garden, but he would never take anyone in there without her express permission. It was getting dark now, and Flavia gazed as the water turned first pink then fiery red all round them as though the azaleas Ben had spoken of were already out. She thought it was the most magical place she had ever been to.

Ben fetched sticks and paper, and lit the fire in the drawing room while Flavia unpacked Elizabeth Cameron's brilliant box of provisions and inspected the larder. Ben had clearly made inroads into what stores there had been. They might have to eat rather oddly but thanks to Aunt Elizabeth they would not starve. It suddenly dawned on her that she had given no thought at all to the length of their stay. She would think about that tomorrow. They had baked beans and fried eggs and mugs of strong tea with long-life milk. Then they sat by the fire and played backgammon.

'Flavia?' asked Ben suddenly.

'Umm?' She was contemplating her next move.

'Do you mind talking about the baby?'

'Well,' said Flavia, 'I haven't talked much so far, because it's felt too awful, too private – except to Aunt Elizabeth. She's special. Sometimes other people want to talk to me about it – like my mother – and I can't. I just absolutely can't. And sometimes I feel I desperately need to talk and talk about it and then I can't think of anything else except the baby.'

'So,' said Ben, 'it's really okay to do what you feel like? It's all right to talk if you want to, but it's all right not to as well?'

'Well, that's what I think anyway,' said Flavia, knowing that the baby was not the only issue.

'That's how I feel about Mum,' said Ben. 'Oh Flavia, I'm glad you're here. It was awful on my own.'

He yawned mightily. Flavia filled hot-water bottles from kettles on the Rayburn and they went upstairs with candles. Ben didn't know how to turn the hot water on.

'Isn't it lovely not being able to wash,' said Ben sleepily as she kissed him good night. He was asleep almost before he finished speaking, but Flavia lay awake in the bedroom next door, wondering what she was really doing here on this island with someone else's runaway child, and listening as the wind got up and started to rage and howl and rattle round the house.

It sounded as if a thousand demons had been released from hell. She went twice to see if Ben was awake and feeling afraid, half hoping he would be, because she felt so very afraid herself, but he never stirred, and she felt very alone with the terrifying wind and her own turbulent thoughts.

XXX

ALISTAIR FORBES HAD arrived home on Friday morning after an overnight flight. He had been negotiating on a particularly sensitive kidnap case in South America, and was utterly exhausted. Because he had left at extremely short notice, as so often happened, he had not had time to clear up the kitchen. His cleaning lady, who normally came in twice a week, had clearly not been near the place since he went away. It was depressing to find unwashed plates and knives in the sink exactly as he had left them. Bowls of hyacinths, a present from Claire Palmer, had dried out and were drooping flabbily over the sides of their pots, letting off a sweet sickly smell of death. There was a huge pile of uninteresting-looking mail on the floor inside the hall, and a layer of dust over everything.

Alistair had refused to let Claire have a key to the house. Had he done so he knew she would certainly have been in during his absence and the place would have been looking spick and span, though she would equally certainly have employed a cleaning agency or her own housekeeper to produce this result. Claire was not one to wield even a duster if she could pay someone else to do it for her, and shortage of money was not one of her problems. She would also, he knew, have taken the opportunity to go through all his private papers. She had been very angry that he had not given her a key, and resented the fact that he only allowed her in the house at all when Johnnie was with her and they were doing joint things with the boys. When they made love – though love was hardly the word – it was always either at Claire's house or on neutral territory such as someone else's house or a hotel. Claire was a very sexy lady, with a great deal of experience and some innovative ideas of her own which left Alistair shaken rather than stirred. Alistair had not instigated the affair; she had arrived in his bedroom and climbed into his bed on a weekend when they were both staying with Christopher and Jane Boynton. He had been in such a state of misery and desolation at the time that he had not even bothered to try to resist her. Flavia was in his head night and day. He ached for her with his body and longed for her with his heart. That he should have fallen so deeply for someone so young and newly married at a time when he himself was now perfectly free was very hard to bear. When he heard from Ben that Flavia was having a baby – and in the way of most school gossip, the boys seemed to have guessed well before they had been told officially – it just underlined what he already sadly accepted in his mind, that as far as he was concerned Flavia Henderson was completely out of court.

Claire made no secret of the fact that she found him wildly attractive, and could not comprehend or accept that he had no wish to form anything other than a casual relationship with her. Before he had gone to South America she had proposed marriage to him – and he had turned her down.

'I simply don't understand you,' she said. 'I give you a terrific time in bed, I find you the sexiest man I've met in years, and it would suit us both perfectly. I'd make you a marvellous wife, do all the things you want me to, look after your kid – and I wouldn't even complain about your absences. I could certainly amuse myself while you were away, as no doubt you could, no questions asked by either of us. An open marriage. What more do you want?'

But Alistair wanted much, much more and was not prepared to settle for less. He knew it would be hopeless to try to explain to Claire, because even if he had told her that he was in love with someone else, she would have been incapable of understanding his scruples in not going after the woman he wanted, let alone the kind of married relationship for which he longed.

She had shrugged her shoulders and said, 'Suit yourself. We'll go on as we are for the moment, but it seems a waste, and you can't expect me to hang about for ever. I suppose it has to do with that son of yours. I think he's a spoilt brat – one shouldn't run one's life to suit one's children.'

A vision of Flavia kissing Ben good night had come up before Alistair and he had felt a profound distaste for Claire.

How Jane Boynton, herself a very sweet person, had come to have such a tough sister as Claire was a puzzle, but then Jane had married into the Boynton family at an early age, and niceness can sometimes be surprisingly catching. While he was away he had vowed that he would end the affair as soon as he got home.

There were several messages on his answerphone. The first was from Big Duncan at Ardvrechan. He was being taken into hospital with an emergency hernia operation, he said. Miss Forbes was away and he thought in her absence he should let Alistair know. He'd left everything in as good order as he could, and asked Wee Duncan to give an eye to the place, but, 'he's no' verra reliable, no' just like other people, ye ken,' and Alistair might want to come up himself. There was a message from Mrs Hawkins, his cleaning lady, to say she had the flu that was going round, and then there were three messages from Claire. Alistair would have been mortified if anyone else had overheard them, and was thankful that Mrs Hawkins had not been in after all: Claire could be extremely crude and didn't give a damn what anyone thought. She quite enjoyed embarrassing people, except, Alistair had noticed, Sir Lance Boynton. She toned herself down considerably when they stayed at Boynton, but Alistair got the feeling that Lance was in no way either deceived or impressed by Claire, though the good-natured and less percipient Pamela probably was, since she was doing everything in her power to promote the match.

Next there was a message from Gervaise: the call had been made the day before the boys were due to go away for half term a week ago; he would like Alistair to call him when he got back, nothing alarming, Ben was well, but there was a difficulty that he needed to discuss with Alistair as soon as possible. Alistair's heart sank. He didn't at all like the sound of that and wondered what Ben had been up to. He guessed that he might have got up against Douglas Butler. Ben dismissively described Spanner as a boring old fart, but Alistair knew that his dislike went much deeper than that.

The next call made his hair stand up at the back of his neck. It was from Ben. The voice was very strained. He played it over twice.

'Dad, I know you're not there, but I've run away. They think

I've been stealing at school but I promise I haven't. I've got to Ardvrechan but Aunt Moy's not here and Big Duncan isn't either.' Here there was a heart-rending gulp. 'I'm okay really – but please, please will you come if you can? I won't do anything stupid.'

Alistair picked up the telephone and dialled the Winsleyhurst number.

Gervaise was just finishing his interview with Rowan Goldberg when Miss Hackett buzzed him to say that Mr Forbes was on the line and it was urgent. He couldn't help admiring Goldberg's loyalty to his friend. It was only when Gervaise and Meg had really impressed on him what dangers and difficulties Ben might be in that they had managed to make him tell the whole story. Gervaise was appalled, and very angry with Irina Goldberg for being such a hopeless and irresponsible parent, but he hadn't the heart to be really cross with the nervous and tearful boy in front of him. Rowan had stammered so much to begin with that he was almost incomprehensible, and it had taken all Meg's gentle calmness to get him to talk coherently.

'I'll see you again later, Rowan,' Gervaise said. 'What you have done is very foolish and wrong but I accept that you thought you were doing the right thing. You are not to discuss this with anyone else at all. Do you understand me?'

A very subdued Goldberg said that he did, and Meg took him off, giving Gervaise a very sympathetic look. She would not have liked to be talking to Ben's father at that moment. She secretly thought Alistair was a very daunting man and did not feel at all at ease with him.

Alistair listened carefully and in silence to Gervaise's full and fair account of what had happened. If he blamed him for suspecting his son of something he hadn't done, he didn't say so, but he cut Gervaise's apologies short.

'What's done is done,' he said. 'You dealt with a difficult situation as best you could. It's bad luck for us all that I was away, but it couldn't be helped. At least I know exactly where Ben is. I'd be very surprised if he does anything foolish. He's been brought up to be very self-reliant and he's in his own surroundings, but I don't like small boys being alone in boats and the loch can be dangerous in bad weather. I shall go straight up there.'

He longed to ask Gervaise what Flavia had thought about the whole incident and was surprised that somehow she had not been able to avert such a near disaster, knowing how close she was to the boy. He managed not to ask to speak to her, hoping against hope that Gervaise might suggest it. For his part, Gervaise was well aware that Alistair must wonder what part Flavia had played in the drama, but an unworthy part of himself that he had not known existed made him desist from mentioning her at all.

As Alistair put the telephone down he looked at the postcard of Millais's girl in the red coat that was still propped up above the fireplace. Claire had picked it up one day, turned it over and read it. 'What a chocolate-boxy picture,' she had commented, raising a scornful eyebrow, 'not unlike a rather chocolate-boxy little girl we've both met. I should chuck that out for starters.' He had wanted to hit her.

Though he was exhausted, Alistair made a quick decision to drive to Scotland rather than catch the night train. It would take him a good ten hours to get even as far as Inverness, bearing in mind that Friday afternoon was not the quickest time to drive out of London; but further north he would risk getting caught by the speed trap cameras on the A9, and reckoned he should be able to make a fast time. There would be little traffic at night and he knew the road like the back of his hand. He would pick up the Ardvrechan Land Rover from Wee Duncan's garage at Buchantilly, where it was always left when Moyra Forbes was away. He hoped Wee Duncan had not suddenly had a rush of blood to the head and locked it away under cover, especially as there would be no Big Duncan to answer a telephone call. Alistair cursed the luck that had taken the old man into hospital at this particular moment. No one could remember his ever being off sick for a day. Aunt Moy could never even persuade him to go away on holiday. 'What would I be doing with one of those?' he would ask, as though it were the most bizarre suggestion. There was also the hazard of going up the loch in the dark if the weather was bad. He knew he could not face hours spent on the train worrying about Ben. If he was driving he might not get there all that much sooner, but at least he would be doing something.

He rang his office, made some necessary arrangements, did a quick repack and was in the car heading across London by three o'clock.

The first hazard he met was a long hold-up on the M1. Alistair chafed as he crawled along. He supposed some lunatic had left it too late to switch lanes where road works had blocked off one carriageway, and had then tried to cut in too late and caused an accident. Alistair was an extremely fast driver himself, and enjoyed taking calculated risks, but he also had great confidence in his own hair's-breadth timing, and was scornful of those with inferior judgement. He listened to Classic FM – Emma Johnson was playing the Finzi Clarinet Concerto, and the thought of this brilliant young musician, who had made such a success of her career, led him to think of Flavia, the last person he needed in his head at the moment. He switched to another frequency and then switched back. There was no way he could escape his longing for Flavia so he might as well wallow in it. There were gale warnings on the weather forecast, especially for Scotland. As he drove further north he could feel the wind getting up: by the time he reached the Carlisle turn-off on the M6 and got on to the A74 it was a serious hazard on the motorway. Alistair cursed. The idea of Ben, alone at Ardvrechan in this sort of weather, made his blood run cold. Pray God he wouldn't be such a fool as to take the boat out in a storm.

He was too experienced an operator to underrate the risk of falling asleep at the wheel, and forced himself to have coffee and a sandwich when he had to stop for petrol. Various bits of debris, including a large piece of roof, were blowing dangerously round the forecourt of the service station. The wind made it difficult to stand. Dawn was breaking by the time he got to Inverness, but the wind was dropping and it was clear that the worst of the gale had blown itself out. He drove out on the A832 Ullapool road with relief – but after he had turned off on the winding road to Buchantilly, he met with a much worse hazard. There was a tree down across the road, and there was nothing for it but to wait for it to be cleared.

By the time he eventually reached the jetty at Kinlochvrechan he was in a state of acute anxiety and it was eleven o'clock in the morning. The sun had come out, and though there was still a stiff breeze and the waters of the loch were rough, he knew he could make it to Ardvrechan. There was only one boat out at anchor, so clearly Ben must have the old Q17 up at the house. He sent up a prayer of thanks. He didn't waste time going up to Duncan's croft, but set about getting the boat in, and felt as though a leaden weight of anxiety had been lifted off his head. It was with surprise and dismay that when at last he came within sight of the house he could see that there was no boat tied up at the island. Over on the far side of the loch the Q17 was bucketing about like a runaway horse. Sick with apprehension Alistair drove over to it at full throttle – but it had clearly broken loose from its moorings and there was no one in it. He tried not to let his imagination run riot. He turned round and roared over to the island, made the boat fast in record time and rushed towards the house.

'Ben?' he shouted wildly. 'Ben, Ben! Where are you?'

There was no reply. He tore through the house like a mad thing, all his ingrained training in keeping cool deserting him in his fear for his son. There were clear signs of recent habitation though; the fire in the drawing room had obviously been used, there were mugs and plates, washed up but not put away, in the kitchen. He knew he must try to think rationally what he should do next – get back up the loch and telephone for help? He opened the front door – and then he heard voices and laughter – joy of joys, unmistakably Ben's laughter. Coming over the long rickety swinging bridge that joined the island to the shore was not one figure but two.

'Ben!' he yelled again and this time it was a shout of triumph.

Ben flew over the bridge and was in his father's arms, being hugged and clutched, laughing and crying simultaneously. For a minute they were completely absorbed in their moment of reunion, but great relief after terrible anxiety can quickly turn to anger and spiral out of control. Alistair suddenly looked up and saw Flavia standing there, and the shock of her presence flipped his control switch completely.

'What the hell are you doing here?' he shouted at her. 'Are you responsible for all this agony we've been through, you bloody little fool? I suppose you planned all this? How dare you?'

All the colour drained from Flavia's face. For a moment she

felt completely winded. Then she got her breath back and a terrible rage came over her.

'You're the most arrogant, ungrateful, hateful man I've ever met,' she screamed back at him. 'I never want to see you again in my life – ever. You can go to hell.'

And she turned and ran back over the precariously swaying bridge like a wild animal, leaving Ben and his father staring after her.

Ben looked at his father in astonishment. 'Oh Dad,' he said reproachfully, 'how could you? You hadn't come, and I was getting desperate and Flavia came all the way from Duntroon to rescue me. Why did you have to shout at her like that?'

Alistair watched Flavia's figure stumbling away up the path out of sight and wondered too.

'I think we'd better do some catching up, old chap,' he said soberly. 'Let's go back into the house. I could do with a mug of coffee.'

'Aren't you going to go after Flavia?' asked Ben, looking at his father with great disapproval for the first time in his life.

'Yes, Ben, I am. Of course I am – but I think I'd better get a few facts sorted out before I face her again.'

'Well, I think that was horrible of you,' said Ben, following him into the house, rigid with indignation. 'You've just been as unfair to her as grotty old Spanner was to me.'

They sat at the kitchen table and while Alistair drank coffee with a tot of whisky in it, which he felt he greatly needed, and ate hunks of home-made Duntroon bread with marmalade, Ben poured out all the sagas of the last weeks.

'I'm terribly sorry about the boat,' said Ben. 'I tied it up when we arrived, but then after we'd unloaded and everything I completely forgot about going back to do the running mooring. When me and Flavia came down this morning it had broken loose and was careering about in the loch, and of course I knew it was all my fault. We got an awful fright, but there was nothing we could do and I wanted to show her everything so we thought we might as well enjoy ourselves till we got rescued. I knew my luck had turned when she came, and I knew you'd come in the end. Are you very angry about it? Will it mean a new boat? Will Aunt Moy be dreadfully upset?'

'Of course she won't – you know what she's like. A gale like that can wreak havoc, and it'll be insured, but you see now why I nag about safety things like that. You'll never forget again, that's for sure, and no, I'm not angry. I don't normally approve of running away, but I understand why you did this and I'm very, very proud of you, Ben. You've had a real adventure – but you mustn't think too hard of Mr Henderson. It must really have looked as if it was you who'd been stealing. People do get things wrong, you know, and suspect an innocent person.'

'Like you over Flavia,' said Ben remorselessly.

'Yes, like me over Flavia. I think I'd better go and put that right now. She can't have disappeared because there's nowhere to go.'

'I'll come too.'

Alistair hesitated. It seemed churlish to leave Ben alone again so soon, but he had things to say to Flavia that were for her ears alone.

'Would you hate it if I left you again just for a little? If I'm going to say sorry properly I might do it better alone.'

This was something Ben could perfectly understand. He often found saying sorry very difficult himself. He nodded.

'Okay. Don't be too long, will you? Shall I get the fire going?'

Alistair eventually found Flavia sitting on a rock below the path, staring out to sea. She had stumbled on for well over a mile in her rage and hurt misery; then she realized she would have to go back eventually, no matter how difficult it would be to swallow her pride, but having stopped she couldn't bring herself to make the move. Her eyes were swollen from weeping, she was cold and looked the picture of misery. He scrambled down behind her.

'Flavia?' he said softly.

She did not turn round. 'Go away,' she said.

He came and sat beside her. 'Would it help if I said I was deeply, dreadfully sorry. That I know I was completely wrong, that Ben has told me everything now, and that I don't know what got into me?'

No answer.

'Flavia, please say you forgive me? It was such a shock to see you. Would it help if I said that you've earned my undying gratitude?'

'Not much,' she said in a whisper.

'Would it help if I said that I love you so much I don't know what to do with myself?' he asked very quietly. 'Would it help if I told you that I think I've loved you since the first moment I saw you? Would it help if I said that I'm not sure I can live without you?'

She turned to him then, her grey eyes, which seemed to change colour like the waters of the loch, enormous in her white face.

'Oh yes,' she said. 'That might help.'

XXXI

ALISTAIR AND FLAVIA walked back hand in hand. Flavia had tripped and floundered up the path an hour earlier; now she might have had wings on her feet. Before they got to the bridge, but still out of sight of the house, he gave her one more kiss. 'Just to be going on with,' he said.

They decided their first priority had to be to go back up the loch and do some telephoning. Alistair offered to go alone, but neither Ben nor Flavia was prepared to lose sight of him for a moment. They sang all the way in the boat, though it was difficult to hear each other above the sound of the engine, and when they arrived they discovered they were all singing something different. It seemed incredibly funny.

The call to Duntroon was not entirely easy; Elizabeth, who answered the telephone, saw no reason why Flavia should not drive back first thing the next morning, and when Flavia had sounded evasive about plans, her easy-going aunt had been unusually sharp. But if the call to Duntroon was difficult the one to Winsleyhurst was much worse, and when Flavia spoke to Gervaise, a knife went through her. He was thankful to know that Ben was safe, and had by now gathered from Colin and Elizabeth that Flavia had gone after him, but something in her voice set alarm bells ringing through every fibre of his being.

'So you'll be safely back at Duntroon tonight then, darling?' asked Gervaise.

'Oh I couldn't make it this evening. It'll be too late and dark, but I'll ring you as soon as I do get there.'

'Like lunchtime tomorrow?'

'Gervaise, I don't know. I might stay on here for a few days. It's all been very traumatic and besides, one of the boats is out of action.'

'Surely that doesn't affect you? Now Alistair's with Ben there can't be any need for you to stay too.' Gervaise echoed what Elizabeth Cameron had just said.

'Well, I'm not sure. We might as well all leave together, and it's such a fascinating place and – and I might be of some use here.'

'I see,' said Gervaise, and after a long pause added drily, 'Then I'm quite sure you will be. Still, it would be nice to have you home – I think it's time I got my wife back.'

'Oh dear,' she said to Alistair. He thought she looked stricken, but they could not discuss it in front of Ben, and Winsleyhurst seemed very far away. By the time they were back at Ardvrechan she was singing again.

'Let's have another feast,' said Ben. 'And then we can have a concert.'

They ate sardines on toast as a main course followed by chocolate biscuits for pudding, and washed it all down with champagne which Alistair produced from Aunt Moy's wine cupboard; not the most conventional mixture perhaps, but they all agreed it was sensational. Then Alistair went over to the piano and started to play old hit numbers from the thirties, 'These Foolish Things' and 'Dancing Cheek to Cheek'. Soon Flavia sat beside him on the second piano stool and played too, not the wild jazz they had improvized together in London, but a gentler mixture, though equally potent and dangerous. Ben, listening happily, curled up in one of the big armchairs, suddenly crashed out with exhaustion, relief and unaccustomed swigs of champagne and had to be half carried up to bed.

'Night, Dad. I knew you'd come,' he murmured as his father tucked him in, but he was really asleep. Alistair stood looking down at his son and listening to Flavia playing: the notes of Poulenc's *Pastourelle* floated up the stairs. Very quietly he closed the door. When he came back to the drawing room she had switched to a *Nocturne* by John Field, and he stood in the doorway, not wanting to break the spell. Then she looked up and their eyes met. Gradually she stopped playing and walked over to the fireplace; they stood, a little apart, looking at each other in the light of the oil lamp and the flickering fire. The moment seemed to go on for ever.

'Will you kiss me again?' she asked, lifting her face.

'Flavia, darling Flavia,' he said. 'I meant what I said to you earlier. I love you so much I don't think I can bear to part with you, but I think you now have to make a choice. Whatever we do someone is going to be terribly hurt, but I don't want to have a quick affair with you. I could stop now – just – if I have to, but I couldn't make love to you tonight and then walk away tomorrow as if this hadn't happened. I want all of you – or nothing. Which is it to be?'

Dulcie's words came back to Flavia: 'Something may happen which will make it obvious,' the old lady had said. 'Life is full of pain and joy – and choices.'

'It ought to be more difficult, but it's not,' she said. 'I simply can't help myself. I have truly tried so hard – I think we both have – but you see I couldn't live without you now either.'

'You told me to go to hell this morning,' said Alistair, laughing down at her and very gently starting to undo the buttons of her shirt. 'Let me take you to heaven with me now.'

'Oh Alistair, I didn't know what I was missing before,' she murmured later, lying in his arms in front of the fire, and this time the moonlight, which now shone through the window on their naked bodies, didn't seem unsympathetic as it had at the folly.

'I thought I was in love with Antoine, but I know now that love had nothing to do with that.'

'You had a great neon sign over your head saying "Unfulfilled",' he teased her, softly starting to kiss her throat, already wanting her again. 'It made every man who saw you long to do something about it.'

They made love again, passionately and hungrily, but afterwards they were content to lie together, talking occasionally, saying some of the things they had never been able to talk about before. She felt there was nothing she could not say to him. She told him about her infatuation with Antoine, the terrible loss of nerve about performing, and then shakily and sadly about the baby, and he held her close and stroked her hair, and let her cry a little. He told her about Claire, and how meaningless it had been, an attempt to drug his pain that hadn't worked; they talked about Ben and how carefully they must handle his feelings, despite his affection for Flavia. She also talked to him about Dulcie, and what an important influence on her life she had always been – but they could neither of them face talking about Gervaise.

They decided to give themselves five days at Ardvrechan – days of pure magic. The storm might never have happened. The loch settled to mirror smoothness and the sun shone. Alistair and Ben took Flavia down the loch to where they knew there was an otter nursery.

'We'll be lucky to see one,' warned Alistair. 'They hardly ever appear on cue.' But luck was with them, and she watched two otters playing, swimming and diving and obviously enjoying themselves to the full. It was hard not to feel they were being given a command performance. There were eider duck bobbing on the water, making their gentle pa-ooh, pa-ooh, pa-ooh calls to each other, and they saw the extraordinary mating courtship display of red-throated divers, racing across the water, half submerged, with necks and heads sticking out at an extraordinary angle.

'They look as if they're pretending to be Loch Ness Monsters,' said Flavia, fascinated. Rock pipits and turnstones were busy on the shore, and there were oystercatchers and ringed plovers. They christened Ben the Turnstone – he spent hours gathering yet more pebbles for his collection, choosing, discarding, grading them for size and colour. Flavia preferred shells, not only collecting the ones that could be gathered on the beach, but looking at those of the tiny live snails that covered the rocks, whose shells were all colours from shiny black to green and orange. She could have spent hours gazing at them.

One day they saw a seal with a live salmon held in its jaws as a Labrador might carry a pheasant. It kept disappearing underwater and each time it came up again the salmon kicked a little less, until finally it was all eaten up. It was rather a gruesome sight but they couldn't drag themselves away. Later they saw the seal lying on its back on the rocks, looking utterly bloated and dangerously distended, clearly sleeping off a Lucullean feast.

'Badly in need of BiSoDol I should think,' said Flavia.

In the evening they played card games with Ben, and discovered a mutual love of poetry. Aunt Moy's taste in books was catholic.

'Listen to this,' said Flavia, holding up a copy of the *Collected Poems* of W. S. Graham: "Blow me a little ladder of sound" – isn't that great? It's something my flute professor read me once, but I've never been able to find it again. I meant to ask him about it only the other day – it's called "Johann Joachim Quantz's Five Lessons" – he was a famous flautist in the eighteenth century who taught Fred the Great and composed lots of flute music. I love this bit too,' and she read:

'Now we must try higher, aware of the terrible
Shapes of silence sitting outside your ear
Anxious to define you and really love you.
Remember silence is curious about its opposite
Element which you shall learn to represent.'

'I think that's wonderful,' said Flavia. 'Sometimes the most important moment is just before you begin to play.'

'Sounds barmy to me,' said Ben.

As well as books, there was a vast collection of records in the house, varying from Monteverdi to Wagner, from Scott Joplin to Cole Porter. One night they rolled the rug back and did a wild Charleston; Flavia very much fancied her own dancing but she had to admit that Alistair was sensational. They had to stop when Ben, whose dancing owed more to enthusiasm than skill, started crashing into the furniture.

At night, after Ben was asleep, she and Alistair made love, and it seemed to Flavia that the wildness of the place and all the harmony of music were in their loving. She would have liked to stay in an Ardvrechan time warp for ever.

Before he had left for South America, Alistair had heard that he'd been made a director of his firm instead of just a consultant. It would not only help financially but would also mean he would have to spend less time abroad. He had to get back to London soon and Flavia and Ben had to go back to Winsleyhurst. They didn't think Ben could stay on long at Winsleyhurst if Flavia were to leave Gervaise for Alistair – that would be a ghastly situation for everyone – but Alistair was adamant that after running away Ben must return for the short amount of term left. They decided not to discuss the future any more until Flavia had seen Gervaise. She dreaded it.

'By the way,' said Flavia to Ben, 'what is this secret you say you know about Spanner?'

'Gross old Spanner has sex with Goldberg's mother. Could you imagine anyone wanting to go to bed with Spanner? Even Goldberg thinks his mum's gone a bit off the rails this time.'

'Ben, you've made it up!'

'Cross my heart. I *saw* them. Goldberg was sick all over his bed when I was staying for a night in the hols, and I went to get his mum. *And,*' said Ben, thoroughly enjoying the attention of his audience, 'when I went in, there was Spanner actually on the bed with her with nothing on. He dived under the bedclothes but Mrs Goldberg was livid. She didn't mind about Spanner, though – she was just furious about the sick. Me and Rowan made up a wonderful joke that she was screwed by a spanner,' and he rolled about laughing. 'That's another reason Spanner wants me sacked,' he went on. 'He knows I know.'

'Well,' said Flavia afterwards to Alistair, 'so much for extra maths coaching. At least I'll have something good to tell Gervaise. He's been dying to get rid of Douglas Butler for ages. This might be an excuse. Poor Betty, fancy being married to that awful unfaithful old lech.'

'Flavia,' said Alistair, 'think what you're saying.'

She looked at him, appalled. 'Unfaithful like me, you mean?'

'Precisely.'

'Oh Alistair – that's horrid.'

'Listen, my love,' he said very seriously, 'all your life you've been loved and sheltered – and approved of. But people aren't going to approve of you now. A lot of people will think what we're doing – what you're doing, not just me – is awful. And it *is* awful for Gervaise. Not everyone will be kind and understanding. Can you face that? There aren't one set of rules for horrors like Spanner and another cosy little set for nice girls like you. It will blow over, but you may be in for a rougher ride than you realize.'

'Yes,' she whispered, looking very sad. 'Yes, I do see. With you I can face anything. But it's a terrible thing I'm planning to do to Gervaise. I know that.'

'We'll face the music together – every kind of music,' he

said, but he wondered if, when it came to the point, she would actually bring herself to wield the knife.

XXXII

DURING FLAVIA'S SO-CALLED convalescence at Duntroon, Gervaise had got into the habit of going over to the sewing room after dinner when Jane and Barbie had giggled their way off duty to join James and Michael at the pub, and Sister had crackled off to dial Amersham. He would find Meg peacefully mending socks or making lists, and she would make him a hot toddy of whisky, and lemon with a good dollop of honey.

He always said, 'I really shouldn't, you know,' and she always said, 'I think it would do you good.'

Sometimes Meg would enquire tentatively after Flavia's health and would ache at the look of misery that would pass over Gervaise's normally cheerful face like a dark cloud crossing a sunlit landscape. Except when they had been jointly absorbed in the dramas about Ben and the missing money, they mostly stuck to safe topics and talked about school affairs in general.

Twenty girls were due to start in the autumn term, and though the idea had originally been mooted by various parents who wanted to simplify family life by educating their sons and daughters together, it now transpired that there were also parents who disliked the idea intensely and were threatening to send their boys elsewhere. Meg and Gervaise discussed it endlessly. Though she'd been so against the idea to start with, Meg was now determined to make it a success for his sake.

Gervaise announced to the staff that Ben was safe and with his father but did not proffer any details, and something about his demeanour prevented anyone from asking, though Spanner's face looked so black all his fuses might have blown.

Gervaise had no illusions about the significance of Flavia's decision to remain on the island with Ben and Alistair, but he hadn't the faintest idea what to do about it. He felt as though his wife was slipping out of his grasp like water running through open fingers.

The evening after Flavia's telephone call from Old Duncan's croft he did not appear in the sewing room to join Meg. After waiting till ten forty-five, greatly daring, Meg went over and tapped softly on his study door. There was no reply. Cautiously she opened it and looked in. Gervaise was sitting at his desk with his head buried in his arms. For one awful moment she thought he might be dead, but when she put her hand on his shoulder he looked up and the despair on his face worked like an instrument of torture on Meg.

'Oh Gervaise, whatever's happened? Do you want to tell me about it? Talking can help.'

'No,' he said. 'I'm so sorry, dear Meg, but I think I just need to be alone.'

'Is there nothing I could do? Shall I get you a drink?'

'I don't think there's anything anyone can do. This is not a school thing – it's purely personal and private and no one can help. But it may sort itself out. Thank you for coming all the same. Good night, Meg.'

She hovered for a moment in an agony of indecision, longing to stay, longing also to shout that his wife should be there to help him; it even crossed her mind that she might try and ring Flavia at Duntroon and tell her she must come back immediately and take this awful unhappiness away from Gervaise. She did not, of course, know that Flavia was at that moment lying blissfully in the arms of Ben Forbes' father on a remote Scottish island.

Three days later, Gervaise, after yet another sleepless night, was shaving when the telephone rang early in the morning. The reflection of his kind, open, humorous face looked back at him from the mirror with tired, troubled eyes. He wished he had a closed, inscrutable dangerous face. He wiped the shaving foam off his chin and reached for the telephone.

'Gervaise? Andrew here. Sorry to ring so early, but we need to speak to Flavia urgently. I rang Duntroon but Colin says she's unobtainable on some island and hasn't been there since Saturday. What on earth's going on?'

'I wish I knew,' said Gervaise untruthfully. 'What's happened?'

'Dulcie died in the night.'

'Oh dear. I'm so very sorry. Flavia will be terribly upset.' His first thought was one of anxiety that she should have another sadness so soon after the loss of the baby, but hard on its heels came the idea that this news must surely bring Flavia back from Scotland.

'I can't ring her,' he said. 'There's no telephone and I haven't spoken to her since Saturday but she did promise she'd try and ring me again today about eleven.'

'Well, tell her to ring Dulcie's London number at once. Hester's gone up already and will be there by then. And Swerve? Tell Flavia to get the hell back down here and stop fooling around.'

'Yes,' said Gervaise, 'yes I will,' though he knew he would be incapable of putting it like that.

Alistair left Flavia alone to make her promised call to Winsleyhurst and took Ben with him to see Wee Duncan about the boat. They had planned that Flavia should go back to Duntroon on Friday while Ben and Alistair went straight to London and that Alistair should then return Ben to school for the last week of term. Neither of them felt it would be right to travel south together, and Alistair knew that after such a dramatic running away, he had to talk to Gervaise about Ben and would find it impossible if Flavia were there. Flavia told herself that as she'd been away so long already, she might as well stay at Duntroon till the holidays. She had not decided how or when she was going to talk to Gervaise. She only knew she dreaded it, and wanted to postpone it for as long as possible. During the holidays there was the concert at Duntroon and she would also be heavily involved with the triennial Orton Music Festival, which was due to take place for a fortnight in April. Apart from concerts and lectures, the school premises were always used to house students for a week's course of music-making, and Flavia had promised to take several classes. She was looking forward to it. Perhaps it could all wait till after that?

When Alistair and Ben returned, Flavia was sitting on the window-sill of Old Duncan's kitchen staring into space, her face as white as her shirt. She had just finished talking to her mother. Hester had gone straight for the jugular.

'*Where are you* and what on *earth* have you been doing?'

'Mum – please just tell me about Dulcie. I can't believe it.'

'Maurice called me early this morning. He and Ina had tea with Dulcie only yesterday and she seemed her usual self – in rather specially good form they thought; some pain from the arthritis, but nothing new. Then apparently she rang for Hilda in the night and asked her to sit and hold her hand. Of course Hilda knew immediately then that something was very wrong and sent for the doctor, but when he got here Dulcie was dead.'

'And Hilda? Oh Mum, poor, poor Hilda. How is she?'

'Not good. I shall stay with her – is it too much to hope you'll come and join me from wherever you are?'

'Of course I'll come. Of course. I'll make a plan as quickly as I can and ring you back.'

'Very considerate of you, darling – that'll be a nice change.' Hester was at her sharpest, but Flavia understood very well that this would be the only way Hester could stop herself from breaking down.

It was early the next morning when Flavia arrived at Dulcie's flat. In the end she and Alistair and Ben had driven back together after all. She had gone first to Duntroon to return the Land Rover and collect a few clothes, and Alistair had come and picked her up after shutting up Ardvrechan. Neither Colin nor Elizabeth asked for any explanations. Alistair drove through most of the night and Flavia spent what little there was left of it at his house. Under the circumstances she felt she could be open about this, though she had no intention of telling anyone that she had actually spent it in his bed. Ironically it was the anniversary of her wedding day, a fact she realized with shame that she had quite forgotten.

As Alistair watched her go into the block of flats where Dulcie lived, he could not rid himself of the fear that Flavia might not be able to bring herself to leave Gervaise.

Hester was still in her dressing gown when she opened the door to Flavia. They clung to each other.

'Oh Mum,' said Flavia. 'Oh Mum. Whatever shall we do without her? Somehow one thought she would go on for ever.'

'Let's go and make some tea. The doctor gave Hilda a sleeping pill and she's still out for the count.'

The kitchen looked incredibly shabby and grubby. Sadly Flavia remembered days when she had enjoyed wonderful toffee-making sessions with Hilda; every surface had gleamed then and it had looked as orderly and shiny as an advertisement for a kitchen in a glossy magazine. Music filled the house in her memory too: Dulcie practising or teaching; Dulcie playing duets with Hester; Flavia herself sitting on Dulcie's knee and picking out tunes on the piano; all sorts of musicians, aspiring or already eminent, making music, filling the house with laughter, and occasionally – it had to be acknowledged – with the temperamental waves of their over-abundant egos. Now it seemed horribly silent. Hester and Flavia sat at the dusty kitchen table and wept into chipped mugs of tea.

'Darling,' said Hester hesitantly, 'the undertakers are coming soon. I hope they arrive before Hilda wakes, but do you want to say your own goodbye to Dulcie or not?'

Flavia looked at her mother, her eyes enormous. 'Should I?'

'There isn't any should. Only you can say – but it won't be frightening. The fear of seeing someone dead is quite different from the reality. It's something you'll have to face one day: we all do. But this may not, for you, be the right time.'

Flavia swallowed. 'I think I will. I owe her that.'

Hester nodded. 'Shall I come in with you?'

'No,' said Flavia. 'Thank you, Mum, but I think I'd like to be alone.'

Hester went with her to Dulcie's bedroom door and opened it. The curtains were drawn back, the early spring sun was slanting across the room and all the lights were switched on. On the dressing table a single candle burned and Hilda's rosary lay beside it. Flavia looked at the bed. Dulcie's face above the folded sheet looked smooth and impersonal as if she had been ironed, but her presence was not there. Her huge personality was conspicuous only by its absence. Flavia felt that Dulcie was already miles away, aeons away.

'Thank you,' she whispered to the absent Dulcie. 'Lend me some of your courage.'

Hilda, always diminutive, seemed to have shrunk and looked more like a bent hairpin than ever. Her frail hands shook.

'I loved her so – but I never told her. I wish I had,' she said to Flavia.

'You didn't need to. She adored you too – we all knew that – but I bet she never told you either.'

'Mind, she could be awkward at times.' Tears trickling from behind her thick pebble glasses, Hilda made the understatement of her life, then followed it like the chorus of a Greek Tragedy with, 'But I wish I'd told her all the same.'

Later in the day, after Dulcie had been taken away, Maurice and Ina arrived. Hester took Ina into the kitchen to see Hilda, and Maurice took Flavia into Dulcie's drawing room. Maurice, a large and normally rather static man, paced round the room. Drama-loving Dulcie, in a fit of irritation at his extreme unflappability had once said crossly, 'The Rock of Gibraltar is like a sponge compared with Maurice.' Flavia wondered what was coming.

'I am Dulcie's executor,' said Maurice. 'This may come as a surprise to you, Flavia, but did you know that you are her chief beneficiary?'

He could see by her stunned expression that she did not.

'There may not be much actual money by the time things are settled. Dulcie was hopeless about money and there will undoubtedly be debts, not to mention a good many subsidiary bequests – but some of her possessions are valuable and those will mostly be yours.'

'Hilda?'

'Hilda is well provided for. What you do with the flat will be up to you.'

'I don't want money.' Flavia twisted her fingers, as she always did when moved or upset.

'Don't knock money if you're lucky enough for it to come your way,' said Maurice briskly. 'Money is bloody handy stuff. It's no guarantee of happiness, of course – nothing can give you that – but you can do things with it – for other people as well as yourself.' He could see she hadn't really taken it in. She got up and put her hand on one of Dulcie's Steinways, running her finger along it, stroking it as if it were alive.

'Would her piano belong to me then?'

'Yes.'

She looked at him with brimming eyes. 'Why me? She had other godchildren.'

'Because she loved you specially. Because she thought you had – possibilities,' said Maurice carefully. He thought Flavia still had surprisingly little idea of the effect she could have on people – perhaps of her dangerous potential to bring heartbreak, but he also thought she had changed in a subtle way and grown up.

'I've known about her will for some time but there are other things. Dulcie has left very explicit instructions for her memorial service. Though there was no obvious medical indication, I think she had a premonition that the end was not far off because she talked to me about all her wishes in the last few weeks. She wants you to be one of the soloists and play for her.'

'Oh Maurice. What an honour – a really huge responsibility.'

'Yes. Half the musical world will be there. It will be a big pressure – I think she meant it to be. Can you take it, Flavia?'

She tilted her chin. 'I shan't let Dulcie down,' she said.

Maurice nodded. 'Don't expect any favours from me, Flavia. If you perform well enough at Dulcie's service, there are some auditions I have in mind for you, some people for whom I'd like you to play, but it will all be up to you.' He held out his arms and Flavia came and leant against him and sheltered in his huge embrace for a long moment.

Later that day she rang Winsleyhurst and gave Gervaise an account of her day and explained that she would like to stay in London till after Dulcie's private funeral. He told her that Ben was back. Alistair had driven him down that morning.

'Where will you be staying tonight, Flavia?' he asked.

'Well, all my things are still at Alistair's house.'

'That isn't what I asked you.'

She hesitated for a moment, then: 'Probably with Trish,' she said eventually. 'I can't stay here. Mum's in the spare room and we could neither of us face sleeping in Dulcie's room. I'll try Trish.'

She had supper with Alistair.

'I've just heard I have to go to South America again next week, which is a great bore,' he told her, spreading her hand out on his knee and stroking each of her fingers with one of his. 'But there's been a call from Aunt Moy. She's back and will have Ben for the holidays. He made an awful fuss about going back to school and couldn't see why he shouldn't go straight to Ardvrechan with her now. I got very angry with him,' admitted Alistair, 'and he was pretty rude back. We had a big row. I think we're both suffering from Flavia withdrawal symptoms – but I intend to go cold turkey on that for a bit. I don't think we should meet again until you have finally resolved everything with Gervaise.'

'Oh Alistair!' She was very shaken. 'Still love me?' she asked into his chest.

'You know I do.'

'Will you give me a little time to – to sort things out?'

'I'll give you until after Dulcie's Memorial Service. But I meant what I said at Ardvrechan. I want all of you – or nothing.'

'Music always excepted?'

'Music excepted – but I won't share you with another man and I don't think Gervaise should have to.'

Alistair, who had taken many risks of different kinds in his life, felt he was staking his all on the most important gamble of his life.

It was late when Flavia eventually arrived at Tricia's flat. She had been surprised to find gregarious Tricia there at such short notice.

'God, you look awful, Trish. Have you got flu or something?'

Tricia shook her head. Her eyes were puffy and swollen, her bubbly fair hair unbrushed.

'No.'

'You haven't given Roddy the push again?'

'No.' A burst of crying. 'He's given it to me,' wailed Tricia.

'Never!' Flavia was truly thunderstruck.

'He has. He says he's absolutely fed up with me. He says I've messed him about once too often – and as far as he's concerned it's all off. It's been a whole week and he hasn't even rung to say sorry yet.'

'Perhaps he isn't sorry?'

Tricia let out a howl like a wolf in *Doctor Zhivago*.

'That's what I'm afraid of.'

'Do you want him back?'

Tricia looked amazed. 'Well, of course I do. The silly nit ought to know that by now.'

'Oh Trish,' said Flavia, 'I do love you but you are an idiot. Ring him up and tell him.'

'But I've *never* done that!'

'Well, tough on you,' said Flavia, laughing and feeling much cheered up, as always, by Tricia. 'Lash out, live dangerously. Try something new – but do hurry up because I've got so much to tell you myself that it'll take all night.' Tricia disappeared into her bedroom.

Over an hour later, when a transformed Tricia, looking as rosy and voluptuous as a portrait by Rubens, burst back into the sitting room to announce that she was engaged to Roddy, she found her prospective audience had crashed out on the sofa, dead to the world.

XXXIII

DULCIE'S CREMATION SERVICE seemed unbearably bleak to Flavia, but Maurice said it was according to her wishes. It was the big memorial service at St Martin-in-the-Fields, now arranged to take place in late May in eight weeks' time, which was to be the celebration of her life. Flavia thought this far too long to wait, but apparently they were lucky to have it so soon, due to the rearrangement of another service previously scheduled for that date. There had been long obituaries in all the major papers.

Gervaise attended the cremation, though Flavia had tried to stop him.

'Please don't dream of coming, darling. You hardly knew Dulcie and anyway you're always so busy on the last few days of term.'

'Not too busy to come and support my wife over something that's important to her,' said Gervaise, and Flavia had been silenced.

While she was at Ardvrechan she had considered writing Gervaise a warning letter, but Alistair had said that was a cop-out.

'He's warned already, I'm sure,' he'd said. 'You owe it him to tell him to his face. You can't duck this one.'

'Do you think I duck things?' she had asked, slightly affronted. There was an uncompromising streak in Alistair that she found both disconcerting and challenging.

After the impersonal little service at the crematorium, Gervaise drove Flavia back to Winsleyhurst. She had wanted to stay on in London, and had a sharp altercation with her mother about it. Hester left her in no doubt about where she thought a wife's place was. Andrew gave her a special hug when he said good bye and then held her by the shoulders and looked at her searchingly.

'Think very, very carefully, Flavia, if you have big decisions coming up,' he said quietly.

'Do you mean about playing at Dulcie's service?'

'No,' said her father. 'Nothing to do with Dulcie's service or your music. Promise me to give yourself time and take a long cool look before you do anything irrevocable?'

'I promise, Pa,' she whispered.

It was in an extremely sober frame of mind that she climbed into the green Lagonda as Gervaise held the door open for her. She thought he looked tired and somehow both older and a little shabbier than when she had last seen him only a few weeks earlier.

Otherwise everything at Winsleyhurst was the same. Almond blossom was out again and the crocuses had turned the grass into a Persian carpet of purple and yellow. Having been through such an emotional upheaval herself, she somehow expected that everyone else would have changed too. It was odd to find the same niggling decisions being discussed with such seriousness. Should the boys start to be called by their Christian names next term, because no one thought girls could be called by their surnames when they arrived in the autumn? Flavia tried hard to look interested.

She told Gervaise about Spanner, and he had been both horrified and half amused. He decided to have a confrontation, but Douglas Butler forestalled him by announcing that he'd been offered a post in a school starting up in Zimbabwe. He would come back to Winsleyhurst for one more term and depart in the autumn. To Gervaise's great relief he didn't even require a reference. Waring's parents refused to accept the fact, despite the boy's own admission, that their son could be either dishonest or a troublemaker and removed him before the end of term in a state of high indignation. There would, of course, be repercussions. They would make trouble with other local parents but Gervaise was philosophical about this; these things were always a nine-day wonder and Pamela Boynton almost certainly carried a lot more clout than Mrs Waring among any socially ambitious parents in the neighbourhood. Pamela told Gervaise that she would be standing firmly behind him. It was hard to imagine her standing any other way. Flavia had a mental image of the tall, droopy figure of Gervaise leaning against a gigantic oak. It comforted her a little to think he might be equally well supported over other troubles.

She decided to wait until the boys had gone before broaching the subject of their future to Gervaise, but once the holidays started she immediately became so involved with the Orton Music Festival, followed by the concert at Duntroon, that she kept putting it off – partly mindful of her promise to her father, but also she told herself, waiting for exactly the right moment. Every time she looked at Gervaise her courage failed her – and terrible inner questions reared unwanted heads. Gervaise came to Duntroon with her for Elizabeth Cameron's concert, which was a great success. Everyone thought Flavia played extremely well but she was not nearly satisfied and felt she had fallen well short of the standard she had set herself for Dulcie's service.

No one at Duntroon mentioned the Ardvrechan episode, though everyone thought about it. Flavia longed to take the Land Rover and go over to see Ben and meet the famous Aunt Moy – but she knew she mustn't. The cold turkey was very cold indeed: there was no word from Alistair at all. She did not even know where he was.

She wondered what she would do if Gervaise tried to make love to her, but the question did not arise because so far he had made no attempt to do so. One thing about her own feelings had changed though: the wicked little insects of irritation had departed and in their place she felt only an aching love and sadness. It was infinitely more painful.

Once the summer term started she practised obsessively. Gervaise was used to her having regular sessions with her flute, but not to the all-absorbing dedication she now showed. She was very sweet to him but he found himself longing for a return of the difficult, touchy Flavia of the weeks of pregnancy.

Meg walked round Flavia like a stiff-legged dog, hostile but not quite prepared to start a fight. Ben was Flavia's only solace, but now that he had started the promised trumpet lessons she saw less of him and felt she had to keep contact to a minimum, which was painful for them both. She longed for Alistair unbearably. It had been bad enough before, but since Ardvrechan she felt she was missing a vital part of herself. She knew very clearly what she wanted – but how great a price was it permissible to make someone else pay?

The day of Dulcie's memorial service was as bright and beautiful as any May day could be, with scudding clouds and the sky blue behind the spire of St Martin-in-the Fields. Outside the church the London traffic roared, and crowds in Trafalgar Square sat about in shirt sleeves, licked cornets and drank cans of Coke – and got bombed by the pigeons. Inside all was cool as the congregation started to arrive early.

The day before, Flavia had stayed behind alone after the rehearsal was over. She had loved the church since her Guildhall days when she had played at the lunchtime concerts given by young musicians. It was here, accompanied by a guitar-playing fellow student, that she had first performed a piece by Ibert – the *Entr'acte*. Here that she had first felt overwhelmed to play where Handel had once played.

It was the quality of light that she loved so much in the church, and which seemed to her now so specially suitable for Dulcie, whose own rooms were always so light and full of flowers. The church was resplendent with flowers too; there were huge arrangements of lilies in pedestals on either side of the aisle.

Dulcie had requested that Flavia should play the first two movements of Bach's Sonata No. 4 and be accompanied by no lesser musicians than Paul Fribourg on the piano and John Barker on the cello – both close friends of Dulcie's. She had also told Maurice that she would like Flavia to play something of her own choosing as well. Paul Fribourg, whom Flavia had known and loved for years, was to play a solo too, but Flavia thought it particularly generous of the brilliant and much younger John Barker to agree to accompany her.

'You realize that Antoine will almost certainly be there?' Maurice had asked her. 'How will you feel about that?'

'Great,' said Flavia, a defiant gleam in her eye. Wonderful. I can't wait to show him a thing or two. I hope he does come,' and Maurice had suddenly felt absolutely confident that Flavia would surpass herself.

'This service seems to be something of a Flavia Cameron benefit concert,' old Paul Fribourg had teased her when they were rehearsing, then catching her agonized expression had added gently, 'And very nice too. We all knew how Dulcie felt about you and how deeply upset she was when you were taken ill. Don't look so sad. We must try and make this a joyful occasion.'

After Paul and John had left, she sat in a pew at the back, looking at the great barrel ceiling, at the cheerful cherubs flying round in summer clouds, and tried to tune in to Dulcie. She thought of all the advice, personal as well as musical, that Dulcie had given her over the years. She thought of the poem she had quoted to Alistair and of Sydney Graham's 'terrible shapes of silence' that seemed now indeed to be sitting outside her ear. I promise I will blow you such a special 'ladder of sound' tomorrow, said Flavia to Dulcie. Tomorrow, too, I will really make my final difficult choice. Help me to choose well.

As she left the church she stood for a moment in front of Sir Gerald Kelly's portrait of Dick Sheppard, once Vicar of St Martin's. Looking at the sensitive compassionate face, she remembered her grandmother telling her once that he had been one of those people of whom it could be said that if his finger even touched your life, then you would in some way be changed. That, in a different way, could certainly be said of Dulcie too.

There was, of course, a huge congregation. Flavia went to sit on the outside of the front pew on the left with her parents and Hilda and Gervaise.

The congregation was not only composed of the musical élite, however. Despite her legendary confrontations and forked tongue, Dulcie had possessed a talent for friendship and people from many walks of life were represented. Flavia recognized the Pakistani couple who had delivered groceries to the flat from their corner shop; Father Donovan, the priest from Hilda's church, with whom Dulcie had waged an argumentative war highly enjoyable to them both, was there, as were the nurses who had latterly helped Hilda heave Dulcie's considerable bulk in and out of bed, and had grown to love her.

When the congregation sang the opening hymn, Dulcie's favourite, 'Be Thou my vision, O Lord of my heart' to the tune of Slane, Flavia realized that she must keep a tight grip on herself if she were to play the Bach as she intended.

She need not have worried. From the first notes she knew that all was more than well. As Hester listened to the three musicians, two so well-known and the third so young and so important to her, she sent up a prayer of pure thankfulness. As they finished the Allegro movement, Paul Fribourg and John Barker exchanged a long look. Like Dulcie, they saw possibilities.

When Maurice went up the beautiful curved stairs of the carved wooden pulpit to read from Kahlil Gibran's passage on death – causing one or two people a frisson of anxiety lest the steps should give way under his weight – Flavia knew that her next big moment was coming up.

'And when you have reached the mountain top, then you shall begin to climb. And when the earth shall claim your limbs, then shall you truly dance,' finished Maurice, and Flavia, a vision of Dulcie at last set free from her painful and unwieldy body, went up again to play her own particular choice, her special offering for her godmother: 'The Dance of the Blessed Spirits' from Gluck's *Orfeo ed Euridice* with an organ accompaniment. There was complete silence as the last notes died away.

Gervaise, looking with pride and longing at his young wife, hoped to catch her eyes so that she could read the message in his own. Earlier Hester and Flavia had found Christina Rossetti's 'Remember' copied in Dulcie's shaky writing, placed between the pages of the battered old copy of *The Book of Common Prayer*, which she always kept by her bed. If Maurice had introduced words from *The Alternative Service Book* for Dulcie's memorial rather than those of 1662, he would have expected to be hit by a thunderbolt at least. Dulcie had made a special mark down the side of the last lines of the sonnet:

Yet if you should forget me for a while
And afterwards remember, do not grieve;
For if the darkness and corruption leave
A vestige of the thoughts that once I had,
Better by far you should forget and smile
Than that you should remember and be sad.

Flavia had certainly not forgotten Dulcie at this moment, far from it, and the brilliant smile she gave was not for her husband. Her gaze was directed to the very back of the church, and she remained looking there for a long moment before rejoining her family in the pew.

'Go forth upon thy journey, Christian soul,' commanded Canon Richards, another old sparring partner of Dulcie's, and Flavia, as she knelt, reached for Hilda's hand and held it. The great words from The Wisdom of Solomon rolled over the congregation: 'But the souls of the righteous are in the hands of God, and there shall no torment touch them.' Maurice had told Flavia that in choosing this, Dulcie had said wryly to him: 'I fear I may not qualify – I've had too much fun in my life – but let's have it all the same.' The choir sang *Ave verum Corpus*, and then the beautiful soprano voice of Loveday Greaves, who had started her career with the ENO, and was now an international star, lifted everyone's hearts with 'Alleluia' from Mozart's *Exsultate jubilate*, and when Paul Fribourg played Dame Myra Hess's arrangement of 'Jesu, Joy of Man's Desiring,' few of those who had truly loved Dulcie were dry-eyed.

As those in the front pews walked down the aisle to the reassuring sound of the organ playing Bach's 'Sheep may Safely Graze' Gervaise looked to the spot where Flavia's gaze had rested – but whoever had been there had slipped out.

This time Flavia stayed up in London for the night. Maurice and Ina were holding open house for all Dulcie's closest friends, but Gervaise begged to be excused and said he really must get back to Winsleyhurst.

'I'll see you tomorrow morning then,' said Flavia, kissing him. He gave her an unfathomable look, and did not tell her that he thought she had played like an angel.

After the gathering at the Fensteins', Flavia did not go to either Tricia or Matt and Di. She went straight round to Alistair's house. When he answered the doorbell, he stood back and held out his arms and she flew into them like a homing pigeon arriving back at its appointed loft. They held each other for a long while without speaking.

Then: 'You came to be with me today,' she said.

'And when you smiled at me you gave me my answer, didn't you, my dear love?'

'Yes,' she said. 'Yes, I did.'

'Flavia, I can't ask you to marry me until you are free, but we have an expression for these arrangements in Scotland that you may know. Will you be my "bidie-in"?'

'Oh, yes,' she said, 'I'll be your bidie-in, all right. For as long as you want me, till death do us part – and whatever anyone else thinks of the arrangement.'

Later they talked about Gervaise. 'I suddenly knew so clearly as I played for Dulcie that I couldn't let our happiness go, couldn't waste it. I thought of Orfeo's lament for Euridice "What is life to me without you?", and I knew that despite what it may cost Gervaise, I just couldn't do it. Dulcie told me that when I found real love, music would find me again, but I knew today that it works the other way round too. I've got my music back – and found you.'

They sat together in silence, holding hands, wanting the moment to go on and on.

'Do you think I'm very sinful?' she asked suddenly.

'It's hard to think of anything as wonderful as our love being a sin. The pain Gervaise will feel – we can't dodge responsibility for that, and that's awful, – but sin? Well, I don't any longer feel sure about sin in this context.'

'No,' she said, 'nor do I. But I think I did something very wrong a year ago when I married Gervaise. It was selfish and cowardly of me. I see that now, and I shall be sorry about that always. He deserves better.'

They talked about Ben. Obviously they could not leave him at Winsleyhurst after the end of this term, even though it would mean yet another change in his life. They did not think he would mind too much, and a day school in London would be a perfectly workable option once Flavia was living with Alistair, but neither of them was under any illusion that Ben would be easy. On the long drive back from Scotland when they had thought he was asleep in the back of the car, he had suddenly said: 'Are you going to marry each other?'

'Flavia's not free to get married,' Alistair had hedged.

'But people get divorced all the time. So, are you?'

'What would you feel if we ever did?' asked Flavia.

'I like it like it is now. I wouldn't like it if you suddenly got like Claire Palmer,' said Ben, and added fiercely: 'And I don't want anyone, ever, to be my mother except Mum.'

'No one could ever be that, Ben,' Flavia had said – but she knew she had been given a warning.

She found Gervaise in his study when she got back. She wondered how on earth she was going to start what she had to say, but in the end he took the initiative.

'Well, Flavia,' he said, looking up as she came in, 'what have you got to tell me?'

'Oh Gervaise, dear darling Gervaise, I think you know.'

'Perhaps I do,' he said, walking over to the window, 'but all the same you'd better tell me.'

Falteringly and sadly she did.

'And our baby?' he asked. 'If that had lived would things have been different then?'

'Perhaps. I thought so. I hope so – but now I'm not sure.'

'I was very slow to see it. I didn't *want* to see it,' he said. 'That night at the folly, that was when you fell for Alistair, wasn't it?'

'No,' she said painfully, truthfully. 'Long before that. Really on New Year's Eve, when I first saw him and danced with him. I should have called our engagement off then. I knew it at the time, but I couldn't face it.'

He shook his head in disbelief at his own blindness. 'That I didn't know.'

'Shall I stay till the end of term?' she asked.

'No,' he said, surprising her. 'No, if you are to go, I think it should be as soon as possible. Like now.'

'Oh Gervaise,' she said, 'I do still love you so much as a person. I always will. You have given me such a lot – we can still go on being friends, can't we?'

It was the first time she had ever seen him look angry. Perhaps it was the first time in his whole life he had ever felt really angry.

'No, Flavia,' he said. 'You are asking too much. You cannot have everything. You have made your decision, you have said what you have to say, and I respect you for that. Don't ask me to give you my blessing too.'

'Will you be all right, though?' It was desperately important to her to hear him say that yes, of course, given time he would be. He did not say it.

'I thought perhaps,' she said, twisting her fingers together, hardly able to speak, fighting the tears, 'I thought perhaps – you and Meg . . .?'

He rounded on her then. 'No,' he said, again with a suppressed fury that amazed her. 'Leave Meg out of it. Don't you offer me Meg like a sort of baby's dummy for me to suck to make you feel better.'

'I'm sorry,' she whispered, 'so desperately sorry.'

She waited for a moment, but there was nothing more to say. She turned and crept upstairs to pack her things. It struck her that apart from clothes and some books and music, there was very little of hers at Winsleyhurst – nothing that could not be packed in suitcases. She had not made a home.

As she drove down the drive, Meg was walking up. Flavia stopped the car and opened the window.

'Meg,' she said, 'will you do something for me?'

'If I can.'

'I think you can. Will you take care of Gervaise for me – try to make sure he's all right? You see I've just told him that I'm leaving him.'

Meg's eyes blazed. 'How could you?' she asked. 'How could you do that, Flavia?'

'I thought you just might be pleased.'

'I love Gervaise,' said Meg. 'How could I want him to suffer like that?'

Flavia opened her mouth to say something more, and then shut it again. Words didn't seem to be helping this morning. She restarted the car, waited for a moment and then drove off.

Meg watched her go down the drive and out of sight. I had a chance once before, she thought, and I missed it. This time I will go for it. I mustn't miss it a second time.

Flavia drove slowly out of the gates of Winsleyhurst, and then accelerated as she took the familiar road to Orton to have what she knew would be another bruising encounter, this time with her mother. She thought of Alistair waiting for her in London.

She would be with him tonight – she hoped for the rest of their lives.

The pain in her heart was acute, but the sun was shining, the birds were singing spring songs – and her heart and her head were full of music.